P9-BZG-682

"Rich in history, culture . . . delightful . . . suspenseful."
—*Winston-Salem Journal*

"Another roistering romp. . . . A deft blend of suspense, history, and humor."
—Bill Sweeney, "Redwood Empire Book Beat"

"Rich historical background and an exciting page-turning mystery."
—*Abilene Reporter-News*

"Davis turns her prodigious talents once again to ancient Rome. . . . Dependable entertainment."
—*Library Journal*

"Lindsey Davis's foray into ancient Rome brings readers both rich historical background and an exciting page-turning mystery."
—*Sunday Life*

"If Travis McGee traveled in time back to treacherous, civilized Rome in A.D. 72, he might be something like Marcus Didius Falco."
— *Publishers Weekly* on
Last Act in Palmyra

"Sam Spade and Philip Marlowe in ancient Rome—some of the best British crime novels coming out at the moment."
—*Kaleidoscope*

Also by Lindsey Davis

THE SILVER PIGS

SHADOWS IN BRONZE

VENUS IN COPPER

THE IRON HAND OF MARS

POSEIDON'S GOLD

LAST ACT IN PALMYRA

TIME TO DEPART

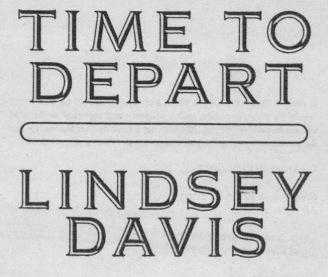

LINDSEY DAVIS

WARNER BOOKS

A Time Warner Company

WARNER BOOKS EDITION

Cover design by Rachel McClain
Cover illustration by Roy Pendleton

Warner Books, Inc.
1271 Avenue of the Americas
New York, NY 10020

Visit our Web site at
http://warnerbooks.com

W A Time Warner Company

Printed in the United States of America

First published in Great Britain in 1995 by Century, Random House UK Ltd., London.
Previously published in hardcover by The Mysterious Press.
First U.S. Paperback Printing: January, 1998

10 9 8 7 6 5 4 3 2 1

Rome: Two Weeks in October, A.D. 72

"It's the City that creates luxury. And out of luxury, inevitably, comes greed, out of greed bursts forth violence, out of violence proliferate all the various kinds of crime and iniquity."

Cicero

Extract from the Family Tree

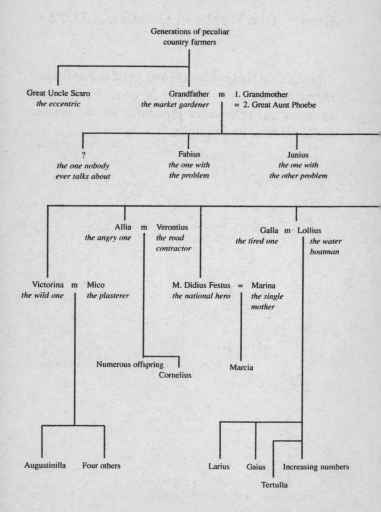

Generations of peculiar
country farmers

Great Uncle Scaro
the eccentric

Grandfather m 1. Grandmother
the market gardener = 2. Great Aunt Phoebe

?
*the one nobody
ever talks about*

Fabius
*the one with
the problem*

Junius
*the one with
the other problem*

Allia m Verontius
the angry one *the road
contractor*

Galla m Lollius
the tired one *the water
boatman*

Victorina m Mico
the wild one *the plasterer*

M. Didius Festus = Marina
the national hero *the single
mother*

Numerous offspring
Cornelius

Marcia

Augustinilla   Four others

Larius   Gaius   Increasing numbers

Tertulla

of Marcus Didius Falco

Generations of sharp
city entrepreneurs

1. Junilla Tacita m Marcus Didius Favonius = 2. Flora
the indomitable one   ("Geminus")   *the caupona owner*

Marcus Didius Falco = Helena Justina
the informer   *the senator's daughter*

Junia m Gaius Bæbius
the superior one   *the customs*
clerks supervisor

Maia m Famia
the sensible one   *the horse vet*

?

Marius Ancus 2 girls

Key: m = Married;
      = = Not exactly married;
      ? = Unknown, never mentioned in public, or a matter of speculation.

Principal Characters

Lalage	refined proprietress of the Bower of Venus
Macra	a young lady at that élite finishing school
Gaius & Phlosis	two extremely helpful boatmen

Low Society (Fountain Court)

Lenia	a blushing bride
Smaractus	her bashful groom
Cassius	a baker whose oven may get too hot
Ennianus	a basket-weaver who may be tangling with trouble
Castus	a newcomer, dealing in old junk
An old bag woman	
Nux	a homeless dog looking for a soft touch
Falco	her target (not as tough as he thinks)
A baby	abandoned, also looking for a nice home with kindly folk

Law and Order (all under suspicion)

Marcus Rubella	tribune of the scrupulous Fourth Cohort of vigiles
L. Petronius Longus	enquiry chief in the XIII region
Arria Silvia	his often furious wife
Their cat	(a cohort joke)
Martinus	a deputy (not for long, he hopes)
Fusculus	an expert on rackets
Linus	on detached duty on the *Aphrodite*
Rufina	the reason Linus has detached himself
Sergius	a happy punishment officer
Porcius	a young recruit (unhappy)
Scythax	an optimistic doctor (public sector)
Tibullinus	a centurion of the dubious Sixth Cohort
Arica	his sidekick (certainly needs kicking)

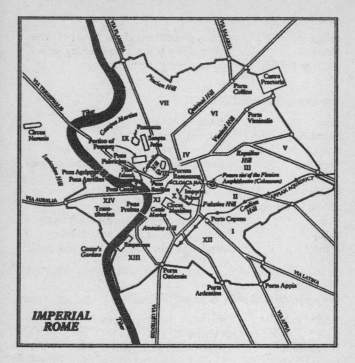

Jurisdictions of the Vigiles Cohorts in Rome:

Coh I	Regions VII & VIII (Via Lata, Forum Romanum)
Coh II	Regions III & V (Isis & Serapis, Esquiline)
Coh III	Regions IV & VI (Temple of Peace, Alta Semita)
Coh IV	Regions XII & XIII (Piscina Publica, Aventine)
Coh V	Regions I & II (Porta Capena, Caelimontium)
Coh VI	Regions X & XI (Palatine, Circus Maximus)
Coh VII	Regions IX & XIV (Circus Flaminius, Transtiberina)

I

"I still can't believe I've put the bastard away for good!" Petronius muttered.

"He's not on the boat yet," Fusculus corrected him. Clearly the Watch's optimist.

There were five of us waiting on a quayside. Mid-October. An hour before dawn. A wakening breeze chilled our tense faces as we huddled in cloaks. The day was making itself ready for action somewhere on the other side of Italy, but here in Portus, Rome's new harbor, it was still fully dark. We could see the huge beacon on the lighthouse flaunting itself, with glimpses of tiny figures tending the fire; pale sheets of flame sometimes lit the statue of Neptune presiding over the entrance. The sea god's illuminated torso stood out strangely in our surroundings. Only the scents of old, hardened rope and rotting fish scales told us we were standing on the grand harbor bowl.

We were five honest, respectable citizens who had been waiting all night for a sixth. *He* had never been honest, though like most criminals he had no difficulty passing himself off as respectable. Roman society had always been readily bamboozled by brazen acts. But now, thanks to Petronius Longus, the man and his crimes had been publicly exposed.

We had been waiting too long. Although nobody said it, we were starting to dread that the big rissole would not show.

The lowlife was called Balbinus.

I had been hearing his name as long as I could remember. It had certainly been notorious when Petronius and I had come home from the army six years before. At that time my old tentmate Petro, being a dutiful type who fancied a good salary, had put himself forward as a public officer; I set up in business alone. He was chasing cabbage thieves through the markets while I was picking through clerks' divorces and tracing stolen art. On the face of it we lived in different worlds, yet we stumbled across the same tragedies and heard the same worrying stories on the streets.

Balbinus was renowned throughout our district as one of the dirtiest underworld organizers ever to gild imperial Rome. The area he terrorized included brothels, wharfside warehouses, the back-doubles on the Aventine slopes, the dark colonnades around the Circus Maximus. He ran jostlers and confidence tricksters; prostitutes and cutpurses; cat burglars and marauding gangs of street beggars with fake blind eyes who could soon spot trouble coming. He kept a couple of safe houses for receiving, set up under the cover of straight businesses. Petronius reckoned that the flow of stolen goods into these dens of illicit commerce rivaled the international trade at the Emporium.

Petro had been trying to nail Balbinus for years. Now, somehow, he had managed to set up a capital charge—and go on to secure a conviction despite all Balbinus' efforts to escape using democratic channels (intimidation and bribes). I had yet to hear the full details. Barely back in Rome from what I liked to describe as a confidential diplomatic mission, I had been roped in tonight as a dependable extra and friend.

"He's not going to come now," I suggested easily, since I knew how stubborn Petro was.

"I'll not risk losing him."

"Right."

"Don't niggle me, Falco."

"You're so conscientious you're tying yourself up in

knots. Listen to someone rational: He'll either have left Rome last evening, in which case we would have seen him by now, or he went to bed first. If that's it, he won't arrive for another hour or two. When's the ship due to leave?"

"The minute he gets here, if I have any control over it."

"With the light," clarified Fusculus in a quiet tone. I guessed my point about our quarry's arrival had already been made to Petro by his men. Since they knew him too, their reaction to my attempt was restrained. They were hoping he would either listen to a pal, or at least give them some entertainment by losing his temper and thumping me.

"I need a drink," I commented.

"Stuff you, Falco. Don't try that one." It was too dark to see his face. All the same, I chuckled; he was weakening.

The trick was not to make an issue of it. I said nothing, and about five minutes afterwards Petronius Longus burst out with an obscenity that I hadn't heard uttered in a public place since we left Britain. Then he growled that he was cold and past caring—and was off to the nearest wine bar for a beaker to console himself.

Nobody chortled. By then we were too relieved that he had given way to gloat over our victory, just as Petro had known we would be. He had a nice sense of timing. Martinus growled, "Better take the bloody barnacle. It'll be his last chance for a long time."

So we bawled out to Linus to stop pretending he was a sailor and to come off the ship and have a drink with us.

II

The atmosphere was thick with lamp smoke; hard to see why, as there was a mean supply of lamps. Something crunched under my boot—either an old oyster shell, or part of a whore's broken necklace. There seemed to be a lot of debris on the floor. Probably best not to investigate.

No one else was in the dump. No customers, anyway. A couple of grimy lasses roused themselves slightly when we tramped inside, but they soon got the message and slumped back into sleep. They looked too exhausted even to be curious. That didn't mean they wouldn't be listening in, but we were not intending any loud indiscretions. There was too much at stake.

We cramped ourselves onto benches, feeling stiff and oversized in our outdoor dress. We were all armed, to the point where it was impossible to be discreet when crowding around small tables. If we tried to pretend we were just carrying Lucanian sausage rolls, someone would have his privates shorn off by an awkwardly placed sword blade. We arranged ourselves with care.

The landlord was an unsmiling, unwelcoming coastal type who had summed us up as we crossed his threshold.

"We were just closing." We must have brought in a suggestion of imminent violence.

"I apologize." Petronius could have used his official status to insist we were served, but as usual he preferred to try his charm first. His brevity probably screamed "law and order." The landlord knew he had no choice. He served us, but made it plain that he hoped we would be leaving quickly. It was too late in the night for trouble.

Well, we agreed with that.

There was tension in all of us. I noticed that Martinus, the cocky bantam who was Petro's second in command, took one deep swig of his drink, then kept going to the doorway and staring out. The others ignored his fidgeting. In the end he parked his rather jutting backside on a stool just beyond the threshold, occasionally calling in some remark to the rest, but watching the waterfront. In Petro's troop even the tame annoyance was a decent officer.

Petronius and I ended up at a table to ourselves.

He had strong bonds with his men. He always led from the front. He pulled his weight in routine inquiries, and on a surveillance he mucked in as one of them. But he and I had been friends for a long time. Between us were even stronger links, forged from when we had met at eighteen and shared a legionary posting to one of the grimmest parts of the Empire while it was earning dismal fame—Britain, in Nero's time, with the Boudiccan Rebellion as our special treat. Now, although for long periods we often failed to meet, when we did we could pick up straightaway, as if we had shared an amphora only last Saturday. And when we entered a wine bar with others it was understood that we two would sit together, very slightly separate from the rest.

Petro gulped his wine, then visibly regretted it. "Jupiter! You could paint that on warts and they'd fall off by dinnertime. . . . So how was the East?"

"Wild women and wicked politics."

"Didius Falco, the world traveler!" He didn't believe a word of it. "What really happened?"

I grinned, then gave him a neat summary of five months' traveling: "I got my ear gnawed by a few camels. Helena was stung by a scorpion and spent a lot of money—much of it my father's, I'm delighted to say." We had brought a quantity of stuff back with us; Petro had promised to help me unload in return for my assistance tonight. "I ended up in a hack job scribbling Greek jokes for second-rate touring actors."

His eyebrows shot up. "I thought you went on a special task for the Palace?"

"The bureaucratic mission rapidly fell through—especially after I found out that Vespasian's Chief Spy had sent a message ahead of me encouraging my hosts to lock me up. Or worse," I concluded gloomily.

"Anacrites? The bastard." Petronius had no time for officials, whatever smooth title they dressed themselves up in. "Did he land you in bad trouble?"

"I survived."

Petronius was frowning. He viewed my career like a kind of blocked gutter that needed a hefty poke with a stick to shift the sludge and get it running properly. He saw himself as the expert with the stick. "What was the point, Falco? What's in it for Vespasian if he destroys a first-class agent?"

"Interesting question." In fact there could be several reasons why the Emperor might feel a foreign jail was just the place for me. I was an upstart who wanted social promotion; since he disapproved of informers, the idea of letting me wear the gold ring and strut like a man of substance had always rankled. Most of the time he owed me money for my undercover services; he would love to renege. Then one of his sons had tender feelings towards a certain young lady who preferred to live with me, while I had a long-term feud with the other. Either Titus or Domitian might have asked their pa to dump me. Besides, who really likes a hireling who handles problems with dispatch, then comes back wearing a happy smile and expecting a huge cash reward?

"I don't know why you work for him," Petronius grumbled angrily.

"I work for myself," I said.

"That's news!"

"That's the truth. Even if the damned secretariat offers me a straight task with a set fee and vast expenses, I won't consider it. From now on, I stick to private commissions—which was what I had to do after I got shoved in shit in Arabia by bloody Anacrites and his devious games."

"You're a dope," Petro answered disbelievingly. "You can't resist the challenge. One nod from the man in purple and you'll scuttle back."

I grabbed the flagon and helped us both to more wine. It still tasted like a cure for swine fever. "Petro, the man in purple didn't try to sell me to a camel trader."

Whatever I thought of the rank of emperor, Vespasian the man was completely straight. Even Petronius grudgingly allowed the point. "So it was the spy, Falco. What's the difference?"

"Who knows? But Anacrites thinks I'm rotting in some desert citadel; this could be the lever I'm looking for to show him up. I'll give my travelogue to Vespasian before the spy finds out I'm alive and back in Rome."

It was good to unload my anger, but there were better things to talk about. "Come to dinner when we get settled back in—bring Silvia and the girls. We'll have a gathering and tell our gripping travelers' tales."

"How's Helena?" Petro remembered to ask when I mentioned his own wife and children.

"Fine. And no, we're not married, or planning it; nor quarreling and planning to separate."

"Any signs of impending fatherhood?"

"Certainly not!" I retorted, like a man who knew how to handle his private life. I hoped Petro would not notice I was bluffing. "When I'm honored, you'll be the first to know. . . . Olympus! Talking to you is like fending off my mother."

"Wonderful woman," he commented in his aggravating way.

I carried on with a feeling of false confidence. "Oh yes, Ma's a credit to the community. If everyone on the Aventine was as stiff-backed as my mother, you'd have no work to do. Unfortunately some of them are called Balbinus Pius—about whom you still owe me an explanation or two."

This time the distraction worked. With a glow of satisfaction Petronius threw back his great head and stretched his long legs under the table. Beaming proudly, he settled down to bring me up to date.

"You realize," Petro began, with mock-heroic grandeur, "we're talking about the most vicious, seditious operator in organized crime who ever fixed his claws on the Aventine?"

"And now *you*'ve caught him!" I grinned admiringly.

He ignored the jesting undertone. "Believe it, Falco!"

I was enjoying myself. Petronius Longus was a stolid, patient worker. I could not remember that I had ever heard him boasting; it was good to see him thrilled by his own success for once.

Inches taller than me to start with, he even seemed to have grown. His quiet manner tended to disguise how powerfully built he was. Slow of step and wry of speech, he could lean on wrongdoers before they even saw him coming, but once Petro applied weight, resistance caved in fast. He ran the watch inquiry team without seeming to exert himself, although as his best friend I happened to know that in private he worried deeply about standards. He achieved the highest. His was a lean, competent squad which gave the public what they paid for and kept the villains on the hop.

He had a calm grip on his domestic life as well. A good Roman: honorific father of three children. He had a small, scathing wife who knew how to make her presence felt, and a much-loved trio of lively little girls. At home he fielded Arria Silvia's sparky temper pretty easily. The children adored him. Even the wife modulated her complaints, knowing she had one piece of fortune that was missing from most marriages: Petro was there because he wanted to be. Both as a family man and as a public officer, he looked easy-going but was utterly reliable.

"Balbinus Pius . . ." he said softly, savoring his triumph.

"Ludicrous name," I commented. "Balbinus the Dutiful! As far as I know his only duty is serving himself. Isn't he the moldy cheese who owns that filthy brothel they call Plato's Academy? And the thieves' kitchens down on the waterside at the back of the Temple of Portunus?"

"Don't speak to me about Plato's. I get a pain in the bladder just thinking about the place. Jupiter knows whose name is scratched on the crumbling title deeds, but you're right; it was Balbinus who had it sewn up. He took a percentage of every transaction in bed, plus whatever the house made on robbing purses or selling 'abandoned' boots and belts. Then, as well as his entertainment interests, he had a nice gold-smith's workshop where stolen goblets could be melted down in minutes; several sweatshops that specialized in putting new braid on tunics that 'fell off' washing lines; numerous tat stalls in the markets, constantly shifting just when I placed a man in the portico watching them; and a couple of counterfeiting factories. If it stank, he owned it," confirmed Petro. "Past tense, though, Falco. One of the bleak facts he has to face today is that a capital conviction means losing all his property."

"I'm sobbing into my napkin."

"Don't upset yourself too much—I'm still not certain we'll net his whole empire. Some of it must be in hidden hoards."

"I bet! Was he expecting to be put away?"

"He wasn't even expecting to be put on trial! This has taken me months of planning, Falco. There was only ever going to be one crack at him, or he'd be screaming 'perse-cution of a citizen!' and I'd be out of a job. But he didn't be-lieve I'd ever find anybody prepared to prosecute."

"So, Lucius Petronius, how did you arrange it?"

"Marcus Didius, there was only one way possible. I found somebody even greedier, and even more of a bastard, than him!"

III

Smiling, Petro passed one big hand over his brown hair. He seemed to have been having it styled more snappily. (Well, it was shorter; that was his barber's creative limit.) His other great paw lay lightly at his waist, where the staff of his office was stuck behind a wide, creased leather belt that I remembered him buying from a shifty Celt in Londinium. Otherwise, apart from the flash haircut, he did not trouble to priss himself up like a man of fashion. On duty it was better to be protected by a leather jerkin that might deflect a knife blade and a thick wool cloak which would shrug off the mud if he hurled himself to the pavement when tackling a runaway. His boots had come up hard on quite a few doorframes too by the looks of them.

"So who was the high-principled, public-minded citizen who squealed about Balbinus?" I asked.

"A donkey's turd called Nonnius."

"Not Nonnius Albius? I thought he was a racketeer himself?"

"He had been. He actually worked with Balbinus, was his chief rent collector. That was what appealed to me."

"Of course! You needed an insider."

"No one else could have done it. Nonnius was ideal."

"But he was a Balbinus boy. How did you sew him up?"

"A sad story." Petro grinned. "He's dying. His doctor had just put the frighteners on. Poor old Nonnius is suffering from terminal rot."

"Something nasty that people don't talk about?"

"Same as his profession!" Petro snarled. Then he told me the story: "Back in the spring, I just happened to learn that Nonnius had been given notice to quit by his pet medicine man—"

"Happened?" This seemed a nice coincidence.

Petro was in full flow and not to be sidetracked by my skepticism. "Nonnius gets informed by some pet Aesculapius that he's finished, but the doctor says he'll last longer if he takes care of himself—no worries, lots of pampering—"

"Expensive!" I was beginning to see Petro's reasoning.

"A life of luxury prescribed! So I get to him when he's just reeling from the bad news, I lend a sympathetic ear, then I put it to him he's spent his life running around for Balbinus while that rat lay on a reading couch counting his winnings—and for what? Now seems the time for a spot of leveling. . . . Since Nonnius has to give up the low life, he soon settles on snatching at the high life to compensate. This appeals to the bastard: taking a litter through the Forum, giving orders to slaves through the window, and greeting fawning admirers who are hoping for free gifts. Even more than that, suddenly he loves the idea of robbing Balbinus."

I laughed shortly. "The loyalty of thieves! So he was prepared to testify?"

"In return for the traditional reward."

"You did a deal?"

"All legal. He appeared before Marponius and twittered like a happy song finch. In return, as a successful prosecutor he can seize a proportion of Balbinus' traceable assets. The only disincentive is that he has to help us trace them. But it's well worth his while to hire accountants. Having been on the money-collecting side himself he knows the occasional fellow with a dodgy abacus, imaginative enough to guess where the loot may be hidden."

"I love it!" I was laughing. We both grabbed more wine, which now tasted almost palatable. "But Petro, you must

have needed to take great care framing the actual charge
against Balbinus. What did you throw at him?"

"Murder. The only count that would have worked."

"Of course. It had to be a capital offense."

"Right. Anything less and he would only end up with a
fine—and however large, a fine wouldn't choke him. He
could shed thousands and hardly feel a tickle."

I didn't say it, but putting Balbinus in court on any charge
that left him free in Rome afterwards would have placed
Petro himself in a very dangerous position. There was no
point dwelling on this feature. He knew all right.

"So who had been topped—and how did you nail Balbinus for the murder?" I didn't suppose he had actually stuck
a dagger in someone personally. "Getting blood spots on his
own tunic was never his style."

"Happy accident," said Petro. "It happened at Plato's
Academy." The brothel we had already mentioned. "They
specialize in fleecing foreign visitors. Some poor Lycian had
been set up to lose his traveling pouch in the floor-creeping
gag. While the girl was giving him the push-and-shove that
he'd paid for, he made the mistake of noticing a rustle in the
straw. Up he jumps, and discovers the whore's accomplice
just reaching for his money. Instead of making a discreet
complaint to the madam, then leaving the brothel with an
apology and a wiser attitude, this fool puts up his fists and
makes a fight for it. The snatcher was so surprised at the Lycian's unsporting behavior that he knifed him on the spot."

I whistled. "Someone should hand out warnings to innocent travelers! But how did you prove it? Surely the
brothel's mother hen was used to denying all knowledge of
trouble?"

"Oh yes. Lalage's well up to it. I'd never have pinned her
down, and I'm not sure I'd even have fancied tackling
her. . . . Thank Jupiter Plato's is on the Sixth Cohort's beat,
and I don't normally have the problem." I saw his point. The
whores who crowded around the Circus Maximus were as
fierce as lynxes, and Lalage, the madam at Plato's, had a
phenomenal reputation. "There was a witness," Petro told
me grimly. "And for the first time in history it was a witness
who managed not to yell at the scene of the crime. So in-

stead of the usual turn-up where the witness gets stabbed too, he hid up in the rafters until he had a chance to run away."

"Unbelievable."

"Better yet, one of my men then found him wandering in shock up on the Hill. He blurted out his tale, and we went straight to Plato's. The Sixth were nowhere in sight—that's normal—so we handled it ourselves. We were able to jump from an alley just as two bouncers were dragging the corpse out through the back door. That pegged the crime to the brothel. So for a start, when we went into court half the Thirteenth-sector Watch had seen Plato's management towing the Lycian to a gutter by the boot-thongs, with Lalage herself holding a lamp. Next we had our witness narrate the stabbing luridly. *He* was a second Lycian who had been smuggled in by the first one. The pair were hoping to slip the girl a copper and get a double spike half-price."

I slapped the table. "Disgraceful! How can you police the city when even the victims are crooks?"

"Falco, I'll live with it! I locked our witness in protective custody, lost the address until he was needed, then produced him at the Basilica in his best tunic to tell how he had trembled in his hiding place and seen all. He identified the prostitute, the madam, and the creeping snatch."

"Do I know the snatch?"

"A weasel called Castus."

It meant nothing. I didn't ask if I knew the prostitute, and Petro didn't bother to embarrass anyone by naming her. "So what about your star witness? What about Nonnius?"

"We were well set up by the time our barrister called him. All Nonnius Albius had to do was to confess his own role as a Balbinus collector, and state that he knew the killer Castus was on the Balbinus payroll. He played his part very prettily—he even produced tallies to show the percentage Balbinus regularly took from stolen purses at the brothel."

"Good value!"

"A prime witness. Our Lycian had come up with some joyful clinchers, like Castus exclaiming as he stabbed the dead man, 'Teach him to argue with Balbinus!' Nonnius then told the jury that all the Balbinus henchmen are routinely ordered to slash if trouble threatens. He had frequently heard Balbinus give those instructions. So we had him for organized crime, profiteering, and conspiracy, resulting in actual death."

"The jury bought it?"

"Marponius had explained to them that he needed their cooperation if he was to be seen as the judge who cleaned up Rome. . . ."

Marponius was the main judge in the murder court. He was keen on his work, and personally ambitious, though not necessarily as blatant as Petronius made out. For one thing, Marponius was not a clever man.

"There were some juicy details," Petro said. "I was threatening Lalage with a range of offenses against the prostitutes' registration rules, so even she went into court to give evidence on our side."

"Couldn't Balbinus buy her off?"

"I reckon she's keen to see him take a trip," opined Petronius. "Lalage would be quite capable of running Plato's on her own. Maybe things were different once, but nowadays she really doesn't need a king of crime creaming off the top of her income." He leaned back and went on with his usual modesty: "Oh, I had some luck in the timing. Balbinus believed himself untouchable, but there was a new mood in the underworld. People were ready to revolt. I noticed the change before he did, that's all."

The point was, Petronius Longus *had* noticed. Many an inquiry captain would have had his nose so close to the pavings he wouldn't have spotted the flies on the balcony.

"Take your credit for sniffing the air," I commanded. "And then for fixing it!"

He smiled quietly.

"So your jury convicted, and Marponius did his own career some good by handing out a death penalty—I presume the Assembly ratified the sentence. Did Balbinus appeal any further?"

"Straight to Vespasian—and it came straight back: negative."

"That's something!" I commented. We were both cynics about the Establishment. "Who signed the chitty?"

"Titus."

"Vespasian must have approved."

"Oh yes." Only the Emperor has the final power of removing life from a Roman citizen, even if the citizen's life smells like a pile of cat's turds. "I was quite impressed by the quick response," Petro admitted. "I don't really know whether Balbinus offered money to officials, but if he tried it he was wasting his time. Things at the Palace seem to be scented like Paestum violets nowadays." One good result of the new Flavian Caesars. Graft had gone over the balcony with Nero, apparently. Petro seemed confident, anyway. "Well it was the result I wanted, so that's that."

"Here we are!" I congratulated him. "Ostia at dawn!"

"Ostia," he agreed, perhaps more cautiously. "Marponius gets a free meal at the Palace; I get a scroll with a friendly message from Titus Caesar; the underworld gets a warning—"

"And Balbinus?"

"Balbinus," growled Petronius Longus bitterly, "gets time to depart."

IV

I suppose it is a comfort to us all—we who carry the privilege of being full citizens of the Empire—to know that except in times of extreme political chaos when civilization is dispensed with, we can do what we like, yet remain untouchable.

It is, of course, a crime for any of us to profiteer while on foreign service; commit parricide; rape a vestal virgin; conspire to assassinate the Emperor; fornicate with another man's slave; or let amphorae drop off our balconies so as to dent fellow citizens' heads. For such evil deeds we can be prosecuted by any righteous free man who is prepared to pay a barrister. We can be invited before a praetor for an embarrassing discussion. If the praetor hates our face, or merely disbelieves our story, we can be sent to trial, and if the jury hates us too we can be convicted. For the worst crimes we can be sentenced to a short social meeting with the public strangler. But, freedom being an inalienable and perpetual state, we cannot be made to endure imprisonment. So while the public strangler is looking up a blank date in his calendar, we can wave him good-bye.

In the days of Sulla so many criminals were skipping punishment, and it was obviously so cheap to operate, that finally the law enshrined this neat dictum: no Roman citizen who was sentenced to the death penalty might be arrested, even after the verdict, until he had been given *time to depart.* It was my right; it was Petro's right; and it was the right of the murderous Balbinus Pius to pack a few bags, assume a smug grin, and flee.

The point is supposed to be that living outside the Empire is, for a citizen, a penalty as savage as death. Balbinus must be quaking. Whoever thought that one up was not a traveling man. I had been outside the Empire, so my verdict was not quite that of a jurist. Outside the Empire can be perfectly livable. Like anywhere, all you need to survive comfortably is slightly more cash than the natives. The sort of criminals who can afford the fare in the first place need have no qualms.

So here we were. Petronius Longus had convicted this mobster of heinous crimes and placed him under sentence of death—but he was not allowed to apply a manacle. Today had been set for the execution. So this morning, while the graybeards from the Senate were tutting away over the decay of public order, Balbinus Pius would stroll out of Rome like a lord and set off for some hideaway. Presumably he had already filled it with golden chalices, with rich Falernian to slosh into them, and with fancy women to smile at him as they poured the happy grape. Petro could do nothing—except make damn sure the bastard went.

Petronius Longus was doing that with the thoroughness his friends in Rome would expect.

Linus, the one dressed as a sailor, had been listening in more closely than the other members of the squad. As his chief started listing for me the measures he was taking, Linus slewed around on his bench and joined us. Linus was to be a key man in enforcing the big rissole's exile.

"Balbinus lives in the Circus Maximus district, unluckily—" Petro began.

"Disaster! The Sixth Cohort run that. Have we hit some boundary nonsense? Does that mean it's out of your watch and you can't cover his house?"

"Discourteous to the local troopers . . ." Petro grinned

slightly. I gathered he was not deterred by a bit of discourtesy to the slouchers in the Sixth. "Obviously it's had to be a joint operation. The Sixth are escorting him here—"

I grinned back. "Assisted by observers from your own cohort?"

"*Accompanied,*" said Petro pedantically. I looked forward to seeing what form this might take.

"Of course you trust them to do the job decently?"

"Does he heck!" scoffed Linus, only half under his breath.

Linus was a young-looking thirty, dressed for his coming role in more layers of tunics than most sailors wear, crumpled boots, a floppy hat his mother had knitted, and a seaman's knife. Below the short sleeves of the tunics his bare arms had a chubby appearance, though none of Petro's men were overweight. Level eyes and a chin square as a spade. I had never met him before, but could see he was lively and keen. A typical Petro recruit.

"So the Sixth carry the big rissole here, then he's handed over to you?" I smiled at Linus. "How far does this slave-driver want you to go with him?"

"All the way," answered Petro for himself.

I shot Linus a look of sympathy, but he shrugged it off. "A lad likes to travel," he commented. "I'll see him land the other side. At least the esteemed Petronius says I don't have to shin up rigging on the journey back."

"Big of him! Where's the rissole going?"

"Heraclea, on the Taurica peninsula."

I whistled. "Was that his choice?"

"Someone made a very strong suggestion," came Petro's dry response. "Someone who *does* have the right to feed him to the arena lions if he fails to listen to the hint." The Emperor.

"Someone has a sense of humor then. Even Ovid only had to go to Moesia."

The world had shrunk since emperors sent salacious poets to cool their hexameters on the lonely shores of the Euxine Sea while other bad citizens were allowed to sail to Gaul and die rich as wine merchants. The Empire stretched far beyond Gaul nowadays. Chersonesus Taurica, even farther away on the Euxine than Ovid's bleak hole, had vivid advantages as a dump for criminals: though technically not a Roman province, we did have a trading presence all along its coast, so Balbinus could be watched—and he would know it. It was also a terrible place to be sent. If he wasn't eaten by brown bears he would die of cold or boredom, and however much money he managed to take with him, there were no luxuries to spend it on.

"It's no summer holiday for you, either," I told Linus. "You'll never get home this side of Saturnalia."

He accepted the news cheerily. "Someone needs to make sure Balbinus doesn't nip off the ship at Tarentum." True. Or Antium, or Puteoli, or Paestum, Buxentum or Rhegium, or Sicily, or at any one of scores of seashore towns in Greece, and the islands, and Asia, that would lie on our criminal's way into exile. Most of these places had an ambiguous form of loyalty towards Rome. Some were run by Roman officials who were only looking for a rest. Many were too remote to be supervised even by officials who liked to throw their weight about. Petronius Longus was rightly distraught about making the penalty stick. Linus, however, seemed to take his responsibility placidly. "This is my big chance to travel. I don't mind wintering at some respectable town in Bithynia, or on the Thracian coast." Petro's stooge had looked at a map, then.

"Will you get your lodging paid, Linus?"

"Within the limits," Petronius uttered somberly, resisting any frivolous suggestion that Linus might be heading for a spree at the state's expense.

"Anything for a bit of peace!" said Linus. Evidently there was a woman involved.

Well, we were all henpecked. Not that most of us would have entertained four or five months beyond the Hellespont at the worst time of year simply to avoid having our ears battered. Linus could not have mastered the gracious art of sloping off to the public baths for half a day (a set of baths you are not known to frequent).

Martinus appeared in the doorway. He gave Petronius a signal that was barely more than a twitch.

"They're coming! Scram, Linus."

With a grin I can still remember, Linus slid from his bench. Keyed up for adventure, he was out of the wine bar and off back to the Chersonesus-bound ship while the rest of us were still bringing our thoughts to bear.

We had paid for the wine. We all left the bar in silence. The landlord closed the door after us. We heard him fasten it with a heavy log, pointedly.

Outside the darkness had altered by several shades. The wind freshened. As we regained the quay Fusculus shook a shin that must have had cramp, while we all adjusted our swords and freed them from our cloaks. Nervously we strained to listen for the sound we really wanted to hear above the creaks of ropes and boards and the plashing of wavelets under buffers, floats, and hulls.

We could make out a movement on the harbor road, though still only faintly. Martinus must have honed his ears for this mission if he had heard something earlier.

Soon the noise clarified and became brisk hoofbeats; then we picked out wheels as well, somewhere in their midst. Almost at once a short cavalcade clattered up, the iron shoes of the horses and mules ringing loud. At the center was an exceptionally smart carriage of the type very wealthy men own for comfortable summer visits to their remote estates—big enough to allow the occupant to eat and write, or to try to forget being shaken by potholes and to sleep. Balbinus was probably not napping on this journey.

A couple of freedmen who must have decided, or been persuaded, that they could not bear to leave their master hopped off the top and began unloading a modest selection of luggage. Balbinus had lost all his slaves. That was part of stripping him of his property. What his freedmen did now was up to them. Soon they would possess more civic rights than he did—though they might still feel they owed familial debts to the master who had once freed them. Whether they saw it that way would depend on how many times he had kicked them for nothing when they were still slaves.

So far the rissole had remained inside his carriage. It was a heavy, four-wheeled special, all gleaming bright coach-work and silver finials, drawn by two lively mules with bronze snaffles and millefiori enamels on their headbands.

The driver enjoyed making play with his triple-thonged whip; the mules took it calmly, though some of our party cantered uneasily when he suddenly cracked the thing above our heads. We were on edge—still waiting for the big moment. Dark curtains across the carriage's windows were hiding the occupant.

Petronius walked forwards to greet the officers of the Sixth watch who had escorted the man from Rome. I stayed at his shoulder. He introduced Arica and Tibullinus, whom he knew. Tibullinus appeared to be the man in charge. He was a truculent, untidy centurion, and I didn't like him much. With them was Porcius, a young recruit of Petro's who had been formally attached to them as an observer. He lost himself among the rest of the Sixth's inquiry team rather rapidly.

While we were going through the formalities, another couple of horses turned up. Their riders slid down; then they too joined us, openly nodding to Petro.

"What's this?" cried Tibullinus, sounding annoyed, though he tried to hide it. "Checking up? On the Sixth?"

"Far be it from me to slander the meticulous Sixth!" Petro assured him. He was a devious bastard when he chose. "Just a couple of lads I told to lend a hand when they'd finished something else. Looks like they only just caught up with you . . ."

Everyone realized his couple of lads had attached themselves to the Sixth and their not-quite prisoner for the whole journey—and that the men of the Sixth had failed to notice they were being tagged. They should have known. It could have been any kind of ambush. We left it at that, before things became too sensitive.

Something was about to happen.

There was a moment's unnatural atmosphere; then everyone straightened and grew watchful. The carriage door creaked as it opened. Then Balbinus emerged.

V

Always the same shock: you come face to face with a murderous master criminal, and he looks like a ribbon-seller.

Balbinus Pius was five feet three digits—definitely not tall. He was looking me in the windpipe, and appeared not to notice that most of the officers present overstripped him by almost a foot. He had an oval head; an expressionless face; wavering eyes; an anxious expression that verged nicely on bewilderment. His manner was quiet, no more threatening than a ladybird.

His hunched shoulders held up a dapper white tunic and short gray cloak. The cloak was pinned extremely neatly on the left shoulder by a round gold brooch set with five garnets. He had healthy pink skin. On the top of his head it was visible through the short, thinning down of near baldness; the bushier stuff above his ears had been lathered with some discreetly piquant lotion. He wore dark gray leather traveling boots. His seal ring was gold, a Greek design of a winged female driving a four-horse chariot. He wore two others for ornament, one set with sapphires and opals, the other openwork, cut from sheet gold with added granulation. He wore the plain wide gold band of the middle rank. He carried no weapons.

I was annoyed, and so was Petro, that Tibullinus, Arica, and some of the other men of the Sixth stepped forwards and shook hands with him, bidding farewell. Words were exchanged. Unable to tolerate it, the rest of us looked away and breathed disapproval. We were reluctant to become part of the conversation. We were resisting being coerced. We had glimpsed the complacency amid which corruption flowers.

"How can you do that?" Martinus spluttered at Arica; Arica had actually slapped Balbinus on the back, as if he were seeing off his own cousin to the army. Martinus always spoke his mind.

"No harm being polite." The Sixth had been supervising Balbinus' movements ever since he went to trial. Contact would have been unavoidable.

The whole group of the Sixth began standing back now that they had delivered the package to us. As soon as he saw them shaking hands with the criminal, Petronius Longus had abandoned any pretense that this was a joint mission. His normal easygoing manner had vanished; I had never seen him so serious. The rest of the climax belonged to him and to the Fourth. Once the Sixth had formally taken their leave, they slunk from the scene.

I said nothing, but I had a sense that Petro's night of triumph had just been spoiled.

The freedmen had taken all the luggage onto the ship. They stayed aboard. We could see sailors assuming their places at the mooring ropes. The captain hovered at the head of the gangplank, impatient to sail now that he had the breeze and approaching light. None of us made any attempt to look for Linus. It was best to forget he was there.

The vessel was a roomy merchantman called the *Aphrodite*. Balbinus would be well set up; there was a cabin for the captain and favored passengers, a latrine hanging over the stern, even a galley where food could be prepared. The *Aphrodite* was half as big again as the ship on which Helena and I had returned from Syria. She needed to be strongly built to make such a long voyage so late in the year.

Now the criminal stood looking hesitant; he seemed uncertain what was expected of him. "Am I to board?"

His doubt did not last. Petronius Longus appeared in front of him, flanked by Martinus and me. The other squad members clustered close, in a tight circle.

"Just a few formalities." It was clear that now that Balbinus was in the care of the Fourth Cohort there would be no hail-fellow hand-shaking. "I've waited a long time, Balbinus," Petro said.

"No doubt you have done your duty, officer." The man spoke with reproach. He still seemed like a tunic-braid salesman—one who had just been told to his amazement that his embroidered Egyptian fancies had leaked crimson dye all over ten togas at some swanky laundry. "I am innocent of the crimes of which I have been accused."

"They all say that," Petronius complained, addressing the sky in despair. "Gods, I hate this hypocrisy! A straight villain always respects a straight arrest. He'll shrug and accept that he's caught. But all you self-justifying types have to make out that you cannot believe anyone could so terribly misjudge you. You convince yourselves all that matters in a civilized society is for men like you to continue your business without interference from officious sods like us. Sods who don't understand." Petronius set his jaw so hard I thought I heard his molars crunch. "Only I do understand!" he sneered. "I understand what you are all too well."

This rant had had no effect. Balbinus' eyes, some color you wouldn't bother to notice, wandered to me. He seemed to realize I was an outsider, and was hoping for some sympathy. "You had your chance," I told him, before he could start whining. "The benefit of a jury trial, in the calm of the Basilica. Six lawyers. A jury of your equals, who heard about your activities without allowing themselves to be sickened. A judge who, even while passing sentence, was polite. Meanwhile, outside, market traders still had their takings grabbed by your rampaging street gangs. Near-destitute old women were being tricked out of their savings. Men who dared to resist your holdup thieves spilled their lifeblood into the gutter. Female slaves were sold into prostitution by angry mistresses after your footpads snatched the shopping money—" Petronius moved slightly. I fell silent.

"Is there anything further you wish to tell me about your business?" Petro's request was formal; a vain hope.

"I am innocent," Balbinus intoned solemnly.

Petro's sarcasm was milder than I expected: "Oh, for a moment I thought you were going to surprise me and admit something."

His men were on edge, wanting to retaliate, wanting something to make them feel good.

Petronius held out his hand, palm upwards. "You can keep what you stand up in. I need your equestrian ring."

With automatic obedience, the big rissole pulled off the badge of his lost social status, struggling to wrench it over his first knuckle bone. He looked puzzled again. "May I have a receipt?"

"No need." Petro took the small band of gold between finger and thumb as if it offended him. He set it edge up on the top of a bollard, then raised one boot. A full inch of layered oxhide stamped down, studded with iron and molded by hard usage to intractable curves that echoed the shape of Petro's foot. I knew, through having stumbled over it on many occasions when drunk, that my old tentmate's massive trotter deserved respect.

Petro crushed the ring into a useless twist. Sneering, he handed it back. The state would forgo that gold.

"You're enjoying this," Fusculus tutted, pretending to admonish his chief. Fitted out with a sense of irony, Fusculus must be the sensitive one.

"I enjoy knowing that I'm never going to see this bastard again."

"Strip him of his rights!" That was Martinus, ever eager for drama and about as sensitive as a dead newt.

Petronius Longus folded his arms. Enjoying this he might be, but he sounded tired: "Tiberius Balbinus Pius, you stand condemned of capital crimes. The laws of Rome grant you time to depart. That is your only prerogative. You are no longer a citizen. You no longer possess equestrian rank, nor the honors attached to that rank. Your property is forfeit to the Treasury and your accusers. Your wife, children, and heirs have no future claims upon it. You shall depart beyond the Empire. You shall never return. If you set foot in any territory governed by Rome, the penalty is death."

"I am innocent!" Balbinus whined.

"You're grime!" roared Petronius. "Get on the boat before I forget myself!"

Balbinus shot him a vindictive look, then walked straight to the ship.

VI

Petro and I regained the quay later that morning. We had snatched a few hours' snoring on a bench in a wine bar that was fractionally more friendly than our previous foray. While we were relaxing the scene had changed completely. It was light. The quays were full of people. After a long, nerve-racking night, the hubbub was a shock.

As we hunted for the *Providentia,* which had brought me home from Syria, we could now make out fully the great man-made harbor basin. This was Portus. Claudius had first enclosed the spectacular new mooring that had replaced the old silted-up basin two miles away at Ostia. Nowadays only shallow-draft barges could use the old port. Portus had taken several decades of construction since Claudius sank the first breakwater—a massive ship once used to carry an obelisk for Caligula. That was now the base of a two-hundred-foot mole holding back the weather and carrying the three-storied lighthouse whose constant beacon announced from the harbor mouth that this was the center of world navigation: one hundred and sixty acres of quiet mooring, to which all the Empire's trade came, eager to cough up harbor tax. I had paid my tax like a good citizen, one whose brother-in-law was a customs officer who liked asking unwanted questions. I was now trying to reclaim my goods.

There was more noise than earlier. Workers were already pouring in from Ostia along the road through the market and flower gardens, or via the Claudian canal (which badly needed widening and dredging): clerks, customs inspectors, owners of vessels and goods, all jostling on the jetties with passengers and porters. We were tired, and the scene was unfamiliar. Somehow the waterfront turmoil stripped us of our normal authority. Petronius and I were battered and cursed along with every other stranger.

"Sorry for getting you into this," I told him ruefully. He was taking it well, however. This was by no means the worst pickle we had been in. Balbinus had put us in a gloomy mood; we were glad to forget him. We applied ourselves to commerce like heroes on behalf of my auctioneer father. He irritated all Hades out of me—but he had at least given us a chance to skive at the seaside for a time.

My father's general habit was to cause me trouble. From the day he had run away from home, when I was still in the tunic of childhood, I had despised pretty well everything he did. I never dealt with him if I could help it, but he had a way of winding himself into my life, however hard I tried to avoid it.

He had known better than to ask me to help him make money from my trip to Syria. On hearing of our exotic destination, he had commissioned Helena instead. Helena Justina, my girlfriend, who had been brought up a senator's daughter, thought Pa was just a likable scamp. She said I was too hard on him. She wanted us all to be friends; this gave Pa a chance to inveigle her into any devious scheme, especially if he could do it behind my back.

Though he claimed to be destitute (a piteous but fake complaint), my father had managed to dispatch Helena with instructions to get me to Tyre if she could—and with a two-hundred-thousand-sesterces banker's draft. She had a free hand to spend this exorbitant sum. He must have trusted her taste. In thirty years he had never given me such leeway with his private funds.

We had naturally been investing for ourselves as well; no

point traveling to one of the Empire's richest markets unless you buy cheap from the caravans. Using Helena's money mainly, plus my own meager savings, we had laden ourselves with enough bales of silk to dress our entire families like Parthian dancing girls and still have some left over to sell. Helena's ex-husband had imported peppers, so we shied off those, but that left plenty of other spices to bring home in casks that hummed with addictive scents. We had purchased Arabian incense and other perfumes. I had acquired a few extras at markets when Helena was not looking. Then finally, just when I believed we were coming home, Helena Justina had coerced me into buying glassware for Papa.

She had made me do the bargaining, though she herself handled a portable abacus with a verve that made the traders sweat. She chose the stock; Helena had a good eye for a flask. Grumbling aside, glass was the desirable commodity. My father knew what he was doing. There were bowls and bottles, jugs and beakers in delicate pinks, metallic greens, sulfurous blues; vases with snakes of molten glass trailing around their elegant throats; tiny perfume flagons like little doves; jugs with furled spouts and fine etching. There was cameo glass, at a price that rivaled the incense. There were even spectacular funeral jars.

All this glass was a serious burden. We had crept home, trembling for the safety of Pa's fragile water sets and dinner bowls. As far as I knew, it was all in one piece when we sailed into Portus on the *Providentia*. All I had to do now was transport it upriver to Rome. If I wanted to remain Helena's private demigod, I had to make sure I did not slip with the bales.

All our own packages had already been taken over to Ostia on mules. I had booked a passage up the Tiber on a barge that was leaving today. Now I was on edge about Pa's damned glass. I did not intend to endure the rest of his lifetime being derided as the son who smashed the equivalent of two hundred thousand pieces of silver. This had to be done right.

Petronius had some sympathy; he was a loyal friend. But he lacked the direct interest I had myself, and I didn't blame

him for that. It was hard enough for *me* to interest myself in
another man's profit margins. Only Helena's pride in her
commission kept me going.

We were having trouble finding transport. We wanted to
take the glass to the old harbor using the canal. Some idiot
(me) had deemed this the best way. No one would hire us a
boat, though. After a couple of hours of fruitless begging,
Petro left me on the jetty, saying I was to keep looking out
for a skiff while he approached the harbor staff and mentioned his official position in a casual manner, hoping to get
us fixed up with reliable rowers that way.

He was gone so long I reckoned he must have slipped off
for breakfast without me. If I was lucky he might bring me
back a squashed roll with a sliver of limp cheese and a quarter of an olive. More likely the rascal would saunter back
whistling and say nothing. Great. The glass had been unloaded from the *Providentia* and left on the quay, so I had to
stay with it.

I had had enough. I tried to sit on a bollard, but they're
never designed to let a backside rest there. While seagulls
squawked scornfully, I cursed my father to Hades and back,
and even muttered about Petronius. I was wasting time here
when I had yet to spend a full day back in Rome. Petro's
caper with the criminal had robbed Helena and me of a
much-longed-for first night together in our own bed. Pa,
lounging with his boots on a lamp table, had told me that he
was "a bit too busy" to visit Ostia. So he had left me to reclaim his goods, which had already cost me enough trouble,
and on which, if I knew him, he would deny Helena her
agent's percentage. Assuming the daft girl had even thought
of asking for a percentage in the first place.

I was all set to kick the glass into the harbor when Destiny took pity. A couple of men in a sturdy boat actually
hailed me and asked if I wanted my goods ferried. I was delighted, though after six years as an informer, I naturally
viewed the offer with caution.

Adopting a suave manner, I made some inquiries. Luckily they had the right answers: They were members of the
rowers' guild, and owned their own craft. They looked like
lads who knew their business. Their names, which I insisted

on knowing, were Gaius and Phlosis. We agreed on a price, and they began loading my precious crates, taking all the care I asked for. There were a lot of crates. When they finished, they had to tell me apologetically that the boat could not take me as well. It did seem pretty low in the water.

Time was running out if I was to catch the barge. Gaius and Phlosis seemed so concerned that I might think they were stealing my collateral, I reluctantly agreed to let them row to Ostia without me while I took one of the regular hired carts. We would meet at the barge; they themselves suggested I didn't pay them until then. This evidence of their honesty clinched the deal.

Tired, and pleased to have sorted myself out without aid from Petro, who could be supercilious about commerce, I was ready to agree to anything sensible. I waved them off.

I was still on the quay, looking around for my friend, when I spotted another skiff. In it I could see Petro, who must have picked up his man Fusculus from somewhere. I waved impatiently. I would now have to explain to the second crew that their services were no longer needed—and if I knew the rules of the Ostian rowers' guild, they would probably demand a disappointment fee.

As I was tapping my toe, Petronius' two rowers suddenly began shouting. Then Petro himself joined in. His boatmen began to row very fast towards Gaius and Phlosis. They tried to speed up. Then, to my amazement, my two handy lads jumped over the side, swam rapidly to the jetty some distance from me, and made off down the quay.

The realization that I had been caught by a swindle fell on me like a cartload of wet sand.

Next moment I was screaming with anxiety over Pa's cargo of glass. Fortunately the inner harbor was sheltered, so there was rarely a swell, and no large ships were maneuvering at that moment. The abandoned skiff had rocked wildly when Gaius and Phlosis dived over the gunnels, but it had stayed afloat. It was collected by Petronius, who had stepped across from his own boat, then held the two craft close together so that Fusculus could scramble across too. Petronius could row; he brought my goods slowly back to me while his own boatmen raced to shore. Still yelling, they jumped out and ran after Gaius and Phlosis.

I didn't care about those thieves; I just wanted Pa's treasure. Petronius threw a rope to me, while Fusculus shook his head over my narrow escape. "You were certainly conned there! A lovely example of the craft rig," he informed me knowingly.

"Oh yes?"

"They steal a boat, then prowl the wharves looking for a sucker who has just arrived at the harbor and needs some goods transferred somewhere. Luckily our own two honest fellows recognized the boat. It belongs to a friend of theirs, so they knew your heroes must have pinched it."

I did not want to hear the depressing details, but I gave him a hand to jump back to dry land. "You're the expert on low tricks, are you, Fusculus?"

"Fusculus is a fervent scholar of the underworld." Petro grinned. Thankfully, he was too good a friend to jeer directly at my mistake.

"Balbinus used to run a gang who specialized in this dodge along the wharves by the Emporium," Fusculus said. "You'd be surprised, Falco, how easily tired travelers can be taken in."

"I'm not surprised at all," I growled.

The two rowers who had exposed the near disaster came back, having failed to catch my lads. We unloaded half the glass from the first boat, then got hot and fractious transferring it to the second one so we could spread the weight between the two and hitch a ride ourselves. Petronius, Fusculus, and I all stuck with the precious cargo right to the barge at Ostia. Not until I had seen every crate transferred did I feel able to relax again.

Exhausted by our adventures, we lay on deck in the autumn sunlight as slowly the barge started to navigate the shoals, creeping up the muddy Tiber into Rome.

VII

Helena Justina had not heard me come home. She was tying in strands of my climbing rose, a thing of long spindly growth that struggled for water and nourishment on the narrow balcony outside my sixth-floor apartment. For a moment I was able to watch her while she remained quite unaware of me.

Helena was tall, straight-backed, dark-haired, and serious. She was five days from her twenty-fifth birthday. The first time I ran across her, married life in the utmost luxury but with an insensitive young senator had left her bitter and withdrawn. She had just divorced him, and made it plain that anyone else who got in her way could expect to be kicked out of it. Don't ask how I got around the problem— but writing my memoirs promised some fun.

Astonishingly, two years of surviving scandal and squalor with me had softened the hard shell. Maybe it was being loved. Now, as she paused rather dreamily to suck at a thorn in her finger, there was a stillness about her. She looked far away, yet unconscious of her own thoughts.

I had neither moved nor made a sound, but she turned quickly. "Marcus?"

We embraced. I buried my face in her soft neck, groaning

with gratitude for the way her strong, sweet face had lit with pleasure when she realized I was there.

All the same, it worried me. I would have to hang a bell inside our entrance door, so nobody else could creep up on her like this. Where we lived was a lawless tenement.

Maybe I needed to find a better place for us.

Helena seemed tired. We were both still drained of energy after traveling home from the East. Coming in and crossing the outer room, I had seen evidence that she must have spent my absence at Ostia unpacking and tidying. My mother or one of my sisters might have dropped in to help, but they fussed around and were likely to have been seen off politely with cinnamon tea and a few tales about our journey. Helena never fussed. She liked to set things just so—and then forget about them.

I pulled her to the rickety wooden bench, which felt even worse than I remembered. Bending down with a curse, I fiddled about with a piece of broken roof tile—which probably meant we had a new leak somewhere—and managed to level up the bench's feet. Then at last we sat quietly together, gazing out across the river.

"Now there's a view!"

She smiled. "You love coming home, Marcus."

"Coming home to you is the best part."

As usual Helena ignored my suggestive gleam—though as usual I could tell she welcomed it. "Did everything go all right at Ostia?"

"More or less. We got back to Rome about an hour ago. Pa finally managed to show an interest. Once I'd done the hard work, he turned up and took charge at the Emporium." Luckily my father actually lived on the riverbank, below the Aventine cliff and only a step from the wharves. "He's got the glass, so make sure he pays you an agency fee."

Helena seemed to smile at my advice. "Did Petronius do what he wanted? And are you now going to tell me what the fuss was about?"

"He was sending a condemned man into exile."

"A real villain?" she asked, lifting her bold eyebrows as she caught my surly tone.

"The worst." Petronius Longus would be horrified at the way I shared such information; I knew he never told his wife anything about his work. Helena and I had always discussed things; for me, the big rissole was unfinished business so long as I was waiting to confide in Helena. "Balbinus Pius. We saw him on to his ship, and one of Petro's men has gone along undercover to see he doesn't hop ashore prematurely. By the way, I asked Petro and Silvia to dinner once we're straight again. Everything in order here?" I didn't bother looking back at the bare room behind me: a small table, three stools, shelves with a few crocks, pots, and beakers, a next-to-useless cooking bench.

"Oh yes."

For the past few months my sister Maia would have valiantly toiled up the six flights from time to time, making sure for us that no one broke in and that Smaractus, my pig of a landlord, had not tried his usual trick of squeezing extra cash from subtenants if he thought I was not here. Maia had also kept the balcony garden watered and had pinched back the herbs, though she drew the line at controlling the rose. She reckoned I had only planted it to get cheap flowers for seducing girls. All my sisters were naturally unfair.

I took charge of Helena's finger, removing the thorn with adept pressure from one thumbnail. My right hand was habitually caressing the two-month-old scar on her forearm, where she had been stung by a scorpion in the Syrian desert.

"I'll be in trouble over your war wound." Both my own mother and Helena's noble parent would blame me for taking her to such a dangerous province and bringing her back scarred for life. . . . And there might be another new situation that would set both our mothers on the alert. Newly home after a whole summer abroad, I did not want to start broaching issues. But I took a slow breath and braced myself. "Maybe there's worse than that in store for me."

Helena showed no reaction; so much for being mysterious.

"I think there's something we need to talk about."

She heard the message in my tone that time. She looked at me askance. "What's wrong, Marcus?"

Before I was ready I heard myself saying: "I'm beginning to suspect I'm going to be a father."

I fixed my gaze on the Ianiculan Mount and waited for her to accept or reject the news.

Helena was silent for a moment, then asked quietly, "Why do you say that?" There was a very slight rasp in her voice.

"Observation." I tried to sound nonchalant. "Matching evidence with probability is my job, after all."

"Well, I'm sure you're the one who knows!" Helena spoke like an angry householder whose chief steward had just accused a favorite slave of raiding the wine cellar. "How do you reckon it happened?"

"The usual way!" Now I sounded tetchy. We had only ourselves to blame. It was a classic failure of contraception—not the alum in wax letting anyone down, but two people failing to bother to use it.

"Oh," she said.

"Oh, indeed! I'm referring to a certain occasion in Palmyra—"

"I remember the date and time."

As I feared, she was sounding far from overjoyed. I decided that my consoling hand on the scorpion scar might be unwelcome; I drew back and folded my arms. Once again I gazed out beyond the Tiber to the Ianiculan Hill, where I sometimes dreamed of owning a villa if Destiny ever forgot that I was the one she liked tormenting with hammer blows. My chance of ever becoming a householder in a quiet and spacious home was in fact ludicrously slim.

"I know you have your position in society to think about," I told Helena, more stiffly than I had intended. "Your family's reputation, and of course your own." Unhelpfully, she made no comment. It tipped me into flippancy: "I'm not asking you to stand by me."

"I will, of course!" Helena insisted, rather bitterly.

"Better not commit yourself," I warned. "When you've had time to think, you may not be too happy about this."

We were not married. She was two ranks above me. We never would be married unless I could persuade the Emperor to promote me to the middle rank—which had been refused once already. One of the Caesars had turned down my request, even though I had earned quite a few favors from the Palace and my father had lent me the qualifying cash. Humbling myself to take the loan from Pa had been hard; I reckoned the Palace owed me more than favors now.

But the Palace was irrelevant. I was in a fix. Plebeians were not supposed to sleep with senators' female relations. I was not a slave, or I would have been dead meat long ago. There was no husband to be affronted, but Helena's father was entitled to view our crime in the same light as adultery. Unless I was much mistaken about the ancient traditions of our *very* traditional city, that gave him the right to execute me personally. Luckily Camillus Verus was a calm man.

"So how do *you* feel, Marcus?"

Fortunately, my life as an informer had trained me to avoid saying what I felt when it could only lead to trouble.

Helena filled in the gap for herself wryly, addressing the sky: "Marcus is a man. He wants an heir, but he doesn't want a scandal."

"Close!" I said it with a smile as if both of us were joking. She knew I was dodging the issue. Applying a serious expression, I altered my story: "It's not me who has to go through with the pregnancy and the dangers of birth." Not to mention enduring the extreme public interest. "What I think takes second place."

"Ho! That will be a novelty. . . . It may not happen," Helena suggested.

"Looks definite to me." Helena had been pregnant with a child of mine before, miscarrying before she had even told me. When I found out, I had vowed never to be left out again. Believe me, keeping track had not been easy. Helena was the kind of girl who lost her temper if she felt she was being watched. "Well, time will show if I'm right."

"And there's plenty of time," she murmured. I sat there wondering: time for what?

The child would be illegitimate, of course. It would take its mother's rank—utterly worthless without a father's pedigree to quote as well. Freed slaves stood a better chance.

We could cope with that, if it ever came to it. What was

likely to break us, one way or another, would happen to us before the poor scrap was even born.

"I don't want to lose you," I stated abruptly.

"You won't."

"Look, I think it's fair to ask what you want to do."

Helena was frowning. "Marcus, why can't you be like other men, who don't want to face up to things?" Maybe she was joking, but she sounded serious. I recognized her expression; she was not prepared to think about this. She was not intending to talk.

"Let me say what I have to." I tried playing the man of the house, knowing this normally only got me laughed at. "I know you. You'll wait until I leave for the Forum, then you'll worry in private. If you choose a course of action, you'll try to do everything alone. I'll have to come chasing after you, like a farm boy left behind at market when the cart sets off for home."

"You'll soon catch up," she answered with a faint smile. "I know you too."

I was remembering the little I knew about what she had gone through, on her own, that other time. It was best not to think about it.

Legally, every day I kept her I was robbing her noble father. Once the results of our fling became apparent, Helena would be strongly encouraged to regularize her life. The obvious solution for her family would be a quick arranged marriage to some senator who was either too stupid to notice this, or plain long-suffering. "Helena, I just want you to promise that if there are decisions to be made, you will let me share in making them."

Suddenly she laughed, a tense and breathy explosion of dry mirth. "I think we took our decisions in Palmyra, Marcus Didius!"

The formality cut like a boning knife. Then, just when I thought I really had lost her, she seized me in a hug. "I love you very much," she exclaimed—and unexpectedly kissed me.

It was no answer.

On the other hand, when a senator's daughter tells a plebeian that she loves him, the man is entitled to feel a certain low pride. After that, it is all too easy to be seduced by the offer of coming indoors for dinner. And there are domestic routines of an even more wicked nature that can be made to follow dinner with a senator's daughter, if you can manage to lure one of these exotic and glorious creatures away from her noble father's house.

VIII

Allowing a woman to sidetrack me was routine. Come the morning, I was still resolute. Plenty of ineffectual clerks had hired me to chase after heartless females who were giving them the silly story; I was used to being offered sensual bribes to make me forget a mission.

Of course, I never accepted the bribes. And of course Helena Justina, that upright, ethical character, would never try to influence me by shameless means. She went to bed with me that night for the same reason she had always done so: because she wanted to. And the next day, I carried on directly facing up to the situation because that was what *I* wanted.

Helena carried on dodging. I had made absolutely no progress in finding out how she felt. That was fine. Her motives defied prediction. That was why I was in love with her; I was tired of predictable women. I could be persistent. Maybe that was why she was in love with me.

Assuming she really was. A shiver as I remembered our lovemaking last night convinced me—at which point I stopped worrying.

I washed my face, rinsed my teeth, and bit my way into a hard bread roll—yesterday's; we lived too far from the street to buy fresh loaves for breakfast. I gulped down some of the warm drink I was preparing for Helena. While she sleepily drank hers in bed, I put on a tunic that had spiced itself up with a gay shower of moth holes and renewed acquaintance with a wrinkled old belt that looked as if it had been tanned from the ox Romulus had used to measure Rome. I dragged a comb into my curls, hit a tangle, and decided to keep the relaxed coiffure that matched my casual clothes. I cleaned my boots and sharpened my knife. I counted my small change—a swift task—then transferred the purse to today's belt.

I kissed Helena, following up with a bit of fumbling under the bedsheet. She accepted the playfulness, laughing at me. "Oh, go and flaunt your Eastern tan where the men show off. . . ." Today she would readily surrender me to the Forum, the baths, even the imperial offices. She knew that when I had had my fill of the city I would come home to her.

After a short tussle with the outer door, which had taken to sticking, I limped downstairs. I had hurt my toe kicking the doorframe and was cursing gently: home again. Everything as I remembered it.

I was absorbing the familiar experience of the ramshackle apartment block; for five floors angry voices reached me from behind curtains and half doors. Two apartments per story; two or three rooms per apartment; two and a half families per dwelling, and as many as five or six people to a room. Sometimes there were fewer occupants, but they ran a business, like the mirror-polisher and the tailor. Sometimes one room contained an old lady who had been the original tenant, now almost forgotten amid the rumbustious invaders to whom Smaractus had sublet parts of her home "to help her with the rent." He was a professional landlord. Nothing he did was to help anybody but himself.

I noticed a few more graffiti gladiators chalked on the poorly rendered walls. There was a smell like wet dog mingling with yesterday's steamed cabbage. Stepping down around one dark corner, I had a narrow escape when I nearly trod on some child's lost pottery horse-on-wheels, which would have skated my foot from under me and probably left me with a broken back. I put the horse on a ledge, alongside a broken rattle and one tiny sandal that had been there when I left for Syria.

The stairs ended outside in a dim nook under two columns that had once made a portico. The rest of this row of columns had long ago fallen down and vanished; it was best not to think about what was happening to the parts of the building they had been meant to support. Now most of the frontage was open, allowing free encroachment from Lenia's laundry. She had the whole ground floor, which according to her included what passed for a pavement and half the dusty road in Fountain Court. Just now her staff were doing the main morning wash, so warm, humid air hit me as I reached the street. Several rows of soaking togas and tunics hung nicely at face height, ready to slap at anyone who tried to leave the building on lawful business.

I went inside to be neighborly. The sweet smell of urine, which was used for bleaching togas, met me like an old acquaintance I was trying to avoid. I had not seen Lenia yet, so when someone else shrieked my name she thrust herself out from the steamy hubbub like some disreputable sand beetle heaving its way above ground. She had armfuls of crumpled garments crushed against her flopping bosom, her chin balanced on top of the smelly pile. Her hair was still an unconvincing red; after the sophisticated henna treatments of the East, it looked hideously brash. The damp air had stuck her long tunic to parts of her body, producing an effect that did little for a man of the world like me.

She staggered towards me with an affectionate cry of "Look! Something nasty's blown in with the road dust!"

"Aphrodite rising from the washtub, sneezing at the wood ash!"

"Falco, you rat's bum."

"What's new, Lenia?" I answered breezily.

"Trade's bad, and the weather's a menace."

"That's hardly new. Have I missed the wedding?"

"Don't make me angry!" She was betrothed to Smaractus, a business arrangement. (Each craved the other's business.) Lenia's contempt for my landlord exceeded even mine, though she had a religious respect for his money. I knew she had carried out a meticulous audit before deciding Smaractus was the man of her dreams. Lenia's dreams were practical. She really intended to go through with it apparently, for after the conventional cursing she added, "The wedding's on the Kalends of November. You're invited so long as you promise to cause a fight with the nut boys and to throw up on his mother." I've seen some sordid things, but the idea of my landlord having a mother set me back somewhat. Lenia saw my look and laughed harshly. "We're going to be desperate for entertainment at this party. The arrangements are driving me mad, Falco. I don't suppose you would read the omens for us?"

"Surely you need a priest?"

Lenia shrieked with outrage. "I wouldn't trust one of those sleazy buggers! Don't forget I've washed their underwear. I'm in enough trouble without having my omens muckcd up. . . . You're a citizcn. You can do it if you're prepared to be a pal."

"A man's duty is to honor the gods for his own household," I intoned, suddenly becoming a master of informed piety.

"You're scared of the job."

"I'm just trying to get out of it."

"Well, you live in the same building."

"No one ever told me it meant peering into a sheep's liver for the damned landlord! That's not in my lease."

"Do it for me, Falco!"

"I'm not some cranky Etruscan weather forecaster." I was losing ground. Lenia, who was a superstitious article, looked genuinely anxious; my old friendship with her was about to take its toll. "Oh, I'll think about it. . . . I told you from the start, woman, you're making a big mistake."

"I told you to mind your own business," quipped Lenia, in her brutal, rasping voice. "I heard you were back from your travels—though this is the first time you've bothered to call on me!"

"Having a lie-in." I managed to beat her to a leering grin.

"Scandalous bastard! Where've you been to this time, and was there profit in it?"

"The East. And of course not."

"You mean you're too tight to tell me."

"I mean I'm not giving Smaractus any excuse to bump my rent up!" That reminded me of something. "This deadly dump is getting too inconvenient, Lenia. I'll have to find somewhere more salubrious to live."

"Oh Great Mother!" Lenia exclaimed immediately. "He's pregnant!"

Taken aback by the shrewdness of her guesswork, I blushed—losing any chance of disguising my plight. "Don't be ridiculous," I lied as brazenly as possible. "I know how to look after myself."

"Didius Falco, I've seen you do a lot of stupid things." That was true. She had known me since my bachelor days. "But I never thought you'd be caught out in the old way!"

It was my turn to say mind your own business, and Lenia's to laugh seditiously.

I changed the subject. "Does your slimy betrothed still own that decrepit property across the court?"

"Smaractus never disposes of a freehold." He never bothered to redevelop a wrecked tenement, either. As an entrepreneur, Smaractus was as dynamic as a slug. "Which property, Falco?"

"The first-floor spread. What's he call it? *'Refined and commodious self-contained apartment at generous rent; sure to be snapped up.'* You with me?"

"The dump he's been advertising on my wall for the past four years? Don't be the fool who does snap it up, Falco. The refined and commodious back section has no floor."

"So what? My shack upstairs hardly has a roof. I'm used to deprivation. Mind if I take a look at the place?"

"Do what you like." Lenia sniffed. "What you see is all there is. He won't do it up for you. He's short of loose change."

"Of course. He's getting married!" I grinned. "Old Smaractus must be spending every day of the week burying his money bags in very deep holes in faraway fields in Latium. If he's got any sense, he'll then lose the map."

I could tell Lenia was on the verge of advising me to jump down the Great Sewer and close the manhole after me, but we were interrupted by a more than usually off-putting messenger.

It was a grubby little girl of about seven years, with large feet and a very small nose. She had a scowling expression that I immediately recognized as similar to my own. She was one of my nieces. I could not remember which niece, though she definitely came from the Didius tribe. She looked like my sister Galla's offspring. They had a truly useless father, and, apart from the eldest, who had sensibly left home, they were a pitiful, struggling crew. Someone had hung one of those bull's-testicle amulets around this one's neck to protect her from harm, though whoever it was had not bothered to teach her to leave her scabs alone or to wipe her nose.

"Oh Juno," rasped Lenia. "Take her out of here, Falco. My customers will think they'll catch something."

"Go away," I greeted the niece convivially.

"Uncle Marcus! Have you brought us any presents?"

"No." I had done, because all my sister's children were in sore need of a devoted, uncomplicated uncle to ruin their characters with ridiculous largesse. I couldn't spoil only the clean and polite ones, though I had no intention of letting the other little brats think me an easy touch. Anyone who came and asked for their ceramic Syrian camel with the nodding head would have to wait a week for it.

"Oh Uncle Marcus!" I felt like a heel, as she intended.

"Cut the grizzling. Listen, what's your name—"

"Tertulla," she supplied, without taking offense.

"What are you after, Tertulla?"

"Grandpa sent me."

"Termites! You haven't found me, then."

"It's urgent, Uncle Marcus!"

"Not as urgent as scratching your elbow—I'm off!"

"He said you'd give me a copper for finding you."

"Well he's wrong." Needing to argue more strongly, I had to resort to blackmail. "Listen, wasn't yesterday the Ides?" One good thing about helping Petronius at Ostia was that we had missed the Festival of the October Horse—once a savage carnival and horse race, now just a complete mess in the streets. It was also the end of the official school holidays. "Shouldn't you be starting school now? Why are you loose today?"

"I don't want to go."

"Tertulla, everyone who has a chance to go to school should be grateful for the privilege." What an insufferable prig. "Leave me alone, or I'm telling your grandma you've bunked off."

My mother was helping with the fees for Galla's children, a pure waste of money. Ma would have stood for a better return gambling on chariot races. What nobody seemed to have noticed was that since I gave my mother financial support, it was *my* cash being flung away.

"Oh Uncle Marcus, don't!"

"Oh nuts. I'm going to."

I was already feeling gloomy. From the first moment Tertulla mentioned my father, I had begun to suspect today might not be all I had been planning. Good-bye, baths; good-bye, swank at the Forum . . . "Grandpa's in trouble. Your friend Petronius told him to get you," my niece cried. Persistence ran in the family, if it involved telling bad news.

Petro knew what I felt about my father. If Pa was in such trouble Petro reckoned even I would help him out, the trouble must really be serious.

IX

The Emporium is a long, secure building close to the Tiber. The barges that creep up from Ostia reach the city with Caesar's Gardens on their left, and a segment of the Aventine district, below the Hill, to their right. Where they meet the left-hand city boundary at the Transtiberina, with a long view upriver towards the Probus Bridge, lying to their right they find the Emporium, a vast indoor market that includes the ancient Aemilian Portico. You can smell it from the water. A blind man would know he had arrived.

Here, anything buildable, wearable, or edible that is produced in any province of the Empire comes to be unloaded at the teeming wharves. The slick stevedores, who are renowned for their filthy tempers and flash off-duty clothing, then crash the goods onto handcarts, dump them in baskets, or wheel about with great sacks on their shoulders, ferrying them inside the greatest indoor market in the world. Cynical sales are conducted, and before the importer has realized he has been rooked by the most devious middlemen in Europe, everything whirls out again to destinations in workshops, warehouses, country estates, or private homes. The money-changers wear happy smiles all day.

Apart from a few commodities like grain, paper, and

spices, which are so precious or are sold in such quantities that they have their own markets elsewhere, you can buy anything at the Emporium. Through his profession, my father was well known there. He no longer involved himself in general sales, for his interest had narrowed to the kind of fine-art trade that is conducted in quieter, highly tasteful surroundings where the purchaser submits to a more leisurely screwing and then pays a more gigantic premium to the auctioneer.

Pa was a character people noticed. Normally I could have asked anybody if they had seen Geminus, and pretty soon someone would have told me which hot-wine stall he was lurking at. I should have been able to find him easily—if only the fierce patrolmen of the Fourth Cohort of vigiles had been letting people in.

The scene was incredible. Nothing like it could ever have happened before. The Emporium lay in the area included by Augustus when he redrew Rome's boundaries because habitation had expanded. I had made the mistake of coming out from the old part through the city walls, using the Lavernal Gate—a spot always busy but today almost impassable. Down in the shadow of the Aventine approaching the Tiber, I had found chaos. It had taken me an hour to force a passage through the people who were clogging up the Ostia Road. By the time I really made it to the wharves beside the river, I knew something highly peculiar must have gone wrong. I was prepared for a scene—though not one evidently caused by my sensible friend Petronius.

It was midmorning. The gates to the Emporium, normally closed at night for security but flung open at first light and kept that way well into the evening, now stood barred. Red-faced members of the watch were drawn up with their backs to the doors. There were a lot of them: Five hundred men formed the half-cohort that patrolled the river side of the Aventine. A proportion were dedicated to fire-watching, and with the special dangers of darkness they were mostly on duty at night. That still left ample cover to combat daylight crime. Now, Petronius must have drawn up all the day roster. The line was holding, but I was glad I was not part of it. A huge, angry crowd was milling about insulting the watch and calling for Petro's head. Occasionally a group rushed forwards, and the line of patrolmen had to link arms and face them out. I could see a small cluster at the far end of the building where Porcius was handing out shields from a wagon.

Petro was nowhere in sight. It seemed wise.

With a spurt of anxiety I shoved my way to the front. "Great gods, what's this? Am I supposed to believe that Petronius Longus, notorious for caution, has suddenly decided to make his name in history as the Man Who Stopped Trade?"

"Shove off, Falco!" muttered Fusculus, who had been trying to argue with four or five score merchants and workmen, many of them foreign and all of them spitting fire.

"Petro sent for me." It was worth a try.

"Petro's not bloody here!" Fusculus told me through bitterly clenched teeth as he pushed back a furious Gallic wine merchant by the simple means of lifting one leg and applying his boot sole firmly to the man's belt buckle. The Fourth Cohort were slightly more sophisticated than others in Rome, but no one argued with them twice. "Petro's in shit. A Praetorian Guard dragged him off to the Palace to explain this mess."

"I may as well get back to bed, then!"

"You do that, Falco. . . ."

The vigiles had their hands full. With so large a crowd, in such an ugly mood, I did not fancy helping them. Luckily, they did not demean themselves by asking. I had a let-out anyway, for I heard my name roared by an unmistakable foghorn, and turned to be greeted by my papa. He clapped me in his arms affectionately. This was not his normal greeting, just showing off before a crowd of foreigners. I shook myself free angrily.

"Marcus! Let's get out of this stew—we've things to discuss!"

I had nothing to discuss with my father. I experienced the usual sense of dread.

He hauled me into a more or less quiet corner around the back of the old Galban granaries. Needless to say, the corner was in a wine bar. After my exhausting passage through the streets I did not object to that, though in an equal world, since he had issued the summons, I would have preferred that he paid the bill. Somehow the chalked piece of tile landed on the table in front of me.

"Oh, thanks, Marcus. Your health!"

My father was a sturdy character of sixty-odd, with a graying thatch of marauding curls and what passed for a twinkle in his untrustworthy dark brown eyes. He went by the name of Geminus, though his real name was Favonius. There was no point in the change; that was typical. Not tall, he was still a commanding presence; people who wanted to annoy me said we looked alike. In fact he was heavier and shiftier. His belly supported a money belt whose weight told its own story. His dark blue tunic was now old enough to be used when he was lifting furniture around warehouses, but the wrecked braid on it, still with traces of silver thread, gave a clue to the style he could afford when relaxing socially. Women liked his grin. He liked most things about women. He had run away with a red-haired one when I was a child, after which he and I could hardly exchange a civil word.

"Your mad crony's caused a bit of a pickle!" One of the few paternal routines he still honored was criticizing my friends.

"He would have had his reasons," I said coldly. I was trying to think of any possible reason for what Petronius had done. "This can't just be a reprisal because some stallholder forgot to pay his market dues."

I have to admit, the thought had struck me that maybe Petro was so proud of himself for capturing Balbinus that he had become a power-crazed maniac. This had always been a Roman trait, at the first hint of success to dream of being deified. It seemed unlikely in Petro's case, however. He was so rational he was positively staid.

"Tertulla said you'd spoken to him," I prodded.

"Oh, you've seen Tertulla? That little mite needs looking after. You're her uncle. Can't you do something?"

"You're her grandfather! Why me?" I felt myself going hot. Trying to instill a sense of duty into Father, who had already abandoned one generation, was hopeless. "Oh Jupiter!

I'll see Galla about it sometime. . . . What's the tale here,
Pa?"

"Disaster." My father enjoyed a spot of misery.

"Well, that's clear! Can we be more specific? Does this
disaster involve a major defeat for the legions in a prestigious foreign war—or just the lupin crop failing in two vil-
lages in Samnium?"

"You're a sarcastic trout! It's this: A gang of robbers burst
in last night and cleaned out half the Emporium." Pa leaned
back on his stool, watching the effect on me. I tried to look
suitably horrified, while still dwelling thoughtfully on my
own fancy rhetoric. He scowled. "Listen, you dozy bastard!
They obviously knew exactly what they wanted—luxury
items in every case. They must have been watching for
weeks, until they knew they could snatch an exquisite
haul then they whipped in, snatched the goods to order,
whipped out, and vanished before anything was noticed."

"So Petronius has shut the building while he investigates
what happened?"

"I suppose so. But you know him; he wasn't saying. He
just looked solemn and closed it."

"So what *did* he say?"

"Stallholders and wharfingers would be let in one by one,
with his man Martinus—"

"Another master of tact!" Martinus, with his high opinion
of himself, was especially dour when dealing with the public.

"To make a list of what was missing." Pa completed his
sentence doggedly.

"Well, that's fair," I said. "Surely those idiots can see that
their best chance of getting their property back will be if
Petronius knows what to look for?"

"Too subtle," replied Pa with the famous flashing grin
that had laid barmaids on their backs from here to the
Flaminian Gate. It only caused irritation in me.

"Too organized!" Petronius had my sympathies. Presumably he had come back from Ostia expecting a short stretch
of peace after his Balbinus coup, only to be dragged from
bed that very night to face one of the worst heists I could remember, in the most important building on his patch. In-

stead of enjoying a glorious rest as a community hero, he now faced working at full stretch for months. Probably with nothing to show at the end; it sounded as if this robbery had been scrupulously planned.

One aspect was still niggling me. "Just as a matter of interest, Pa—why did Petronius tell you to send for me?"

My father put on his reliable look—always a depressing portent. "Oh . . . he reckoned you might help me get back my glass."

He had slipped it in as delicately as a fishmonger filleting a mullet.

"They stole your glass?" I could not accept this. "The glass Helena bought for you? That I nursed all the way back from Syria?" I lost my temper. "Pa, when I left it with you, you told me you were carting the whole lot straight back to the Saepta!" The Saepta Julia, up by the Plain of Mars, was the jewelry quarter where Pa had his office and warehouse. It was very well guarded.

"Stop roaring."

"I will not! How could you be so damned careless?"

I knew exactly how. Traipsing to the Saepta with a wagon would have taken him an hour or two. Since he only lived two minutes from the Emporium, he had gone home and put his feet up instead, leaving the glass that we had nursed so carefully to look after itself for the night.

Pa glanced over one shoulder and lowered his voice. "The Emporium should have been safe enough. It was just temporary."

"Now it's temporarily lost!" There was something shifty about him. My lava eruption checked in midflow. "I thought you said this lift was planned? That they knew just what they were going for? How could anybody know that you had half a treasury in Syrian dinnerware, coincidentally brought home by me that very evening and locked up there for only one night?"

Pa looked offended. "They must have found it by chance."

"Oh, donkey's balls!"

"There's no need to be coarse."

I was doing worse than that: I was taking a stand. "Now listen, Pa, let's get something straight. This loss is your affair. I don't want to hear any nonsense like you'll not pay Helena because you never took delivery—"

"Stuff you!" scoffed Pa. "I'd never cheat that girl, and you know it." It was probably true. He had a sickening respect for Helena's rank, and a wild hope she would make him a grandfather of senators one day. This was not the moment to tell him he was halfway home on that one. In fact, that was when I started hoping we would have a girl. "Look, son, I know how to shrug off a reverse. If the glass is gone for good I'll have to carry the loss and keep smiling. But after you buzzed off last night, I looked through the boxes. It was beautiful quality—"

"Helena can pick out a tasty jug."

"Too right. And I'm damned if I'll let it go without a fight. I want you to help track it down for me."

I had already worked out what he wanted. I had my answer ready too: "I have to earn. I'll need a fee. I'll need expenses."

"Oh we can come to some arrangement," murmured Pa in his airy fashion. He knew Helena would be so upset when she heard this that I would probably end up searching for him for free. He also knew that finding stolen art was my specialty, so he had come to the best man. Other people would be after my services too. Pa had got to me first, before anyone else who had suffered losses today— anyone who might actually pay me—could claim my time.

I downed my wine, then shoved the bill across the table pointedly. If he was paying my expenses he could start with the one for entertaining him. "I'm off then."

"Beginning already?" Pa had the grace to look impressed. "Do you know where to look?"

"That's right." Well, I knew how to lie well.

In fact, I had only one plan at this stage: Petronius Longus had been hauled to the Palace by the imperial guard. He was in grave trouble. After all the times he had criticized the way I carried out my own work, I could stand watching him squirm. I was off to see how he tried to convince the Emperor that he knew what he was doing.

Besides, Petro was my oldest friend. There was a risk he was about to lose his job for today's action. If I could, I would help him bluff his way out of that.

X

I marched up the Clivus Victoriae to the old Palace of Tiberius, where the bureaucrats still had their offices.

Petronius Longus was sitting on a bench in a corridor. He had been there long enough to start looking worried. His face was pale. He was leaning forwards with his knees apart, staring at his upturned palms. I saw him twitch as I arrived. He pretended to look suave. I thumped his shoulder and berthed alongside.

"Lucius Petronius—the man who brought Rome to a standstill!"

"Don't harass me, Falco!"

"Don't fidget. I'm here to back you up."

"I can manage."

"Well, you can manage to get yourself into a fix."

"I don't need a nursemaid."

"No, you need a friend at court." He knew I was right.

"You've been there, I take it, Falco? What's going on now?"

"Fusculus is keeping the crowds penned out. Porcius is distributing riot shields. I didn't see Martinus. Pa told me the gist of last night's disaster."

"He lost that glass of yours, he says." Petro knew my fa-

ther well enough to allow for possible deception. I was un-
perturbed by the insult to the family name. It had never
stood high, least of all in respect of Papa. "They were a
sharp crowd of thieves, Falco. I don't like the smell of it.
Geminus lost his glass; we know that was quality.
Calpurnius was deprived of a huge haul of porphyry that
also only came in yesterday. Someone else lost ivory." I
wondered what, if anything, was special about goods landed
yesterday. "Martinus is collecting full details, but we can see
the losses are serious."

"I thought the Emporium was guarded at night?"

Petro growled in the back of his throat. "All hit over the
head and laid out in a line like dead sardines, tied up and
gagged."

"Neat. Too neat?" I queried thoughtfully. "An inside job,
maybe?"

"Possibly." Petro had thought of it. "I'll work some of the
guards over. When I get the chance."

"If!" I grinned, reminding him that his position was about
to be tested. "This could be your big chance to meet the Emperor."

"I've met him." Petro was terse. "I met him with you,
Falco! On the famous occasion when he offered you a fortune to keep quiet about a scandal, but you opted for the
high moral ground and threw away the cash."

"Sorry." I had not forgotten refusing the fortune, merely
that Petro had been there watching me play the fool. I had
made the mistake of uncovering a plot that impinged too
closely on the imperial family; struck by an urgent need to
protect his son Domitian, Vespasian had rashly promised me
advancement, a ploy he now regretted, probably. It had been
pointless in any case, given that I had turned the offer down
in a high-handed manner. "Nobody buys my silence."

"Hah!" Petronius knew the only loser had been myself.

Suddenly a chamberlain slid out through a curtain and
gave Petro the nod.

I stood up too. "I'm with him." The official had recognized me. If he thought I was trouble he was too well
groomed to let it show.

"Didius Falco." He greeted me smoothly. The two Praetorian Guards flanking the doorway gave no sign of hearing what was said, but I knew they would now let me pass inside without tying my arms in a Hercules knot. I had no wish to approach anyone of regal status looking flustered after a fight. I knew, even though we were not in the right part of the Palace, that we were about to meet regality; hence the Praetorians.

Petronius had shot towards the curtain the minute he was signaled. Before he could object, I stepped past him and entered the audience chamber. He grabbed the curtain and bounced in after me.

Petronius would have been expecting an office, one full of people perhaps, but all with the kind of status he felt free to ignore. I heard him utter something, then cut it off short. It was a lofty room full of scribes. But there was one other, very particular occupant. Petro choked. Even though I had warned him, he had not seriously expected that he would meet the Emperor.

Vespasian was reclining on a reading couch, glancing over a note tablet. His craggy face was unmistakable; he had certainly not bothered to demand a flattering portrait when he approved the new coin issue.

There was no pomp. The couch was against a side wall, as if it had been placed there for casual visitors. The whole impression was that the lord of the Empire had just dropped in and made himself at home in someone else's cubbyhole.

Centrally, there was the long table, covered with scrolls and piles of tablets. Secretaries were stationed there with their styli. They were scratching away very fast, but the speed was unforced. A young slave, smart though not particularly handsome, stood quietly near the Emperor, a napkin over one arm. In fact, Vespasian was pouring his own drink—half a cup, just to wet his whistle. He left it on a bronze pedestal so that he was free to stare at us.

He was a big, easygoing, competent character. An organizer, he had the direct glance of a blacksmith, with the country-born arrogance that reminded me of my grandfather. He knew what he believed. He said what he thought. People acted on what he said. They did it nowadays because they had to, but people had been jumping when Vespasian barked since long before he was Emperor.

He had held all the civil magistracies and the highest military ranks. Every post in his career through the *cursus honorum* had been screwed out on merit and in the face of Establishment prejudice. Now he held the final post available. The Establishment was still prejudiced against him, but he need not care.

He wore the purple; it was his entitlement. With it he had neither wreath nor jewels. For him the best adornment of rank was acute native intelligence. That was aimed at us. An uncomfortable experience.

"Falco! What are you doing here, and who's your big bodyguard?"

I walked forwards. "I act as his guardian actually, sir." Petronius, annoyed at my joke, followed me; I shoved him to the front. "This is my friend Lucius Petronius Longus, whom you want to see: the inquiry captain of the Aventine sector in the Fourth Cohort of the vigiles. He's one of the best—but he's also the happy fellow who shut the Emporium today."

Vespasian Augustus stared at Petronius. Petronius looked self-conscious, then thought better of it and stared boldly at the floor. It was marble, a tasteful acreage in black and white. The tesselations had been laid by a sharp tiler.

"That took nerve!" commented the Emperor. Petronius looked up again, and grinned slightly. He would be all right. I folded my arms and beamed at him like a proud trainer showing off his best gladiator.

"I apologize for any inconvenience, sir." Petronius always sounded good. He had a mellow voice and a calm delivery. He gave a trustworthy impression. That explained his success with civic selection boards, and with women.

"Apologies may not be enough," replied Vespasian. Unlike selection boards and women, he could spot a rogue. "How do you know Falco?"

"Colleagues from the Second Augusta, sir." Our legion was one Vespasian himself had once led. Both Petro and I allowed ourselves a certain cockiness.

"Really." The Second had disgraced itself since Vespasian's day. Regretfully, we all let the subject drop. "You two work in different areas now."

"We both strive for law and order, sir." A bit too pious, I thought. Petro could get away with it perhaps, since Vespasian had not known him long. "Which is what I was doing today after the robbery at the Emporium." Petronius liked to gallop straight to the point. The concept of first being weighed up through friendly chatter was so alien to his blunt nature that he was rushing the interview.

"You wanted to assess the damage before people trampled everywhere." Vespasian could assimilate information swiftly; he rapped out the explanation as if it were obvious. I saw Petro flush slightly. He now realized he had plunged in too fast. Given our relative positions in this conversation, forcing the pace was rude. Being rude to an Emperor was the first step to having a lion sniff your bum. "Why?" asked the Emperor coolly, "could you not have made the merchants responsible for alerting you to their losses in due course? It is in their own interests to provide the information. They will want you to retrieve the stolen goods. So why cause a riot?"

Petronius looked alarmed. He had done things his own way. It was a way that would work, so he had not bothered with alternatives. Alternatives tend to be messy. Just thinking about them wastes time.

"Closing the market sounds crude," he admitted. "I was thinking ahead, sir. It was clear we were dealing with a highly organized gang. They had already made fools of everyone involved with security at the Emporium." He paused. Vespasian quietly indicated that he could go on. Petro got into his stride: "My immediate reaction was that the raid was so well done they wouldn't stop there. We'll see them again—either at the Emporium, or elsewhere. At this moment they have the advantage of me. I need all the facts—and I need them rapidly. Today I had to discover everything I could about the methods used—how they had identified the goods in advance, for instance. This was no ordinary robbery. The haul was exceptional, and I prophesy big trouble in Rome."

Without actually answering the original question, Petronius Longus had managed to put the situation in context. He came out of it well, too. I knew it was bluff, but he looked like a man who was planning well.

"You expect a repetition of today?"

"I fear it, sir."

The Emperor leaned forwards suddenly. "Were you expecting *this*?"

Petronius did not flinch from the fierce question. "No, sir. But I had felt *something* might happen."

"Why?"

"A power vacuum has been created in the criminal fraternity."

"How? Oh, Balbinus Pius, of course. You were responsible for that."

This time Petro was startled. He had not realized that the tablet which Vespasian had been reading when we entered would have been his brief from the secretariat: a swift summary of events today, an account of Petro's career, a résumé of the Balbinus case, even polite suggestions for handling this interview.

I stepped in: "Petronius Longus is too modest to regale you with his success, sir. He was indeed the officer who convicted Balbinus. He found an opportunity to do it, and he saw matters through. He's too good a man to stop there. He thought ahead, and considered the effect on Rome."

Vespasian gave no sign of having heard me, though he certainly had. He looked at Petro, who was quite capable of sliding out of this. While I burbled, he had already marshaled his thoughts: "Sir, I realized the size of the Emporium heist meant there would be political implications."

"Political?" We had the Emperor's full attention. He himself had stepped into a power vacuum when he wrested the throne from the various contenders and settled in to remedy the oddities of Nero's reign and the devastation of the ensuing civil war. He had yet to prove himself. He was working hard, but the benefits of good government take longer than the ravages of bad to become apparent. His grasp on power was still precarious.

I suggested dryly, "Robbery on a grand scale casts doubt upon the government's effectiveness, sir."

"No, it casts doubt on the effectiveness of the watch!" retorted the Emperor.

Petronius was visibly annoyed with me. "Sir, it will cause grumbles, I realize. But I take this theft as a signal. It was very bold. Some element is declaring open war—"

"On whom?" rapped the Emperor. "You? Me?"

"On the watch, certainly," Petro replied slowly. "On the state by implication. And probably on other major thieves. Given that context, I should say that it is likely to involve more than one city sector—"

"That's beyond your scope!" Vespasian had an old-fashioned regard for the limits of office. Immediately he reined Petro in: "That calls for a coordinated strategy."

"Yes, sir," agreed Petronus, looking meek. "I was, of course, intending to alert my cohort tribune and the Prefect of the City, sir." The lying shark!

Vespasian thought about it. "I'd better see your tribune. I'd better see them all." He gave a slight nod to some sideliner in a white tunic. This silent, virtually invisible official was more than just a secretary. Notes were being made briefly on a tablet, but these were the notes of a man taking instructions. He knew the first rule of administration: Always cover yourself. "Conference. After lunch. Warn Titus." The Emperor spoke offhandedly, though both Petro and I had a sense of starting far more than we had bargained for. He turned back to us. "That still leaves the riot to diffuse. What do you suggest?"

Knowing that the man who starts a riot rarely thinks about how he will stop it, I thought best to offer ideas myself. "You could mollify the discontent to some degree by announcing compensation, sir."

"Compensation?"

I had done it now. I had used a naughty word.

XI

"Thanks a lot, Falco!"

We were back on the bench in the corridor. The chamberlain who shepherded visitors was looking curious. The white-tunic-clad official strode off. Vespasian's mention of lunch told us that the "few minutes" we had been told to wait would be several hours. Petronius was furious. "Well if that was helping, thanks, Falco! Thanks to you mentioning money, the poor old buffer's had to rush to his bedroom for a quiet lie-down!"

"Forget it," I assured Petro. "Vespasian's famously tight, but he won't faint at the mere mention. If he hates our suggestion he'll say no."

"*Your* suggestion," Petro inserted. I ignored it.

We were silent for a while, mulling over events past and recent. "What in Hades have you got me into here?" Petro grumbled.

"At some point later, when we want to be having our dinner, we'll find ourselves advising a committee on the fine points of managing crime."

"I just want to get back to my case."

"This could be the most promising assignment of your life."

"Stuff it," Petro growled.

It was in fact lunchtime when things started to happen. First the white tunic came and collected us. He wanted to pick our brains. We allowed it, but made sure we shared his lunch.

He introduced himself as Tiberius Claudius Laeta. Evidently a Palace freedman of great status, he had possession of a room that was twice as big as my whole apartment. There, when Vespasian didn't need a minion to push around, the good Laeta could sit and pick his nose. There, too, persons of lesser status brought him trayloads of sustenance.

"Nice!" we said.

"It's a living," he replied. There was only one winecup, but Petro quickly found a couple of dusty extras hidden behind some scroll boxes. The clerk tried to look impressed with our initiative as, smiling like happy new cronies, we poured his flagon for him. Since the wine was free, it proved good enough even for Petro. Laeta raised his cup to us, looking pleased to have company. Being top clerk, which he obviously was, can be a lonely life. "So! I gather you're Falco, one of Anacrites' men?"

"I'm Falco," I answered patiently. "I'm my own man."

"Sorry. I understood you worked for the bureau that we don't talk about."

"I have worked for the Emperor. I found the rewards unrealistic, and I don't plan any more."

"Ah!" The good Laeta managed to say this with an air of discretion, while implying that whatever bureau *he* served was scheming to put the Chief Spy on the rim of a live volcano and give him a big shove. "Maybe you would find it more rewarding working for us."

"Maybe," I said, fairly peacefully. If it upset Anacrites, I would consider anything.

Claudius Laeta gave me a considered stare, then turned to Petronius. Petro had been stolidly putting away a platter of cold artichoke hearts. As his attention was demanded by our host, I myself started on Laeta's dish of anchovies. "And you are Petronius Longus, of the Aventine Watch?" Petro nodded, still chewing. "Do set me straight about the vigiles. I confuse them with the Urban Cohorts. . . ."

"Easily done." Petronius filled him in politely. Replete, he leaned back on a stool and gave Laeta his lecture for new recruits: "This is how law and order works in Rome: Top of the heap you have the Praetorian Guard; Cohorts One to Nine, commanded by the Praetorian Prefect, barracked at the Praetorian Camp. Fully armed. Duties: one, guarding the Emperor; two, ceremonial swank. They are a hand-picked élite, and full of themselves. Next in line and tacked onto them are Cohorts Ten to Twelve, known as the Urbans. Commanded by the Urban Prefect—a senator—who is basically the city manager. Routinely armed with sword and knife. Their unofficial job description is *to repress the mob.* Duties officially: to keep the peace, keep their ears open, and keep the Urban Prefect informed of absolutely everything."

"Spying?" Laeta queried dryly. "I thought Anacrites did that."

"He spies on them while they're spying on us," I suggested.

"And at the bottom," Petro continued, "doing all the real work, you have the vigiles, commanded by the Prefect of the Vigiles. Unarmed, but run on military lines. Seven cohorts, each led by a tribune who is an ex-chief centurion; each with seven centurions who do the foot patrols. Rome has fourteen administrative regions. Each cohort looks after two. Duties: everything those flash bastards at the Praetorian Camp won't lower themselves to touch."

"So in the Aventine Watch you cover the Twelfth and Thirteenth regions?"

"Yes. We're the Fourth Cohort."

"And your tribune is?"

"Marcus Rubella." Petro rarely spoke of the tribune, whom he cordially dismissed as a legionary has-been who should have stuck to square-bashing.

"An equestrian?"

"Bought it with his discharge grant. Almost enough rank now to be a master criminal," Petro replied dryly, thinking of Balbinus Pius.

"And the main role of the vigiles is fire-watching?"

"*One* role." Petro hated to be thought of as a mere fire-man. "Yes, but since that involves patrolling the streets at night, when most crimes are committed, our remit expanded. We apprehend street thieves and housebreakers, round up runaway slaves, keep custodians of tenements and warehouses up to the mark. We spend a lot of effort controlling the baths. Clothes stealing is a big problem."

"So you remain a proletarian squad?" Laeta was falling into the administrator's trap of obsession with titles and rank.

"We are freedmen and honest citizens," snarled Petro, clearly not amused.

"Oh quite. And what's your own position?"

"Casework," said Petro. "I head the inquiry team for the Thirteenth district. The foot patrols pound the pavements, sniffing for smoke and apprehending wrongdoers if they meet them face-to-face. They're competent for basic tasks like thrashing householders who let stoves fall over. But each cohort has an officer like myself with a small team of agents doing house-to-house searches and general follow-up. Two, in fact, one per district. Between us, we trace the stolen goblets and investigate who hit the barmaid over the head with a plank."

"Reporting to the tribune?"

"Partly. We do a lot for the Prefect's office as well. Any case where more than a public whipping is called for has to go forward to him. The Prefect has a full staff, including a registrar for various lists of undesirables, and an interrogation officer—"

"He carries out the torturing?"

"We find brute force can be counterproductive," Petro replied: the official disclaimer.

I laughed bitterly. "Tell that to a hard case who has just had his privates squeezed in the little back room!"

Petronius chose not to hear me.

"So . . ." Laeta moved on. "Tell me your anxieties about the Emporium raid. Your theory is that we have an organized and daring gang moving in on the city center? I'd like to know how much of Rome is threatened."

"Who can say?" Petronius knew better than to give neat summaries. Criminals don't follow neat rules. "I'd reckon all the central watches ought to be put on alert."

Laeta made a note. "So what is your assessment of the threat?"

"They are aiming at commodities," Petro answered confidently. "It will be wharves and stores—not, I think, the general food markets. This affects the Thirteenth region mainly, but also the Eleventh and Twelfth, which include some specialist warehouses. I doubt if the granaries are vulnerable."

"Why not?"

"With the state corn dole for the poor and the rich living off grain from their own estates, where's the scope for a black market? The bastards might take a swipe at the paper warehouse on the Quirinal. The Saepta Julia will also be a target. The jewelers should be warned." Laeta was absorbing all this assiduously.

He had a warm almond omelette under a cover, so we divided that up into three for him and shared it around. Soon the food tray was empty.

Laeta then excused himself. We were allowed to put our feet up in his luxurious bolt-hole until required.

"This is a right mess, Falco!" Petro tested the flagon, but we had already drained it. "I don't want a bunch of amateurs all over my patch."

"Don't burst your pod. It was you who made yourself out to be a master of criminal intelligence."

"Hercules Victor! How was I to know a passing thought would be turned into an issue, with secretaries running around like rabbits and a full intersectional conference on major crime being thrown together the same day?"

I grinned at him kindly. "Well, you've learned something useful here: Keep your thoughts to yourself!"

Rooting among the scroll boxes, I discovered a slim alabastron of red wine that Laeta had already unbunged and half drunk on some previous occasion. We unbunged it again and helped ourselves. I replaced the container just where I had found it, so Laeta would not think we had been prying among his personal stuff.

We took it in turns to nod off.

Instinct told us when to rouse ourselves. This we had learned primarily while watching for mustachioed Britons to jump out from broom bushes. In fact, the Britons had never jumped us. But the instinct had proved useful for warning us of bad-tempered centurions who didn't think it was funny if the footsloggers on guard duty happened to lean against a parapet to discuss whether the Greens were having their best season ever in the chariot races at home. At any event, when Claudius Laeta bustled back to fetch us, we were neither leaning nor dozing, but had washed our hands and faces in a bowl that a flunky had brought for Laeta's use, then combed our hair like a couple of swanks going to a party, and sat ourselves up like men who could be relied upon.

"Ah, there you are. . . ." Laeta gazed around his room nervously, as if he expected to find vandalism. "The old man's gone across to his own quarters. We'll have to make the trip to the Golden House."

I smiled. "Lucius Petronius and I would welcome a stroll in the fresh air."

Laeta looked worried a second time, as if he was wondering what we had been up to that could necessitate a breather.

Nero had set out his Golden House across the whole of Central Rome. Via a garden that filled the entire valley of the Forum, he had linked the old palace of the Caesars to a new complex completed for him by masters of architectural innovation and decor. Our conference was held in the new part. I had seen it before. It still made me gasp.

To reach it, we had come down from the Palatine, through the cool, guarded cryptoporticus, and walked across the eastern end of the Forum, past the Vestals' House and the Sweating Fountain, then around the mess that had recently been the Great Lake dominating the country gardens that Nero had created in the bowl of the Palatine and Esquiline hills. The lake was now a gigantic hole where Vespasian had inaugurated his promised amphitheater. On the Oppian crest beyond it still stood Nero's fantastic palace. It was too opulent for the new Flavian dynasty, who had restrained good taste, yet too costly and too exquisite to pull down. To build another palace when Rome itself lay in ruins would look a worse extravagance than Nero's. So Vespasian and his sons were living here. At least they could blame their mad predecessor.

Claudius Laeta led us through a maze of marble-clad entrance halls and tall, intensely decorated corridors. I think we were in the east wing; the west seemed to be the private quarters. Guards nodded Laeta past, and he found his way with ease. To a stranger, the Golden House was deliberately bewildering. Rooms and passageways succeeded one another in a seemingly random profusion. The eye was dazzled with gilt and the gleam of the finest polished marble; the brain was bemused by twists and turns; the ear was assaulted by the continual music of water in fountains and cascades. Petronius stumbled into me as he tried to stare up at the minutely painted ceilings while Laeta hurried us along. Finally, we took a dart to the left, glimpsed an apsidal hall, whipped past another room, and stepped into the famous fabulous octagonal dining room.

In Nero's day people came here for orgies; just our luck to arrive when times had changed and the best we could get was a crime conference.

The room was full of light. There was an open aspect to the south, with a heart-stopping view that we would not be gazing at. There was a theatrical cascade (turned off). There were curtained side rooms in which scenes of revolting debauchery had once occurred (now empty). Above our heads had been the legendary revolving ivory ceiling that had showered gifts down upon lucky diners (dismantled; no presents for us).

Already assembled were Vespasian and his elder son, Titus, seated on thrones. Petronius would like the thrones. He approved of formality. Titus, a younger version of his father but with a jolly hint of chubbiness, gave me a pleasant nod; I showed my teeth politely. Calm administrators were handing them last-minute briefs.

Other officials were just arriving with us. Summoned from their lunches were both the Urban Prefect, who thought he ran the city, and the Prefect of the Vigiles, who really did the work. Each had a fleet of office minions who were shuttled into the side rooms. To speak up for them (since they kept themselves unencumbered by practical knowledge), the prefects had brought all seven tribunes of the vigiles cohorts, including Rubella, the Fourth Cohort's own top man, to whom Petro was supposed to report any problems before they became public. Rubella had brought a paper cone of sunflower seeds, which he continued to munch surreptitiously. Despite Petro's scorn, I thought he looked pleasingly human.

Present, though not named in the record, was Anacrites, the Chief Spy.

"Falco!" His light eyes flickered nervously as he realized that I was alive, and deep in this unexpected enterprise. He did not ask how I had enjoyed his Eastern fiasco. When I was ready, I would report to Vespasian personally, and my comments would be unrestrained by loyalty to the man who sent me there.

"Excuse me," I answered coldly. "I'm presenting a report. . . ."

Claudius Laeta must have overheard, for he waved Petro and me up close to him; his position was nearest the Emperor. On Vespasian's behalf he was chairing the meeting. What was said is, of course, confidential. The minutes ran to half a closely written scroll. In confidence, of course, what happened was:

The regular officials conducted business briskly. They were held up sometimes by tribunes holding forth on personal theories that had nothing to do with the issue and were sometimes incomprehensible (unminuted). Once or twice a prefect ventured a trite remark (paraphrased succinctly by the secretary). Petronius Longus gave a clear account of his belief that with the removal of Balbinus, some new crime lord had seized the initiative. (This, pretty well verbatim, took up most of the record.) Petro had moved in the course of that morning from a man who was talking his way out of trouble to one who looked a contender for a laurel crown. He took it well. Petronius had the right skeptical attitude.

I found myself being consulted by Vespasian as his expert on life in the streets; I managed to produce some ideas that had a ring of good sense, though I foresaw problems explaining later to Helena Justina exactly what I had said.

Anacrites was suddenly asked by Titus what his professional intelligence team had noticed. He offered nothing but waffle. His team was useless, unaware of pretty well everything that went on in Rome. The Urban Prefect gleefully stepped in and pretended *his* spies had spotted worrying signs of unrest. Asked to be more specific, he was soon floundering.

It took two hours of debate before the Emperor was satisfied. The problem—if it existed—was to be tackled with energy (though no extra men would be drafted in). The Prefect of the Vigiles would coordinate a special investigation, reporting to the Urban Prefect, who would report to Titus Caesar. Petronius Longus, reporting to Rubella, reporting to the Prefect of the Vigiles, would identify the Emporium thieves, then evaluate whether they were a one-time strike or a more widespread threat. He had the right to advise any cohort tribune of a perceived danger in a particular sector, and all had a duty to assist him if required.

Anacrites was allocated no activity, though as a courteous gesture Titus said it was assumed the intelligence network would "keep a watching brief." We all knew this traditional phrase. It meant they were to keep out of the way.

As an exceptional measure only (this was heavily stressed by Vespasian), compensation would be offered to those traders at the Emporium who had lost goods last night, so long as their names appeared on the official list. Martinus had brought this for Petronius, sent in via a flunky. Vespasian, who knew how to dodge fiddles, told a copy clerk to duplicate the list for him immediately.

I found myself assigned as a supernumerary officer, to work alongside Petronius. As usual with meetings, I came away not entirely clear what I was supposed to do.

XII

"So Marcus, you went out for a quiet stroll up and down the Forum," mused Helena, passing a platter of cheese savories to Silvia. "By the time you came home, there was a major epidemic of crime, an imperial commission, and both of you hearty fellows had become special inquiry officers?"

"Beats shopping for radishes," I commented, though since we had guests, I had done that too. A householder has to be versatile.

"Working together will be nice for them," remarked Arria Silvia. Petro's wife was petite and pretty. A bright, dainty girl with ribbons binding her hair, she was the kind I had once thought I wanted—until Petro acquired Silvia. She had a habit of stating the obvious; I suppose he found it comforting. They had been married for about seven years, and with three children to secure them in affection (or whatever it was), the union looked likely to last. I had therefore decided to put aside my reaction to Silvia. Which was that she brought me out in a rash.

Helena seemed able to get along with her, though their friendship lacked the warmth that I had noticed flowering naturally between Helena and my sister Maia, for instance. "I hope you two won't quarrel," Helena said to me, smiling quietly. The shrewd one, mine. Whether or not he recognized what she meant, Petronius did not respond but went out to the balcony, where he lifted up his eldest daughter so she could pee into one of my pots of bulbs. This would probably kill them, but I said nothing. He was a competent, uncomplicated father. A lesson to all of us.

I had the other two girls on my lap, playing with toys we had brought them. We were a happy party, stuffed with food and still enjoying a fine wine Petronius had donated from his extensive collection. Petro and Silvia had spent the early evening with us, laughing over stories of our travels in Syria. Friends do so love to hear about you suffering from ghastly climates, crooked money-changers, and intense pain from poisonous arachnids. Saves them going on holiday themselves.

There had been so much to say about the scorpion nipping Helena and other lively memories, that she and I had managed to avoid mentioning the one item that Silvia would think important: that we too might become a family.

I won't say Helena and I were sneakily pleased to keep it a secret. It was too much of an issue; we were not ready to laugh about it. But we were close enough friends for Helena to let me see her wry expression as Silvia prattled cheerfully about her own little girls. Silvia was hinting that it was about time Helena started to feel jealous yearnings. Eventually I caught Helena's eye privately and winked at her. Silvia saw me do it. She shot a mock-scandalized look at Petronius, thinking I was being amorous. Petro pretended, as usual, that he had no idea at all what was going on.

The wink remained as a moment of stillness between Helena and me.

The women were taking a greater interest in our new task than either Petro or I wanted. Silvia had realized that Helena Justina was used to more free consultation than Petronius allowed her. She plunged in, picking over issues as tenaciously as she had earlier torn apart her chicken wings in peppered wine sauce.

Petronius and I had been allies for a long time. While Silvia speculated, we just talked quietly among ourselves.

"I want you to come over the road later, Petro. There's a property Smaractus is offering on the market. It's a dump, but a better one than this if it was done up a bit."

"Done up a bit?" Petro squinted at me as if he had just caught me stealing wine jars from caupona counters. "Will Smaractus invest in improvements?"

"No, but I'm determined to find another place for us, even if I have to renovate a wreck myself."

"I've not heard about this!" said Helena, taking one of Petro's girls from me. The other scampered off to play on the balcony. "Shouldn't I be the one to inspect the real estate?"

"And why can't you find another landlord?" Silvia put in.

I grinned at Helena. "The person who needs to inspect it is the kind associate who will be helping me install the new windows and floorboards!"

"Forget it!" exclaimed Petro, looking appalled.

"You're a good carpenter."

Helena laughed. "And he *was* a good friend!"

"I'm going to have my hands full with this initiative against the Emporium thieves," said Petronius firmly. Sometimes he would help out in my crazy schemes; sometimes he didn't want to know. I let it drop. He was too stubborn to change his mind.

"So why has our bijou niche here lost its charm after so long?" Helena asked, with the air of a Fury lightly fingering her scourge.

"I'm getting old. My legs are hating the stairs." My beloved gave me a very sweet smile that meant I was toying with serious trouble.

"You should try it with three children hanging around your neck!" Silvia's remark was too close for comfort; I was dreading it with just one, particularly on Helena's behalf in the long months before our shrimp was born. I could already hear helpful relatives suggesting she should live somewhere more accessible, hoping that would be the first step to her leaving me for good.

Presumably Helena realized why I wanted a better billet. She leaned back on her stool, cradling Tadia, and gave me a

long stare. It was a challenge to tell Petro and Silvia the situation we were in. I returned the stare but stayed silent.

"Now doesn't Helena look good holding a baby!" Silvia
rebuked me, clearly not even suspecting the truth. I had denied it to Petro, and he must have passed this on. Feeling
mild pangs of guilt on his behalf, I condescended to survey
Helena. She was wearing blue, with a tasteful row of
bracelets covering her scarred arm, and silver earrings on
which I had squandered a week's earnings one day in
Palmyra just because I knew she was enjoying herself traveling the world with me.

She did look good. She looked healthy, calm, and sure of
herself. As she gripped the child—who was trying to fling
herself to the floor to see if landing hard on boards would
hurt—Helena's big brown beautiful eyes sent me another
dare.

I stayed calm. I never let Silvia see how much she annoyed me. And I tried not to let Helena discover how her
challenges made me feel jittery. "The first time I ever saw
Helena, she was holding a child."

"I don't remember that."

"The British procurator's daughter."

"Oh, Aunt Camilla's eldest!" She did remember now; her
blush told me. "Flavia."

"Flavia!" I agreed, grinning at her. I could see she had re-
called the scene: a polite family group, educated after-din-
ner people discussing whether it might rain the next day,
then I prowled in, newly landed in the province, flexing my
class prejudice and intending to break bones if anyone offered me any pleasantries.

"What was *he* doing?" said Silvia, giggling.

"Scowling," replied Helena patiently. "He looked as if a
Titan had just stepped on his foot and crushed his big toe. I
was staying with nice people who had been very kind to me;
then this hero turned up, like Milo of Croton looking for a
tree to split with his fist. He was exhausted, miserable, and
exasperated by his work—"

"Sounds normal!"

"But he still managed to be rude to me."

"The lout!"

"In a way that made me want to—"

"Go to bed with me?" I offered.

"Prove you wrong!" Helena roared, still hotheaded at the thought.

When I met her in Britain she had thoroughly overturned me: I had started out believing her stuck-up, strict, ill humored, uncharitable and untouchable; then I fell for her so hard I was barely able to believe my luck when she did go to bed with me.

"And what were you after, Falco?" Silvia was half hoping for a salacious answer.

I wanted Helena as my partner for life. That was too shocking to mention to a prim little piece like Silvia. I reached for the fruit bowl and savagely bit a pear.

"We're still waiting to hear about this task you two have for the Emperor!" Making Silvia change the subject was simplicity itself. If you ignored one remark she came out with something different. That did not mean you liked it better.

I saw Petro frown slightly. We both wanted to let things ride. We still had to maneuver for position, and we didn't need women helping us.

"Which of you is taking the lead in this venture?" Helena asked curiously. She could always find really awkward questions.

"I am," said Petro.

"Excuse me!" I had wanted to sort this out privately with him, but we were now trapped. "I work independently. I don't take orders from anyone."

"I'm head of the special inquiry," said Petro. "You'll have to work with me."

"My commission comes direct from Vespasian. He always gives me a free hand."

"Not in my district."

"I hadn't foreseen any conflict."

"You hadn't been thinking, then!" muttered Helena.

"There's no conflict," Petronius said calmly.

"Oh no. It's all pretty clear. You intend to be planning the work, giving the orders, and leading the team. That leaves me sweeping the office."

Suddenly he grinned. "Sounds fair—and I suppose you're competent!"

"I can wield a broom," I agreed, though I was conceding nothing.

"We can work something out," Petronius murmured airily.

"Oh, we can operate in tandem. We've been friends for a long time." That was why it was impossible for either of us to be in sole charge, of course. Helena had seen that immediately.

"Of course," confirmed Petro, with the briefest of smiles.

Nothing was settled, but we left it at that to avoid a furious argument.

XIII

Fountain Court on a quiet October evening had its usual soiled and sultry charm. A faint pall of black smoke from the lampblack ovens drifted languidly five feet above the lane, looking for passersby with clean togas or tunics to smudge. Amid its acrid tang lingered scents of sulfur from the laundry and rancid fat frying. Cassius, the baker, had been making veal pies earlier—with too much juniper, by the smell. Above us people had hung bedding over their balconies, or sat there airing their fat backsides over a parapet while they shouted abuse at members of their family hidden indoors. Some idiot was hammering madly. A weary young girl staggered past us, almost unable to walk under the weight of the long garlands of flowers she had spent all day weaving for dinner parties in louche, wealthy homes.

A thin scruffy dog sat outside Lenia's, waiting for someone softhearted it could follow home.

"Don't look," I commanded Helena. I took her hand as we crossed the dusty street to ask Cassius to give us the key to the empty apartment.

Cassius was a genial fellow, though he had never deigned to notice that Helena Justina was attached to me. He sold her loaves, at more or less reasonable prices; he chucked me the occasional stale roll while we swapped gossip. But even when Helena appeared in his shop with her noble fist grasped in mine, Cassius gave no acknowledgment that he was addressing a couple. He must regard us as unsuitable; well, he was not alone. I thought we were unsuitable myself—not that that would stop me.

"Ho, Falco!"

"Got the key for upstairs?"

"What idiot wants that?"

"Well, I'll have a look—"

"Hah!" chipped Cassius, as if I had dared to suggest one of his whole grain crescent baps had a spot of mold.

Refusing to be put off, we made him go for the key, which had been abandoned for so long he had lost it somewhere behind a mountain of sacks in his flour store. While we waited for him to track down the nail he had hung it on, I hunted for interesting crumbs in the bread roll display baskets, and grinned at Helena.

"It's right, you know. You looked quite at home that time I saw you with Aelia Camilla's little girl. A natural!"

"Flavia was not my child," said Helena, in a cold voice.

Cassius came back, armed with an iron key the size of a ratchet on some dockyard winding gear. Being nosy, he made sure he kept hold of it and came with us up the dilapidated stone steps beside his shop. Not many of the treads were completely broken away; if you kept near the wall it was almost safe. Using both hands, Cassius struggled to turn the key in a rusted lock. Failing, we discovered the easiest way in was to push open the back edge of the door and squeeze through the matted spiderwebs that had been acting as hinges.

It was very dark. Cassius boldly crossed to a window and threw back a shutter; it dropped off in his hand. He cursed as the heavy wood crashed to the floor, leaving splinters in his fingers and grazing his leg on the way.

"Frankly," Helena decided at once, "this seems a bit too elegant for us!"

It was out of the question. Deeply depressed, I insisted on seeing everything.

"Who lives upstairs, Cassius?"

"No one. The other apartments are even worse than this. Mind you, I saw some old bag woman poking round this afternoon."

Disaster. The last thing we needed was vagrants for close neighbors. I was trying to become more respectable.

Huge sheets of plaster hung away from the wall slats, which themselves bowed inwards alarmingly. The floors dipped several inches every time we trod the boards, which we did very delicately. The joists must have gone. Since the floor joists should have been tying the whole building together, this was serious. All the internal doors were missing. So, as Lenia had warned me, was the floor in the back rooms.

"What's that down there?"

"My log store," said Cassius. True. We could see the logs through his ceiling. Presumably when Cassius was loading his oven, sometime before dawn, anyone upstairs would hear him rolling the logs about.

The place was derelict. We would not be asking for a lease from Smaractus. Cassius lost interest and left to tend his leg, which was now bleeding badly. "Is this your dog down here, Falco?"

"Certainly not. Chuck a rock at him."

"It's a girl."

"She's still not mine—and she's not going to be!"

Helena and I stayed, too dispirited to shift. She gazed at me. She knew exactly why I was looking at property, but unless she acknowledged being pregnant, she could not discuss my project. For once, I had the upper hand.

"Sorry," I said.

"Why? Nothing's lost."

"I was convinced this dump had been on the market so long I could walk in and pay Smaractus in old nuts."

"Oh, he'd be delighted to find a tenant!" Helena laughed. "Can we mend it? You're very practical, Marcus—"

"Jupiter! This needs major building work—it's far beyond my scope."

"I thought you liked a challenge?"

"Thanks for the faith! This whole block should be torn

down. I don't know why Cassius sticks it. He's risking his life every day." Like much of Rome.

"At least we could get fresh bread." Helena pretended to muse. "We could reach down through the floor for it without getting out of bed. . . ."

"No, we can't live above a bakery. Apart from the fire risk—"

"The oven is separate, in the street."

"So are the mills, with a damned donkey braying and the endless rumble of grinding querns! Don't fool about, lady. Think of the cooking smells. Bread's fine, but when Cassius has baked his loaves he uses the ovens to heat offal pies in nasty gravy for the entire street. I should have thought of that."

Helena had wandered to the window. She stood on tiptoe, leaning out for the view, while she changed the subject: "I don't like this trouble between you and Petronius."

"There's no trouble."

"There's going to be."

"I've known Petro a long time."

"And it's a long time since you worked together. When you did, it was back in the army, and you were both taking orders from somebody else."

"I can take orders. I take them from you all the time."

She chortled seditiously. I joined her at the window and caused a diversion, trying to nudge her off balance. She slipped an arm around me to save herself, then kept it there in a friendly fashion while we both looked out.

This side of Fountain Court was lower down the hillside than where we lived, so we were almost opposite the familiar streetside row of lockups: the stationery supplier, the barber, the funeral parlor, small pavement businesses in a gloomy colonnade below five stories of identical apartments, some overpaid architect's notion of thoughtful design. Few architects permit themselves to live in their own tenements.

"Is that our block?"

"No, the one next door."

"There's a letting notice, Marcus."

"I think it's for one of the shops on the ground floor."

Helena's sharp eyes had spotted the kind of street graffiti you usually ignore. I walked her downstairs and across the road to check up. The chalked advertisement was for a workshop. It called itself *"well-set-out artisan premises with advantageous living accommodation,"* but it was a damp booth with an impossible stairway to a disgusting loft. It's true there was a small domestic apartment attached, but the two-room tenancy was for five years. Who could say how many offspring I might have accidentally fathered by that time, and how much space I should be needing to house them all?

Shivering, I let Helena lead me out to Fountain Court. The scruffy dog had found us again, and was staring at me hopefully. She must have worked out who was the soft one.

Since the barber had no customers, we dumped ourselves pessimistically on two of his stools. He grumbled briefly, then went indoors for a lie-down, his favorite occupation anyway.

"You know we can live anywhere," Helena said quietly. "I have money—"

"No. I'll pay the rent."

As a senator's daughter she owned far less than her two brothers, but if she allied herself with anyone respectable there was a large dowry still kicking around from her previous failed marriage, plus various legacies from female relations who had spotted her special character. I had never let myself discover the exact extent of Helena's wealth. I didn't want to upset myself. And I never wanted to find myself a kept man.

"So what are we looking for?" She was being tactful now, refraining from comment on my proud self-respect. Naturally, I found it maddening.

"That's obvious. Somewhere we don't risk scum breaking in. Where perverts who come to see me about business won't make trouble for you. And more space."

"Space for a cradle, and seats for all your sisters when they come cooing over the item in it?" Helena's voice was dry. She knew how to soften me up.

"More seats would be useful." I smiled. "I like to entertain."

"You like to get me annoyed!"

"I like you in any mood." I ran one finger down her neck, just tickling the skin beneath the braid on her gown. She lowered her chin suddenly, trapping my finger. I thought about pulling her closer and kissing her, but I was too depressed. To provide a public spectacle you need to be feeling confident.

From her position with her head tucked down, Helena was looking across Fountain Court. I felt her interest shift. Gazing at the sky, I warned the gods: "Watch out, you loafers on Olympus. Somebody's just had a bright idea!"

Then Helena asked, in the curious tone that had so often led to trouble, "Who lives above the basket shop?"

The basket-weaver occupied a lockup two along from Cassius the baker. He shared his frontage with a cereal-seller—another quiet trade, and fairly free of smelly nuisances. Above them rose a typical tenement, similar to ours and with the same kind of underpaid, overworked occupants. There was no letting sign, but the shutters on the first-floor apartment were closed, as they always had been to my knowledge. I had never seen anybody going in.

"Well spotted!" I murmured thoughtfully.

Right there, opposite Lenia's laundry, we could have found our next home.

XIV

The basket-weaver, a wiry gent in a tawny tunic whom I knew by sight, told us the apartment above him belonged to his shop. He had never occupied the upstairs because he only bunked temporarily in Fountain Court. He lived on the Campagna, kept his family there, and intended to retire to the country when he remembered to stop coming to town every week. The rooms above were in fact impossible to live in, being filled up with rubble and junk. Smaractus was too mean to clear them out. Instead, the idle bastard had negotiated a reduced rent. It suited the basket-weaver. Now it suited me.

Helena and I peered in warily. It was very dark. After living on the sixth floor, anywhere near ground level was bound to be. No balcony; no view; no garden, of course; no cooking facilities. Water from a fountain a street away. A public latrine at the end of our own street. Baths and temples on the Aventine. Street markets in any direction. My existing office within shouting range across the lane. It had three rooms—a gain of one on what we were used to—and a whole array of little cubbyholes.

"Pot stores!" cried Helena. "I love it!"

"Cradle space!" I grinned.

*   *   *

Smaractus, my landlord, was a person I avoided. I lost
my temper just thinking about that fungus. I had intended
to discuss matters peacefully with Lenia, but I foolishly
chose a time when her insalubrious betrothed had dropped
in with a wine flagon.

I refused to drink with him. I'll take a free tipple from
most people, but I'm a civilized man; I do discriminate.
Below the line I drew in those days lay unrepentant murderers, corrupt tax-gatherers, rapists, and Smaractus.

Luckily, I knew I made him nervous. There had been a
time he always brought two gladiators from the gym he ran
whenever he risked his neck in Fountain Court; with Lenia
to defend him from aggrieved tenants, he had taken to dis-
pensing with the muscle. A good idea; poor Asiacus and
Rodan were so badly nourished they needed to conserve
their strength. The big daft darlings would never stagger
into the arena after a day fighting me. For Smaractus I was
a difficult proposition. I was lean and hard, and I hated his
guts. As I crossed the threshold I heard his voice, so I had
time to apply what Helena called my Milo of Croton look.

"Falco is going to read the sheep's liver at the wedding
for us!" Lenia simpered, incongruously playing the eager
young bride. He couldn't have been there for more than a
few minutes, but she was well into the wine. Who could
blame her?

"Better watch out!" I warned him. He realized that if I
took the augury this might be a double-edged favor. A bad
omen could ruin his happiness. A *really* bad omen, and
Lenia might back out before he got the ring on her, depriv-
ing him of her well-filled strongboxes. Being sick on his
mother as Lenia had asked me was nothing to the fun I
could have with a cooperative ewe.

"He's nice and cheap," said Lenia to him, as if explaining why I seemed a good idea. I was on her side too, though
we refrained from mentioning that. "I see the little dog's
found you, Falco. We call it Nux."

"I'm not taking in a stray."

"Oh no? So when did you change your attitude?"

Smaractus muttered that I lacked experience as a priest,

and I retorted that I knew quite enough to pontificate on *his* marriage. Lenia shoved a winecup into my hand. I shoved it back.

With the business formalities over, we could get down to cheating each other.

I knew Smaractus would try to swing some fiddle if he heard we were the basket-weaver's subtenants. One way out was to avoid telling him. Unfortunately, now that he was betrothed to Lenia he was always littering up the neighborhood; he was bound to spot us going in and out. This needed care—or blatant blackmail. To start with I ranted at him about the dilapidated rooms above Cassius. "Somebody's going to tell the aediles that place is a danger to passersby, and you'll be ordered to demolish the lot before it falls in the street!" Smaractus would do anything to avoid pulling down a property, because by law he would have to replace it with something equal or better. (The idea of making more money from higher rents afterwards was too sophisticated for his moldy old sponge of a brain.)

"Who would stir up trouble like that?" He sneered. I smiled courteously, while Lenia kicked his foot to explain what I was getting at. He would be limping for a week.

"Wasn't it you I saw talking to the trug-seller?" Lenia asked me. You couldn't squeeze a pimple in Fountain Court without three people telling you to leave yourself alone.

"I'm going to help him clear out his upper floor."

"Why's that?" demanded Smaractus suspiciously.

"Because I'm a kindhearted fellow."

I waited until he was about to explode with curiosity; then I told him what I had just agreed with the cane-weaver: I would clear out the apartment and in return live there rent-free. Once we moved in, I would keep an eye on the lockup when it was closed, allowing the weaver greater freedom to buzz off to his family.

Smaractus was nonplussed by this news. The word "rent-free" was not in a landlord's vocabulary. I explained what it meant. He then used some phrases that proved what I had always suspected: He had been brought up by runaway trireme slaves in an unlicensed abattoir.

"I'm glad you approve," I told him. Then I left, while he was still choking on his wine.

XV

Next morning I presented myself at the Aventine Watch. The Fourth Cohort had its tribunal headquarters in the Twelfth region, the Piscina Publica, which most people deemed more salubrious. Alongside the HQ was a station house for the foot patrols, where their fire-fighting equipment was stored. To cover their other patch, the Thirteenth region, they had a second station house, to which Petronius bunked off whenever possible. That was where he kept an office staffed by his casework team of plainclothes inquiry agents and scribes. They had a lockup for people who were caught in the act by the foot patrols or who sensibly chose to confess as soon as challenged, plus a room for more detailed questioning. It was small, but had interesting iron devices hung on all the walls. And there was just space to get a good swing with a boot.

Fusculus was outside the office, helping an old woman compose a petition. They had a bench in the portico for local people who came with complaints. The duty clerk, a lanky youth who never said much, leaned down and worked grit out of his left sandal while Fusculus very patiently went through the procedure for the crone: "I can't write it for you. Only you know the facts. You want to start off: *To Lucius Petronius Longus, chief inquirer of the Thir-teenth region . . .* Don't worry. The scribes will put that bit automatically. *From . . .* Then say who you are, and tell us details of your loss. *On the Ides of October,* or whenever it was—"

"Yesterday."

Fusculus kicked the clerk into action. *"The day after the Ides, there was stolen from me . . ."*

"A bedcover." The woman had caught on rapidly, as they do when they have persuaded some handsome young fellow to work for them. "By a street gang who removed it from my balcony. In Conch Court, off Armilustrum Street."

"Worth?" Fusculus managed to squeeze in.

"A denarius!" She was probably guessing.

"How long had you had it?" demanded Fusculus suspiciously. "What was this treasure made of?"

"Wool! The most serviceable wool. I'd had it twenty years—"

"Put: *worth a dupondius!* Then the usual formula: *I therefore request that you give instructions for an inquiry into the matter. . . .*"

As the clerk began to write, Fusculus nodded me indoors. He was a round, happy fellow, about thirty-five years old and a hundred and eighty pounds. Balding on top, the rest of his hair ran around his skull in horizontal ridges. It had remained dark, and he had almost black eyes. Though rotund, he looked extremely fit.

"If you're after Petro, he'll be in later. He went out with the night patrol," Fusculus announced. "He's convinced there will be another gigantic raid. Martinus is on duty. He's gone back to the Emporium to check on some things."

"I can wait." Fusculus grinned slightly. Most people didn't bother with Martinus. "So what's on, Fusculus?"

"Seems pretty quiet. The day patrol is out looking into a possible theft from the Temple of Ceres. We've got scratchers doing statues at the Library of Asinius—"

"Scratchers?"

"Lifting off the gilding. Then a tanner's allegedly poisoning the air by the Aqua Marcia. Normally it's poisoning the water . . . Anyway, we can get him for noxious smells and shift his workshop to the Transtiberina, but somebody's got to go there and actually sniff the air while he's working. Street fight by the Trigeminal Gate—be over by the time the lads can get down the Clivus Publicus. Three apparently responsible citizens have laid separate reports of seeing a wolf by the Temple of Luna."

"Probably a large cat," I suggested.

"On the usual form it will turn out to be a small, timid tabby!" Fusculus chortled. "Escaped bears and panthers we pass straight on to the Urban Cohorts—well, at least those bastards are armed. And we let them catch senators' sons' pet crocodiles that have escaped from the rainwater tank. But a 'wolf' we usually have a look at. Just in case it's suckling heroic twins, you know."

"Oh, you'd want to be in on the action then!"

"Right! More boringly, we have an abandoned dead horse in the Cattle Market forum, which will have to be cleared with fire-breaking tackle. Meanwhile, we've got a bunch of runaway slaves in the lockup waiting for owners to collect them. There are also two careless householders for me to interview. They were picked up by the fire-watchers last night for allowing fire or smoke in their premises. The first-timer will be let off with a warning; another has been dragged in before, so *he* has to prove it was an accident, or he'll be thrashed."

"Who does that?"

"Sergius!" said Fusculus gleefully. I had met Sergius. He enjoyed his work. "Then we've a third would-be arsonist in the cell who is definitely on his way."

"On his way?"

"To the Prefect. He's a stupid sod of a jeweler who constantly leaves unattended lamps swinging in the breeze in his colonnade."

"So what'll he get?"

"A hefty fine. I'm taking him over to headquarters to be processed. Maybe you'd better come with me. Rubella wants a welcoming word." Rubella was the Fourth's tribune.

I grinned. "Am I going to enjoy this?"

"What do you think?" Fusculus twinkled. As he collected his cudgel, the arsonist, and some official notes about the prisoner's misdemeanors, he continued filling me in. Obviously he was a thoughtful type, and one who enjoyed lecturing. "Apart from all that, it's work as normal—which means not doing it because of more urgent priorities. We have an ongoing investigation of a secret religion that will have to be delayed *again* because of the new task, as will our long-term granary fire protection program, our anti-toga-theft campaign at the baths, and keeping up the lists of undesirables."

"What undesirables are those?" I asked, curious about what kind of degenerate earned a formal state record.

Fusculus looked rather shy. "Oh well, you know we have to assist the aediles with their registers. Bars and brothels."

"Somehow, Fusculus, I don't think bars and brothels were what you meant!"

"Mathematicians and astrologers," he confessed. I looked faintly surprised. "Anyone who leans towards the occult or magic has a question mark over them in the public order stakes. Philosophers especially."

"Oh, flagrantly seditious!"

"So I'm told. I'm not saying we believe the principle, Falco, but we like to be ready in case the Emperor demands a purge. Under Nero it was Christians. That's eased off lately, so we can go back to actors."

"Disgusting degenerates!" I did not reveal that I had just spent three months working with a theatrical troupe. "Who else?"

"Greek shopkeepers."

"Now that's a new one. What's wrong with them?"

"They keep their booths open night and day. It's reckoned unfair on the locals. That can lead to trouble, so we keep lists to tell us quickly who to lock up when a row flares and dung starts being hurled about."

Somehow I didn't suppose he kept matching details of the local businessmen who complained.

"I'm sure it's a relief to all honest citizens to know you stay vigilant!" Sarcasm was breaking through as I sensed there was more. "And is there anybody else who threatens public order so badly you keep them under surveillance and maintain their names on secret lists?"

"Informers," Fusculus admitted, looking resigned.

XVI

Rubella was still eating sunflower seeds.

He looked about fifty. Must have been, to have put in a full stint in the legions. He had been a chief centurion; that takes sticking power as well as a clean nose. Once he would have been about my level socially. Twenty years had pushed him on: promotion the whole way in the legions, discharge with honor, and buying himself into the middle rank. Now he commanded a thousand men; poor quality, it's true—the vigiles were ex-slaves for the most part—but if he continued to dodge disasters he could aspire to the Urban Cohorts, and maybe even the Praetorian Guard. Rubella was made—though he had spent his whole useful life getting there.

He was big physically; quiet; not tired by life. His gray hair was still close-cropped in the military manner, giving him a tough appearance. His strength was enough to move an ox aside merely by leaning on it. The knowledge soothed him. Rubella took the world at his own pace. He was utterly composed.

Fusculus introduced me. Rubella forced himself to pause between the seeds. "Thanks for coming over. I like to induct new attachments personally. Welcome to the squad, Falco."

The tribune's welcome was deceptive. Like Petro, he didn't

want me near the squad. He seemed friendly, but it was a barely concealed front. I was an outsider. Uninvited. Liable to uncover private grief.

Some officials would have made me talk about my work for the Emperor. Rubella must have been told of my past career. He might have picked it over, full of prejudice and seeking to belittle me. Instead he ignored that side completely, a worse insult.

"You're an old colleague of Petronius'."

"We go back ten years."

"Same legion?"

"Second Augusta. Britain."

"A good man," said Rubella. "Absolutely straight . . ." His mind seemed somewhere else. "I've been having a talk with Petro about this task with the gangsters. He suggested I assign you to looking up some past history."

I noticed the subtle way Rubella had put himself in charge of allocating duties. Clearly it wouldn't just be Petro and me haggling over the booty. Rubella wanted in. Any moment I expected the Prefect of the Vigiles to put an oar in the stream too. Then there was probably the Fourth Cohort's interrogation officer—Petro's immediate superior—to contend with. And no doubt each of the seven cohort centurions thought himself top man on the Aventine. If I wanted work, I would have to grapple for it.

"Past history?" I asked, giving nothing away. If a client paid I would look up birth certificates or wills, but it was not my favorite activity.

"You have skills we should be using." I noticed his dismissive tone. I had plenty of skills available. Informing needs rugged persistence, intelligence, intuition, and hard feet. "Attention to detail," Rubella selected.

"Oh, dear. I feel like a rather plain barmaid when offered as a chat-up line, 'I like you, you're different from the other girls . . .' "

Rubella stared at me. Apparently he had as much sense of humor as a centipede. He couldn't take an interruption either. "Petro doesn't agree, but I think we should send you to meet Nonnius."

"The nark who used to work with Balbinus? The rent-collector whose testimony put the big rissole away?"

"We have an excuse to intervene. The man is involved with tracing Balbinus' assets—"

"Oh, I'm thrilled!" I was annoyed. I let it show. "So while there's juicy work on the streets, I'm to be sitting with an abacus playing at audits!"

"No. There already is an auditor." He had failed to notice I was ready to explode. "A priest from the Temple of Saturn is representing the state's interest."

He could represent the Establishment on this inquiry too, if blinking at profit-and-loss columns was supposed to be my fate. "I can contribute something more useful than spotting a few dodgy figures on a balance sheet!"

"I hope so! You were assigned to us with a reputation, Falco. You'll want to sustain the myth." Rubella was smiling now. He could. All he had to do was munch endless seeds in his official throne of office while minions scurried in the dust. He knew he had riled me; he was openly enjoying it. "Do I detect a problem with rank? I bet when you were in the army you hated your centurion!"

"I don't expect he liked me much either." Aware of the goad, I came under control at once. Maybe he was trying to pack me back to the Palace with a complaint that I was uncooperative. If he imagined he could shed me before we had started, tough. I wasn't intending to play.

Rubella walked away from the fight. Barely pausing, he reiterated, "Past history, yes. If we believe that the gangsters who robbed the Emporium have dropped into a hole that formed after Balbinus was removed, maybe we should have a look at what existed before the hole."

The man made sense. My mind leaped, and I threw in quickly, "Whoever ploughed the Emporium was lined up and waiting to go. Balbinus had only taken ship the night before. Someone could hardly wait to announce there was a new criminal regime."

"They were effective," Rubella commented. His manner was restrained. He looked like a cook who hopes the pudding will get stirred if he just stands gazing at the bowl.

"They knew how to get things done," I agreed. "Maybe it

is someone from the Balbinus organization—maybe even Nonnius himself."

"That's an interesting suggestion," Rubella murmured, apparently taking no interest at all.

Suddenly I quite liked being given Nonnius to tackle. I said I would visit him at once; Fusculus offered to come with me and effect the introductions.

At the door, I paused. Rubella was busy opening a new cone of sunflower seeds. "Tribune, a question. How much am I allowed to say to Nonnius?"

He looked back at me almost dreamily. "Anything you like."

"He turned state evidence. Doesn't that mean he gets treated with circumspection?"

"He's a hardened criminal," said Rubella. "He knows the numbers on the dice. Balbinus has been safely put away. Nonnius is no use to the state now, not unless he comes up with further evidence. If he helps you, you may feel it is appropriate to behave respectfully. If not, feel free to trample his toes."

"Fine." I could trample toes. I could even be respectful if the situation really warranted. I had one more question. It concerned another sensitive area. "Does Petronius know that I'm being given a wider brief than he suggested?"

"You can tell him when you see him," said Marcus Rubella, like a man who really did not know he had just put the lid down on a very old friendship. He was still smiling benignly as I shut the door.

He could be one of those dark types who like to pretend they never lift a digit, while all the time they have a swift comprehension of events, a warm grasp of human relationships, and an incisive grip on their duties in public life. He could be loyal, trustworthy, and intelligent.

On the other hand, he could be just as he appeared: a lazy, carefree, overpromoted swine.

XVII

Nonnius lived in the Twelfth region—about two streets from Helena Justina's father. Which proves that money can buy you respectable neighbors—or a house next door to criminals. It was no better than where I lived. The criminals in the Capena Gate sector just happened to be richer and more vicious than the ones in Fountain Court.

The senator was a millionaire; he had to be. This was the rough-and-ready qualification for the job. Well, nobody needs exorbitant talents like judgment, or even a sense of honor, to vote in an assembly three times a month. But possessing a million is useful, I'm told, and the Camillus family lived comfortable lives. Helena's mother wore her semiprecious jasper necklace just to visit her manicurist.

Nonnius Albius had been chief rent-runner for a master criminal. The qualifications for *his* job were simple: persistence and a brutal temperament. For employing these over thirty years of violent activity, he had earned the right to live in the Capena Gate area, just like a senator, and to own his own freehold, which in fact many a senator has mortgaged away. His house, which looked modest but was nothing of the kind, had a subdued portico, which carefully refrained from drawing attention to itself, where callers had to wait while a growling porter who had only peered at them through a fierce iron grille took news of their arrival indoors.

"It's like visiting a consul!" I marveled.

Fusculus looked wry. "Except that Nonnius' bodyguards are better groomed and more polite than consuls' lictors tend to be."

There were stone urns with well-watered laurel bushes just like those at Helena's father's abode. Clearly, the topiary tub supplier at the Capena Gate didn't care who his customers were.

"What did you make of Rubella?" queried Fusculus as we still tapped our boot heels in the unobtrusive portico while the porter went off to vet us. "A bit of a complicated character?"

"He has a secret sorrow."

"Oh! What's that, Falco?"

"How would I know? It's a secret."

Petro's team had investigated too many inarticulate inadequates. None of his lads could spot a joke coming. "Oh, I thought you were in on something."

"No," I explained gently. "I just get a deep sexual thrill from speculating wildly about people I have only just met."

Fusculus gave me a nervous look.

Nonnius was, as everybody knew, a dying man. We could tell it was true because when we were let in we found him lying on a reading couch—but *not* reading—while he slowly ate a bowl of exquisite purple-bloomed plums. These were the hand-picked fruits, weeping unctuous amber, that are sent to console invalids by their deeply anxious friends. Perhaps thinking of your friends laying out silver by the purseload takes your mind off the pain.

The bowl they were in was a cracker too: a wide bronze comport two feet across, with three linked dolphins forming a handsome foot and with seahorse handles. The bowl was far too heavy for a sick man to lift, so it was held for Nonnius by an even-featured eight-year-old Mauretanian slave boy in a very short, topless tunic with gold fringes all around the hem. The child had gilded nipples, and his eyes were elongated with kohl like a god on an Egyptian scarab. My mother wouldn't have taken him on even to scrub turnips.

Nonnius himself had a lean face with an aristocratically hooked nose, big ears, and a scrawny neck. He could have modeled for a statue of a republican orator. In the old Roman manner, he had features that could be called "full of character": pinched lips, and all the signs of a filthy temper if his dinner was late.

He was about sixty and pretty well bald. Despite being so poorly, he had managed to shave; to make it more bearable his barber had aided the process with a precociously scented balsam. His tunic was plain white, but scrupulously clean. He wore no gems. His boots looked like old favorites. I mean, they looked as if they had already kicked in the kidneys of several hundred tardy payers, and were still greased daily in case they found a chance of kicking more. Everything about him said that if we annoyed him, the man would cheerfully kick *us*.

Fusculus introduced me. We had fixed a story: "Didius Falco has a roving commission, in a supervisory capacity, working alongside the public auditor."

Nobody believed it, but that didn't matter.

"I'm sorry to learn you're off color," I mouthed sympathetically. "I may need to go through some figures eventually, but I'll try to limit the agony. I don't want to tire you—"

"You being funny?" Nonnius had a voice that sounded polite, until you noticed threads of a raw accent running through it. He had been brought up on the Tiber waterfront. Any semblance of culture was as incongruous as a butcher calmly discussing Heraclitus' theory of all things being in a state of eternal flux just as he cleavered the ribs of a dead ox. I knew one like that once; big ideas, but overprone to making up the weight with fat.

"I was told you had to take it easy. . . ."

"Raiding Balbinus' accounts seems to have given me a new lease on life!" It could just have been the desperate jest of a genuine deathbed case. I was trying to decide if the bastard was really ill. Nonnius noticed, so he let out a pathetic cough. The exotic slave child rushed to wipe his brow for him. The tot was well trained in more than flirting his fringes, apparently.

"Is the Treasury man helping you?" I asked.

"Not a lot." That sounded like most Treasury men. "Want to see him?" Nonnius appeared perfectly equable. "I put him in a room of his own where he can play with the balls on his abacus to his heart's content."

"No thanks. So what's the score so far?" I tossed at him unexpectedly.

He had it pat: "Two million, and still counting."

I let out a low whistle. "That's a whole bunch of radishes!" He looked satisfied, but said nothing. "Very pleasant for you," I prompted.

"If I can get at it. Balbinus tried to lock it in a cupboard out of reach."

"Not the old 'present to wife's brother' trick?"

He gave me a respectful gleam. "Haven't come across that one! No: 'dowry to daughter's husband.'"

I shook my head. "Met it before. I took a jurist's advice, and the news is bad: You can't touch the coinage. So long as the marriage lasts, it has passed away from the family. Title to the dowry goes with the title to the girl. The husband owns both, with no legal responsibility to the father-in-law."

"Maybe they'll divorce!" sneered the ex-rent-collector, in a tone that suggested heavy whacks might be used to end the marriage. Once a muscleman, always a thug.

"If the dowry was big enough, love will triumph," I warned. "Cash in hand tends to make husbands romantic."

"Then I'll have to explain to the girl that her husband's an empty conker shell."

"Oh, I think she must have noticed that!" Fusculus put in. He glanced at me, promising to elaborate on the gossip later.

I saw Nonnius looking between us, trying to work out how Fusculus and I were in league. None of the vigiles wore uniforms. The foot patrols were kitted out in red tunics as a livery to help them force a right-of-way to the fountains during a fire, but Petro's agents dressed much as he did, in dark colors with only a whip or cudgel to reveal their status, and with boots that were tough enough to serve as an extra weapon. They and I were indistinguishable. I wore my normal work clothes too: a tunic the color of mushroom gravy, a liverish belt, and boots that knew their way around.

The room was full of working boots. There were enough soles and studs to subdue a crowd of rioting fishmongers in five minutes flat. Only the slave boy, in his embroidered Persian slippers, failed to match up to the rest of us.

"What's your background?" Nonnius demanded of me, bluntly suspicious.

"I'm an informer, basically. I take on specials for the Emperor."

"That stinks!"

"Not as much as enforcing for organized crime!"

I was pleased to see he did not care for me standing up to him. His tone became peevish. "If you've finished insulting me, I've got enough to do chasing my stake from the Balbinus case."

"Stay busy!" I advised.

He laughed briefly. "I gather your 'roving commission' will not include helping me!"

I wanted to tackle the area that Rubella had called past history, the one that had big implications for the future. "I need to rove in other directions."

"What do you want with me?"

"Information."

"Of course. You're an informer! Are you buying?" he tried brazenly.

"Not from a jury-fixer!"

"So what are you looking for, Falco?" Nonnius asked, ignoring the insult this time as he tried to startle me.

I could play that game. "Whether it's you who masterminded the Emporium heist."

It failed to nettle him. "I heard about that," he said softly. So had most of Rome, so I couldn't accuse him of unnatural inside knowledge. Not yet anyway. I was starting to feel that if he *had* been involved, handing him over to justice would give me great pleasure. I had a distinct feeling that he knew more than he ought. But crooks enjoy making you feel that.

"Somebody could hardly wait for Balbinus to leave town," I told him. "They snatched the inside lane of the racecourse—and they want everyone to know who's driving to win."

"Looks that way," he agreed, like a convivial friend humoring me.

"Was it you?"

"I'm a sick man."

"As I said earlier"—I smiled—"I'm very sorry to hear that, Nonnius Albius. . . . I've been away. I missed your famous court appearance, so let's run over a few things."

He looked sulky. "I said my piece, and I'm finished."

"Oh, yes. I heard you're quite an orator—"

At this point Fusculus, who had been watching with amused patience, suddenly cracked with anger and had to butt in: "Get a grindstone and sharpen up, Nonnius! You're a committed songbird now. Tell the man what he needs to know!"

"Or what?" jeered the patient, showing us the ugly glower that must have been forced on countless debtors. "I'm dying. You can't frighten me."

"We all die," Fusculus replied. He was a quiet, calm philosopher. "Some of us try to avoid being hung up in chains in the Banqueting Chamber first, while Sergius gives his whip an airing."

Nonnius was hard to terrify. He had probably devised and carried out more excruciating tortures than we two innocents could even imagine. "Forget it, shave-tail! That's the frightener you use for schoolboys filching oysters off barrows." He glared at Fusculus suddenly. "I know you!"

"I've been involved in the Balbinus case."

"Oh yes, one of the Fourth Cohort's brave esparto grass boys!" This was the traditional rude nickname for the foot patrols, after the mats they were issued with for smothering blazes. Used of Petro's team, who thought themselves above fire fighting, it was doubly rude. (All the worse, because the esparto mats were regarded as useless anyway.)

I managed to break in before things got too hot. "Tell me about how the Balbinus empire worked."

"A pleasure, young man!" Nonnius decided to treat me as the reasonable person in our party in order to show up Fusculus. The latter settled back again, quite content to simmer down. "What do you want, Falco?"

"I know Balbinus was the uncrowned king of rat thieves and porch-crawlers. He ran small-time crime as an industry and had drop shops on every street corner to process the loot. I haven't even mentioned the brothels or the illicit gaming houses yet—"

"He could run an estate," Nonnius conceded, with visible pride at being an associate.

"With your help." He accepted the smarm. I choked back my disgust. "It was more than stealing scarves from washing lines, however."

"Balbinus was big enough to have carried off the Emporium raid," Nonnius agreed. "Were he still in Rome!"

"But sadly he's traveling. . . . So who might have inherited his talent? We'll take it that you personally have retired to lead a blameless life." Nonnius allowed that lie too. "Were there any other big boys in the gang who could be showing a flash presence now?"

"Your sidekick ought to know names." Nonnius sneered nastily. "He helped close down the show!"

Fusculus acknowledged it with his normal grace, refusing to lose his temper this time. "They all had cheap nicknames," he said quietly to me, before running off one of his competent lists: "The Miller was the most sordid; he did the killings. The more brutal, the more he liked it. Little Icarus thought he could fly above the rest, the joke being that he was a complete no-hoper. Same for Julius Caesar. He was one of those madmen who think they're an emperor. Laurels would get the blight pretty quickly on his greasy head. The others I knew were called Verdigris and the Fly."

We looked at Nonnius for confirmation; he shrugged, pretending at last to be impressed. "Clever boy!"

"And where are they all now?" I asked.

"All gone to the country when the trial came off."

"Quiet holidays in Latium? You reckon that's true?" I put to Fusculus.

He nodded. "Minding goats."

Petro would have kept tabs on them as far as possible. "So, Nonnius, those were the centurions, and now they're living in rural retirement like a legion's colony of veterans. . . . Who were the big rivals to your dirty group?"

"We did not allow rivals!"

I could believe that.

There was no need to press the point. Better to think about the other criminal gangs after we left him. I sensed that Nonnius was taking a gloating delight in my interest in the rivals—who undoubtedly existed, even though Balbinus Pius must have done his best to strong-arm them out of his territory. I saw no need to gratify the rent-collector's pernicious taste for making trouble.

"We'll be in touch," I said, trying to make it sound worrying.

"Don't wait too long." Nonnius leered. "I'm a sick man!"

"If the Fourth wants you, we'll find you in Hades." Fusculus chortled. A pleasant threat, which somehow carried a darker tone than his mild, cheery nature led one to expect. Petronius knew how to pick his men.

Fusculus and I left then, without bothering to make contact with the Temple of Saturn auditor.

XVIII

When we returned to the station house, Petronius had just come in. At the same time his deputy, Martinus, had gone off duty, so Petro was in an affable mood. In our absence the day patrol had brought in two suspected lodging house thieves, and a man who kept an unleashed dog that had bitten a woman and a child (the "suspected wolf" from the Temple of Luna). Petro told Fusculus to do the interrogations on these.

"What, *all* of them, Chief?"

"Even the dog."

Fusculus and I exchanged a grin. It was his punishment for palling up with me. Petronius wanted to keep me on a very tight rein—one that could be personally jerked by him.

"And you can stop smirking!" he snarled at me. "I've seen Rubella. I know you're setting up special little escapades that I haven't agreed to!"

Looking innocent, I made sure I told him how friendly my chat with his triune had been, and how I had been given a free hand to interview Nonnius.

"Bastard," Petro commented, though it was fairly automatic. "You're welcome to the rent-collector. I warn you, he's a snake nesting in a midden heap. Be careful where you shove your garden fork." He relaxed. "What did you think of Rubella?"

Assessing the tribune seemed to be a cohort obsession. It's the same anywhere that has a hierarchy. Everyone spends a lot of time debating whether their supervisor is just an ineffectual layabout who needs a diagram in triplicate before he can wipe his backside clean—or whether he's so poisonous he's actually corrupt.

"Snide," I said. "Could be more dangerous than he looks. He can make a sharp judgment. It was like being interviewed by a crap fortune-teller. Rubella chewed some magic seeds, then informed me that as a legionary I didn't like my centurion."

Petro feigned an admiring look. "Well, he was right there!" We both laughed. Our centurion in the Second Augusta had been a brutal lag named Stollicus; both Petro and I were constantly at loggerheads with him. Stollicus reckoned we were a pair of unkempt, unreliable troublemakers who were deliberately ruining his own chances of promotion by dragging down his century. *We* said he marked down our personnel reports unfairly. Rather than waiting to find out after twenty years of failing to make centurion ourselves, we manufactured invalidity discharges and left him to it. Last I heard he was tormenting the local populace in Nicopolis. Interestingly, he was still a centurion. Maybe we really had been successful in blighting his life. It was a pleasing thought.

"Your honorable tribune spoke as if it were a promise to find out who our centurion was, and ask."

"He loves handing out some hint of blackmail that sounds like a joke but might not be," scoffed Petro.

"Oh well," I teased. "At least he won't have any trouble tracing Stollicus. He will have already found him once, to ask about you!"

Thinking about our military careers, we were silent for a moment, and allies again. Perhaps, being more mature now, we wondered whether it might have been wiser to placate the official and salvage our rights.

Perhaps not. Petronius and I both believed the same: Only crawlers get a fair character reference. Decent characters don't bother to argue. For one thing, the truly decent know that life is never fair.

Changing the subject, Petro asked, "Did you get anywhere with Nonnius?"

"No. He swears the Emporium raider isn't him."

"Hah! That was why," Petro explained, fairly mildly, "I myself wasn't going to bother to visit him."

"All right. I just thought I'd been assigned here to volunteer for the embarrassing jobs, so I might as well get on with one."

"*Io!* You're going to be a treasure."

"Oh yes. You'll be asking for a permanent informer on the complement. . . . So what lying ex-mobster do you reckon we should tackle next?"

Petro looked thoughtful. "I've had Martinus doing the rounds of the other big operators. They all deny involvement, of course. The only hope is that one of them will finger the real culprit out of spite. But Martinus can handle that. Why should we upset ourselves? The only trouble is, he's slow. Martinus reckons never to break into more than a decorous stroll. Asking three gang warlords where they were on a certain Thursday night will take him about five weeks. But left to himself he'll tell us in due course if anything has an abnormal whiff."

"You trust him?"

"He has a reasonable nose—with expert guidance from his senior officer!"

"So while he's sniffing villains extremely cautiously, what do we two speedy boys get up to? Investigating the races?"

"Depends . . ." Petro looked whimsical. "Do you see this as an office job, or will you take a mystery assignment that could ruin your health and your reputation?"

"Oh, the office job for me!" I lied. If I had realized what mystery assignment he meant, I might have stuck to this joke.

"That's a pity. I thought we could go visiting my auntie." A very old euphemism. Petronius Longus did not mean his auntie Sedina with the big behind and the flower stall.

"A brothel?"

"Not just any old brothel."

"Ooh! A *special* brothel!"

"I do have my standards, Marcus Didius! You don't have to come with me—"

"True, you're a big lad."

"If Helena wouldn't like it—"

I grinned gently. "She'd probably want to come too. The first time I slept with Helena Justina, we'd been to a brothel earlier that night."

Petronius snorted disapprovingly. "I didn't know Helena Justina was that kind of girl!" He thought I had been implying she had once been one of those senatorial stiffs who descend on bawdyhouses for a thrill.

"We were just passing through. . . ." Calling his bluff could be easy. "Oh, get wise. Helena could have been a vestal virgin if she hadn't met her heart's delight in me." I shook my head at him. He winced. I didn't worry him by mentioning the rest of the story. "So where is this palace of delight you're luring me to? The dives in the Suburra where the practices are ancient and the whores positively mummified? The out-of-town cabins where runaway slaves solicit travelers for a bit of brass? Or the lousy dens of push-and-shove in the deeply plebeian Patrician Street?"

"Home ground. Down by the Circus."

"Oh Jupiter! You can catch something just thinking about those filthy holes."

"Shut your brain off, then. You get by without thinking often enough. . . . We've had a hard morning. I thought we deserved an afternoon of exotic entertainment with the exquisite Lalage!"

"I'll buy you lunch first," I offered promptly. Petro accepted, agreeing with me that we needed to build up our strength before we went.

XIX

We had entered the Eleventh region. It was outside Petro's area, although he said it was unnecessary to make a courtesy call on the Sixth Cohort, who patrolled here. His was the career in public service, so I let him decide. I could tell he didn't like the Sixth. He was enjoying the fact we had sneaked into their patch privately, on the excuse of our special task.

Most prostitutes around the Circus Maximus are pavement crawlers and portico practitioners. They hang about during and after the races, preying on men whose appetites for excitement have been aroused by watching arena crashes. (Or men who have just come out hoping to waste money and don't fancy any of today's track runners.) Some of these women give themselves an air of moral rectitude by parading near temples, but the trade is the same: up against a wall, with the penalties of theft, a guilty conscience, and disease.

The brothel known as Plato's Academy offered a few advantages. At Plato's, unless you were a nice boy who liked clean bedding, you could at least do the deed horizontally. Theft and the scald were still hazards. Your conscience was your own affair.

Petronius and I carried out a reconnoiter of Plato's. I won't say we were nervous, but the place did have a lush reputation even by Roman standards. We wanted to be sure of ourselves. We walked to the Circus, scowled at the dark-eyed girls who hooted lewd suggestions after us from the colonnades, and ventured into a maze of lanes at the south end of the hippodrome. We stationed ourselves at a street-side drink stall opposite. While we decorated the marble with cups of the worst wine I had drunk in Rome for several years, I risked some chilled peas. Petro asked for brains; excitement had always made him go peculiar.

The peas were completely tasteless. The brains didn't look as if they had ever been up to much either, even allowing for the fact that calves don't devise encyclopedias. Whatever they tasted like, something made Petro say gloomily, "There's a rumor Vespasian wants to ban the sale of hot food in the streets."

"Well, that'll solve one of life's great dilemmas: to go hungry or get the runs."

"The latrine-keepers are hopping with worry."

"Well, they're always on the go."

The chat was meant to divert the stallholder while we sized up our destination.

Officially, Plato's appeared, from a very faint painted sign above the lintel, to be called the Bower of Venus. Depressed cherubs swinging on garlands at either end of the sign attempted to reinforce the dainty-sounding message. To reassure tourists who had been recommended in the vernacular, a larger chalked banner gave its common name at eye level, just alongside a stone Priapus with a horrible erection, for those who either could not read or were in too much of a hurry to stand about deciphering mere lettering. On the opposite side of the doorway, another slogan announced COME AND GET WHAT EVERY MAN WANTS, with a graphic doodle which made it plain that this did not mean a modest woman, an unexpected legacy, and a tranquil life. For all but the tragically shortsighted, there could be no doubt which trade was carried on within the drab-looking premises.

There was a lumbering oak door, propped open with two

staves. It looked too slumped on its hinges to be closed. No doubt it never was.

This portal was barely a couple of yards from us, diagonally up the dirty street. Through it marched a regular line of last-time-before-recall soldiers, straight-off-the-ship sailors, slaves, freedmen, and small businessmen. Some of the sailors felt obliged to make a bit of noise. An occasional character who looked like an olive oil salesman or corn chandler's understeward had the grace to appear furtive and only slipped inside at the last moment. Most men just strode in clinking their coins. Even while we were eating, one or two we already recognized strode back out and carried on in the same direction as if they had merely stepped inside to say hello to their old mothers. Business at Plato's must be matter-of-fact and brisk.

"I suppose there's a difference," Petro commented in his dark, philosophical voice, "between men who come because it's not allowed, and those who come because it is."

"I'm not with you."

"One kind who buy it actually get a thrill from the guilt. That's not Plato's trade. Around here, you purchase a whore in between picking up a chicken for supper and putting your boots in at the cobbler's to have a strap mended."

"Daily shopping!" I was feeling silly. "Do you think the madam lets you feel the girl first, to convince yourself she's ripe?"

He dug me in the ribs. "We're like recruits again, wondering what went on in the *canabae* outside Isca fort!"

I could not quite tell whether my old comrade Lucius Petronius thought this comparison was reprehensible, or a positive hoot. "I think I know what went on in the *canabae*," I said gravely. "I'll explain it to you some day, when you've got a lot of listening time." This time I sidestepped and managed to avoid his elbow before it had a chance to cause a bruise.

We were so near to the open doorway we could hear the bargaining as customers arranged their treats. The bug-eyed foreigners were obvious. So were the Roman goldfinches, men with too many sesterces in their purses, picked like flowers in the Forum by affable pimps; they had been lured here to be gulled, fleeced, and if possible heavily black-mailed. Otherwise it was impossible to tell which of the crumpled tunics who entered were straightforward cus-tomers, which wanted to defy the antigambling laws with a few games of soldiers, and which were small-time members of the criminal underworld gathering to exchange news of likely homes to burgle.

Not many women were visible in the vicinity.

"Too busy?" I speculated.

"Their conditions of employment don't encourage pop-ping out for a length of hair ribbon." Petro meant the pros-titutes at Plato's were slaves.

We had finished our lunch. We paid, leaving a meager tip. It was what the barman expected, but he roused himself to spit with disgust after us. Petro said over his shoulder, "Do that again, and you'll lose your food license." The man retorted something we could not quite catch.

We crossed the street, and glanced at one another. We had a justifiable job to do, but inevitably felt like conspirators.

"If my mother gets to hear of this, I'm blaming you."

"Falco, it's not your mother you should be worried about."

He was wrong about that, but it was no time to block the entrance arguing. We went in.

A flaunty piece in the scarlet toga that was the strict legal badge of her trade was taking the money and fixing the arrangements. It was not a requirement that the toga should be vermilion and make her blaze like a corn poppy, nor that she wear it within the brothel; this lady liked to defy the law by obeying it with too much flourish. None of the other girls we glimpsed inside were in togas, though in fact most of them were not wearing many of their clothes—if they possessed any. The doorkeeper was watched over by a hound-dog male whom she sensibly ignored. He couldn't have bounced a feather ball, let alone a determined rioter. Having a dozy protector did not seem to cause her much anxiety. She looked like a girl with a good uppercut.

"Afternoon, boys. I haven't seen you before. I'm Macra,

and I'm here to see you enjoy yourselves." It was the kind of aggressive sales talk I dread.

"He's Falco, I'm Petronius, and we're with the vigiles," announced Petronius immediately. I had been wondering how he would handle that aspect.

"We're always pleased to see the hornets. . . ." She must have been chosen for her manners, though her tone managed a sneer. Her eyes sharpened slightly as she weighed up what we expected. We could see her deciding we were definitely not foot patrol. Nor were we Sixth Cohort, the regulars for this district, whom she was bound to know. She had soon worked out *Prefect's office,* or *tribunal staff,* from which she made the inevitable smooth transferral to *troublemakers*. Clearly a young lady of some initiative, her reaction was: *Find out what they want, and humor them.* "This is a decent house, with all clean young girls. I can choose you something a bit special," she offered. "We like to do business with the forces of law and order." Her gaze flickered to the hound dog. Even we could see he was supposed to run for reinforcements at this point, but he was no help.

"Something special," repeated Petronius thoughtfully.

On the assumption he was welcoming the offer, Macra cheered up. "As it's your first time being entertained here, it will be on the house. May I recommend Itia. She's a lovely creature, a freeborn girl who normally only works on private hire. One at a time suit you? For both together we would have to make a small charge, I'm afraid."

"Freeborn?" asked Petro. "So you can tell me which aedile she's listed with, and her registration number?" Any freeborn woman who wished to shed her reputation could work as a prostitute, so long as she formally declared her profession and put herself outside the reach of the adultery laws.

As soon as Petro's attitude became clearer, Macra kicked the sleepy bouncer, who condescended to show an interest. He stood up.

"Sit down," said Petronius pleasantly. The man sat down again.

Macra took a very deep breath. "If you scream I'll knock

your head off," said Petro, still in a level tone. "I can't abide loud noises. We're here to see Lalage."

Macra managed to defer screaming. "Lalage is engaged at the moment." It would be her stock rejoinder. The madam is never available.

"Don't panic. We're not asking to query a bill."

"Very funny! Is she expecting you?" Another tactic.

"She's a brothel-keeper," said Petro. "Her whole life must be spent expecting questions from the law! Do you want fish pickle on it? Stop stalling. There's no point."

"I shall go and inquire," the girl informed him pompously. "Kindly wait just here."

"No. You'll take us," Petronius corrected. "Hit the grit." She pretended not to know the expression. "*Walk, Macra!*"

With a curse she didn't much bother to muffle, the girl led us in, swinging her hips in a parody of a seductive dance. Artfully untidy tangles of black hair swished on her bare shoulders. Her heels clattered loudly. She was grimy, and not very pretty, though she did have a certain style.

We passed a series of dim cubicles. Crudely obscene pictures above the doors made a feeble attempt at suggesting erotic art. The grunts we overheard were far from high culture. One customer was washing himself from a ewer, so minimal hygiene must be provided for. There were cloak pegs and a sign to the latrine.

A small slave boy with a trayful of flagons dashed past us and dived into a room like an inn's refectory, where low-class men were crouched about tables, either gambling or conspiring. Petro halfheartedly started to investigate, but the door swung across behind the slave, and he gave up. Maybe it was just the weekly meeting of the chicken feed suppliers' guild.

Up narrow steps we found a corridor with doors to larger rooms for higher-paying customers. We could hear a tabor being thumped, and smell insidious smoke. By now we had realized that Plato's was much more extensive than its street frontage suggested. It also provided for a varied clientele. I reckoned there were probably other ways in and out of it too.

The odor of burning bay leaves gave way to imitation frankincense. I coughed slightly, and Petronius grimaced. Further on Macra led us through a veritable banqueting hall. It had a sunken floor; Jove knows what orgies were carried out there. Tired flower petals still lay squashed on the steps. There was a statue of two entwined figures who appeared to have more than two full sets of procreative organs, though, as we said afterwards, we might have been misled by some scraps of leftover garland and the fact that a stone goat was also participating.

The corridor grew darker. From a room at what must have been the farthermost end of the building came sounds of an unexpectedly professional flute. Macra knocked, then kept the half-open door against her hip so we could not see past her. With a rapid apology, she relayed who we were. A woman's voice swore briefly, then said, "I'm sorry for the intrusion. Look after him nicely please, Macra."

There was an angry movement. A half-naked teenage girl flutist pushed past Macra and vanished. Then a magistrate we could not fail to recognize walked out.

He did not deign to greet us. Petronius gave an ironic salute, and I squeezed against the wall so as not to dirty His Honor's purple stripes as he rushed by. The Very Important Patrician ignored these courtesies. Maybe that was because he was famous for his devotion to a cultured, highly connected, slightly older (but immensely wealthy) wife.

Macra sneered at us and flung open the door, releasing natural daylight amid curious wafts of violets and hydromel. She twirled off after the magistrate. We walked in to meet Lalage.

She had the face of a once very beautiful woman, painted so thickly you could hardly detect the sweetness it still carried. She wore a yellow silk gown, which she was casually readjusting after most of it had been removed to allow access to an oiled and perfumed body that made two honest citizens gulp. Her headdress contained Oriental pearls an empress would die for; her necklace was of mixed sapphires and amethysts; her arms were sheathed in bracelets of Greek gold filigree. Her eyes were angry. She did not welcome us to her establishment, or offer us a glass of the strong honeyed wine.

The notorious Lalage had a scar on her delicate left ear. It brought back nostalgic memories. She was pretending to be an elegant Oriental courtesan, but I knew exactly where this precious pullet came from. I had met her before.

"**W**ill this take long?" Her voice had all the fluting charm of pebbles in vinegar cleaning out a blackened skillet. "We're expecting guests."

"Lycians, maybe?" asked Petronius.

"You've got a nerve." She was still pinning folds of her dress, more interested in how it draped than in dealing with us. "This had better be good," she snapped, looking up abruptly. "Luckily, we'd finished, or I'd kill you for interrupting that customer. He's my best client."

"Who gets a personal service," Petro commented.

"He knows this is where he'll receive the best!" Lalage smirked. I noticed her giving us a thorough squint: Petronius solid, tough, and hostile; me less tall, but just as tough and even more disparaging.

"Left his lictors at home, did he?" I asked, in an offensive tone. I was referring to the mighty man's state-employed bodyguard; they were supposed to escort him everywhere, showing the axes and rods that symbolized his power to chastise. Or as Petro used to say, symbolizing what a big donkey he was.

"We're looking after the lictors."

"I bet! Lictors usually know how to park their rods," I said.

"A man should always take his lictors, Marcus Didius," Petro reproved me gravely.

"Oh, true, Lucius Petronius," I corrected myself formally. "Leaving your lictors at home is the right way to make the wife suspicious."

"And he's a magistrate, so he must be a clever man! He'll know how to bluff the old broomstick he left at home in his atrium. Besides, I expect the lictors only keep quiet about his habits, provided they get theirs—"

"Spare me the comedy!" Lalage interrupted. She swung her bare feet to the floor and sat up on the edge of her couch, an ornate affair with bronze curlicues all over it, dripping with cushions of the type that are described as "feminine." I could think of several women who would shove Lalage out of a window and fling her tasseled and pleated pink fripperies after her—not so much for moral reasons, but in disgust at her decor.

With a shimmer and tinkle of jewelry, she folded her fine arms and waited.

Petronius and I had deliberately stood at opposite ends of the room, so she had to turn her head to face whoever was speaking. In more fragile company it was a tactic to cause alarm. I suspected Lalage had had plenty of practice in dealing with two men at once. Still, we went through the routine, and she let us play.

"We need to ask you some questions," Petro began.

"Don't you mean *more* questions? I thought the damned business with the Lycians was all sorted out." She assumed we had come about the murdered tourist whose death had formed the basis of the Balbinus trial.

"This is not about the Lycians."

"Afraid I can't help you then."

"Afraid you'd better. Do you want a raid?" Petronius asked. "I daresay we could find a few kidnapped minors working your cubicles. Or unlicensed freeborns. Are you absolutely certain you comply scrupulously with the hygiene regulations? Is any food being supplied on the premises? If so, are you licensed for hot meals? Who *exactly* were those shady characters Falco and I saw huddled downstairs?"

Petronius tended to stick stolidly to his remit, but this

could take poking with a fancier baton. "How about a scandal?" I chimed in. "Senior magistrate named; society divorce ensues; shocked officials say they have seen nothing like it since Caligula's excesses. That should make a few entries in the *Daily Gazette*!"

"Good for trade." Lalage shrugged. Annoyingly, she was right. Such a story might limit her upper-class clients for a while, but others would flock. She decided to defy Petro. "Anyway, you work in the Thirteenth. This is the Eleventh; it's out of your jurisdiction. I'm not going to be raided," she assured him serenely. "The Bower of Venus has an excellent relationship with the local boys."

Petro's voice grated. "Excellent as tar!"

"They look after us very prettily."

"I'm not the Sixth Cohort. I don't take oily handshakes, and I don't want half an hour with a dubious haybag on one of your flea-ridden blankets—"

"Of course you don't. You're a hero, and your cohort's incorruptible! Something more select?" Lalage then rasped at Petro, with an affected attitude. "Does the most excellent sir have interesting tastes?"

"Shut it, Lalage!"

"Juno! Have I just met the one and only member of the vigiles who's not on the take?"

Petro ignored it. We were not investigating graft. If anyone tackled that problem, it would need more than two agents, and they would want to be wearing Scythian chain mail. "Hear my words. I'm not touting for a free tickle, and you're in danger of finding the brothel closed down and yourself back as a pavior again."

"I was *never* a streetwalker!" the madam exclaimed with true horror.

I took a turn in the conversation. "This is the real business," I warned her. "Unless we get cooperation, you'll find yourself making an appearance before the eagle's beak!"

"Nice oratory. So what's the catch?"

"Be clever. My colleague's easily upset."

She turned lustrous eyes on me. Her manner altered. She had had fifteen years of practice, and I felt my breath falter. "So what about you?" she murmured.

"He has a very respectable girlfriend," Petronius shot in rapidly.

"Oh I see! Why keep a pig and honk yourself?" Her eyes never left me. If I looked at her, the pressure was serious, and if I stared back, I could no longer see Petro. This was where separating ourselves at two ends of the room could leave one of us vulnerable. Lalage knew how to make feeling vulnerable seem exciting. She was still relaying the promising smile, and I was freely admiring the act. She had once been a genuine looker. She was soiled, but still attractive. Well-worn glory has its own allure. Virginity's a bland commodity.

The skirmish was brief, however. "You seem to be a man of taste," she said.

"I like to bask at my own fire." I liked rather more than that, and what suited my taste was not sold by the hour. My girl could never be bought.

Lalage dropped the subject, though not without a sneer. "Well thanks for making it sound like an apology!"

"Aventine etiquette."

She gave me a sharper look, but I chose to pretend I had said nothing significant. She still did not know what I was hinting; she had seen too many men to remember who I was. I felt her lose interest—leaving me with a strong sense of unfinished business.

Unexpectedly she spun back to Petro: "I haven't got all day! What do you want?"

She was using our own separation routine; letting one relax, then trying to catch him off guard. Petro managed to avoid being thrown. His chin came up, but he turned it into a surly gesture by sweeping back his straight hair with one hand, like a dandy who didn't reckon on letting a mere woman make him jump. "To discuss the Emporium heist."

"Oh that was a loud one!" She rolled her eyes. They were still very beautiful: wide-set, large, dark as a winter evening, and melting with suggestiveness. Personally, I liked eyes with a more subtle challenge. But Lalage had nice eyes.

Petronius had noticed them, though only a close friend would know it. "Yes, they're talking about it everywhere— but nobody's whispering who did the dirty deed."

"Who do you think did it?" Lalage asked, pretending to flatter him.

"I haven't time to waste thinking. I want names."

She tried the innocent-little-woman trick: "Well what makes you believe I might know anything about thieves?"

Petro's temper was running short now. His teeth had locked. "You mean, apart from the fact that your downstairs parlor is full of sneaks who follow funerals to rob the mourners, door-knock thieves who work the rush-the-porter game, balcony-crawlers, basement rats, and that little runt who hangs the fake fly in peoples' faces, then slits their purse thongs while they're brushing it away?"

I was impressed. We had only glimpsed the trading room for a moment. Petro must have sharp eyes. He certainly knew the streets.

And I knew him. I recognized the signs; he felt uneasy with the location and was working up to dragging Lalage over to his station house. If she had been a well-bred schoolgirl who had never spoken to a public official, he might have stood a chance. But he ought to realize what a fool he would look, trying to put an armlock on a glittering saffron butterfly who would shriek abuse at him all the way to the Aventine. Arresting a brothel madam is never discreet.

"Are you talking raids again?" Lalage laughed. She knew he had lost his grip enough to give her the upper hand.

"He knows better," I assured her. "By the time we can bring the espartos in, the joint will be clean. Macra probably gave the word straight after she finished massaging your magistrate."

"Well, I do hope she was thorough." The madam grinned shamelessly. "A person of his status doesn't expect to be hustled!"

It seemed to me it was time the man was hustled out of office. Rome would never be cleaned up if every time Petronius brought a mugger to court, the bad character could smile at a judge who had shared the ewer where he washed his privates after his Tuesday afternoon binge. The fellowship of Plato's had insidious tentacles. In fact, that was only one aspect of our visit today that had an aura of ambidextrous ethics. The smack of sticky payments seemed to be lurking everywhere.

Lalage's diversion failed. Petronius Longus was strictly unamused. "Who's your landlord now?" he sprang on her. "Who runs this place since Nonnius did his singing from the high twig and Balbinus Pius took a sail?"

"What sort of a question's that?"

"Well it's not about who has decorating rights under your building tenancy. Who's the mighty man behind you, Lalage?"

"I don't go in for boys' stuff."

"Stifle the innuendo! Who's giving Plato protection? We proved in court that Balbinus used to cream off his percentage, so who skims Plato's now?"

"Nobody. Who needs it? I'm running everything myself."

It was what we already suspected. Petronius screwed the corner of his mouth. "This had better be honest gen."

"Who needs a man?" scoffed Lalage lightly. "I had it up to here with the old system. Balbinus demanded an exorbitant cut, then I was constantly giving presents to Nonnius to stop him breaking up the furniture—all in return for a supposed service we never saw. Any trouble had to be sorted out by my own staff. What happened when the Lycian blew away was typical—we tried to clear up ourselves. I was doing the hard work, and Balbinus was just milking the business. That's over. The only commerce I'm interested in now is when men are paying me!"

"Someone will try to take over his position," Petronius insisted.

"Let them try!"

"If it hasn't happened yet, now Balbinus has left Rome you'll meet with pressure eventually. When it happens, I want to know."

"Sorry," she answered acidly. "You're in the same bumboat as all my customers: You'll get what you pay for—and no more!"

"That's closer to what I call a bargain," Petronius responded, in his normal, level tone. "For the big item, I'll be buying."

She heaved her bosom, setting up ripples of light from the

jewelry. The effect was less worrying than the eye trick, but highly professional. "How much?"

"What it's worth. But I don't want shoddy goods or fakes."

"You don't want much." The last comment was amiable bluster. They had reached the real center of the discussion; the terms were understood and more or less accepted by both sides. Whether that meant Lalage would ever produce any information was another matter.

"Bring me the name I need, and you won't regret it. You'll find me at the station house in the Thirteenth," Petro announced politely.

"Oh, go away." She sneered, addressing me as if her patience with him had run out. "And take the Big Unsusceptible with you!"

We were leaving. I turned back at the last moment to add a courtesy of my own. Giving the famous whore a generous smile, I said, "I'm glad to see your ear healed up!"

While she and Petronius were thinking about it, I grabbed him by the elbow and we fled.

XXI

We emerged unscathed, though I for one wanted to head for the nearest respectable bathhouse.

"What was the crack about the lug, Falco?"

I just grinned and looked mysterious.

The place seemed much emptier than when we arrived. News spreads.

The girl Macra was standing back at the outside door. She looked edgy, but when she saw we were leaving peacefully she relaxed. As we passed her I heard a young child's cry. Macra noticed my surprise. "Things happen, Falco!"

"I thought you were organized in places like this." Some brothels were *so* organized, their expertise had led to them operating as neighborhood abortionists.

"Losing a baby's illegal, isn't it, officer?" Macra gurgled at Petronius. He looked tense. We all knew it would be a long time before anyone bothered to take a prostitute to court for this. The unborn are protected if there's a legacy in it; the unborn with shameless mothers have few rights.

"Like to see around the nursery?" the girl then offered Petro. There was a distinct undertone of offering him a pre-pubertal tidbit. He declined in silence, and she giggled.

"You're a hard man to tempt! Maybe I'll have to come and see you in your station house."

"Maybe I'll show you the cell!" Petro growled in annoyance. A mistake.

"It's a promise!" Macra shrieked. "We know a client in the vigiles who does *amazing* things with chains during 'interviews.' "

Petronius had had enough. He took out his note tablet formally: "And who would that be?"

"Well, do you believe"—she leered at him—"his name seems to just escape me. . . ."

"You're a lying little flirt," Petronius told her, fairly pleasantly. He put away the note tablet. We stepped out into the street with her jibes ringing along the narrow passage at our backs.

"So that's a brothel!" Petro said, and we both nudged each other, grinning at an old joke from the past.

We had hesitated, lacking plans. We should not have laughed. Laughing on a brothel doorstep can lead to disaster. Never do it before you have taken a careful look in both directions down the street.

Somebody we knew was coming towards us. Petro and I were already helpless. It was too late to make off discreetly; *far* too late to look less like guilty men.

Approaching down the narrow lane, crying loudly, was a little girl with big feet and a dirty face. She was seven years old, in a tunic she had outgrown months ago; with it she wore a cheap glass bracelet that a kind uncle had brought her from abroad, and an extravagant amulet against the evil eye. The evil eye had not been averted; the child was being dragged along by a small, fierce old lady with a pinched mouth who had an expression of moral outrage even before she spotted us. Spot us she did, of course, just as we two emerged like utter layabouts from Plato's Academy.

The little girl was in deep trouble for playing truant. She was glad to see anyone else she could drag down to Hades with her. She knew we were exactly the distraction she needed.

"There's Uncle Marcus!" She stopped crying at once.

Her jailer stopped walking. Petro and I had been reprobates in our youth, but nobody in Rome knew that. Petro and
I had not been stupid. We were reprobates abroad.

We had just blown our cover. My niece Tertulla stared at
us. She knew that even bunking off school after her grandma
had pinched and scraped to pay for it failed to match our disgrace. We knew it too.

"Petronius Longus!" cried the old lady in frank amazement, too horrified even to mention me. Petro was renowned
as a good husband and family man, so this disaster would be
blamed on me.

"Good afternoon," murmured Petro shyly, trying to pretend he had not been chortling, or if he had it was only because he had just heard a *very* funny but perfectly tasteful
story about an aspect of local politics. With great presence
of mind, he embarked upon explaining that we could not
make ourselves available to escort people to a safer neighborhood, owing to a message he'd just received about a crisis over at the station house.

At the same moment a flying figure whom I recognized as
my fraught sister Galla came hurrying down the lane, crying, "Oh you've found the little horror!" Galla spent half her
life oblivious to what her children might be getting up to,
and the rest in guilty hysterics after somebody stupid had
told her.

"I found more than that!" came the terse reply, as a pair
of unmatchedly contemptuous eyes finally fixed themselves
on me.

There was nowhere to hide.

"Hello, Mother," I said.

XXIII

When I walked into my apartment, I found someone standing in the doorway from the balcony. Her dark hair shone in the sunlight behind her; she had left its warmth immediately she heard my footfall.

She was full of grace and serenity. She wore a simple dress in blue, with a late October rosebud in a pin on the top seam. If she had used perfume, it was so discreet that only the favored fellow who kissed her neck would be aware of it. A silver ring worn on her left hand showed her loyalty to whoever he was. *She* was everything that a woman should be.

I gave her a courteous nod.

"People will be racing to tell you," I said, "that Petronius and I spent an hour in a brothel near the Circus Maximus this afternoon. It's famous for offering disgusting services as bribes to the vigiles. We were witnessed coming out nudging each other guiltily, and with happy grin."

"I know," she said.

"I was afraid of that."

"I daresay!"

The slender links of one bracelet slipped over her fine wrist as she lightly held a scroll. Her feet were bare. She, who should have been cushioned on swansdown amid some great man's marble colonnades, had been reading in the warm sun, high above the squalor of the Aventine where she lived with me.

I selected a cool and formal tone. "People overreact sometimes. I was with Petro when he reached his own house and couldn't make his wife answer the door. A neighbor shoved her head through a shutter and bawled, 'She's taken the children to her mother's and your dinner's been thrown at the cat.' I had to help him pick the lock. He loves that cat; he insisted on going in to look for it."

She smiled. "Every hero should have a tragic flaw." I happened to know she didn't care for cats. I suspected she despised heroics too.

I thought it best to maintain a serious approach. "Despite his pleading, I felt unable to escort him to fetch Arria Silvia from her mother's lair."

"Did you leave him by himself, then?"

"He was all right. He had his cat. . . ." Something caught in my throat. "I wanted to make sure you were still here."

"I'm here."

"I'm glad."

It was midafternoon. I had been as quick as possible, but I had gone to bathe. Now I was clean. Every inch of me was oiled and scraped, but I felt as if I walked in grime.

"Were you worried?" I asked.

Her dark eyes were fixed on me with a steadiness my heart was failing to match. "I do worry when I hear you're in a brothel," she told me in a low voice.

"I worry when I go into a brothel myself." For some reason, I suddenly felt clean again. I smiled at her with special warmth.

"You have to do your work, Marcus." There was a shade of resigned amusement lurking deep in Helena Justina's gaze. It seemed to me she had deliberately placed it there. While she waited for me she had taken her decision: Either we could fight, and she would only end up feeling more wretched than when she started, or she would make it be like this. "So what did you think of the brothel?" she asked quietly.

"It was a dump. They didn't have a monkey. I wouldn't take a senator's daughter near the place."

"The monkey in the one we ran through was a chimpanzee," she reminded me. Her tone was serious, but the seriousness was a joke.

Sometimes we did fight. Sometimes, because she wanted me too badly to use reason, I could make her quarrel bitterly. Other times, the intelligence with which she handled me was breathtaking. She set trust between us like a plank, and I just walked straight across.

I could see a very faint twist at the corners of her mouth. If I chose to do it now, with merely a look in my eyes I would be able to make her smile.

I crossed the room. I came right up to her and took her by the waist. A slight color stained her cheeks, echoing the unopened rose pinned to her dress. As I had suspected, the perfume was there for somebody who knew her well enough to come close enough to treat her tenderly. Not many had ever had that privilege. I breathed slowly. A whisper of cinnamon crept over me, not just any perfume, but one I particularly liked. It was fresh, only recently applied.

I let myself enjoy looking at her for a while. She enjoyed herself letting me drown gently in old memories and new expectations. I must have dropped my hand without intending it. I felt her fingers entwine in mine. I drew up both our hands and held hers hard against my chest.

The room was silent. Even the street noise beyond the balcony seemed far away.

Helena leaned forward and brushed my mouth with a kiss. Then, with no flutes or incense or sticky wines, without needing to negotiate a price, without even needing words, we went to bed.

XXIV

By the time consciousness reasserted itself, my sister Galla had told my sister Junia, who had rushed to relate the tale to Allia, who—since she could no longer exclaim with Victorina, who was dead—told Maia. Maia and Allia normally did not get on, but this was an emergency; Allia was almost last in the queue, and she was bursting to amaze somebody with the news of my latest offense. Maia, who alone among them had a conscience, first decided to leave us alone with our trouble. Then, since she was a friend to Helena, she set off for our apartment to make sure nobody had left home over it. Had rapid action been necessary, Maia would have comforted anyone she found sobbing, then rushed out to look for the runaway.

While she was still on her way to us, I was rousing myself.

"Thank you."

"What for?"

"The sweet gift of your love."

"Oh, that!" Helena smiled. I had to close my eyes, or I would have been in bed with her until nightfall.

Then she asked me, wanting answers this time, about our visit to Plato's Academy. I rolled over on my back, with my arms behind my head. She lay with her cheek against my chest while I told her my impressions, ending with the fact that I had known Lalage long ago.

Helena laughed at the story. "Did you tell her?"

"No! But I left a few hints to worry her."

Helena was more interested in the results of our official inquiries: "Did you believe her when she claimed she was going to resist having the place 'protected' by a male criminal?"

"I suppose so. To call her competent would be an understatement! She can run the brothel and easily beat up anyone who tries to interfere."

"So maybe," suggested Helena, "she was telling you more than you think."

"Such as?"

"Maybe *she* would like to take over where Balbinus left off."

"Well, we've agreed she wants to run her own empire. Are you suggesting something more?"

"Why not?"

"Lalage control the gangs?" It was an alarming thought.

"Think about it," said Helena.

I was silent, but she must have known I always took her suggestions seriously. Grumpily I accepted this one, though it was against my will. If we could say Nonnius Albius had stepped into the space left by his former chief, things would be much simpler both to prove and to put right. If we needed to consider newcomers, let alone women, the affair assumed unwelcome complexity.

Wanting to make sure I had listened, Helena sprang up excitedly, leaning over me on her elbows. Then I noticed her expression change. With a sudden mutter she turned away out of bed and left me. She scampered next door, and I heard her being sick.

I followed, waited until the worst was over, then put an arm around her and sponged her face. Our eyes met. I gave her the look of a man who was being more reasonable than she deserved.

"Don't say anything!" she commanded, still white-lipped.

"Wouldn't dream of it."

"It can't be something we ate at dinner disagreeing with me, because we forgot to have any dinner."

"Just as well, apparently."

"So it seems you were right," she admitted, in a neutral voice.

Then Maia's voice exclaimed from the door, "Well, congratulations! It's a secret, I daresay."

"Unless you tell somebody," I answered, biting back a curse.

"Oh, trust me!" Maia smiled, deliberately looking unreliable.

She came in, a neat, curly-haired woman wearing her good cloak and nicest sandals so she could make a real occasion of simpering at the trouble I had caused. "Put her on the bed and lay her flat," she advised. "Well, this is it!" she chirped at Helena helpfully. "You've really done it now!"

"Oh, thanks, Maia!" I commented, as Helena struggled upright and I started clearing up.

Helena groaned. "Tell me how long this is going to last, Maia."

"All your life," snarled Maia. She had four children, or five if you counted her husband, who needed more looking after than the rest. "Half the time you're lying down exhausted, and the rest you just wish you could be. As far as I can tell, it goes on forever. When I'm dead I'll come back and tell you if it improves then."

"That's what I was afraid of," Helena answered. "First the pain, and then your whole life taken over . . ."

They both seemed to be joking about it, but there was a real edge. Helena and my youngest sister were on very friendly terms; when they talked, especially about men, there was a fierce undertone of criticism. It made me feel left out. Left out, and thoroughly to blame.

"We can have a nurse," I offered. "Helena, my darling, if it makes you feel better, I'll even set aside my principles and let you pay for her."

This piece of piety did not soothe the situation. I decided it was time to go out. I put up the excuse of emptying the rubbish pail, grabbed it, and sauntered downstairs whistling, leaving the pair of them to enjoy themselves grumbling. I wasn't going far. I would use up the rest of the evening at the new apartment on the other side of Fountain Court. Having a second home to escape to began to seem a good idea.

I felt shaken. Faced with definite evidence that I was becoming a father, I needed to be alone somewhere so I could think.

I had chosen a good moment. The basket-weaver hailed me with news that a man he knew who hired out carts was bringing one around for me, something he had volunteered when I talked to him previously. The cart could only be driven here at night because of the vehicle curfew, and as I would be keeping it for a few days while I cleared the property, arrangements were required. I wanted to use the cart as a temporary rubbish skip. For this to work we had to put it up on blocks and take the wheels off, or someone was bound to make off with it. That was no easy task. Then we had to manhandle the wheels inside the weaver's shop and chain them together for added security. My troubles had only just started. In the short time that the weaver, the carter, and I were in the shop making the wheels safe, some joker stowed half a woodwormy bed frame and a broken cupboard in the skip.

We dragged them out and towed them a few strides farther, leaving them outside the empty lockup on the other side of the road, so the aediles would not make us (or anybody who knew us) pay for clearing the street. Luckily, Maia came down at that point, so I told her to send her eldest boy, and I'd give him a copper or two to act as a guard.

"I'll send him tomorrow," Maia promised. "You can have Marius when he's finished school, but if you want a watchman earlier in the day you'll have to pinch one of Galla's or Allia's horrible lot."

"Marius can miss a few lessons."

"He won't. Marius *likes* school!" Maia's children were encouragingly well behaved. Since I felt disinclined to bring more vandals and loafers into the world, this cheered me up. Maybe, despite all the evidence I saw daily in

Rome, parenthood could work out well. Maybe I too could father a studious, polite little person who would be a credit to the family. "Put a cloth on top overnight. Famia reckons that makes a skip invisible."

Famia, her husband, was a lazy swine; trust him to realize people are so idle they would rather lose a chance of dumping their waste in someone else's bin than apply a bit of exertion uncovering the container first.

Maia hugged me rather unexpectedly. In our large family she was the only one younger than me; we had always been fairly close. "You'll make a wonderful father!"

I pointed out that there were a great many uncertainties before ever I got that far.

After Maia left, I started hauling debris from the first-floor apartment. The weaver, who told me his name was Ennianus, assured me he would love to be some help, but apparently he had a bad back that not many people knew about. I said it was lucky that selling baskets didn't call for much bending and lifting; then he shambled off.

I didn't need him. I rolled my tunic sleeves up to my shoulders and set to like a man who has something disturbing to forget about. Although autumn had arrived, the nights were still light long enough for me to put in an hour or two of heavy work. The whole first-floor apartment was crammed with dirty old junk—though I came across no dead bodies or other unpleasant remains. It was hard work, but could have been much worse.

Smaractus must have let his handymen use this place sometimes as a materials store. There were half-buckets of good nails lurking under the warped scaffold boards, and bits of mangled joist timber. One of his halfwits had left behind a perfectly decent adze that would find a welcome place in my own toolbag. They were a feckless lot. Dustsheeting had gone moldy through being folded up while wet. Pulleys had rusted solid. Paint had gone hard in uncovered kettles. They never took home an empty wine flask or filthy food wrapper if they could stuff it under the unusable tangles of hoisting rope. There were unopened sacks of substances that had set like rock so it was impossible to identify the contents; nothing was labeled, of course. Smaractus never bought from a regular builders' merchant, but acquired oddments from contractors who had already been paid once by some innocent householder who had never heard of demanding to keep spare materials.

I cleared one room and used it to store any stuff I could reclaim. By the end of the evening I had made good headway and left pleased with my work. One more stint would reduce the apartment to a shell, then Helena and I could start thinking about what was needed next. I had not found many bad mending jobs to do. The decor would probably be a pleasure to tackle once I had braced myself to start. Living in the kind of hovels I did, I had never had much call to be a dado and fresco man, so this would be something new. Everywhere needed a furious scrubbing, but it struck me that while I was attached to the Fourth Cohort I might be able to wangle help from the firefighters to bring the water in. . . .

On my final trip down to street level, I found I had been donated an old bench and a soaking wet counterpane in my rubbish skip. I turfed them out, then covered the skip, and roped it too. I went to the nearest baths to cleanse myself of dust and sweat, mentally adding sweet oil and a strigil to the list of things I would bring across next time I came to work. After I rinsed the dirt from my hair, I also added a comb to the list.

It was dark when I made my way back up Fountain Court. I felt tired but satisfied, as you do after hard labor. My muscles were stretched, but I had relaxed at the baths. I felt on top of life. Playing the thorough type, I stepped over to look under the cover and check my skip again.

In the gloom I nearly didn't see what was there. If I had still been tipping rubbish in, I would not have noticed a thing. That was somebody's intention. Rome being the city it is, whoever put the young baby in the cart meant him no good. He was cute, and gurgling trustingly, but a baby who gets dumped by his keeper does not easily acquire another—not unless he is grabbed by a woman who is purposely watching the middens in case someone abandons an unwanted newborn. Nobody in Fountain Court felt that desperate. Whoever ditched this little one had left him to die. They would not have expected anybody else to pick him up and take him home.

Since it was me who found him, that was what I did.

wearing it much longer than he should, however. That kind of babywear usually belongs to families where the children are changed regularly, almost certainly by a nurse; this baby had not been cleaned up, perhaps for days. He was soiled and sore. I was handling him gingerly.

"Poor little fellow needs a bath."

"I'll find you a big bowl." Helena snorted. She was definitely not going to help.

"Luckily, you've come to a home where the women are fierce but the men understand it's not your fault," I told him. When I talked, he hardly seemed aware of me. I tickled his chin, and he did condescend to wave his feet and hands about.

He was a very quiet baby. Something about him was too subdued. I frowned, and Helena, who had by then brought me a bowl of warm water, looked at me closely the way she did when she thought I was drawing conclusions. "Do you think he has been mistreated?"

I had lain him on his back on a tunic on the table while I took the clothes off him. He was not afraid of being handled. He was plump, a good weight. There were no bruises or unhappy marks on him.

"Well, he looks unharmed. But there's something odd," I mused. "He's too old, for one thing. Unwanted babies are abandoned at birth. This lost mite must be nearly a year old. Who keeps a child so long, looks after him, grows fond of him—and *then* carefully pushes him under a canvas in a rubbish skip?"

"Someone who knows it's *your* skip!" suggested Helena dryly.

"How could they? I only got it tonight. And if they wanted me to find him, why wait until I'd finished work, covered it up, and could not be expected to look inside again? I only found him by accident. He could have died of exposure or been gnawed by rats or anything."

Helena was examining a loose cord around his neck, a twisted skein of colored material. "What do you think this is? It's very fine thread," she said, unraveling it partially. "One of the strands could be gold."

"He's had an amulet, probably. But where's it gone?"

XXV

"**O**nly you could do this!" Helena groaned.

"Your lucky day!" I told the babe. "Here's a nice lady who only wants to cuddle you. Listen to me. She's a pushover for big brown eyes and a showy grin—"

"This is no good, Marcus."

"Very true. I'm determined to be firm. I'm not allowing other people's unwanted goods in my rubbish skip. I paid for it, and I've got plenty of clutter to shift for myself—"

"Marcus!"

"All right, but once I picked him up and took him out, what was I supposed to do? Lay him down in the gutter and just walk off?"

Helena sighed. "Of course not."

"He'll have to find himself a berth somewhere. This is just a temporary reprieve." It had a callous ring.

I noticed Helena made no attempt to come and take the child. He stared at me, as if he realized this could be the big tricky moment in his life. He was quite a few months old, enough to take notice of his surroundings anyway.

He looked healthy. His hair, which was dark and slightly curled, had been trimmed neatly. He wore a proper little tunic, in white, with embroidery at the neck. He had been

"Too valuable to throw away with the child!" Helena Justina was growing angry now. "Some person felt able to abandon the baby—but made sure they kept his bulla."

"Perhaps they removed it because it might have identified him?"

She shook her head sadly, commenting, "This never happens in stories. The lost child always has a jewel very carefully left with it so years later it can be proved to be the missing heir." She softened slightly. "Maybe his mother cannot keep him, but has preserved his amulet as a memento."

"I hope it breaks her heart! We'll make sure we keep his tunic," I said. "I'll get Lenia to wash it, and I'll ask her if any of the laundry girls have seen it before. If they have, they are bound to remember the embroidery."

"Do you think he's a local baby?"

"Who knows?"

Somebody knew. If I had had more time, I might have traced his parents, but the rubbish skip babe had picked the wrong moment to be dropped on me. Working with Petronius on the Emporium heist was going to take up all my energies. In any case, finding parents who don't want their babies is a dead-end job.

I had done the child a favor, but in the long run he might not thank me for it. He had been found in a district so poor that we who lived there could hardly keep ourselves alive. On the Aventine, three times as many children died in infancy as those who survived, and many of the survivors grew up with no life worth speaking of. There was little hope for him, even if I did find somebody to take him in. Who that could be I had no idea. Helena and I had our own troubles; at this stage we were certainly not available to foster unknown orphans. There were too many children already in my family. Although no member of the Didius clan would be made to suffer this child's fate, finding space for an extra who had no claim on us was inconceivable.

We could sell him as a slave, of course. He wouldn't be overjoyed about that.

The baby seemed to like being washed. The sensation appeared to reassure him, and when Helena allowed her guard to slip and started a gentle splashing game, he seemed to know he was expected to chuckle and play along with her. "He's not a slave's baby," I observed. "He's already been among feckless time-wasters who throw water all over the room!"

Helena let me haul him out, though she did find a towel to dry him on. He must have decided that now he could start in with the serious demands: food, preferably. We had patted him all over, allowing him a few more tickles on the way, and rolled him in a stole while we thought about where we could stow him safely overnight. Then the babe decided to assert himself and began roaring.

Unluckily for Helena, that was the moment when the Palace slave arrived to ask me to an urgent confidential meeting with the Emperor's eldest son.

I managed not to grin as I kissed Helena tenderly, apologized for bunking off—and left her to cope.

XXVI

Rome was full of litters taking the wealthy out to dinner. It was, therefore, also full of harshly squabbling voices, as the slaves carrying the litters vied for road space with the heavy carts delivering necessities that were now permitted to enter the city. Flutes and harps occasionally tweedled above the havoc. Around the temples and courts in the Forum I noticed the good-time girls, the night moths, already hovering. There seemed to be more than usual. Maybe I had prostitutes on the brain.

I was being taken to the Golden House. The slave made inquiries at the marble-clad entrance, while Praetorians gave us nasty looks. I was led in to the west wing, the private apartments where I had never been before. Once past the Guards, there was a quiet atmosphere. It was like entering a friendly home, though one with sumptuous embellishments.

Titus was in a garden. The state bedrooms were all designed to face across the Forum valley, with views that would once have included the Great Lake and which now took in the building site of the Flavian amphitheater. Behind them, decorously lit with outdoor lamps, lay this private, interior court. It was dominated by an immense porphyry vase but also contained pieces of statuary chosen to delight Nero.

The planting was tasteful, the topiary pristine, the seclusion divine.

The Emperor's heir and colleague was sitting with a woman who must have been nearly forty years older than him. Since he was a handsome man in his thirties who was currently unmarried, my imagination leaped wildly. She couldn't be his mother; Vespasian's wife was dead. The Chief Vestal Virgin would be a regular visitor at the Palace, but this elderly biddy wasn't dressed as a vestal. They had been talking together pleasantly. When he saw me being brought through the colonnade, Titus began rising as if he meant to excuse himself for our discussion, but the woman held out a hand to prevent him. He then kissed her cheek before she herself rose and left him. This could mean only one thing.

Her name was Caenis. She was Vespasian's freedwoman mistress. As far as I knew, Caenis did not interfere in politics, although any woman whom Vespasian had cherished for forty years and whom Titus treated respectfully must have the potential for enormous influence. The freedwoman was a scandal waiting to happen, but the cool glance she gave me said that scandal stood no chance.

As she passed me, I stood aside meekly. Her intelligent gaze and upright carriage reminded me of Helena.

"Marcus Didius!" Titus Caesar greeted me like a personal friend. He had noticed me looking at his noble father's not so noble ladyfriend. "I was telling Caenis your story. She was listening very sympathetically."

I was pleased the Emperor's mistress found details of my life entertaining, though I noticed that Titus had not introduced us so the lady could award me a bag of gold, a kindly word, and my heart's desire.

"Are you well?" Titus was asking, as if my health were of major significance to world events. I said I was. "And how is the splendid daughter of the excellent Camillus?"

Titus Caesar had in the past looked at Helena as if he found her as attractive as I did. This was one reason why she and I had been spending time abroad, in case he decided his famous fling with the Queen of Judaea was completely doomed and looked around Rome for a replacement. While

Helena would make a perfect substitute for a beautiful, spirited, and slightly naughty royal, this would leave me bereft and with little hope that Queen Berenice would fancy me as a quid pro quo. So I was resisting a swap. I thanked him for asking, then made damn sure he knew the truth: "Helena Justina is fit, flourishing—and doing me the immeasurable honor of carrying my heir."

If he drew an unexpected breath, he disguised it well. "I congratulate you both!" Titus Caesar had the knack of sounding as if he meant exactly what he said.

"Thank you, sir," I replied, a mite somberly.

There was a small pause. Titus gazed at the dimly visible topiary. I restrained any urge to feel smug. Putting one over on the Emperor's elder son was not clever. Everyone knew Titus had a very pleasant temperament, but he could also have me sent down to Hades by the short route.

"This will be a difficult time for you, Falco. Is there anything I can do to assist?"

"I don't think so, sir. I did once make Helena and her parents a rather rash promise to improve myself socially and marry her—but your brother tells me the equestrian rank is to be kept select, and I am not the right material."

"Domitian said so?" Titus appeared unaware of it. I didn't blame him. Rome was full of eager self-improvers; he could not expect to keep daily track of all of us. However, it might have been sensible to watch the ones that his family had kicked in the teeth.

"Obviously, you will not wish to overrule your brother, sir."

"Oh obviously not," Titus agreed, though I detected exasperation that his brother had chosen to antagonize me. He was publicly loyal to Domitian, but his private opinion might be interesting. "So you have been having a bad time lately? I discover you went to Nabataea, on the state's behalf, and encountered difficulties?"

"There was no difficulty with Nabataea," I told him. "Only with the shark who sent me there."

"Anacrites! I'd like to hear your side of the story sometime," Titus offered in a friendly tone. That left me worrying exactly what side of the story Anacrites had already told.

I said nothing. Titus had known me long enough to realize when I was angry. Sometimes complaints have more effect if you make people sweat. "My father would welcome a report—if you will consider it." I love to see a prince pleading. "We do need a confidential assessment of the situation in the desert."

I smiled. Without a word, I produced a slim scroll from my tunic. Helena, smart girl, had not only forced me to write up my findings, but tonight she had guessed that I might find occasion to hand in my homework. This way, Anacrites took no credit. He would not even know what I had said.

"Thank you," said Titus gently, balancing the scroll between his well-manicured fingers. "You always serve us well, Falco. Both my father and I have a high opinion of your judgment and trustworthiness." In fact, they hated informers, and only used me when desperate. This must be leading somewhere. "Do you want to tell me about the problems you encountered?"

It was an invitation to land Anacrites in mule dung. Needless to say I took the sophisticated option: sheer stupidity. "It's not important, Caesar. I survived."

"I think it is important." Titus was acknowledging that spies receive speedy justice in hostile foreign kingdoms. "You were sent incognito, and somebody accidentally exposed you."

"Deliberately exposed me," I corrected in a mild tone.

"Do you want an inquiry into that?"

"Best not find out." I sneered. "Anacrites is too dangerous to dismiss. Better for him the telling demotion: say, conducting a very long survey of ordering procedures for sanitary materials in the public works domain."

Titus had always privately enjoyed my cynicism. He ran both hands through his neat hair. "Falco, why is it when I talk to you I always end up wondering whether I can stand the pace?" He knew why. He was the Emperor's son, and would be Emperor himself. Few people would ever again offer him a decent argument.

"I'm a sterling debater, Caesar."

"And modest!"

I produced a gracious shrug. "And the only kind of fool who'll risk offending you." He accepted it, and laughed.

"And have you been paid for your work?" Titus then asked narrowly. Whatever Vespasian and he wanted from me next must be spectacularly unpleasant.

"Please don't trouble yourself. When the omens are right for the accounts clerks, I shall draw my standard fee, Caesar."

"There will be an addition," Titus remarked.

"That's most kind." I was convinced something big was coming.

The pleasantries had been cleared away. Titus admitted that there was a reason why I had been summoned at night, without any record-takers present. He said the matter was confidential and sensitive; I could have guessed both. However, I had not guessed what I was being asked to undertake. And when I knew, I hated it.

"What I am going to say to you must remain a complete secret. Nobody—*nobody*, Falco, however close to you—is to be told what we discuss."

I nodded. You commit yourself to this kind of nonsense like a lamb. That's the trouble with secrets. Until you know what they are, how can you tell whether your ethical element approves of them?

"Marcus Rubella," Titus began crisply, "is a recent appointment to the tribunate of the vigiles." Quite so. Vespasian's man. The city cohorts must be reckoned to be fairly loyal, since even while his predecessor and rival, Vitellius, had ruled Rome, Vespasian's brother Sabinus had been Prefect of the City. Sabinus, a popular man trying to keep the peace in impossible times, inspired lasting respect. To reinforce that, officers throughout the civil institution in Rome were now, like those in the legions, being changed as the new Emperor handed out rewards and replacements where applicable.

"I met Rubella," I said conversationally.

"I know that," Titus said. A bad feeling was already creeping over me.

"Seemed an interesting character."

Titus smiled. "That must be some kind of cautious short-hand—Rubella said much the same about you." So, since interviewing me only that morning, Marcus Rubella, the tribune of Petro's cohort, had been talking to Titus. Another evil sensation hit me somewhere in the lower gut.

"This is rather unpleasant," Titus explained inexorably. "Rubella is disturbed about the low level of ethics among his men."

Of course I had seen it coming, but I drew a harsh breath. "Rubella thinks the *Fourth* accept bribery?"

"Does that surprise you, Falco?"

"I know one of them," I confessed.

"I am aware of that."

"I know him well."

"And?"

And I could not stomach the suggestion that Petro might even be under suspicion. "It's impossible." Titus was waiting for me to elaborate. "The man I know, my friend Lucius Petronius, is an impeccable character. You saw him at the meeting yesterday; you must have judged his quality. He is the man who has just expelled from Rome a major criminal. Balbinus Pius would never have been brought to justice without him."

"True. Were it not for that," Titus said, "he would be under a cloud with the rest, and there would be no question of asking you to assist us. We are assuming that Petronius Longus need not feature in Rubella's concern. However, Petronius must not be made aware of our inquiries until he is formally ruled out, and perhaps not even then."

"This stinks," I said. "You want me to spy on the Fourth—"

"Not only them," Titus broke in. "Your special assignment is to involve any relevant regions of the city. What Rubella has reported about his own cohort may apply elsewhere—his may not even be the worst problem. I want you to take a close look at any cohort you come into contact with."

That was better. I had already gathered from Petro a feeling that some of the rest were much less choosy in their habits than his own team. But if I was not allowed to tell him what I was doing, it would be difficult to pry this kind of information from him. If I was underhand and he found out later, he would be outraged. Rightly so.

"Sir, this could damage my most valued friendship."

"I apologize if so. But I believe you are capable of handling it." Oh, thanks! "You were selected as particularly suitable. In fact, we have been awaiting your return from the East."

I managed a grin. "So that was how you found out where I was!" Nice thought: the great ones wanting me for something else—and Anacrites having to own up that he had probably disposed of me. How happy they must all have been when my boots touched Italy again. "The Fourth Cohort trust me, sir. Because of my friendship with their inquiry captain."

"Exactly," Titus insisted. "This is a far better disguise than if Rubella put in a special agent, someone who would inevitably be identified as Rubella's man."

"Very convenient!" I saw his point; that only made it worse. "And is the graft Rubella suspects a general problem, or does it relate somehow to the Emporium heist?"

"Rubella thinks it may be relevant. The robbery occurred so swiftly after the criminal Balbinus left Rome."

"Jupiter! It's a mess if he's right."

"Rubella's a good officer. You will need to take extreme care, Falco."

"Do you trust Marcus Rubella?" I shot at Titus unexpectedly.

"Rubella is a known commodity." He accepted my suspicion indulgently. "We trust him as much as we trust you, Falco."

If that was a joke, it was in bad taste.

"If you will do this—" Titus began to say, but I was so angry with the mission that I cut him short.

"Don't make promises," I snarled, remembering how his brother Domitian had done me down when I asked for a just reward. "I've had them before. I'll do the job. I'll do it well if I can." Better me than some idiot from the spy network. "Whatever you think of informers, rewarding me would be a sign of respect for my reliability, which you say you value.

Maybe one day you will think about that, but in any case, I have to ask you this, Caesar: If as a result of this distasteful assignment I end up in a back alley with a knife in my ribs, I hope at least you will remember my family."

Titus Caesar inclined his head in agreement. He was known as a romantic. He must have understood which member of my family I meant. Maybe, since he really was a romantic, he even had some idea of her distress if she ever lost me.

He was famous for his courtesy, so we had to end with further pleasantries. I slid mine in first: "Please convey my regards to your father, sir."

"Thank you. It must be Helena Justina's birthday soon," Titus offered in return. He liked to remind me that he knew when Helena's birthday was. One year he had even tried to inveigle himself into the family festivities.

"The day after tomorrow," I said firmly, as if it were in my every thought.

"Do congratulate her from me."

I forced my teeth into a show of gratitude.

I had not forgotten her birthday. Nowadays I even knew the date myself. For once I had managed to buy her a rather fine present. I had been trying not to think about that. Added to the various complex tasks that had been laid on me since I returned to Rome, it was one problem too many.

Helena's present had been hidden among the Syrian glass that was stolen from my father in the Emporium heist.

XXVII

The streets were quieter, and dark. There was a chill in the air at night as autumn made its presence felt. I would have welcomed a cloak, though mainly it was what Titus had said that caused my shivering.

I had to cross the Forum, negotiate the Palatine, and climb the Aventine. I walked steadily, keeping away from doorways and glancing down any alleys that I passed. I stuck to streets I knew. Where there was space for more than one person I went straight up the center of the road. When I heard anybody who must realize I was there, I made sure my tread was confident. If the other person did not appear to have noticed me, I kept quiet.

I had a lot to think about. Domestic events alone were enough to take up all my energy: a pregnant girlfriend who still had to decide how she wanted to react; her family; my family. Then there were the hours of work I needed to put in on the new first-floor apartment; my friend Lenia's wedding, in which I was expected to participate as a convivial priest; and now the baby I had discovered in my skip. Just sorting out the foundling might take a week—a week I didn't have to spare for him.

Somehow, too, I had to find a replacement birthday gift

for Helena. I was short of cash (partly because I had spent so much on the now stolen original). There was an obvious solution, but it was one that niggled me: I would have to ask Pa to find me a tasteful antique in his warehouse, one he was prepared to let me buy at cost. For Helena he would probably do it—and for Helena, so would I without quibbling—but the process would be horrible. I felt tense just imagining what I would have to go through in the bargain with Pa.

And now Titus had asked me to break faith with Petronius. I hated this. I was also angry that I was supposed to be on my own with it. The only person who would know anything about my filthy task was the tribune Marcus Rubella, and he was not the type I chose for consoling little chats. But even if I wanted it, seeking him out was impossible. If I tried nipping into the tribune's office to mull over my findings, all sorts of rumors would immediately start.

Luckily, I could talk to Helena. Although Titus had forbidden me to tell anyone about this, one exception could not be overruled. Whatever the jokes about keeping wives in ignorance, a Roman expected his domestic partner to bear his children, keep the store cupboard keys, quarrel with his mother, and, if required, to share his confidence. The fact that Brutus failed to confess to Porcia what he was planning on the Ides of March just shows you why Brutus ended up as dead mutton at Philippi.

Helena and I had always shared thoughts. She told me about feelings nobody would imagine she had. I rarely told her my feelings, because she guessed them anyway. I discussed my work. Openness was our pact. Neither Titus nor Vespasian could interfere with that.

I had plenty of company on the streets that night. A couple of times I noticed groups of dubious characters huddled around the folding doors of lockup shops. Once there were scuffles above me as climbers scaled balconies on their way to upstairs burglaries. A woman called out, offering her services in a voice that reeked of dishonesty; having passed by in silence, I spotted her male accomplice in the next lane, hanging about waiting for her to bring a client for him to beat up and rob. A shadowy figure slipped from the back of a moving delivery cart, carrying a bundle. Slaves escorting a rich man's litter were sporting ripped tunics and black eyes, having been mugged despite their sticks and lanterns. All normal. Rome was itself. No livelier than usual. Eventually I heard the tramp of the vigiles' foot patrol; someone in the shadows laughed at the sound dismissively.

There were still lamps in the laundry. The slurred voices of Lenia and Smaractus were arguing dismally: all normal there, too. I reached in through a shutter to steal a light, then called good night, scaring the pair witless. They were too drunk to do much. Lenia cursed, but I was already heading up the stairs before they could try to lure me indoors to ramble about their wedding plans. I was not in the mood for a long wrangle about what color sheep to sacrifice. I was not in the mood for Smaractus: end of tale.

The lamp helped me avoid obstacles. Smaractus ought to have provided light if he wasn't intending to keep the stairs clear of toys and rubbish. As I mounted the stairs, my useless, sestertius-grubbing, dupondius-pinching landlord became the focus of my entire catalogue of frustrations and anxieties. If he had appeared in person, I would have knocked his head off. . . .

Movement in a corner attracted my eye. I reached for my knife, then decided a rat was about to tear out past me and got ready to boot it. The shuffle subsided; it was probably the mongrel Lenia called Nux. The scrawny bundle of misplaced hopefulness whimpered once, but I carried on upstairs.

When I reached home, I saw that Helena Justina must be in bed. A dim taper provided a glow by which I found the skip baby in a basket that looked as if it came from Ennianus across the road. Helena had tucked the child up safely; somehow she must have fed him too, for he was placid, though whimpering slightly. I picked him up and took him out to the balcony to say goodnight to Rome. He smelled clean now, and slightly milky. He had a little burp on my shoulder; I joined in with a nicely controlled belch, showing him how to do it properly.

After I put him back I noticed a bowl of cold fish and lettuce left on the table for me. I ate, pouring myself a cup of water. I blew out his taper to save the baby from fire, then found my way in darkness to my own bed.

Helena must have been asleep, but she stirred as I crawled in beside her. Somehow she realized how deeply disturbed my talk with Titus had made me. She held me while I told her the story, and calmed me down as I started to rant.

"Why do I always have to get the filthy jobs?"

"You're an informer. Finding unpleasant information is what you do."

"Maybe I'm tired of being despised. I'm tired of being a fool to myself. Maybe I should change my work."

"To do what?" Helena murmured, in a reasonable tone. "Do you see yourself selling purses or plucking ducks?"

"I hate women who reprove me with their sensible attitude when I'm trying to curse madly!"

"I know you do. I love you even when you hate me. Go to sleep," she said, wrapping herself around me so I could no longer jump about in the bed. I sighed, submitting to her good sense. About three breaths later I dropped off into a heavy slumber. In my dreams I knew that Helena Justina was lying awake, worrying for me over what I had to do.

By that time the first victim would already have been tortured and murdered, and his body dumped.

XXVIII

Petro's whistle from the street woke me. Within the apartment it was still dark.

We had been friends so long he could rouse me even from outside and six flights down. I knew it was him. When I dragged myself to the balcony parapet and looked over, he was standing below with one of the foot patrol. I could tell from the top of his head that he was cursing me for taking so long to appear. I whistled back, and he glanced up. He waved urgently. I didn't stop to shout questions, but ran down to him, pulling on clothes as I went.

"Morning, Petro. No problem with your cat, I hope?"

He growled. "Stollicus was right, Falco! You're an irritating, insolent, dozy dog."

"Stollicus just misunderstood my charm. What's up?"

"Body in the Forum Boarium. Sounds like problems."

I let my curiosity ride. In the time it had taken me to come downstairs, Petro and the foot patroller had already strolled impatiently halfway along the lane. The three of us walked briskly to the end of Fountain Court, then hurried downhill, picking up Fusculus from his house. Petro must have banged on his door on the way to collect me, and he was waiting for us, rotund and unreasonably bright for the time of day.

"Morning, Chief. How's the cat?"

"Fusculus, I'm not in the mood."

Neither Fusculus nor the vigilis who was with us grinned. Petro's men knew how to irritate a senior officer without needing to smirk.

At the end of the Clivus Publicus we saw Martinus emerging from his tenement, summoned by another member of the vigiles. "Don't ask about the cat," warned Fusculus. Martinus lifted a wry eyebrow in a significant fashion and said nothing in a way that drove Petro mad. Martinus *was* allowed a grin, since he had had to forgo the joke. Petronius, who had the longest legs among us, lengthened his stride so the rest of us were forced to step out.

It was barely dawn. The pale light, empty streets, and our echoing footfalls increased the air of urgency. We came down past the Temple of Ceres into the damp gray mist along the river.

"Why does this always happen before I've had my breakfast?" Petro grumbled.

"They dump the corpse in the dark, then the dawn patrol discovers it at first light," Martinus explained. Petronius had not needed him to say this. Martinus went in for pedantry. As a result, Petronius went in for thinking that Martinus needed to be washed out with a violent enema.

It crossed my mind that I could do Petro a favor by naming his deputy as a bribe-taker and having him removed. In fact, if my interest in truth had inclined to the inaccurate, I could have wreaked havoc in the watch. I could finger anyone I took against; it would be hard to disprove. Even though none of them knew the position, I felt sour.

"Petro, they do it on purpose, to stop you enjoying your morning. . . . Do we know who this dumped corpse is?" I asked.

Petronius glanced back at the patrolman who had been with him at Fountain Court. "Not yet," Petro said. He seemed to be keeping something back.

"Who found the remains?"

"One of the Sixth's patrols. It's in their patch." That explained Petro's restrained attitude. He kept his counsel in front of men from another cohort. But he did condescend to mutter, "There seems to be a connection with the Emporium."

We had reached the scene of the crime—or at least where the victim had ended up. Our pace slowed, and we left further questions to answer themselves.

The Forum Boarium lies in the Eleventh region, immediately below the Capitol, between the river and the starting gate end of the Circus Maximus. It is part of the Velabrum. Once the marsh where Romulus and Remus were supposedly found by the shepherd, it has a long history. There must have been a landing place and a market here since long before Romulus grew up and identified the Seven Hills as an ideal development site. The rectangular Temple of Portunus marked the ancient use as a harbor of the riverbank between the Aemilian and Sublician bridges. The diminutive round Temple of Hercules Victor was later, a cute initiative in marble that dated from the time when shrines started to become decorative and, according to my grandfather, morals declined.

The meat market had its own decidedly off-putting flavor. Owing to the presence of the body, it had not yet been set up for the day, which made it appear even shabbier. There was a mess of hurdles everywhere. I never liked walking through it, for the putrid smell of drying animal blood always hung about. The disgusting odor filled the air this morning so strongly, I felt sick.

Right in the center of the area a small group of fire-watchers were conversing in a huddle near a body on the ground. Farther away a couple of street-sweepers stood gawping, leaning on flat-headed brooms. Market traders, kept back from their normal business, hung about talking in low voices, some of them warming their hands around little cups of hot spiced wine. The first arrivals of cattle were jammed in a pen on the riverside. They were lowing with distress; maybe they sensed even more trouble than the slaughter that awaited them.

We walked across to the corpse. The vigiles drew back and watched us as we looked down at their find. The two who had come to fetch us joined their colleagues. As they let officers take charge of their discovery they were wary, and disbelieving of our so-called expertise. We inspected the body in silence. It was a bad experience.

We were looking at a man, age indeterminate, probably not young. He lay on his front, with arms and legs neatly outstretched like a starfish—not the attitude of any accidental death. We could see at once that he had been tortured. He was barefoot, wearing what might once have been a white tunic. The tunic was almost completely soaked in blood. Its material also bore signs of what seemed to be scorching. There were marks of a thrashing on his calves. His arms were badly bruised and had been slashed with knives. People with perverted natures had really enjoyed themselves here, and their victim must have died slowly.

We could see nothing above the neck. At some point during his terrible adventure last night, his head had been crammed inside a large bronze pot. The pot was still on the corpse.

XXIX

Martinus made a loop of his neckscarf. He bent over the victim and pulled it up by an arm, then dragged at the corpse until one shoulder twisted and the body turned over. The metal pot scraped piercingly on grit. There was less blood on the front of the tunic, but a great deal of dirt, as if the body had been dragged about face down. The pot stayed in place, wedged on by a cloak shoved inside. If the man had not been dead when they covered his head, he must have been suffocating while they tortured him.

Petronius strode over to the vigiles. "How did you find him?"

"On our last round," said their leader, stressing that it was now time they went off duty. "We came upon him just where he is."

"Had you been around here earlier?"

"When our shift started. He wasn't here then. We hadn't been back during the night. We check the temples for vagrants, but apart from that we don't get much to do in the Boarium. The smell of dead meat puts off courting couples."

"Dear, dear!" Petronius tutted to me. "Lovers are becoming so fastidious. . . ."

The patrolman gave him a sideways look, then continued

somberly: "There's nothing to pinch, and nothing to go up in smoke. So if there's no one about we forget it. We've got plenty of worse trouble spots."

"This is the Eleventh region. What made you come for me?"

"The pot."

"The pot?"

"A list was circulated to all the cohorts yesterday: things to watch for from that robbery. Anything we spotted being disposed of, you were the special contact name." The patrolman grinned slightly. He had very stained teeth. "Nobody mentioned that the funeral urns might be full!"

Petro's face set. He rarely joked about murder. "You're referring to the Emporium losses? Was a pot like this on the list?"

The man Petro was talking to stared at him pityingly. "I seem to remember 'Etruscan bronze vessels: set comprising jugs, ladle, suspension hooks, and *double-handled wine bowl*,' sir!"

"Right!" said Petronius, managing to sound crisp. "Well spotted, lads."

He came back to us. We had been standing in silence, listening in. He checked with Martinus in a low voice. "Was stuff like this on our list?"

Martinus shrugged. "Could be. I only drew up the list. You know how many items were on it. I didn't know I was meant to learn it off by heart." Sensing the chief's disapproval, he had second thoughts. "Maybe. Could well have been."

Petro turned to me. "You're the antiques expert, Falco. Is this Etruscan?"

He really needed Pa to discuss bronzes. I walked to the top of the corpse's head and viewed the item more or less the right way up. It was a large, open-topped bowl, with two handles, as the patrolman said, each fixed with two attachment plates and cast with satyrs' heads in relief. Handsome. Probably robbed from a tomb. My father would adore it; my mother would call it "too good to use."

"It looks extremely ancient. One thing I do know," I conceded. "This is a highly valuable pot. I personally would not stuff even my favorite granny into it."

Petronius looked at me. "Who would abandon something like that, Falco?"

"Someone who knew what it was worth. Upending our friend in the pot was a statement: We killed him because of the robbery—and here's an item to prove the point."

"What point?" asked Fusculus.

Petro supplied it: "We're the big boys now."

Martinus pondered, "So who's the man who wasn't quite big enough? The man in the pot?"

I poked at the handsome crater, attempting to remove it with the toe of my boot. No luck. Like a naughty child egged on by an even naughtier brother, this corpse had ended up completely stuck. I had been jammed in a pot myself once. Remembering could still raise panic. I had had to be worked loose using cold water and olive oil. I could still hear my ma soothing me quietly while she eased my ears out—and feel the great whack she had given me as soon as I was free.

At least with a dead man there was no need to mess about being gentle on the ears.

I squatted on my haunches, grabbed the two handles, and twisted off the vase. I threw it aside, letting it ding heavily across the blood-soaked pavings. My father would have yelled in horror, and no doubt the owner would complain loudly about the dents I had caused. But I felt no twinge of conscience. It had been used in the torture of a human being. Its beauty was soiled. Its price had slumped.

The idea of touching the corpse made us all recoil. Gingerly, I tugged away the cloak from around the dead man's head.

In fact, apart from discoloration, the face was unmarked. We recognized him instantly. If he had been wearing his boots instead of being barefoot, I would probably have known him earlier. It was Nonnius Albius.

XXX

Petronius took charge in his quiet, resigned way.

"Martinus, you're the king of the stolen property list. Take the nice Etruscan wine bowl to its owner to identify. Maybe you should wash off the blood a bit first. I need sensible answers. Don't give him a chance to get hysterical."

"I'll have to go to the station house and look up who owns it." Martinus could be bone idle.

"I don't care how you set about the job," Petro said, restraining himself.

"What if the man wants his bowl back?" asked Fusculus, to calm things.

Petro shrugged. "Suits me. I can't see us needing to use it as evidence. If it could answer questions, I'd put it on a stool and start wheedling, but I reckon the pot's a hostile witness. . . ."

He fell silent, though at first he pretended not to notice that a new group of figures were marching into the square. Fusculus groaned quietly. I recognized Tibullinus, the centurion from the Sixth Cohort whom I had not much taken to. He must have been told about the body. He and his sidekick, Arica, came briskly across, flanked by a small honor guard.

They folded their arms and stood watching us with a cocky air.

Petro forced himself to look up and gave Tibullinus a brief nod. "Your patch, but it's one for us—direct bearing on the post-Balbinus inquiry. The pot comes from the Emporium haul, and the victim was my chief suspect."

"Looks like poor old Nonnius," Tibullinus remarked to Arica. Arica tutted in mock-tragic style. Making a deliberate survey of all his wounds, they sucked their teeth; then they grinned. Tibullinus viciously kicked an arm straight. They had a callousness that the men of the Fourth lacked. While Petro's group had no tolerance for a gangster's enforcer while he was alive, they still showed grim respect for his mangled body.

Then I overheard Martinus say openly to Arica, "Some people are going to be grieving that they've lost their paymaster!" It was a jibe, though I could not tell from his tone whether his feelings were jealous or reproving.

Arica and Tibullinus barely glanced at one another. It was Petro who seemed angry, and who brushed the comment aside. "I assume you're happy for me to take this one on." His colleagues made a theatrical show of standing aside for him. It may have been accidental, but Petronius then virtually turned his back on them. He gave orders in a low voice: "Fusculus, get some help and shift the remains. I don't want the whole city talking about this. If it's meant to cause public comment, I'm going to disappoint them. Whip it out of sight. Nab one of the hurdles and carry him to the station house for the time being. Maybe Scythax could take a look. He might be able to tell us something about what went on—though it's fairly obvious."

Petro seemed too tense for comfort. I noticed the Sixth, having made their presence known like generals on a battlefield, were now melting from the scene. Petro started relaxing as soon as they left.

"Who's Scythax?" I put in.

"A medico attached to our patrols." The vigiles always had doctors on the squad; they looked after the patrolmen, whose work led to frequent injuries, and when there were bad fires or building collapses they tended civilian victims at the scene. "Falco, I think you and I should go to the victim's home. Martinus, if you are going to the station house, send a detachment to meet us at the Nonnius place. I'll have to search it, and probably guard it afterwards. Mind you, Rubella won't be happy to allow us the men. . . ."

Mention of Rubella made me go quiet.

On the way to the Capena Gate, we bought bread rolls and munched as we walked. Luckily, sight of a corpse always stopped Petro wanting to talk. He must have assumed I was reacting the same way.

We strolled the length of the Circus on the north side, then around its end under the Appian and Marcian aqueducts. As we emerged from their shadow, shopkeepers were unlocking their booths and washing the pavements. There were some decent residential streets, but they were interspersed with rougher ones. Interestingly, it was an area of mixed jurisdiction by the vigiles. The First region, which we were just entering, was looked after by the Fifth Cohort, yet we were quite near to the Twelfth region, which as part of the Aventine came under the Fourth. We were also very close to the much seedier quarter where Plato's Academy lurked. That was in the Circus Maximus region, the Eleventh, and like the Forum Boarium it was prowled by the Sixth Cohort.

"Petro, does the fact that three different groups of vigiles are responsible for this triangle have any bearing on the crime that's rife?"

"Probably," he said. I could not tell him that according to Rubella criminality occurred among the vigiles themselves.

"Do you work closely together?"

"Not if we can help it."

"Any reason?" I was hoping there would be one.

"I've enough to do without wasting effort on 'intercohort cooperation!'" Petro sneered.

"Strikes me the cohorts all have different characters?"

"Right. The Fifth are dull, the Sixth are bastards, and, as you know, we in the Fourth are unsung heroes with a mature and efficient approach!"

I just hoped I could show that that was the truth.

I took a deep breath. "Are Tibullinus and Arica on the take?"

"Probably," said Petro shortly. Something in his manner made me reluctant to ask more.

As we neared the street we wanted, a familiar figure hailed me.

"Marcus!"

"Quintus! I heard you were back from Germany. Oh, this is good. Petro, let me introduce you to Camillus Justinus."

Justinus was Helena's younger brother, a slight, boyish lad of twenty-odd. Today he was in civilian dress—a pristine white tunic and rather casually draped toga. The last time I saw him he had been in tribunal uniform, in the army on the Rhine. I myself had been there on a mission for Vespasian, one Justinus had joined in, acquitting himself bravely. I knew he had been recalled and was now expected to work through the stages of upper-class civilian life, probably ending in the Senate when he reached twenty-five. Despite that, I liked him. We embraced like brothers, and I chaffed him about his position.

"That's right. I've been brought back home to be a good boy, and to start planning to cadge votes."

"Don't worry. The Senate's a doddle. All you have to do is learn to say 'Gods, what a stench!' every time you appear in a crowd, while keeping your teeth bared in a friendly smile in case any of the plebs can lip-read."

"Well, it's a few years away yet. . . ." Justinus sighed. "I was hoping to see you. I think I'm in love with an actress."

Petro and I turned to one another and groaned.

"Why do the young always have to make the old mistakes?" I asked. Petro shook his head sadly. Petro and I had been friends with a few stage performers in our day, but now we had responsibilities. (We were too old, too cynical, and too careful with our cash.)

"I think you may know her—" Justinus tried.

"Very probably!" exclaimed Petronius, as if it was nothing to be proud of. Since getting married, he had turned highly self-righteous. I suspected it was a deliberate pose. He hadn't really changed.

"Quintus, don't ask me any favors to do with entertainers! I'm in enough trouble with your family."

Justinus slipped into his infectious grin. "That's true—and heading for more! If I see you I am to invite you and Helena to dinner on her birthday. Tomorrow," he spelled out annoyingly. That reminded me about my lost birthday present problem, and I cursed to myself. "What you don't know," continued Helena's favorite brother, "is that someone else has come home from abroad. Somebody who doesn't take kindly to having his sister living with an informer, and who keeps describing in tortuous detail what he would like to do to you."

"Aelianus?"

"Aelianus." The other brother, whom I had never met but already disliked. His views on me were plain too; he had written them to his sister with great acrimony. The distress he had caused Helena was more than I could think about.

"Looks as if we're heading for a wonderful evening!" I commented.

Quintus Camillus Justinus, an odd soul who happened to believe I was quite good for his sister, gave me a formal salute. "You can, of course, rely on my unstinted support, Marcus Didius!"

"Oh, thanks!" I said.

He would make a good politician: It was a blatant bribe. So now I had to find time to introduce a senator's son to an actress, then watch him ruin his previously immaculate reputation in a scandalous love affair. No doubt afterwards I would be expected to help this young man tour the city trying to win votes.

Petronius and I were admitted to the Nonnius house by the porter as soon as we shouted our arrival. He seemed relieved that we had turned up to take charge. He came out to greet us carrying a temporary screen and watched us examine the front door, which had been battered open last night so efficiently that little of it now remained. "They came in a cart with a ram on it. A pointed tree trunk mounted on a frame. They pulled it back on a sling, then let go—it crashed right through."

Petro and I winced. This was real siege warfare. No house in Rome would be safe from such artillery—and only a daring gang would risk taking that kind of illegal weapon openly through the streets.

The house was silent now. Nonnius had been unmarried and had no known relatives. With him gone, domestic management would come to a full stop.

We walked about unhindered, finding few of the slaves who had been in evidence the last time I visited. Maybe some had run away, either eager to be free or simply terrified. In strict law, when a man was murdered, his slaves were subjected to statutory torture to make them identify his murderer. Any who had denied him assistance would be punished severely. If he was murdered in his own house, his slaves were bound to be the first suspects.

The porter was the most helpful. He freely confessed that strange men had come to the house after dark, had broken down the door suddenly and violently, and rushed past him. He had hidden in his cubicle. Sometime later the men had left. A long time after that he had ventured out. He learned from the others that Nonnius had been dragged away.

None of the other slaves would admit to having seen what was done to their master. At last we found the little Negro who had been his personal attendant; the child was still hiding under a bedroom couch, crazy with fear. He must know the truth, but we got nothing from him but whimpering. Some of the cohort had turned up by then, brought here by Fusculus. Petronius, not unkindly, put the child in the charge of one of them and ordered him to be brought to the station house.

"Put a blanket or something around him!" Petro's lip curled in distaste at the little black boy's fluttery skirt and bare, gilded chest. "Try to convince him we're not going to beat him up."

"Growing soft, Chief?"

"He's palpitating like a run-down leveret. We'll get nothing if he drops dead on us. . . . Now let's do a regular search."

We drew some conclusions from the search. Nonnius had been in bed. Boots were in the bedroom, thrown in different directions, and tunics lay on a stool. The bed stood askew, as if it had been jerked violently; its coverlet had fallen half on the floor. We reckoned he had been surprised and snatched while asleep, or at least only partly awake. Whether he was alive or dead when they took him from the house was debatable, though Petronius decided on him being still alive. There was only a small amount of blood on the bedclothes and the floor—not enough to have been caused by the mass of wounds we had seen on the body.

We should probably only ever find out where they had taken him if somebody confessed. We might never know. What had happened to him in the hour or so that followed his abduction we could all imagine clearly. Most of us preferred not to think about it.

XXXI

As we were leaving the Nonnius mansion, someone else made the mistake of trying to arrive. We were keyed up in investigating mode, and surrounded him. He was a lean fellow in a smart white tunic, carrying a leather satchel.

"May we look in the bag, sir?" The man handed it over to Fusculus with a rather dry expression. It was full of tweezers, spatulas, and stoneware medicine jars. "What's your name?"

"Alexander. I am the householder's doctor."

We relaxed, but our humor was harsh. "Well, he won't need you now!"

"The patient has suffered a fatal dose of being beaten up."

"Terminal knife wounds."

"Irreversible death."

"I see," commented the doctor, no doubt thinking of his lost fees.

Petronius, who had not spoken to him before this, said, "I respect your relationship with your patient, but you will understand my inquiries are very serious. Did Nonnius say anything to you in confidence that might tell us who may have done this?" To judge from his careful phrasing, Petro had had trouble extracting information from doctors.

"I don't believe he did."

"Well, you are free to go then."

"Thank you."

Something about the man's manner was oddly restrained. He seemed hardly surprised to have lost his patient in this appalling way. Perhaps that was because he knew what line of business Nonnius had been in. Or perhaps there was another cause.

"There was something peculiar there," I suggested, as we all walked back to the patrol house.

"He's a doctor," Petro assured me calmly. "They're always peculiar."

If I had not known him better I might have thought something in Petro's own manner seemed oddly restrained too. In view of my special investigation for Titus, I wanted Petronius to behave in ways I understood.

At the station house Petro's young assistant, Porcius, was in deep trouble with a woman. Luckily for him, she was extremely old and not worth creating a fuss about. It was another stolen bedcover case; somebody was going around with a hook on a stick targeting ancient dames who were too bent to chase after a thief. Porcius was trying to write a report for this one; we could see he would be helpless for the rest of the morning unless rescued.

"See the clerk," Petro told her curtly.

"The clerk's a dozy mule!" She must have been here before. "This nice young man is looking after me."

Porcius was a new recruit. He was desperate to arrest as many wrongdoers as possible, but had no idea of how to dodge time-wasters. Petro was unimpressed. "This nice young man has more important things to do."

"See the clerk, please," muttered Porcius, looking embarrassed.

Indoors we found a nasty scene: A large boulder was lying in the center of the floor, along with the broken shutter it had been thrown through last night and the wreckage of a stool. Petro sighed, and said to me, "As you see, sometimes the locals chuck worse things at us than cabbages."

"They poked some brassica stalks through the cell air

hole too," Porcius told him. "People around here do seem to think we're short of greens."

"Well, next time forget charitable deeds for grannies, and try to find out who hates the vigiles!"

"That's easy." Fusculus grinned, rolling the boulder towards the door. "*Everyone* does."

He roared for the foot patrol to stop counting their esparto mats in the fire-fighting equipment store and come to remove the debris from indoors.

Trying to regain Petro's approval, Porcius announced nervously, "One of the centurions had been sitting just where it landed, but luckily he'd just gone for a pee. It would have killed him otherwise."

Petronius, who had merely been frowning with annoyance, checked slightly. "Right. This looks bad. Fusculus, put the word around the whole cohort: Keep alert. We could be in for a dangerous time."

Frowning, he turned into the small room he used for interrogations, only to find two of the foot patrol's most recent prisoners. One of them was shouting and throwing himself about, nearly throttling himself with the giant ring chained around his neck. The other stayed sullenly silent, a middle-class fire offender who was pretending this was all a nightmare from which a smart lawyer would extract him, probably with compensation for insult and slander. (I could tell from Petro's irritated expression the man was probably right.) With them, huddled on a bench, was the minute black slave from the Nonnius house.

Petro fumed at the chaos. "Shut up!" he bawled abruptly at the half-mad drunken man who was shouting: surprised, the fellow obeyed instantly. "Fusculus, start asking questions and see if we can let these prisoners go. Unless they're hard nuts, we need the space. Porcius, get Fusculus to tell you what we know happened to Nonnius Albius, then I want you to take this little lad somewhere quiet and make friends with him. If you can deal with indignant grannies, you can handle terrified tots. Win his confidence, then find out what he saw when his master was attacked. He's not arrested, but if he witnessed anything useful I'll want him put somewhere very safe after he's talked."

Since there was nowhere else private, Petro and I went out for a conference at the chophouse just across the street.

"So what do you think, Falco?"

I chewed a stuffed vine leaf, trying not to think about its consistency and taste. This job promised an endless parade of lukewarm, stand-up food taken squashed against the cracked counters of unhygienic foodshops. Petro did not come from a family that provided lunch baskets. When we were in the legions, he was always the one who never hid spare marching bread in his tunic, though he soon learned to pinch mine. I spat out a rough bit. "It looks as if the Emporium robbery may have been organized by Nonnius—and that somebody else has punished him rather publicly for daring to think big."

We both considered that, eating gloomily.

"Alternatively—" I offered.

Petro groaned. "Knowing you, I might have known the easy answer wasn't enough. Alternatively?"

"Nonnius had nothing to do with the raid. Some swine just thinks it would be convenient if the Emporium do was *blamed* on him, to take the heat off them."

"Bit stupid," argued Petro. "So long as Nonnius was alive he was a suspect. Now when these others do a raid, they've no cover and I'll be sure it's them."

"If you ever find out who they are."

"I love a chirpy optimist."

"Helena thinks we should be looking at Lalage for the Emporium."

Petronius laughed dismissively, then fell silent. Helena Justina's wild ideas had a way of turning themselves over in your head so they soon seemed completely rational. I myself had stopped even thinking they were wild. I had known her to be right too many times.

Petro tried looking at me as if I were daft either to share information with my girlfriend, or to indulge her mad suggestions. Eventually this palled too. "Suppose that was right, Falco. Suppose Lalage did want to take over running the gangs. Why would she kill Nonnius?"

"She hated him. She had scores to settle. He had leaned

on her too heavily when he was collecting for Balbinus. And then he left her with the problem when the Lycian was murdered at Plato's. Besides, if she is ambitious, maybe Nonnius guessed that and tried to apply pressure. He could have blackmailed her and demanded a cut. Since he'd already squealed once in court, he was a formidable threat; he only had to say he would inform on her too. She'd know he could very well mean it."

"True."

We were both uneasy. There was not enough to go on. We could only speculate. And although we were both good at making the facts fit in a situation, there was always the unexpected waiting to confound us. Like me, Petro had probably lost count of the times he had found out that the facts he had been working on for months were only marginal. The final story could be wildly different from any theories he had so carefully pieced together.

"Want any more to eat?"

I shook my head. "No thanks. I had to leave without even saying good morning to Helena. If nothing else turns up, I'll be going home for lunch. Won't you?"

"Suppose so."

My question had been ironic. I knew Petro always ignored lunch. He went home for dinner with his children in the evening, and sometimes he slipped off if there were a definite household job to do, like mending a window. He enjoyed carpentry. Otherwise, Petronius Longus was the type whose domestic life ran smoothest when he stayed out part of the night with the patrols, then lingered at the station house most of the day on follow-up. This applied most of all when Arria Silvia was furious with him for some reason.

I grinned. "Though you might need to feed the cat again."

He refused to rise.

It was still too early for lunch. A wise man doesn't stroll home halfway through the morning as if he has nothing else to do. He allows time for the cheese and olives to be bought and set out on the table, then he comes in looking as if he has made a special effort to fit in being with his family.

We discussed what we could do. Other than plug away

with routine questioning, the answer seemed to be, not much. "I really hate this part," fretted Petro. "Just sitting back, waiting for a tribe of rats to spring something."

"They'll make a mistake in the end."

"And how many have to suffer in the meantime?" He felt responsible.

"We both know it will be as few as you can make it. Listen, Rubella wanted me to check up on the Balbinus background in case anything was relevant to what's going on now." At my mention of Rubella, Petro scoffed, though in a fairly routine manner. He had no particular grouse. He just hated officers.

He would hate Rubella rather more personally if he ever found out that thanks to him I was spying on the cohort for suspected graft.

I tried again. "What about the Balbinus men?"

Petro answered this one quite calmly. "As far as I know, Little Icarus, the Miller, and all the rest of the mob are still out of Rome. Lying low. I have a pet squealer who lets me know their movements. I can nose him out and check, but if they had been seen in the city he would almost certainly have come to sell me the information."

"When I interviewed Nonnius, there was mention of the Balbinus family, which sounded interesting."

Again Petro favored me with a short bark of laughter. "The wife's a mean bitch. Flaccida."

"And there's a daughter?"

"The lovely Milvia! Their only child. She had education and culture lavished on her—a classic case of crooks with too much money trying to better themselves through their offspring."

"Brought up like a vestal. So did she go to the bad?" I asked dryly. I had seen that happen.

"Funnily enough, not apparently. Milvia turned out as innocent as rosebuds—if you believe her version. She claims she never knew what her papa did for a living. She's been married off to an equestrian who had some money of his own—one Florius, son of a minor official. Florius never intended himself to be better than anyone. He goes to the races most of the time. I don't think he's ever been known to do anything else."

"So he's not involved in criminal activities?"

"Other than having more money to bet with than anyone deserves, no."

"There was a large dowry then."

"Probably," said Petro. "Balbinus kept the details obscure. Suffice it to say, Milvia and Florius live in style, apparently having little to do with each other but both content to stick it out in harness. This leads me to suppose there is cash which they want to keep their hands on."

"Fascinating. I might go and see these colorful folk."

"I thought you might."

Petronius would probably have come with me, but just then a messenger from Rubella hurried up. Since Nonnius had been a judicial informer of some importance, his sudden death had caused questions from on high. Rubella wanted Petronius at the cohort headquarters to prepare a report.

Petro growled. "This is how crimes go unsolved! Instead of asking painful questions of villains, I spend my time helping Rubella make up lies. Falco, if you're wandering among the Balbinus set, you ought to have a witness with you. I can't spare anyone just now. Wait until this afternoon, and I'll find someone."

"I don't need a nanny."

"Take a witness!" he growled. "With this bunch it's policy."

"Is that why Fusculus made sure he came with me when I went to see Nonnius?"

"Fusculus is a decent, well-trained agent."

Trained to interfere with me, apparently. Annoyed, I found the thought of cheese and olives reasserting itself. "Well, if I have to wait for a minder, I'll nip off home. Send whoever it is to Fountain Court, will you?"

"You're getting soft!" He snorted.

I wanted to explain that Helena was pregnant, but it seemed too soon after I had so firmly denied it. With yet more guilt depressing me, I left him to pacify his tribune while I sauntered off to see my girl.

XXXII

A small, serious figure greeted me as I turned into Fountain Court.

"Uncle Marcus! May Mercury, god of the crossroads, ever watch over you!"

Only Maia's eldest boy, Marius, ever sounded off so formally. He was a good-looking, extremely solemn little person, eight years old and completely self-possessed.

"*Io*, Marius! I was not expecting you until after afternoon school. Are you particularly fond of me, or just very short of money for pastries?"

"I've organized a rota for you. Cornelius will be on guard duty this afternoon, then Ancus. You should pay me, and I'll do the sharing out." Maia had made all her children excellent foremen. Both I and my rubbish were in safe hands. But his mind appeared to be somewhere else. "We have a crisis," he announced, as if I were a partner in disaster. Marius believed in the sanctity of personal relationships: I was family; I would help.

The best help to offer was the sacred art of spotting trouble and bunking off the other way. "Well, I'm very busy on official business. But I'm always available if you need advice."

"I'm afraid I'm heading for a row," confessed Marius, walking with me towards the apartment. "I expect you would like me to tell you what has transpired."

"Frankly, Marius, one more problem and I'll buckle."

"I rather hoped I could rely on you," he said gloomily. Short of bopping him on the head with a baton and sprinting for cover, I was trapped.

"You're a hard master! Have you ever thought of becoming a bailiff?"

"No, I think I shall be a rhetoric teacher. I have the mind for it."

Had he not borne his father's eyes (in a less bleary vision), I might have wondered whether Marius had been found under the parapet of a bridge. Still, maybe young sobersides would grow up and fall in love with a tinker's byblow, then run off to be a harp player.

I doubted it. Full of calm assurance, Marius saw the pitfalls of eccentricity and had simply turned his back on them. Sad really. The mind he spoke of with such respect deserved a more colorful fate.

We had reached the laundry. "I'm going up, Marius. If you've something to tell me, this is the moment."

"Tertulla's disappeared again."

"Why fret? It happens all the time. Anyway, your grandma's taken her in hand."

"It's true. This time I'll get the blame for it."

"Nobody could possibly blame you for Tertulla, Marius. She's your cousin, not your sister, and she's beyond help. You're not responsible." I wondered if he knew he had been supposed to be named Marcus, after me. When his father was sent to register his birth, Famia had dropped into several wine bars on the way to the Censor's Office; then he had misread the note Maia had sent him out with. This would have been bad enough once, but he had repeated his triumph when he registered his second son as Ancus instead of Aulus. When Maia gave birth to her daughters, she dragged herself to the Censor's with him and made sure things were done right.

"Uncle Marcus, I think I'd better tell you what has happened." The sight of a child confiding his problems was too much. Marius must have been relying on this, the cunning brat.

I sighed. "You ought to be at home having your dinner."

"I'm frightened to go."

He didn't look very frightened, but it was unlike him to say it. "Walk upstairs with me, then."

"Tertulla hasn't run away. She's too scared of Grandma. Grandma put me in charge of seeing her to school. It was really annoying. And then I was supposed to march her to lunch at her mother's house—"

"So she did go to school in the morning?"

"No, of course not!" scoffed Marius impatiently, scuttling after me around the third bend. "She skipped off as soon as we arrived, but she promised to meet us all outside after lessons."

"So what happened?"

"She never showed up. I think something bad has happened. I need you, Uncle Marcus. We'll have to conduct a search."

"Tertulla's a minx, and she's forgotten the time. She'll turn up."

Marius shook his head. He had the same curls as me and Pa, yet somehow managed to make his look neat. I ought to ask him for hairdressing tips sometime. "Look, Uncle, I have an interest in this problem, since I shall be blamed for losing her. If you agree to search, I'll help you."

"I don't agree!" I told him cheerfully. We had reached the apartment; I led him indoors. "But I don't agree with a future rhetoric teacher being made a scapegoat for one of Galla's rascals, either. Now here's Helena—"

"Oh, good!" exclaimed Marius, with no attempt to disguise his relief. "Somebody who will know what we should do!"

Helena came in from the balcony. She was carrying the skip baby. I grinned approvingly, but it was my nephew who risked his neck. Maia must have been talking at home about our own impending family, because as soon as Marius saw the baby he shrieked, "Oh goodness, Helena! Has Uncle Marcus brought you one in advance to practice on?"

She was not pleased.

XXXIII

I did not wait for Petro's promised agent to come with me to see the Balbinus relatives. My domestic cares were so pressing, it seemed necessary to leave home as soon as I had swallowed lunch. I did take a witness, however.

"I miss you, Marcus," Helena had complained.

This was an aspect of living together that had always worried me. Born into a class where the women spent their days surrounded by scores of slaves and visited by flocks of friends, Helena was bound to feel isolated. Senators' daughters were offered no other respectable daytime occupation than taking mint tea together, and though many preferred to forget being respectable and hung around gladiators, Helena was not that type. Living with me in a sixth-floor apartment must be frightening—especially when she often woke up to find I had rushed out without leaving a note of my plans. Some girls in this position might get too friendly with the janitor. Luckily Smaractus had never provided one. But if I wanted to keep her, I would have to produce some other option.

"I miss you too." It sounded glib.

"Oh yes? And that's why you have deigned to come home?"

"That, and I have to wait to be supplied with a witness."
A thought struck me. "You could take notes and listen as
well as some silly coot from the vigiles." She looked surprised. "Wear a plain dress and no necklaces. Bring a stylus, and don't interrupt. I hate a secretary who talks smart."

So Helena came with me. She was not one for staying at
home with the domestic cares, either.

It suited me to start investigating without one of Petro's
minders lurking at my elbow, breathing my air, then reporting everything I did straight back to him. It certainly suited
me to be out with my lass—more like leisure than work.

We sent Marius home to Maia's, telling him to confess
his loss of Tertulla and to promise that if the girl were still
missing this evening, Helena and I would organize a search
from Fountain Court. Marius looked happier about owning
up. He knew nobody would thump him once I was involved; they would rather wait for a chance of thumping
me. We made him take the skip baby to his mother's for the
afternoon. It was leading a busy life. Helena had found a
wet nurse to feed it sometimes, while in between it went to
Ma's house to be weaned on the gluey polenta that had produced my sisters, me, and numerous sturdy grandchildren.

"Your mother agrees with me; there's something odd
about the baby," Helena said.

"You'd seem odd if you found yourself abandoned in a
rubbish skip on the Aventine. Incidentally, I met Justinus
this morning. He's in love with an actress, but I'll try to
cure him of it. We are invited to a birthday dinner with your
parents. I'm to have the extreme pleasure of being introduced to Aelianus."

"Oh no!" cried Helena. "I wanted my birthday to be
fun!"

I always enjoyed discovering that relationships in patrician homes were as terrible as those in my own low family.

"There will be fun," I promised. "Watching your mother
trying to be polite to me while your father hankers to nip off
and hide in his library, your friendly brother nags me to
teach him flirting with floozies, and your nasty brother
flicks sauce in my eye should provide hours of jollity."

"You go," Helena urged despondently. "I think I'll stay at home."

Flaccida, the Balbinus wife, lived in a gorgeous gem of town architecture just south of the Circus Maximus, at the Temple of Ceres end. It was a rare residential block in the Eleventh district—well placed for the crime empire Balbinus had run along the Tiber waterfront. It lay in the lee of the Aventine but on a piece of land that was patrolled, along with the racecourse itself, not by Petro's cohort but by the Sixth.

At least, Flaccida was living there this week. A huge notice advertised that the spread was for sale, confiscated straight after the trial verdict. Flaccida would be moving house soon.

Indoors, everything echoed. The place was virtually empty, and it was not done for stylish effect. Only the fixed assets remained to show the opulent lifestyle master criminals enjoy: ravishing yardages of mosaic floor, endless perspectives in top-quality wall painting, meticulously plastered ceilings, fascinating shell grottoes that housed well-maintained fountains. Even the birdbaths were gilded.

"Nice place!" I remarked, though for me the columns were too massive and the artwork too frenetic.

"It was nicer when it was full."

Flaccida was a short, thin woman, a blonde of sorts, about forty-five. From twenty strides away she would have looked fabulous. At six feet she showed signs of a troubled past. She wore a gown in material so fine its threads were tearing under the weight of its jeweled fastenings. Her face and hair were a triumph of cosmetic attention. But her eyes were restless and suspicious. Her mouth set in a hard, straight line. Her hands seemed too big for her arms. Size mattered here. On both wrists she wore bangles that were trying too hard to tell people how much they cost, and on her fingers two full rows of high-budget rings.

Naturally, Flaccida was giving us the eyeball. I reckoned we would pass; whereas Helena had dressed down for the occasion, I had dressed up. Smartness always helps in gain-ing access to the houses of the wealthy. Anyone with a clean face is acceptable to thugs.

I wore my best white tunic, newly laundered, and even a toga, which I knew how to handle with an air. A recent shave and a faint splash of pomade announced status, a bold lie. A money purse clicked on my belt, and I was flaunting my great-uncle's massive obsidian finger ring. Helena had followed me quietly. She was also in white, a straight gown with sewn sleeves and a plain woollen belt. She usually fixed her hair very simply, and she wore no jewels today apart from one insignificant silver ring that she never took off. Some might imagine her a slave. I tried to view her as a highly trained freedwoman inherited from an aunt. Helena herself seemed quite at ease, without being explained away.

I found a bland smile. "I am working closely with Marcus Rubella, the tribune of the Fourth Cohort of vigiles."

"So you're in the Prefect's Office?" Flaccida's voice had a smoky rasp that came from a misspent life in ill-lit places.

"Not really. I normally represent a more senior outfit. . . ." Leaving it vague was easy. Half the time I didn't know who I was working for myself. "I have some news to break, and I need to ask some questions."

She pinched her mouth, but did gesture me impatiently to a seat. Her movements lacked grace. She dumped herself on a couch, while I took its partner. They were handsome pieces in silver, with winged griffin armrests and sinuous backs, but they looked slightly too small for the room. We had found Flaccida in one more or less furnished salon, though as I settled in I noticed bare curtain rods. Shadowed lines on the wall showed where display shelves had been removed. Dark marks on the ceiling spoke of candelabra, though there were none now.

Helena had perched on the other end of my couch, with a note tablet on her knees. "My assistant may take a few notes," I informed Flaccida, who replied with a gesture of indifference. Interesting that she accepted Helena's presence so readily.

"What's this about?"

"Your husband, partly."

"My husband is abroad."

"Yes; I met him briefly as he was leaving. So how will you manage? I notice the house is up for sale."

"I shall be living with my daughter and son-in-law." Her tone was dry enough to elicit any sympathy we could find for her. She was still too young for that option. She was neither a widow nor divorced. Moving in with the youngsters was not going to work. Something about her manner suggested she would not even try to cooperate.

"Your daughter must be a great comfort," I said. Without meeting her, I felt sorry for the girl.

"Get on with what you came for," Flaccida snapped. "What's the news you mentioned? Has somebody died?" Watching for any reaction, I told her it was Nonnius Albius. "That traitor!" She said it fairly quietly. I happened to catch Helena's eye, and reckoned she thought that Flaccida had already known.

"I suppose you're glad to hear it?"

"Correct." She was still speaking in a flat tone. "He ruined my life."

I decided not to waste my breath mentioning all the people whose lives had been ruined by the crime empire her husband had run. "Nonnius was murdered, Flaccida. Do you know anything about it?"

"Only that I'd give whoever did it a laurel wreath."

"He was tortured first. It was very unpleasant. I could tell you the details."

"Oh I'd like that." She spoke with a disturbing mixture of contempt and enjoyment. I found myself wondering whether Flaccida would herself be capable of ramming a wine bowl on a man's head and having the rest of him mutilated while he choked. She sat very still, scrutinizing me through half-closed eyes. It was easy to imagine her presiding over horror.

Various pale maids were sitting in on the interview. A rapid scan indicated that most were undernourished, several had bruised arms, and one bore the remnants of a black eye. Flaccida's immaculate coiffure had been achieved with a level of violence that would not disgrace a gladiators' training school.

"Were you aware what kind of business your husband ran?"

"What I know is my affair."

I kept trying. "Have you seen any of the men who used to work with him recently? The Miller? Little Icarus? Julius Caesar, and that lot?"

"No. I never mixed with the workforce."

"Is it true they are all out of Rome?"

"So I heard. Driven out by the vigiles."

"So you cannot say if any of them were behind the recent theft from the Emporium?"

"Oh, was there a theft?" cooed Flaccida, this time scarcely concealing her prior knowledge. The raid had certainly not been announced in the *Daily Gazette* as a national triumph, but word had galloped around the bathouse circuit the same day. Flaccida was just giving us the routine false innocence of a regular villain.

"A big one. Someone who wants to be *very* big must have organized it." Flaccida herself, for instance. If she had done it, though, she knew better than to signal the fact. I wondered how she would react to the notion of a female rival. "Do you know Lalage?"

"Lalage?"

"Keeps the brothel called Plato's Academy." Helena, who had not previously heard the popular name for the Bower of Venus, stifled a giggle. "She's a business contact of your husband's."

"Oh yes. I think I've met her." They were probably best friends, but Flaccida would never admit it under official questioning. She would lie, even if there was no reason to do so. Lying was her way of life.

"Do you think Lalage might be trying to take over where your husband was forced to leave off?"

"How should I know? You'd better ask her."

"Oh, I've done that. She knows how to lie as well as you." I changed tack wearily: "Let's start again. Nonnius Albius, your husband's one-time associate, turned him in. It could be suggested that now your husband has left the Empire, you may be acting as his agent of revenge against Nonnius."

This charge, though unproven, could go straight into the

mouth of a prosecutor in a court of law. Flaccida started fighting back seriously. "You have no right to make such suggestions to an unsupported woman." Legally this was true. A woman had to have a male representative to speak for her in public. The answer was well rehearsed too. Not many women I knew would raise that objection. But not many of my associates needed to shelter behind the law.

"Quite right. I apologize."

"Shall I strike the question from the record?" Helena interrupted demurely.

"I shouldn't think it matters, since the lady has not answered it."

Helena smiled gently at my anger. She suggested, in a way that sounded straightforward but was actually skeptical, "Perhaps Flaccida has a guardian acting for her now her husband is away?"

"I have a guardian and a battery of barristers, and if you want to ask questions about the business," barked Flaccida, using the word "business" as if the family were engaged merely in carving cameos or in scallop fishing, "you can go through the proper procedures."

"Make an appointment?" I grinned, but my tone was bitter. "Send a prior written list of queries to some pompous toga who charges me five hundred just to tell me you cannot comment? Expect a writ for slander if I mention this discussion in public? Find myself barred from the Basilica Julia on some frivolous charge? Discover no one in the Forum wants to talk to me? Lose my clothes every time I go to the bath, find my mother's rent has been put up threefold, receive a summons from the army board of deserters, have mule dung shoveled into my doorway?"

"You've done this before." Flaccida smiled. She was quite blatant.

"Oh, I know how intimidation by the powerful works."

"Lucky for you, you didn't tell me what your name is!"

"The name's Falco." I could have used an alias. I refused to be dragged down to the level of fear these operators used. If they wanted to humiliate me, they would have to find me first. My normal clients were sadder and seedier; I was not well known among major criminals.

"And who's your friend?" This Flaccida was nasty work. It was a threat against Helena—and not a subtle one.

"No one you should tangle with," I answered coolly.

"Unusual to see an official with a female scribe!"

"She's an unusual scribe."

"I assume you sleep with her?"

"So long as it doesn't affect her handwriting . . ." I rose. "I'm not intending to bother you further. I don't like wasting effort."

"I don't like you," Flaccida told me frankly. "Don't harass me again!"

I said to Helena, "Make a note that the wife of Balbinus Pius refused to answer routine questions, then described polite inquiry by a civil investigator as 'harassment.' "

"Get out!" The more or less blonde sneered.

In some circles the women are more fearsome than the men.

XXXIV

"Oh, you really made a mess of that!" Helena Justina was furious with me. "Is that how you normally conduct interviews?"

"Well, yes. With slight variations."

"For instance, sometimes people throw you out right at the start?"

"Sometimes they never even let me in," I admitted. "But it can be easier than that was."

"Oh? Sometimes the women are all over you?"

"Naturally a handsome lad like me gets used to asking questions while fending off attention."

"Don't fool yourself. She slaughtered you!" growled Helena.

"Oh I wouldn't say that. But what a hard-faced hag! At least she gave us the full flavor of life among the big-time crooks: lies, threats, and legal bullying."

We were standing in the street outside Flaccida's house, having a warm set-to. I didn't mind. Arguing with Helena always cheered me up. So long as she thought I was worth fighting, life still held some hope.

"You learned nothing from her, but you told her all the lines of inquiry you're pursuing—plus the fact you can't

prove *any* of them! This is no good at all," Helena continued
crossly. "We'll have to go and see the daughter. We'll have
to go fast, before the mother sends to warn her, and when we
get there, leave the talking to me this time!"

Investigating with Helena as my partner was wonderful
fun. I gave way gracefully, and we marched off to see the
girl.

Milvia and her gambling husband, Florius, lived pretty
close to her parents' house. Perhaps that was how Balbinus
had come to notice the young equestrian on whom he had
foisted his daughter. At any event, this house was even
larger and more elaborate than the one where Flaccida had
seen us off. That probably meant we should expect an even
more rapid dispatch here.

The husband was out. The girl saw us. She was about
twenty, dark, sharp-faced, very pretty. Nothing at all like either of her parents. She was dressed in an extremely expensive gown of deep purple silk weave, with panels of
silver-thread embroidery. None too practical for eating pears
in a sloppy honey sauce, which was what she was doing.
Somehow I doubted whether young Milvia had ever worried
about a laundry bill. Her jeweler was more tasteful than her
mother's; she was decked out in a complete set of antique
Greek gold, including a neat little stephane on her crisply
curled hair.

She saw us without any chaperone, so I could not check
whether the maids who wielded the curling tongs in this
mansion had to endure being thrashed if they misplaced a
ringlet. Milvia had a bright, intelligent expression that suggested she could manage staff by guile. Or bribe them, anyway.

Taking charge firmly, Helena proffered a smile that would
polish sideboards. "I do apologize for bothering you—you
must have lots to do. This is Didius Falco, who is conducting inquiries on behalf of an important committee. He'll be
sitting here quietly while we have our chat, but you don't
need to worry about him. It was thought that you might prefer to be interviewed by a woman, so that's why I'm here."

"Anything I can do to help!" promised the bright-eyed,

innocent daughter of gangsters, as if she was agreeing to assist in raising a subscription for a new shrine to Juno Matrona.

"Well, perhaps I can just make sure that I'm clear on one or two details. . . . You're Balbina Milvia, daughter of Balbinus Pius and Cornella Flaccida, now married to Gaius Florius Oppicus?"

"Ooh, that's me!" Apparently it was a great delight for little wide-eyes to find herself so well documented.

"Of course," said Helena kindly, "your recent family difficulties are known. It must have been a shock to discover the serious charges against your father?"

The pretty face clouded; the sweet mouth pouted slightly. "I don't believe it," Milvia protested. "It's all lies made up by wicked enemies."

Helena spoke in a low, stern voice. "I wonder how you think your father made such enemies, though?" The girl shuddered. "We cannot help our relations," Helena sympathized. "And sometimes it's hardest for those who are closest to see the truth. I know this from personal experience." Helena had had an uncle who dabbled in treason, not to mention the husband she divorced, who had been a maniacal social menace. "I understand that your father did ensure *you* had a perfect upbringing. I'm sure your husband thinks so too."

"Florius and I are very close."

"That's wonderful." As this conversation proceeded I was more and more glad it was not me being obliged to maintain a sickly expression in the face of so much mush. I reckoned the girl was a complete sham. So long as she kept up the act consistently, it would be difficult to prove, however. "My dear, you're clearly a credit to Rome, and I'm sure"—Helena smiled serenely—"I can rely on you to help our inquiries. . . ."

"Oh, I'd love to be of use," lilted the creditable citizen, stroking the lovely skirts that had been acquired for her with the proceeds of theft and extortion. "Unfortunately, I know nothing at all about anything."

"You may know more than you think!" Helena informed

her decisively. "Let me just ask a few questions, and we'll see."

"Oh, whatever you want."

I personally wanted to upend the innocent protester over a knobbly log and thrash a conscience into her. Helena restrained herself. "Let's think about your father's associates, Milvia. I'm sure you won't know this, but Nonnius Albius, who used to be your father's chief assistant, has just been found dead in rather ugly circumstances."

"Oh, goodness!"

"Have you seen Nonnius, or heard anything about him, since your father's trial?"

"Oh no!" burbled the dainty one.

"But you did know him?"

"He was a kind of uncle to me when I was small. I still can't believe the terrible things he's supposed to have done. And I can't believe he meant to go into court and make up those stories about Papa. His illness must have affected him. As soon as he did it, I knew neither Mama nor I could ever meet him again. Mama hates him."

"Yes, she told us that." Somehow Helena made it sound as if she thought Flaccida and Nonnius must have been having a torrid affair. Whether little Milvia was receptive to this much irony seemed doubtful, but I was enjoying myself. "Now," Helena continued strictly, "I want to ask you about some of the other members of your father's business. What can you tell me about people called Little Icarus and—who else is there, Falco?"

"The Miller, Julius Caesar—no relation, I'm told—and a couple of thugs called Verdigris and the Fly."

"Ooh, I don't know any of them!" I knew from Petro that Balbinus used to run his empire from home; the thugs I mentioned must have been in and out of his house all the time. Milvia was either lying, or very dim indeed. "They sound horrible—"

"They are," I said tersely.

Milvia turned to Helena, looking flustered and seeking protection. "Tell him I don't have anything to do with such people."

"She doesn't have anything to do with such people," Helena told me dryly. Milvia had the grace to look worried that her interrogator was so unmoved. Helena Justina possessed natural politeness (when she chose to employ it). Underneath she was shrewd and tough. Normally it was me she liked to screw to the floor with the toughness; watching her tackle someone else made a pleasant change. I had to admit she was doing it well—even though the answers were disappointing. "Tell me now," Helena continued relentlessly, "have you ever met a rather exotic businesswoman called Lalage?"

"I don't think so. What business is she in?"

"She keeps a brothel." Helena's voice was calm.

"Oh no!" shrieked the shocked moppet. "I've never met anyone like that!"

"Neither have I," said Helena reprovingly. "But one ought to be aware that such places and people exist."

"Especially," I interjected, "when such places have funded one's education and stocked one's dowry chest! If she denies knowledge of rents from brothels, ask Balbina Milvia where she thinks her family's money came from."

Helena gave Milvia a questioning look, and the girl muttered, "From some kind of trade, I suppose."

"Very good. From selling stolen property, and percentages on prostitution."

"Excuse me, Falco." It was Helena's interview; I subsided quietly. "Is trading your husband's background!?" Helena queried thoughtfully.

"I believe his father was a tax-farmer."

I nearly burst out laughing. For the first time ever, I felt tax-farming was a clean occupation.

"And what does Florius do?" asked Helena.

"Oh, Florius doesn't need to work."

"That must be nice for him. How does he spend his time, Milvia?"

"Oh, this and that. Whatever men do. I don't need to set spies on him!"

"Why? Don't you care?" I challenged her. "He might be with women."

She blushed prettily. "I know he's not. He's socializing with his men friends."

"Any chance the men friends he's so pally with might be criminals?"

"No." Again Milvia threw an anguished appeal at Helena, as if she hoped for protection from my unjust accusation. "Florius goes to the baths, and the races, and he talks with people in the Forum, and looks at art in the porticoes—"

"Nice!" I said. It did not preclude a career in crime as well. All those activities were routine features of Roman life—and all could provide ideal cover for organizing a major network in the underworld.

"So Florius is a man of the world," mused Helena. "A man of affairs." Florius kept his hands clean while he spent what his own forebears had earned and what his wife with the nasty relations had brought him in return for sharing his respectability. He sounded a typical middle-class parasite.

"Who is your father's heir?" I asked abruptly.

"Oh goodness, I have no idea!" Thanks, Milvia. Well up to standard.

At this point a slave entered, bearing a salver on which were presented the young lady's midafternoon tipple and the dainty bronze cup she was to drink it from. Milvia handed over her empty fruit bowl (a heavy gilt item with finely chased bacchanal scenes). The maid poured her a dash of rich-looking red wine, headily infused with spices that clogged the strainer that filtered them. Cold water was added from a glass jug. We were invited to join her, but we both refused. Helena drank only with me; I never drank with other women when Helena was present. I also hated to have my wine thinned down so much.

"What a wonderful water jug!" cried Helena, who rarely commented on chattels when we visited strangers' homes.

"Do you like it?" Milvia grabbed it from the tray, poured the contents into a vase of flowers, and handed it to Helena. "Do accept it as a present!"

The offer was so spontaneous, I found it hard to think she was bribing us. The maid looked unsurprised. Balbina Milvia must be one of those girls who showered overexpensive gifts on everyone she came into contact with. The only child of people who moved in a restricted and secretive circle, a circle from which she herself had been shielded, she probably found it hard to make acquaintances. Her husband had little to do with her. Their social life was no doubt limited. If we could have believed she was genuinely ignorant of her father's world, we might have felt quite sorry for the girl.

Even I managed a smile as Helena turned to show me the beautiful jug. "You're very generous. This is a fine piece. Did you buy it in Rome?"

"A family friend gave it to my husband."

"Somebody with excellent taste. Who was that?" I kept my voice light as I took the article from Helena.

"Oh, just a well-wisher. I don't know his name."

"Won't your husband mind you giving it away?"

"He didn't seem to like it much. We haven't had it long," replied Milvia.

About two days, I reckoned. I decided not to press the point until I had consulted Petronius, but sooner or later guileless little Milvia would have to supply the well-wisher's name. When Petro saw what she had handed over so gaily, he would probably want to search her house for more—and it would not be because he admired her choice of wineware.

What I was carefully holding was a delicate glass water jug in a translucent white, around which trailed fine spirals of dark blue; it had a twisted, twin-thread applied handle and a neat, pinched spout.

"Very fine," Helena repeated. "I should say that it was Syrian, wouldn't you, Marcus Didius?"

"Undoubtedly." I could say more. Unless it was a double, this was one of the pieces Helena had bought at Tyre for my father, one taken in the Emporium raid.

I would not normally have permitted a stranger to make a present to Helena Justina. On this occasion there was no argument. We took the jug away with us.

XXXV

"Well, that's how to do it." Helena preened herself as we walked back over the Aventine towards Fountain Court.

"I'm deeply impressed! If I had only approached the mother with your conciliatory line, who knows what luxuries we might have acquired for the home!" I made the idea of a present from Flaccida sound disgusting.

Helena ducked under a row of buckets hanging in a shop portico. "I admit our discovery was an accident. I'm not unreasonable."

"You're a gem."

"Well, I prized out more information than you did."

"You got no information, Helena! The mother refused to help us; the daughter batted her fine lashes, promised to give us anything we asked for, but then denied any knowledge to give. Different tactic; same useless results."

"She seems genuine, Marcus. She cannot have known the water jug was stolen."

"She cannot have known it was stolen from *us*!" I corrected her. I sounded like some old pedantic Roman paterfamilias. Helena skipped down a curbstone and laughed at me.

I couldn't skip. I was carrying the stolen jug.

While Helena repaired to Maia's to collect our abandoned baby and check whether Tertulla had turned up again, I took the glassware to the station house and exhibited the gorgeous thing. Petro weighed it in his great paw, while I sweated pints in case he dropped it. "What's this?"

"A present from Milvia. Last time I saw this, it belonged to Pa."

"You've questioned Milvia? That's quick. I only just sent Porcius over to your house."

"I work fast," I said smoothly, not telling him I took my own witness. "The girl claims she and Florius had it as a 'gift from a well-wisher.' "

"Believe her?"

"I stopped believing girls when I was about fourteen."

My old friend was not a man who rushed in without preparation. He thought this through carefully. "The glass jug was one Geminus had stolen. Now it's been found with Milvia and Florius, but we don't know how it came there—"

"It's always possible sweet little Milvia acquired it legitimately," I pointed out. "An innocent purchase, or genuine gift."

"Don't annoy me, Falco! But it might be all she has."

"I hope not. There was a matching beaker set," I remembered bitterly.

Petro carried on doggedly, now instructing his men: "I don't want to force the issue and bungle it, but I do want to see what else they've got. What we'll do is conduct house searches of all the major criminals, then we'll add in Flaccida and Milvia. We'll go in as if it was a routine result of the Emporium raid. We'll probably net a few interesting trophies anyway, so it won't be wasted. Falco won't be there. We won't mention Milvia's water jug at this stage."

"That sounds sensible. There's been time for the raiders to share out the loot, but I'd assumed most of it would go for sale."

"Falco's right," Petro conceded. "We'll raid a few hot-property shops at the same time." Turning to Martinus, he added, "Try to find out what new receivers have opened up recently, so we don't miss any."

"Keep your eyes peeled for one item that is not on your theft list," I said gloomily. "It's gold, and it cost a fortune, believe me!" I described Helena's birthday present carefully, while they all listened with expressions of rapt attention— all of them mocking my extravagance. "It was among Pa's load of glass, but he won't have mentioned it to Martinus because he didn't know I had hidden it."

"Bribe for a mistress?" inquired Fusculus, looking innocent.

"Birthday gift for Helena. I've got a day to find it—or pay up twice."

"Why not explain to Helena and hope to find the original soon?" Petro suggested. "That girl is strangely understanding where you're concerned."

"Helena is not the problem. I have to come up with something, and it has to be spectacular so her damned family don't sneer. Her mother, for one, will be expecting me to let Helena down."

"Oh, it's the *mother* he's trying to impress!" Petro murmured wickedly to Fusculus.

Fusculus sagged his jaw into a sorrowful grimace. "Explain to the man, Chief—the mother *never* comes around!"

Since I was not needed for the searches, I left Petro and Fusculus shaking their heads over my predicament while I set off on errands of my own. The jug stayed at the station house, which was just as well, or it might have ended up in pieces before the day ended.

I called at my father's house, knowing he would be at the Saepta Julia. That suited me. I left messages with his domestic staff saying we had recovered one of his Syrian treasures, and explaining about my need for a gift for Helena. Now Pa would know it was her birthday; he would try to inflict himself on us to celebrate, but as we were promised at her parents' house we could escape that. Leaving, I popped in at Mother's. She was out too, but I made sure a nosy neighbor saw me so word would reach Ma. Brilliant. I had made duty calls on both my parents, without the trouble of seeing either.

Back to Fountain Court. I waved at Cassius, noticing that somebody had suddenly taken over the ground-floor shop lease opposite his bakery, the one Helena and I had looked at briefly before we spotted our preferred new abode. Some sort of mixed hardware was now being offered for sale from the lockup, though I didn't take note of what. My own new let, which I ran up to and inspected by daylight, was looking as if we could make something respectable of it. At street level, the skip had lost several items to desperate scavengers, but I had gained a little more; I was winning on that. I now felt like a juggler who was keeping the balls in the air. Overconfident, I made the mistake of letting Lenia see me as I crossed to walk upstairs.

"Falco! We need to discuss arrangements!"

"Like, how can you be persuaded to jilt the bridegroom?"

"You never give up."

"I don't want to find myself in two months' time being harassed to suggest grounds for divorce so you can claw your dowry back. Getting evidence on Smaractus will be more sordid than anything I've ever had to do."

"He's just a colorful character." Lenia sulked.

"He's a disaster."

"He just needs to settle down."

"In a dung heap," I said.

After that I was allowed to leave without discussing the auguries at all.

I took the stairs at a cheerful pace, pausing only to instruct the stray dog called Nux not to follow me up. She was a tufty mongrel in several colors, with limpidly soulful eyes. Something about her big furry paws and her whiskery face had a dangerous appeal. I sped off fast to discourage her.

By now it was well into the afternoon, so everywhere was fairly quiet in the lull after siesta and before the men's baths grew busy. The apartments I passed sounded more peaceful than they were sometimes; fewer screaming children, fewer distressed adults. The smells seemed less obnoxious. I could almost convince myself that though the building was shabby and overcrowded, its landlord did deserve a chance at normal life. . . . This was no good. Being dragged in to act at the nuptials was shaking my cynical view. I knew what it was: Playing the priest for Lenia and Smaractus was making me feel responsible for their future well-being.

Cursing, I leaped up the stairs on the fourth and fifth flights several at a time. I wanted to leave the laundry and its crazy proprietress behind as fast as possible. At the top I slowed. An automatic instinct for caution led me to silence my steps.

Somebody else was making a noise, though. As I reached the final landing I heard a man shouting anxiously. Then Helena screamed, "No! Oh no!"

I crossed the landing in two strides. The door stood open. I shot through it, out of breath from the stairs, yet ready for anything.

The voice I had heard belonged to Porcius, Petro's young recruit. He was holding up one hand, trying to calm the situation. It was well beyond him. Two ugly brutes whose violent intentions were unmistakable had invaded the apartment, probably not long before I arrived. One leering thug, a huge collection of sinew, was laughing at Porcius as the lad tried to reason with him. The other man was menacing Helena; he was holding our rubbish-skip baby by his tiny wrists and swinging him backwards and forwards like a pegged napkin on a windy washing line.

"I'm not Falco, and that's not their child!" Porcius attempted valiantly.

From the doorway I roared, "*I'm Falco!*"

The giant spun to face me, a terrifying prospect. I had pulled out my knife, but I had to drop it. The small man hurled something at me. I dropped my knife because I had to catch his missile—and I had to catch it right: the bastard had thrown the babe at me.

XXXVI

I caught him and turned him upright. The baby was screaming, but I didn't think he had broken any bones or been
crushed. Still, he wanted everyone to know he was outraged.
Without letting my eyes give away my intentions, I tried
frantically to think of somewhere I could put him down. The
only place was the table; I could not get to it.

Fighting for time, I tried to calm the atmosphere. "Good
afternoon!" I saluted the unknown visitors. "Are you melon-
sellers, or just passing financiers trying to interest us in a fa-
vorably priced loan?" The two bullies stared. A jest was my
only weapon now; they looked unimpressed. Meanwhile,
the skip baby grabbed me around the throat in a strangle-
hold, but he did stop crying. "I'm afraid you must leave," I
continued hoarsely. "My doctor has advised me against acid
fruit, and we're a household that avoids debt on religious
grounds."

"You're Falco!" It was the small man who owned the
voice. The brain it went with must be a slow one. His voice
was harsh, his tone arrogant. His friend didn't need to talk.
The large fellow only had to stand there pulling and clicking
his finger joints in order to contribute to this conversation
quite successfully.

I managed to loosen the babe's grip and snatched some air. "What do you want?"

"A word." I could tell what they really wanted was to kick me in the ribs. The smaller man spat deliberately into a dish of newly peeled boiled eggs. These were very unpleasant people. Helena seethed, and he grinned at her.

He was exceptionally small. Not a dwarf; perfectly proportioned, but a good foot less than average. A statue would not have revealed his problem, but not even his mother would want to commission a statue of this villain. They could afford it, though, judging by the torque-style bracelets on his upper arms. And he wore signet rings so solid they were more like growths than jewelry.

"Who sent you?"

"You don't need to know."

"I'll find out." I glanced at Helena. "Something tells me, love, that somewhere today we upset someone!"

"You're upsetting us!" the first man commented.

"And you're going to back off!" growled the wide man. His voice rumbled deeply, rich with the remembered pleasure of torturing people who ignored what he said. Shaved hair and unclean skin were his badges of toughness. Massive shoulders were bursting through the strained skeins of a worn-out tunic. He liked to show his teeth in a neat white rectangle when he talked. He nearly filled the room.

"Back off what?" I answered pleasantly. "Exactly which group of uncompromising social misfits have you been sent to represent?"

I saw Helena close her eyes in despair, thinking this the wrong attitude. Apologizing meekly would have done no better, and I knew it. The men had come to terrorize us; they would not leave until they saw us cowering. They would enjoy inflicting pain. With a pregnant woman, an innocent rookie, and a baby to answer for, my main interest was making sure it was me they chose to damage.

There were two of them and three of us, but we were outranked in power. There seemed no way I could get us out of this, yet I had to try. I would have liked to tackle the small man first, but there was no space to move; my scope for action was limited.

I said, "I think you should leave." Then I passed the baby to Porcius and squared up as the wide man came for me.

It was like being tackled by an altar stone on legs. Like a marble slab full in the guts, he caught me in a wrestling hug. His grip was unbearable, and he was not even trying yet.

The baby screamed again. The small man spun around to Helena. He grabbed her. Porcius slipped the child out onto the balcony; then he jumped on Helena's attacker from behind and tried to pull him off. Porcius was yelling, which might have brought help, had any one of my fellow tenants been the type to notice murder happening. They were deaf. We had to sort this out ourselves.

The others' skirmishing did slightly distract my man. I forced my elbows outwards just enough to get my hands down low. I used the squeeze. I used both hands. The wide man's face creased into an angry grimace, but my attempt to pestle his privates had no other visible effect. I was for it. He lifted me off my feet merely by expanding his chest. He would have raised me overhead, but the room was too small. Turning slowly, he prepared to crash me against a wall instead. I glimpsed Porcius staggering backwards; he had yanked the small man away from Helena. They fell against us; the wide man changed his mind about making wall decoration out of me; Porcius and his captive bounced off again.

The wide man kept his hold, but swung me back the other way. Now I was to be a weapon; he was intending to attack Porcius using me as a battering ram.

Suddenly Helena grasped a hot pan of broth from the cooking bench. She upended the vessel over the small man so that the scalding liquid flowed down his face and neck.

Porcius saw her coming; he let go and sprang back just in time. The small man became a shrieking mess. The wide one shifted his grip on me. He seemed genuinely troubled by his friend's cries of agony. I was fighting back now. I was doing everything right. It was hopeless—like trying to mold set concrete with bare hands.

Porcius rushed back, punched the small man a few times, then he and Helena started battering the fellow to chase him out of doors, Helena now trying to brain him with the pan's red-hot iron base. He was still yelling, and trying to get away. Somehow he found my fallen knife. Next minute he was crouching and making vicious feints with the blade. Helena and Porcius pressed back against the balcony door. Even scalded and trying to pluck boiling hot lentils from his tunic neck, he was dangerous.

I was in deep trouble. Every move I made brought me closer to asphyxiation. I pushed the heel of one hand beneath the wide man's chin, forcing his head back as far as possible. He pulled a face like a demonic mask, but continued to crush me. My other arm seemed useless; he had badly mauled it. I started losing consciousness.

Then I was aware of other people rushing up the stairs outside. Helena was crying out for help. I heard tramping feet. Suddenly something flew through the air to fasten itself on the great arm that was crushing my head. The wide man yelled and tried to shake himself free; I slid to the floor. My savior was Nux; her jaws clamped on my attacker, though she still growled loudly.

The room filled up with shrieking women. The small man dropped the knife; I grabbed it. I lurched to my feet. Without waiting, I plunged my knife into the side of the wide man's neck. It was a poor blow. There was no time to aim, and he was too large to stop with one stab wound anyway. But it hurt. The blood gushed—always worrying.

"You're dead!" I snarled (though I doubted it). He brushed at the cut like a man swatting wine flies—one-handed, because the dog Nux was still hanging on to his other arm with rigidly clenched jaws. The more he hurled her about, the more fiercely the creature clung on.

A boy slipped through the crush—my nephew Marius. He leaped for the balcony and let out a piercing whistle. "Up here, officers—and be quick!" He was apparently calling down to a troop of vigiles.

It was all too much. A landing full of extra witnesses—my mother, sister Maia, and Marius—was unwelcome even to our visitors. There was no space for beating anyone up properly. And now Marius had summoned further help. The two of them decided that if the vigiles were coming up they had better rush down. With a mighty effort, the wide one forced the dog's jaws apart and flung her to the floor.

"Be wise, idiot!" he shouted at me. Then both men took a run for the door (chased by the little dog, barking ferociously). They barged past Ma and Maia, and thundered downstairs.

Porcius grabbed the dog by its neck fur and dragged her in as he slammed the door. Nux flung herself against it, still trying to chase the villains. Now tearful, Marius threw himself on me. "There, there! They've gone now, Marius."

"When they reach ground level they'll realize I was whistling at thin air."

When they reached ground level, they would be exhausted. One was covered in blood, even if his wounds were far from fatal. The other was quite seriously scalded. "Trust me; they've gone. You were a brave boy."

"They'll be back," commented Ma.

"Not tonight."

We took precautions; then we men started clearing up while the women exclaimed over the incident. I thanked the recruit for his help. "You're a bright lad, Porcius! Where did Petro discover you?"

"I was a cold-meat-seller's son."

"Wanted to clean up society?"

"Wanted to get away from pickled brains!"

Helena had brought in the baby from his refuge on the balcony. She passed him to me; I jiggled him comfortingly, using one arm, though I soon handed him to Ma, for reasons of my own. As his screaming subsided, I watched Helena anxiously. Her face was white, but she seemed calm as she swept her hair up tidily and refixed two side combs just above her ears. We two would talk after the rest had left.

As I felt my body surreptitiously, checking for permanent damage, I notice Ma staring at Helena. There was nothing to suggest Helena was feeling bilious, but Ma's face tightened. Sometimes she piped up at once when she recognized a secret; sometimes it pleased her more to keep quiet. I winked at Helena. Ma said nothing. She didn't know we knew she knew.

Helena looked around the disordered room. Catching her

eye, the little dog leaped straight into her arms, licking her frantically. As a jumper it could have won a crown at the Olympic Games.

"I am not adopting a dog." I tried instructing them both sternly.

Helena still clutched the mad bundle of fur. The dog was full of life. Well, she was now that she saw a chance of worming her way into a cozy home. "Of course not," Ma said, finding a space to sit down and recover. "But the dog seems to have adopted you!"

"Maybe you could train her to guard your clothes at the baths," suggested Porcius. "We get a lot of theft. It can be very embarrassing to come out naked and find your tunic's gone."

"Nobody pinches old rags like the tunics I wear!"

Ma and Maia were fussing over Marius. Glad to have someone even younger to look down on, Porcius chucked his chin. "You're a quick thinker, Marius! If your uncle's still in this business when you grow up, you could make him a fine assistant."

"I'm going to teach rhetoric," insisted Marius. "I'm grooming my brother to work with our uncle."

"Ancus?" I laughed at the way I was being set up. "Will he be any good?"

"He's useless," Marius said.

Life's a basket of eggs; I invariably pick out the one that's cracked.

Ma and Maia had arrived at a lucky moment, but now that I had time to think about it I knew there must be a reason, one I didn't like. "Thanks for interrupting the festivities, but what brought you? Don't tell me Tertulla's still lost?" They nodded, looking grim. Maia reminded me I had promised to organize a search party, and gave me the fabulous news that most of my brothers-in-law—a crass gang of idlers and idiots—would be turning up shortly to assist. I groaned. "Look, she's always running off. I've got enough on at the moment. Does a naughty child call for all this fuss?"

"She's seven years old," Maia rebuked me. In silence we all thought about the brutal assaults that could be inflicted on a child.

"Something's happened." Mother pursed her lips. "If you can't help us, perhaps you can suggest what the rest of us can do?"

"I'll help!" I snarled.

"Oh you're busy. We don't want to trouble you!"

"I said I'll help!"

Porcius looked curious. "Is this something for the vigiles?"

"Missing child."

"We've had a lot of those lately."

"Do they turn up?" I asked.

"They seem to. The parents arrive in hysterics demanding house-to-house investigations; then they come in again looking sheepish, and saying the little one was just at Auntie's, or out looking for excitement. . . ." That would have sorted the issue, had he not gone on to report, "Petro did think there might be a pattern, but we've never had time to look into it."

I said, "Anyone who kidnaps Tertulla will hand her back pretty quick."

"Don't joke," retorted Helena, beating Maia to it by half a breath.

Sighing, I promised to draw up a regular plan for searching. To start with, Helena and my sister could prepare a description for the vigiles. We might as well involve the patrols.

I would have showed more enthusiasm, but I was trying to hide the fact I was in pain and next to panicking myself. My left arm still hung limp. I was afraid I had suffered permanent harm from the wide man. Porcius finally noticed my distracted air. "Oh, Falco! You've been nadgered—something's up with your collarbone."

I raised an eyebrow. That was still working, anyway. "You a medical man?"

Porcius said, "Recognizing damage was the first part of our training in the vigiles."

Helena was upset, mostly because she herself had failed to notice my disablement. Porcius told her he would fetch Scythax, the cohort doctor, to look at me. Suddenly I was being treated like an invalid. When Helena went into the bedroom for a blanket to wrap me in, I told Porcius in a low voice that we ought to have followed the intruders and tried to discover who they were.

Porcius looked dismayed, but then he smiled. He was tall, well built in a youthful way, and had a rosy glow beneath his outdoor tan. Helping out in the fight, he seemed to have gained confidence. "I think I know who they were," he assured me. "I haven't met them before, but I bet those two were the Miller and Little Icarus."

I was right. I had offended someone—someone I should have left alone. The problem with Tertulla might have to wait. This was far more serious.

XXXVII

Porcius went off to fetch Scythax and report to Petronius the bad developments.

Porcius and I had exchanged a few thoughts: "If you're right, and I have every confidence in your judgment, Porcius"—he blushed happily—"we now know that some of the Balbinus men are back in Rome. That probably means they all are."

"That makes them suspects for the Emporium raid," offered the young recruit. A fast thinker. Good material. Even in the aftermath of a fight he was piecing together the evidence.

I was thinking myself. "Interviewing Lalage, I was with Petro as a member of the cohort. She has no reason to single me out for special treatment. Apart from Nonnius—who's out of it—the Balbinus females are the only people I've visited on my own. The fact that it's the Miller and Little Icarus who were sent to put me off does point to this being in the family." I was convinced this had happened because I had asked too many questions of Flaccida and Milvia. The speed with which they had tracked me down was worrying. I kept that to myself. "Maybe we can forget the other gangs. Maybe Petro cut the head off the Balbinus organization, but the body's still active. We'll have to find out who's running it now, Porcius." For the safety of my household, we needed to find out fast.

"Do you really think it could be the wife or the daughter, Falco?"

"Or the son-in-law. I haven't met him yet."

"Or Lalage," Helena put in, refusing to give up her theory. "She could easily have taken over the services of the Miller and company."

Porcius and I exchanged a surreptitious glance. Face it: It was easier for us to accept that the Balbinus organization had been hijacked by his deadbeat thugs themselves than that it was masterminded by women. Even women as hard-baked as Flaccida and Lalage.

Neither Porcius nor I were intending to say this to Helena Justina. She came from the same stern mold that had produced the warrior queen Tanaquil, Cornelia, Volumnia, Livia, and other tough matrons who had never had it mentioned to them that they were supposed to be inferior to men. Personally, I like women with ideas. But you have to be genteel when you're teaching a recruit about life on the streets.

"The Miller and Little Icarus can't be very bright," Helena said. "They were frightening, but if they have sneaked back to Rome to run the show they ought to lie low, not draw attention to themselves. Flaccida struck me as clever enough to realize that."

"Right! So we're back with Lalage as the queen of intelligent activity!" I smiled at her.

Or with somebody we had not thought of yet.

Scythax came quickly. Porcius had made it to the station house in one piece. I had warned him to keep his eyes peeled when he hit street level. He must have told his story with some urgency, for the physician was with us by return. Porcius came back with him, to show him the right house. Petro had sent two members of the foot patrol as guards too. He had recognized the danger I was in.

Scythax was a brusque Oriental freedman who seemed to suspect malingering. This was understandable. The vigiles patrolmen were always trying to dodge off sick; given the dangers of their work, no one could blame them. Scythax expected people to cry ouch as soon he entered a room; he viewed "headaches," "bad backs," and "old knee trouble" with little patience. He had heard it all before. To get sympathy from Scythax you had to produce a bright red rash or a hernia, something visible or proddable.

He did concede that my shoulder and arm were genuinely out of action. He was delighted to inform me the shoulder joint was merely dislocated. His treatment would be to manipulate it back into place.

He did this. "Manipulate" had sounded a gentle enough word. In fact the maneuver involved working on me with a brute force that the Miller would have been proud of. I should have realized that when Scythax told Helena and Ma to grip my feet so I couldn't kick out, while Porcius was to throw himself on my chest with all his weight. Scythax immediately attacked me, bracing his foot against the wall as he leaned back and pulled.

It worked. It hurt. It hurt a lot. Even Ma had to sit down fanning herself, and Helena was openly in tears.

"There's no fee," Scythax condescended amiably.

My mother and my girlfriend both made comments that seemed to surprise him.

To smooth over the angry atmosphere (since he really had mended my shoulder), I managed to gasp, "Did you see the body the patrol brought in this morning?"

"Nonnius Albius?"

"You know of him?"

Scythax peered at me rather wryly, packing away his equipment. "I keep abreast of the cohort's work."

"So what did you think?"

"What Petronius Longus suggested: the man had been tormented, mostly while he was still alive. Many of the wounds were not fatal in themselves. Somebody had inflicted them to cause pain—it looked like punishment. That fits his position as a squealer who had betrayed his chief."

And it called for the same list of suspects as the people who might have taken over afterwards: the Balbinus women, the other gang members, and Lalage.

"He was very ill," I mentioned, as the doctor reached the

door. "Were you able to tell what might have been wrong with him?"

Scythax reacted oddly. An expression that could almost have been amusement crossed his face; then he said, "Nothing much."

"He was supposed to be dying!" Helena exclaimed in surprise. "That was the whole reason Petronius was able to persuade him to give evidence."

"Really?" The freedman was dry. "His doctor must have been mistaken."

"His doctor's called Alexander." I was already growing suspicious. "I met him at the house. He seemed as competent as any other Aesculapius."

"Oh, Alexander is an excellent doctor," Scythax assured me gravely.

"Do you know him, Scythax?"

I was prepared for rivalry, or professional solidarity, but not for what I learned instead: "He is my brother," said Scythax.

Then he smiled at us like a man who was far too long in the tooth to comment, and left.

I caught the eye of Petro's impressionable recruit. His mouth had dropped open as he worked out, slightly slower than I did, the implication of the cohort doctor's last remark. I said softly, "That's a lesson to you, Porcius. You're working for a man who is not what he seems. I'm talking about Petronius Longus. He has a mild-mannered reputation—behind which lurks the most devious, evil-minded investigation officer anywhere in Rome!"

XXXVIII

Maia was the kind of organizer generals love. She had put terror into the men of our family. Their response to her instructions to converge on Fountain Court to search for little Tertulla was mindless obedience; even Marius, the dedicated scholar, had abandoned his grammar homework. I was impressed. My brothers-in-law arrived all at once—all except the water boatman, Lollius. He was the missing child's father. It was too much to expect that creep to take an interest. Not even Galla, his wife, ever expected any support from Lollius.

The other four were bad enough. What a gang! In order of my sisters' seniority, they were:

Mico. The unemployed, unemployable plasterer. Pasty-faced and eternally perky. He was bringing up five children on his own, now his wife Victorina had died. He was doing it badly. Everyone felt obliged to say at least he was trying. The children would have stood more chance of surviving if he sailed off to Sicily and never came back. But Mico defended his useless role like a fighter. He would never give up.

Verontius. Allia's treasure. A shifty, untrustworthy road contractor who smelt of fish pickle and unwashed armpits.

You would think he had been heaving shovels all day long when all he really did was codge together contracts. No wonder he sweated. The lengths he went to to defraud the government were tortuous. A glance at Verontius looking half-asleep and guilty was enough to explain all the potholes in the Via Appia.

Gaius Baebius. Utter tedium. A ponderous customs clerk organizer who thought he knew it all. He knew nothing, especially about home improvements, a subject on which he liked to expound for hours. Gaius Baebius had brought Ajax, his and Junia's spoiled, uncontrollable watchdog. Apparently some clown had decided Ajax could sniff one of Tertulla's shoes, then trace her movements. Gaius and Ajax arrived in a lather of paws and untidy black fur; then we had to lock Nux in my bedroom to stop Ajax attacking her (he already had a history of violence).

Famia. Maia's darling was the best of the bunch, though I have to report Famia was a slit-eyed, red-nosed drunk who would have regularly cheated on Maia if he could have found the energy. While she brought up their children, he whiled away his life as a chariot horse vet. He worked for the Greens. I support the Blues. Our relationship could not and did not flourish.

Everyone milled around noisily to start with. Some of the brothers-in-law looked as if they had hoped we would give up the idea of a search and all sit down with an amphora. Helena disabused them crisply. Then we had the inevitable jokes about the skip baby, mostly suggesting he was some unfortunate relic of my bachelor past. I dealt with that one. There was one good side to my male relations. Since they were married to my sisters, they had all learned to be swiftly subdued by sarcasm.

As there was no one else at home to look after the children (except his old mother, who had gone to play dice tonight at a caupona by the Temple of Isis), Mico had brought his three youngest. These unpleasant mites had to be kept amused, given copious drinks, and protected from Gaius and Junia's dog.

"He loves children!" protested Gaius Baebius, as Ajax

strained at the flimsy string on his collar and tried to reduce Mico's family to something he could bury under Gaius' home-built sun-yourself pilastered breakfast patio. Then Ajax was offered a shoe, so he could do his stuff as a tracker. He just worried the shoe, thinking it was a dead rat. Gaius Baebius blustered about, looking embarrassed and blaming everyone else.

Helena took charge, supported by young Marius. They gave each brother-in-law a sector to search, and ordered them to question shopkeepers and locals whether anyone had seen Tertulla earlier that day; then they organized my various nephews to act as runners if any information were found.

"You coming, Falco?"

"Marcus has been gated." Helena made out that I had been seriously wounded that day. I know how to look pale in a crisis; I had been in the army for seven years. The mob dispersed without me. Gaius took his watchdog. Mico's children clung to their father and left with him. Silence descended. Helena started spooning porridge into the skip baby. It would be a long, messy process. I went into my bedroom for a quiet lie-down. I wanted to think about the interesting information that the physician who had told Nonnius Albius he was dying had lied to him, and that that physician just happened to have a brother working in the public sector—alongside Petronius.

As soon as I stretched out, easing my sore arm, Nux jumped straight on the end and settled as if she thought it was her role in life to sleep on her master's bed.

"Stop warming my feet. I'm not your master!"

Nux opened one eye, put out a long pink tongue, and wagged her tail enthusiastically.

XXXIX

The brothers-in-law took their time. They had probably all met around the corner and gone into a wine shop to relax.

It gave me an opportunity to walk over to the new apartment and carry on with its clearance. My sore arm made work difficult, but Helena had come to help. Even with a couple of guards loitering on the stairs, there was no way I intended leaving her alone. Not now that the vicious Balbinus mob knew where we were.

Nux trotted happily after us. I shut her out, but we could hear her lying right outside the door, snuffling under it as she waited for me to reemerge.

"She adores you!" Helena laughed.

"It won't do her any good."

"The hardhearted hero! Still"—Helena was smiling—"you once took that defensive attitude with me."

"Nonsense. I was the one slavering outside doors, begging you to let me in."

"I was frightened of what might happen if I did."

"So was I, lady!"

I was grinning at her. I had never quite lost that quick thump of the heart whenever I thought where our relationship might be taking us.

We had to open the door to carry out the last of the rubbish, so then the dog got in. I was forced to whistle her after me, rather than leave an untried animal alone with the skip babe. Between the two of them they had me in knots.

As we worked I discussed with Helena my theory about Nonnius being set up by Petronius.

"Was that illegal, Marcus?"

"Doubt it."

"Entrapment?"

"Nonnius was the fool to believe his physician, that's all."

"What if he had found out? Presumably when he failed to die of his 'fatal' disease, he would eventually have realized the diagnosis was at fault."

"He couldn't complain. Had he lived, he would have been enjoying his share of the Balbinus estate as a direct result."

"He's a clever man, your friend Petronius."

"The quiet ones are the worst," I said.

While we were still in our new lodging, Petro himself turned up to inspect how much damage the Miller and Icarus had wreaked on me. He started out anxious, but once he had looked me over his broad face became happier. "So you're off our necks for a while, Falco? How long will the convalescence be?"

"Forget it! Here, lug this bale down to the skip for me." He complied obligingly while I enjoyed myself playing the man in charge. "What your investigation needs is brainwork; there's nothing wrong with my head."

Trotting down to the skip, he pulled a face as if he were questioning that, so when he passed me I thumped him with my good arm to prove I could still be active; then I laid into him with jibes about how he had put one over on Nonnius. He merely smiled in his annoying way.

"Has Silvia come home again yet?" Helena called down after us.

"Oh yes."

He seemed surprised she asked. I could imagine how he had talked himself out of trouble and won Silvia around. Petronius had had years of practice in softening up his angry wife.

Returning upstairs for more rubbish, Petro changed the subject. "Was Porcius any use in the scrap?"

"Perfectly adequate. A sound one, I'd say."

"Bit raw." Petro rarely complimented his men until he had thoroughly tested them. Though he wanted to hear good news about the lad, his voice carried a doubtful tone.

"He seems impressed by his senior officer's deviousness!"

Once again Petronius carried on as if he had no idea what I meant. He glanced around the apartment, which was now almost clear. "This place is better than your usual standard, but it's filthy, Falco. Helena can't live here."

"All it needs is a good scrub," Helena demurred loyally.

I dug Petro in the ribs. "As a friend, you might offer the foot patrols to help bring the water up."

Petro barked with scornful laughter. "If you want a favor from the bloody firefighters, you'll have to ask them yourself!"

He had found the stuff that I had salvaged from Smaractus' workmen, and dived in with a whoop. Immediately he started sorting out wood nails and pieces of good timber. When it came to carpentry, he was a worse scavenger than I was.

"Just take anything you want!" I snorted, grabbing back a pair of metal pincers.

"Thanks, Falco!"

"Petro, did Porcius tell you about Marcus' missing niece?" Helena broke in as we rummaged on the floor. "We are starting to think she may have been abducted. Is it true this has happened other times?"

"We've had a spate. I thought there was something in it because they were all from wealthy families." Petro grinned. "With due respect to the Didius clan, this must be unconnected!"

"Pa has cash," I pointed out tersely.

"Your father's not exactly known for family loyalty. I wouldn't hold out any chances for the kidnapper who tried squeezing Geminus. Be fair. Can you see him coughing up a ransom for one of your sisters' horrors?"

"Maybe." Or maybe not.

"Most of the other lost sprats were sweet little moppets. Parents would gladly pay to get them back. Plus one baby lifted from a very exalted cradle, finally said to have been 'merely taken by a nurse to show to a friend.' "

"Believe it?"

"No."

"Were you allowed to interview the nurse?"

"Of course not. We might have actually learned something!"

"And every single child turned up?"

"Apparently."

"Were there any leads we could follow?"

"Only that the cases were all south of the Circus. I checked, but none of the other cohorts were having the same stuff happening. I tried working out a theory that somebody who normally hangs around the Aventine and wouldn't be noticed was snatching. The parents refused to cooperate, so I was in the dark and let it slide. I have enough to do."

Helena murmured thoughtfully, "Would you be prepared to tell me some of the parents' names?"

"You're not intending to see them!" Petro waited for a denial, but received none. "Are you going to allow this, Falco?" His attitude towards women was as traditional as mine was relaxed. The odd thing was, his surly paternalism had always done him more good—at least until I met Helena. Petro couldn't compete with that.

I grinned. "I draw the line at her questioning suspects." This overlooked the fact that I had taken her with me to assist that very afternoon. A dangerous gleam lit Helena's soft eyes. "But there's no harm in her visiting respectable victims."

"Oh thanks!" muttered Helena. Definitely *not* a traditionalist.

"It's highly irregular," complained Petronius.

He was weakening. Helena Justina had one great advantage over us: She could approach snooty families on equal terms; she was probably superior to most of them. We could see how her mind was working, but she politely told us anyway: "I can say I begged their addresses because we are desperate about our own missing child. If they believe I am asking as a private individual, they may just confide more than they were prepared to tell the vigiles."

Petro abandoned resistance. "Going to play the distraught mother?"

Helena gave him a straight look. "Good practice, Petro. I'll be hysterical for real reasons soon enough."

He glanced at me. I shrugged. "Yes, it's true. I would have told you."

"Oh really? What you actually told me was some lie about this not happening!" He made as if to leave in a huff, but at the last moment picked up the skip baby, who had been reclining like a pharaoh on a sack of old rags. Petro, the dedicated father of three, leaned against the outside doorframe, showing off his expertise. The babe, tolerant as ever, accepted that big tough men are full of soppy talk. "Hello, cheeky fellow, what are you doing with these two eccentrics?"

I was just explaining that when I wasn't being thumped by desperadoes, I was trying to find the babe's guardians for him when Martinus arrived in Fountain Court. From our first-floor landing, we saw him before he spotted us. Initially Petronius ducked back indoors, pretending to hide. Across the lane Martinus started jabbering something to Lenia. Seeing the slowcoach Martinus in a hurry changed Petro's mind.

He went out onto the steps and whistled. Nux barked at him loudly. Lenia shouted abuse across the street. Heads shot out of windows to gape. Passersby stopped in their tracks. Casual shoppers listened brazenly. This was the Fourth Cohort at its discreet, efficient best; soon the whole Aventine would know what was up. Any chance of solving the problem by using an element of surprise was lost before we even heard what the problem was.

Martinus turned towards us. Excitedly the deputy shouted his message: There had just been a heavy raid—in broad daylight—by a gang who had ransacked the goldsmiths in the Saepta Julia. The size of the haul, the speed of the attack, and the efficiency of the robbers bore marked similarities to the raid at the Emporium. The Seventh Cohort were in charge, but Petronius was expected to attend.

Petro had run down almost to the street before he cursed and remembered he was still holding the skip baby. He leaped back three steps at a time with his long spider's legs, shoved the child into my arms, then hared off again. I passed the baby to Helena, instructed Nux to stay and guard them, then set off after Petronius.

I was wearing the wrong boots for hurrying, but I had no intention of missing this.

XL

There was much less commotion at the Saepta than we had seen at the Emporium. Goldsmiths are a more secretive lot than merchants. They were wary of making a fuss about their stock even after it had been wrenched from them. None of them wanted to confess, especially to each other, exactly what they possessed, let alone what they had lost. They merely stood around the ground floor and the upper balcony looking deeply glum.

Petronius made sure he reminded them that Vespasian had said he was compensating the Emporium merchants as an exceptional measure. The goldsmiths had been warned to take care, Petro declared. If they had failed to secure their premises despite the formal notification of a need for extra vigilance, they would have to stand the loss.

This went down like a gladiators' strike at a five-day festival. Hoping to avoid inflated claims, Martinus started trooping around the jewelers to make up another of his lists. Maybe the Emperor would agree to token compensation after all. More likely, he would confine himself to issuing a strict reprimand to the Prefect of the Vigiles for neglecting to prevent another robbery. The Prefect would take it out on the tribune of the Seventh Cohort, who was responsible for the Saepta, and on Marcus Rubella, tribune of the Fourth, who was in charge of the special initiative for catching the gang. Rubella would land on Petronius like a barrel of bricks from a great height.

I absorbed the size of the raid, which was phenomenal. That was all I needed to know. The next stage of action would be routine: taking endless details and asking questions of hostile witnesses whose information would probably prove pointless. Spotting my father, I dragged him into his office. "There's enough grief here! Let's keep out of the way."

Pa had lost nothing this time. The robbers had stormed through the building, swiping jewels and precious metalwork. They had had a strict menu of items to lift. Furniture and fancy lamps were off their agenda. Pa looked miffed.

"No bloody taste!"

"Be grateful, you villain."

"I like to put it about that my stuff is desirable."

"Any connoisseur of mock-marble tables with one foot missing can see yours are up with the best! Any collector who wants twenty identical statuettes of a muse on Mount Helicon—one or two with chipped noses—will come rushing straight here. . . . Did you get my message?"

"Some garbled jabbering from my steward."

Pa's steward was perfectly competent, as I happened to know. Like Pa's stock, his staff turned out to be better quality than you thought at first glance. I reiterated patiently, "We found one of the glass jugs."

"Oh?" He could hardly force himself to express an interest. I knew why it was. He would rather claim the Emperor's compensation, cash in hand, than enjoy owning and selling the treasures we had taken so much trouble to bring home. He made me furious.

"You give me a pain in the brain, Pa! What about what I said about a present for Helena?"

"That was a gorgeous piece you got her."

"You mean you found it?" I was beside myself.

"I had a very good look at the glass in the boxes that first night. I thought I told you."

"Then I wish you'd taken it out and kept it safe for me!"

"How was I to know it was a present for Helena?"

"It was wrapped in one of my old tunics. You should have realized."

"I thought you were secreting away a bribe for some fancy bit."

"Oh for heavens' sake! I hate to flirt and fornicate."

"Jupiter, that's new!"

"Don't judge me by your own low behavior!" I felt so annoyed with him I could not bear to stay and haggle over a replacement, even though I needed a present by the next morning. With a brief curse—my usual salutation—I brushed aside Pa's offer of a drink and stormed off home.

By the time I returned to Fountain Court it was dark. I put aside my anger; I had to give my attention to keeping alert. A loose chicken scuttled across my feet in a panic, frightening me too. There were the usual feeble lamps flickering like extremely tired glowworms on the porches of the bakery, the basket shop, and one or two others. Only the funeral parlor was ablaze with cheerful strings of lights; offering a brilliant welcome was their idea of comforting the bereaved. In one deeply shadowed doorway two figures were locked together; hard to see whether it was a pair of lovers steadfastly taking their pleasure or a mugger throttling a victim. In keeping with the traditions of our area, I did not inquire. I had once helped a youth who was being raped by a carter, only to have him steal my purse while his attacker was giving me a black eye. Not a setup; just a typical Aventine reward for my overfriendliness.

I was walking up the laundry side of the lane, which was normally quieter. This brought me to the ground-floor lockup alongside the barber's, the set of rooms that had previously been advertised to let. The new tenants had made fast work of moving in. There was a dim lantern with a dirty horn shutter swinging from an awning support, by the light of which I could make out masses of intriguing stuff for sale. A faint chalked sign above the entrance now advertised: THE LUMBER ROOM: BARGAINS APLENTY AND GIFTS FULL OF CHARM.

This was my last hope of acquiring a birthday present for the girl I adored. Even better, I could possibly get something cheap. I had nothing to lose, so I rapped on a cauldron hanging by the doorway, and went in.

XLI

If you liked jumble, it was a wondrous glory hole. As soon as I squeezed in through the folding doors, which had been nearly closed, I knew this was the sort of cavern that cried out for half a day's perusal. It all looked extremely casual. There were enough mixed sacks of pictures and crocks to give the impression the proprietor had lost any chance of knowing his stock—holding out the tantalizing hope of unsuspected valuables for which the sharp-eyed browser could offer a copper, intending to sell on to a more discerning dealer at twenty times the price. My father always called these places rubbish dumps; his disdain only made me like them more.

By the light of a few tiny oil lamps I tried to familiarize myself. Dust filled the air. There was a smell which I recognized from the house sales my father organized after people had died, that faintly upsetting aroma of old things newly disturbed. The confined space was very warm. From the rear of the building came a succession of muffled noises, not quite domestic in character.

I brushed through a strung-up cascade of belts, some with extraordinary buckles. Then I nearly stepped on a dismantled chariot wheel. Sandals and boots were knotted on ropes like onions. They bulged on the walls amid hookfuls of skillets and drainers that hung in colonies like shellfish on a groyne. Around my feet were teetering piles of bowls and platters. To reach the gloom where the counter groaned under mounds of cloth items—old clothes and household drapes, apparently— required steering a path through the tableware; huge baskets of ironmongery that leaned against the serving island, keeping you at a distance. Little stands dripped bead necklaces. Caskets stood open to show off glittering finger rings. There were bronze flagons, black metal cups that could well clean up into silver, and an astonishing candelabra that reached the roof.

I wondered where the proprietor got his stuff. On the off chance, I kept an eye out for Syrian glass.

A figure emerged suddenly from the rear, making me jump. He looked flustered and suspicious, as if I had invaded a shop that was really closed for the night. I stuck one thumb in my belt and applied an unthreatening air.

"Evening. This is quite a collection! I bet you don't even know what you've got." It was intended as a compliment; he took it as an insult, I could see.

The man was slight and seedy-looking. I had seen this type in many a dark boothful of paraphernalia before. I never know how they live. They never seem to want to part with any goods from their untidy selection, and if you bring anything to offer for sale, they despise that too.

This one had lanky strings of hair covering his ears, though the dome of his head was bald. His skin was like old cheese rind, the sort at which even sparrows turn up their beaks when you find it behind a cupboard and throw it out. He looked insignificant. I tried to tell myself he was a pent-up ball of energy and intelligence. I failed.

"Mind if I look around?"

He condescended to allow it, but appeared about as happy as if I had told him I represented the aedile in charge of licenses. "Anything special you're looking for?" he forced himself to demand. He definitely had the gloom of a man whose credentials were being checked—one who knew he had not paid the right bribes to be in the clear.

"I'll know it if I see it."

I wanted to browse; he just wanted me to leave. The fact
that he stood there watching meant that things which had
once looked attractive rapidly lost their interest. I started
noticing chips and dents the minute I picked up an item; then
I felt embarrassed about putting it straight down. He had no
idea how to sell. Even if he suspected I was an evening op-
portunist looking for goods to lift, he could have watched
me without letting it show. Anyone would think I had
slouched in with a hook on a stick or a large swag bag.

I lost myself for a long time in a basket of handles, brack-
ets, and hinges. Eventually I straightened up. "Do you sell
any decent-quality jewelry?"

"I don't have much in stock at the moment." He meant, if
any ever came in he sold it straight on to a specialist jeweler
who could present it on a pretty display and charge more.
"My partner reclaims precious metal, and we have a good
craftsman who can make it up into anything you want. We
could commission you a piece."

"In gold?"

"Oh yes."

"Would you guarantee the purity?"

"All our work goes out with a certificate."

Anyone who "reclaims" metal can probably forge documents too, but it sounded a reasonable offer. That only made
me feel more worried. This was a prime opportunity for
them to pinch the materials, if I supplied any, or for me to
pay a lot of money for work that entirely lacked artistry.

"What's your name?"

"Castus."

"Maybe we can do business, Castus."

I hated the normal class of jeweler. I hated their prices and
the stuck-up way they sneered at me. I really would have
liked to give some smaller firm a chance. But Helena was
special. Feeling like a louse, I promised to decide more
clearly what I wanted and come back later with instructions.
Then I left the shop. Poor Castus obviously knew I was just
a time-waster.

Back at home, Helena was in bed. I knew pregnant
women have to rest a lot. When I suggested this, Helena re-

torted that she had just decided I was an unreliable wanderer it was no use waiting up for.

I sat on the edge of the bed, holding the skip baby, who had been awake when I came in. He gazed back with his normal, quiet, trusting expression. I had a bad conscience about this one. I kept forgetting him. I kept forgetting my niece Tertulla too. There was madness on the Aventine, a two-way traffic in youth. Some children were being abandoned; some were being snatched. I tried to make a connection, but nothing jumped out at me.

I pushed Nux off the end of the bed; she crept closer along the floor, and since she was shy of fussing me while I was acting stern, she licked the baby's foot instead.

"That's a good sign." Helena smiled.

"She's good with children!" We both giggled, thinking of Gaius Baebius making this wild claim as he fought to hold his struggling hound, Ajax.

Helena told me the brothers-in-law had achieved nothing in the search for little Tertulla (no surprise). The last sighting of her must have been soon after Marius had left her, in a street only two away from Fountain Court. Gaius Baebius had offered to come again tomorrow to continue searching. He and Junia had no children of their own, but he was a good-hearted soul. That had never made him easier to like.

I sighed. Trying to think what I could do about this, I stretched on top of the coverlet alongside Helena. I was still holding the babe. Next thing, the damned dog started creeping up over the edge too, one paw at a time. There was hardly room for all of us. At this rate we would need a bigger bed.

Tertulla might have to wait. She had been missing most of the day, and we were now into the night. I knew what that meant. I was perfectly aware of the dangers she might be in. She was certainly frightened. She might be hurt. Or dead. But without a lead to follow, I had little chance of doing anything.

I was her uncle. I was head of her mother's household, since Pa was an absconding scoundrel and the child's own father was a complete deadbeat whom even Galla threw out whenever possible. It was my role to find the child. Dear gods, I hated this kind of responsibility.

"Let me try," Helena urged, snuggling up to me. "I'll speak to the parents of the other so-called missing children. Marcus, you can't do everything."

I turned my head and gazed at her sadly. "You're beautiful!"

"What's that for?" She was suspicious at once. "What's happened?"

I closed my eyes wearily. This had to be confession time. "I can't do anything right. I bought you a wonderful present for once—and it's been stolen from me."

"Oh no! Oh my darling."

"It was marvelous. Something I'd probably never be able to better." I was really depressed. "I've been trying to replace it, but I can't find anything I like as much."

"Ah, Marcus . . . It doesn't matter. Come to bed properly."

"I didn't want to have to tell you this."

"It's not your fault."

"I'm supposed to be catching the bastards. I thought I'd get it back."

"You will," she said. I loved her faith, but it was terrifying. Helena put her arms around me. I began to feel drowsy straightaway. That was no good. I had too much to worry about. If I dozed I would have bad dreams. I might as well just stay awake and ruin my chances of sorting out anything by making myself completely exhausted for tomorrow.

Tomorrow was going to be a difficult day. "Helena Justina, what are we going to tell your mother when she asks you what you had from me?"

"I shall just smile mysteriously and say it's a secret."

Helena's mother would take this for a salacious reference to the child we were expecting. Once she knew of it. "Well what, if it isn't too much to ask, are we going to tell your mother about starting a family?"

"Don't worry."

"I do worry. I've bungled enough things. I'd like to handle this with decorum and tact."

"I'll tell her that was my birthday present." Exactly as I feared: *"He's made me pregnant. What more do you want?"*

What a wonderful household. A hopeless informer, a girl he should not be living with, a strange little foundling baby, and a dog I didn't want. And somehow between the four of us, we were trying to solve half the conspiracies in Rome.

By next morning there was another crime for us. During the night, Alexander, the doctor who had told Nonnius he was dying, was found by the watch lying in his open surgery. The place was a wreck and he was surrounded by scattered instruments and spilled medicines. His throat had been cut with one of his own scalpels. Various disgusting experiments had been perpetrated on him first. His brother, Scythax, the Fourth Cohort's medico, happened to be out with the night patrol that came across the corpse.

XLII

Helena's birthday. My poor girl loyally spent her time trying to find my lost niece. She set about interviewing all the Aventine householders who had reported missing children. Gaius Baebius had turned up just as I was myself leaving home, so I found a piece of rope in my skip to tie Ajax to a pillar in the laundry portico, then arranged with Gaius that he would stick close to Helena. It was protection for her, something I could not spare time to provide myself, and kept him out of trouble too.

Lenia bawled something angrily about the dog.

"Leave off, Lenia. If I'm to provide your augury, you owe me a favor or two."

"Don't push your luck, Falco! Seems to me you're using this as an excuse to behave like a complete tyrant."

"Don't underestimate the lies I'll have to make up."

"If you feel like that I'll find somebody else."

"I wish you would."

Nobody else would do it, we both knew. Every lockup shopkeeper in Fountain Court had already given himself a hernia laughing at the thought of me having to suffer under the sacrificial veil.

Dear gods. That was another problem: I would have to acquire a headdress to parade in at the altar on the wedding day.

"Gaius Baebius, you look like a man with a sense of duty. Have you got a priest's veil?"

"Of course." My brother-in-law smirked. Trust him. What a pious operator. How could even Junia have married him? (Answer: for his customs salary. Do not ask me, however, how a placid lump like Gaius ever married a spiteful stick like her.) "Marcus Didius, I am hoping to be elected to the college of the Augustales soon."

Official religion. Oh spare me, Gaius! "Excellent fellow! And thanks for the loan of your bonce sheet," I cried, setting off in the opposite direction from Helena and him at a fast pace. I could see him looking puzzled; Helena would explain. If I knew Gaius Baebius, lending me his head veil would make him think he had the right to attend Lenia's nuptials. Things were looking up. He and Junia were bound to bring their dog; Ajax was their child substitute, treated as one of the family. Maybe Ajax could be trained to bite the bride's beloved. Maybe, if the gods were *very* kind, they would give me time to train Ajax myself.

Walking to the station house, I enjoyed myself, thinking of fierce canine teeth being sunk into my landlord's most personal assets on his wedding day.

I already knew how my own day would be unfolding. Fusculus had called at the apartment early to break the news of the doctor's murder. He said Petro had been up half the night pursuing investigations into the Saepta thefts. When he heard of Alexander's murder, he had given up and gone home to grab a hasty nap. The plan was for us all to meet at midmorning in order to tackle the new disaster after the crew had rested and were fresh.

This gave me a couple of hours to spare. Time for serious preparations: I went to the gymnasium and put in some wrestling and weapons practice. Given the grim state of Rome, it seemed a good idea.

I had forgotten about my shoulder. That very promptly sent me out of the gym and into the massage room.

"You're full of flab," complained Glaucus, the proprietor,

who acted as my personal trainer whenever I allowed him access.

"Get me into condition then."

"In *half an hour*, Falco?"

"Half an hour is all I have."

"You're slow, you're weak, you're dopy. It's going to take me months to undo this. I hope you're not planning anything dangerous in the near future."

"Just tackling a gang of vicious murderers. And mind it, man. I had a dislocated shoulder poked back yesterday."

"Jupiter, Juno, and Minerva! I presume," moaned Glaucus sarcastically, "somebody also landed some heavy blows to the soft part of your head?"

I do like to approach threatening situations with such warm encouragement.

Petronius Longus was in a filthy mood. "What in Hades is wrong with these bastards? Can't they give us time to run ourselves into the ground on one job before they have to jump up like flea-bitten rabbits? Time was you could rely on growing thoroughly depressed with your first case before some cluck decided to throw the next at you. . . ."

He was just ranting. I could understand why.

He had Scythax in the interrogation room. The poor man was so deeply in shock, he seemed drunk. Every few minutes he wandered out muttering a confused suggestion, or asking the same question he had put to us three times already. "What did they think they were achieving? Why did they have to torture him? Why, oh why?"

"Revenge, Scythax. Porcius, make yourself useful. Go in there and sit with him."

"Just talk to him," counseled Fusculus in a low voice. "Or if he talks about his brother, just nod and listen."

As the nervous recruit obediently led the grief-stricken man indoors again, Petro covered his face briefly. "I can't send him home. Oh gods on Olympus, Falco! What a mess. He lived with his brother. He'll go mad in those surroundings. Besides, these bastards may be looking for Scythax too."

"The patrol couldn't hold him back," Fusculus told me.

"The door was ajar. As soon as Scythax saw the situation, he was in like an arrow, howling and covered with blood himself. They had a terrible time dragging him away from Alexander and getting him back here. He still keeps trying to return to the surgery."

Everyone present was white-faced. There was plenty to do, but they were sitting together in the patrol house, impotent. They saw violence daily, hideous death far too frequently. This had struck too close. This affected one of them. This—though nobody had yet mentioned it—was something their own work had caused. Alexander *might* have been attacked by a deranged patient, but we all thought this was directly related to his false diagnosis of Nonnius Albius.

We spent a day trying to make sense of it. First we all said there was no point going to look at the surgery—or no point *all* of us going. We all went. It seemed a gesture of respect. We had to force ourselves to see what the man had endured. Petronius imposed it on himself as a punishment. Some of the others made it serve as an apology. I went because I knew from experience that if you don't, you never stop worrying whether there was some clue you could have spotted if you had been there. We badly needed evidence. The squad was so shaken up that any clues there were might easily be missed or misinterpreted.

Young Porcius was the only one who actually vomited. The scene knocked back his composure completely; there was nothing for it but to send him to the station house to sit with Scythax again. By the end of the day, the youngster was a gibbering wreck, but we had too much else to think about. He was given sympathy, but no one could nursemaid him.

"The chief's heartbroken," Martinus muttered to me. Even he had lost all his cockiness.

"I've never seen him so bad," Fusculus agreed dolefully.

I was his friend. They all seemed to want to tell me about Petro's distressed state. I could hardly bear it. I needed nobody to tell me. He was as foul-tempered as I had ever seen him—except once, during the Boudiccan Rebellion in Britain. He was older now. He knew more obscene words, and more painful ways to take out his anger on people nearby.

I would have hauled him out for a drink, but in the mood he was in, he would have stayed knocking it back until he passed out or killed himself.

By the afternoon we had exhausted ourselves asking questions. Several innocent householders had gone off to complain to the Prefect's Office about the way they had been pushed around and bawled at. Nobody had seen or heard anything suspicious, either last night or the previous day. Nobody knew anything. Nobody wanted to know. Everyone had caught a whiff of gangster involvement. Everyone was terrified.

We all believed the same people had killed both Alexander and Nonnius. Even that simple fact was hard to prove. The evidence denied it. One victim had been abducted; one was killed at home. One was a declared informant; the other had been sensibly discreet. The methods used were completely different. The message sent out seemed less flagrant the second time. Apart from the fact both murders happened at night—like most crimes in Rome—only the violence inflicted was common to both. Only instinct and experience convinced us we were right to link the two deaths. But it all made sense if we decided that Nonnius had been killed as an act of revenge for betraying Balbinus, and Alexander had died because someone found out it was his telling Nonnius he was dying that had led to that villain's "reform."

The public baths were opening by the time the investigation broke up for the day. The scent of wood smoke on the damp October air gave an autumnal gloom and added to our melancholy mood. We were no further forward. There was a sense that we would spend this coming night waiting for more deaths. We were losing. The villains had all the dice running for them.

With a set face, Petronius ordered the body's removal—to an undertaker this time, not the station house, where the dead man's distraught brother was still being looked after. He then arranged for members of the foot patrol to be brought in to clean up and leave the surgery neat. Fusculus volunteered to oversee that. He seemed to need something to fill his time. Petro thanked him, then sent the rest home.

I saw Petronius to his house. He said almost nothing as we walked. I left him at his door. His wife let him in. She glanced at his drawn features, then her chin went up, but she made no comment. Maybe she even gave me a half-concealed nod. Arria Silvia loved to rant, but if ever Petro looked beaten she rushed to protect him. So Silvia took over, and I was not needed. As the door closed, leaving me alone in the street, I felt momentarily lost.

It had been a terrible day. I had seen Rome's underbelly, smelled the matted filth beneath the ravening wolf. It was nothing new, but it forced me to face the lack of hope that lives alongside crime. This was the true face of the Caesars' marble city: not Corinthian acanthus leaves and perfect gilt-lettered inscriptions, but a quiet man killed horrendously in the home and workplace he shared with his brother; a vicious revenge thrust on the one-time slave who had learned a respected profession, then repaid his freedom and citizenship with a single act of assistance to the law. Not all the fine civic building programs in the world would ever displace the raw forces that drive most of humankind. This was the true city: greed, corruption, and violence.

It was dusk as I made my way to Fountain Court. My heart lay heavy. And for me, the day was nowhere near over yet. I still had to put on a smile and a toga—then go out to dinner with my girlfriend's family.

XLIII

Once we got past the porter, who had always viewed me like a door-to-door lupin-seller who was aiming to snatch silverware, it was an occasion to remember. The hosts were so considerate that guests felt free to behave badly. Helena Justina's birthday, in the consulship of whoever it was, laid the foundation for many happy years of family recrimination. For once, it was not my family involved.

Being a mere private citizen, my manners were the best on display. As soon as I escorted Helena from the carrying chair I had grudgingly hired, I turned to find her mother right behind me waiting to knock me aside and embrace the birthday girl. I kissed the matron's cheek (smoothly oiled and scented) with grave formality. She was a tall woman who had not expected me to tackle her, so the maneuver required dexterity. She was even more surprised than I was.

"Julia Justa, greetings and thanks. Twenty-five years ago today you gave the world a great treasure!" I might not be the ideal son-in-law, but I knew how to press a rather nice soapstone casket of balsam into a lady's receptive hands.

"Thank you, Marcus Didius. What a pretty speech." Julia Justa was a mistress of elegant hypocrisy. Then her expression froze. "Why," queried Helena's mother icily "is my daughter carrying a child?" Helena had brought the skip babe.

"Oh, Marcus found him in a rubbish skip!" cried Helena Justina breezily. "But there's another child I'm carrying that you'll want to hear about."

This was hardly the tact and decorum I had tried to plan. On the other hand, nobody could say that it was my fault.

I had a side bet with the Fourth Cohort that the night would end with women in tears and men losing teeth. (Or the other way around.) Before we even crossed the threshold, there was some jostling for position among the female element.

Helena's mother wore leaf-green silk with an embroidered stole; Helena wore not merely silk, but a fabulous cloth from Palmyra woven in multiple patterns of purple, brown, deep red, and white. Helena's mother wore an expensive parure of golden scrolls and droplets set with a clutch of evenly matched emeralds; Helena wore an armful of bangles, and absolutely enormous Indian pearls. Helena's mother was scented with highly refined cinnamon perfume, the one Helena herself often wore; Helena tonight wore a few vivid dabs of a precious liquor containing frankincense. She also had the gracious air of a daughter who had won.

We men were in white. We started in togas, though we soon flung them off. Helena's father had his fond, faintly cautious expression. Her brother Aelianus boasted a scowl and a Spanish belt. I had been smartened up until I felt like a whole guild of shoemakers on their big day out.

Justinus had failed to appear that night. Everyone knew he must be mooning around Pompey's Theater. "He won't forget," his mother assured us as she led us indoors. He might. (The actress might be exceptional, and she might choose tonight to notice him.) Helena and I gulped, then prayed for him.

While the women rushed away to share urgent news, I was led off for a predinner winecup with the Senator (honeyed mulsum, strictly traditional; makes you feel sick without letting you get drunk). Camillus Verus was shrewd and intelligent, with a diffident manner. He did what was necessary, and didn't waste effort on the rest. I liked him. It mattered to me that he should be able to tolerate me. At least he knew the strength of my feelings for Helena.

The Camillus family were certainly patrician when viewed from my own perspective, though there were no consuls or generals in their ancestry. They were rich—though their wealth was in land, and my father probably owned far more portable collateral. Their house was spacious and detached, a lived-in town villa with water and drainage but rather tired decor. Lacking expensive works of art, they relied on old-fashioned features for domestic tranquillity. Tonight the courtyard fountains were splashing merrily, but we needed more than that to cool the air as the Senator introduced me to his elder son.

Aelianus was two years younger than Helena, two years older than Justinus. He looked much like his father—sprouting straight hair and slightly stooped shoulders. More chunky than Justinus and Helena and heavier-featured, he was less good-looking as a result. His abysmal manners were a patrician cliché. Luckily I had never expected a senator's son to approve of me. That was fine; it let me off trying to like him.

"So you're the man who's been pushing my young brother's career along!" exclaimed Aelianus.

Nearly a decade his senior, and worth ten times more in useful qualities, I refused to agitate myself. "Quintus has a warm personality and a fine intellect. People like him, and he's interested in everything—naturally such a man stands no chance in public life! Unlike you, I'm sure." Well done, Falco; an insult, but nicely ambiguous.

Young Justinus stood every chance, in fact. But I don't stir up trouble; close relatives can usually find enough things to be jealous about.

"And did you get him interested in the theater too?" his brother sneered.

It was the Senator himself who said, "He selects his own hobbies—like all of you." That had to be a fatherly dig; I sat back and wondered what dubious activities the pious Aelianus liked. If he gave me any trouble, this would be something to find out.

"Let's hope my brother's hobby doesn't last—or my sister's, either!"

There were now so many stars alongside Justinus' name on the army list, a scandal might just make him appear more intriguing to the public. I refrained from saying that. Aelianus had completed his own military service rather dully; then a year as a governor's unpaid aide-de-camp in Baetica had failed to give him luster. On the other hand, none of that had been his own fault. Luck stepped around me pretty smartly too, so I said kindly, "Don't be jealous. Your brother was just in the right province, at the right time."

"And of course he knew you."

Again there was an unpleasant, scornful note. Aelianus was naïve enough to expect me to flare up. Instead his father said mildly, "That was indeed fortunate. When Marcus was sent on one of his peculiarly demanding missions, your brother was able to join him."

"Did you approve of that?" Aelianus demanded accusingly. "I've heard what Justinus got up to in Germany was damned dangerous."

"I didn't know until it was over," Camillus replied honestly.

The young man was bursting with outraged dignity. "There are things we ought to get straight." The Senator and I glanced at one another, then let him get on with it. He needed to make a racket. That was easier than arguing. "This man is a common informer." I noticed he found it impossible to use even my formal name. "The situation with my sister is damaging our family." He meant that it might reflect on his own career.

The Senator looked annoyed. Whatever he thought about his finely bred daughter absconding with a piece of rough cheese, he always put the best face on it. "Falco is an imperial agent. He has the confidence of the Emperor."

"But Vespasian hates informers."

I laughed. "Except when he needs them."

The younger Camillus was still sounding off pompously. "I have seen no public recognition of the role of 'imperial agent.' It carries no official title or salary. And as I under-

stand it, although there was once talk of a substantial reward, it has failed to materialize."

I made an effort to avoid reacting. I had promised Helena
not to involve myself in conversations that might end with
my fist shattering her brother's jaw.

Camillus Senior looked embarrassed. "Falco's work is
necessarily secret. Don't be offensive to our guest." He tried
gamely to change the subject: "You look in good form, Marcus. Travel suits you."

"You should see me in my Palmyrene trousers and embroidered hat. . . ." I sighed. Chitchat on Oriental matters
would dodge the problem but not solve it. "Your son is quite
right, Senator. I *was* promised social advancement, and it
has been refused."

Camillus must have heard about it from Helena. As a
member of the Establishment, he seemed to feel personally
responsible. He scratched his nose; light gleamed on a
workaday garnet signet ring. "It's a misunderstanding, Marcus. It can be resolved."

"No, Domitian Caesar gave me a very clear ruling, and
when I discussed the matter with Titus last week he was unable to change that."

"Titus told me," answered the Senator. "Rulings do tend
to become immutable if they involve denying just rewards!"
His sense of humor was always refreshingly dry. "Well, tell
me if I can help. . . . I gather you're working on the law-and-
order issue at present?" So much for keeping the post-Balbinus investigation confidential.

"Yes, I'm on the special commission."

Camillus noticed my dark mood. "Not enjoying it?"

"Mixed feelings; mixed loyalties." The conversation had
shifted. The Senator and I were talking at a level that now
excluded Aelianus. I went back to one aspect of what Camillus had said: "I'm asking myself how much of my personal
chat with Titus Caesar he passed on, sir? Has he preempted
a private discussion I intended to have with you?"

Camillus smiled, waving a hand in acceptance of the fact
that he had been told he was to be a grandfather by someone
other than me. "I realized Titus was being premature."

"I'm sorry for it. You know how things work, sir."

"You had to seize your opportunity," he agreed. Well, for Helena's sake he would want me to have tried. Our relationship stayed easy. "Are you pleased?" he asked. I let a grin answer him. Then we both stopped looking so delighted, as like dutiful men we both considered the perils to Helena.

"I still think something can be sorted out for you, Marcus." Vespasian, like any good Roman, had his private clique of friends who advised him; the Senator was one of them, once close, and still consulted. It could be made to work on my behalf—if I could accept having strings pulled. The Senator knew my feelings about that. "Will you let me speak to the old man?"

"Better not." I smiled. Even with his personal interest, it was gracious of him to offer. But I had to do this myself. "My new assignment is a complex one. Let's see the results before I call in imperial favors!"

"Maybe you'd better leave my sister alone, then." Aelianus grappled himself back into the discussion even though unsure of its content.

"I note your advice," I said pleasantly. Suddenly I was too angry to carry on fielding his jibes. "I'm sorry you're distressed. I can see it must have been difficult, coming home from abroad to find that the respectable family you had left behind was now tainted with scandal." He began to speak. I stabbed the air with my finger. "The scandal I mean has nothing to do with your sister. I refer to the sad mess which brought me into contact with the Camilli in the first place, when various of your noble relations—now fortunately dead—engaged in a treasonous attempt of staggering ineptitude! Camillus Aelianus, before you embark on public life I suggest you ask your father to explain just how much the Emperor allowed to be covered up."

The jaw of the not so noble Aelianus had dropped open. Clearly he had not realized I knew about his family's near disgrace.

"Excuse me." I apologized briefly to his father, for I normally tried not to mention all this.

"Was the cover-up organized by you?" Aelianus was

catching on. But now he assumed Helena Justina had been presented to me in return for my silence.

"My job is to expose things. Still, I'm glad we had this opportunity to clear the air. . . . Philosophical insights are traditionally brought to light by men drinking at a symposium." Trying to improve the atmosphere, I raised my cup.

Aelianus glowered at me. "What exactly do you do, Falco?" Sometimes I wondered that myself.

"Nice of you to ask this time, before condemning me! I do what's needed—what nobody else is able or willing to tackle."

"Do you kill people?" He had no finesse.

"Not regularly. It's too much trouble making my peace with the gods afterwards."

I avoided looking at the Senator. He was sitting very silent. The last time I remembered killing a man, it was a thug who attacked Helena on her father's own doorstep. Camillus saw me do it. But there were other deaths, closely connected to that, which the Senator and I never talked about.

"It's a glorious thought." Aelianus was still sneering. "Some dogged lone operator attempting to right society's wrong without praise or pay!"

"Pure foolishness," I agreed briefly.

"Why do it?"

"Oh, the hope of gain."

"Strength of character?" The family irony had not entirely bypassed Aelianus.

"You've found me out. I'm a soft touch for ethical actions."

"And it's a short cut to the women too?"

"The very best of them . . . You'd better grit your teeth. I know I've found a good one, and I'm here to stay. My relationship with your sister is permanent. And you're going to be an uncle to an informer's son or daughter by next spring!"

Aelianus was still spluttering with disgust when Julia Justa and Helena sailed back to join us.

XLIV

Repairing to the dining room enabled me to lighten the mood with tasteful praise for a recent repaint (heavy stuff, black dadoes and perspectives in deep red and gold). They must have been taken in by a contractor who dreamed of decorating Oriental tombs.

The Senator's wife declared coolly that we would dine now, without Justinus. She showed no particular emotion after her conversation with Helena about our coming baby; she must have been prepared for it. So much so that she had taken over the skip orphan as if to accustom herself to playing with a child she would rather avoid. Her sole concern now was to get through the celebration without embarrassment. The noble Julia had the suffering air of a woman who was doing her best even though everyone around her seemed determined to ruin her carefully planned day.

She had a fine sense of decency. I made sure I stepped forwards and handed her kindly to her dining couch. In return, Julia Justa politely insisted that I take the couch next to her. I was assuming the air of a guest who was a *very* close family friend. One reason I did this was to annoy Aelianus by letting him think he had been superseded—in his own home and in front of all the slaves and family freedmen and -

women—by his sister's unsuitable lover flagrantly adopting the role of a respected son-in-law.

I managed to maintain the fraud of gravitas right up until I caught Helena's eyes. I lost control when she winked at me.

Food and wine always help. Besides, it was Helena's birthday, and we were people who all loved her. (Even her tense brother must have cared for her as much as his own right to a scandal-free public life.)

The food was probably better than that normally served in that cash-strapped household. I was particularly taken by the lobster dumplings, which came in the first course along with Colymbadian olives and various pork nuggets. Helena and I managed to put in a fair ration of travelers' tales concerning food, enabling us to sidestep the dubious theatrical aspect of our tour in Syria. The centerpiece of the main course was a small whole boar in nut sauce, a dish which I freely admitted rarely featured in the cook's repertoire at my own house.

"We don't often have it here!" admitted the Senator, helping me to a vintage that I described as "suave."

"Don't you mean smooth?" Aelianus was still trying to be caustic even when he had the bright blue stains of peas indigo spilled down his tunic. I had already pointed this out, while passing on my tip that worldly diners refuse tidbits served in squid's ink.

"No, I mean warm and sophisticated with a cynically dangerous undertone that may trip some of us down stairs before the night's up."

"Are you a connoisseur, Falco?"

"No, but I drink with one. I know the rhetoric," I said, warning him off if he meant to indulge in snobbery. "My friend Petronius Longus can convincingly distinguish between Falernian from the hilltops, the middle slopes, and the plain. I can't, though I'm always pleased to let him serve me samples as he tries to train my palate. . . . His dream is to get hold of some vinum Oppianum."

Aelianus was sufficiently tipsy to admit his ignorance: "What's that?"

"It was a legendary year, named after the consul, of course: Oppianus, the man who killed Gaius Gracchus."

"Why, that must be nearly two centuries old!" exclaimed the Senator. "If he finds any, try to get me a taste!"

"It may happen. According to Petronius, the vintage was so good stocks were hoarded, and they occasionally surface."

"Would it be drinkable?" Helena asked.

"Probably not. A buff like Petro would gulp down the sludge, and get drunk on the mere cachet."

"Buffs don't gulp." She laughed, correcting me. "Buffs breathe, savor, mull, then compete at producing flowery descriptions—"

"And get very sick."

The Senator laughed, enjoying our repartee. "Try this, Marcus. It's Guaranum, only produced in a very small quantity from the ridge above Baiae, where the air must be salty, the earth sulfurous, and the grapes encouraged by the happy screams of the girls being seduced by gigolos in the bathing spa."

"Oh really, Decimus!" mouthed Julia Justa, though her goblet was out for a refill. She graciously received her wine from her husband, then returned her attention to the skip babe, whose quiet demeanor in public had endeared him to her. She was shaking his rattle, a pottery pig with pebbles inside that Helena had bought from a market stall.

"Oh, Mama!" Aelianus shuddered. "He could have come from anywhere."

Angry, I had to bury my nose in my cup. Luckily the Guaranum was rich and full-bodied, a consoling wine.

"His clothes were fine quality. We think he came from a good home," Helena countered coldly. "Not that that's important; the child is lost, and something must be done for him." Her mother, who had known Helena long enough, deftly ignored the implication that something should be done by the Camilli.

"If his home was as good as all that," Aelianus persisted, "there would be a public outcry from the people he was stolen from."

"I doubt it!" his mother said abruptly. She moved the rattle, first shaking it to one side, then bringing it in front of the child's face. We watched him react by waving his hands. Helena's mother was an intelligent woman. She had spotted what even mine had missed. The babe did not respond until the rattle actually came into his view. Then Julia Justa told us crisply, "His family may have lost him deliberately. This baby is deaf!"

I dropped my head, covering my eyes. If he was deaf at birth, he would be dumb too. He was damned. People would write him off as an idiot. There was no chance of finding him a civilized home.

"Jupiter, Falco!" Aelianus crowed. "Whatever are you going to do?"

"Oh, do stop sniping!" His mother turned on her couch back to the table. "Marcus will produce an apt, elegant solution. Marcus always does." It was difficult to tell whether she was reproving her son, or grumbling about me.

I raised my winecup to the lady and watched Helena frowning over the child's sad plight. We were two ticks away from giving him a home ourselves.

I was saved by a distraction. The useless door porter had let a drunk into the house. A tall, shyly attractive young man wandered into the dining room, crashing into a side table on his way; Quintus Camillus Justinus had finally shown up.

Blinking in the lamplight, he bent to kiss his mother, not a good thought. He then tickled the sole of Helena's foot, causing her to kick out wildly. She caught Aelianus a nasty blow on the ear as he sat up to say something insulting. With the intense care of the far from sober, Justinus placed two packages before his sister, then made a sudden lunge and kissed her too. Helena biffed him away.

Impervious to atmosphere, Justinus regained his balance like a tightrope walker, then staggered around the couches and threw himself on the empty one alongside me. I braced myself as he flung an arm across my shoulders. "Marcus! How are you surviving the party?" He was beyond help.

I made soothing noises while Helena sent me urgent signals to feed him. Since it was me he would throw up on, I had an interest in limiting his intake.

"Sorry, I'm a trifle tardy. I've been in the Saepta looking for a gift."

My heart sank even further. "*Where* at the Saepta?" I already had glimmerings of why young Justinus was late and drunk tonight.

"Oh, you'll know, Falco! I was wandering, then I saw a name I recognized and introduced myself. . . . A wonderful auctioneer," Justinus told his brother. Aelianus was grinning; the son whose sins still lay undiscovered watching the debauched noisily sink himself. I absorbed the ominous news that it was my not-so-wonderful pa who had been filling up the golden boy.

Helena broke in brightly. "We missed you! Sweetheart, is this my gift?"

"The small one," Justinus enunciated clearly. "A bijou from your devoted brother."

"Thank you very much."

"The large heavy item is sent to you with compliments from my excellent friend Didius Geminus."

"Is that," jeered Aelianus, "the man who gave you so much wine?"

"My father," I snapped. Julia Justa's face had frozen. I pressed on feebly. "Didius Geminus likes his customers in a weak state. I counsel you, Aelianus, against tippling with an auctioneer. As you see, your brother now needs a quiet lie-down—and the gods only know what he's spent!"

"Very reasonable," Justinus burbled happily. He at least had taken my advice. He was lying down. Unhappily, it was in the sweetmeat display.

We left him there. It seemed kindest.

Helena tried to look jolly as she unwrapped her brother's gift. It was an extremely attractive mirror, decorated in Celtic style with magnificent swirls and curlicues of foliage. She examined her face in it, trying to forget her younger brother's condition.

"And your father has sent Helena a present too, Marcus!" Julia Justa was much cheered by thinking the Didius family knew about buying off would-be relations. Helena obediently unwrapped it.

"My father thinks a lot of Helena," I said weakly.

That was evident. Pa had sent her a highly superior (wincingly expensive) jewel casket. Not too big—nothing brash—but a beautiful example of cedarwood. Every corner had elaborate bronze fittings; there were miniature feet, a neat fastener, and a perfect lock with a swinging escutcheon.

"Oh, the darling!" Oh the bastard. He had completely ignored my own predicament. Not even a word of apology.

It seemed a moment for toasts. Wine was being poured by slaves who wanted a chance to crane at the young mistress's gifts. Various hairpin pots and tweezer sets were also being proffered by ancient slaves who had once nursed her. "Happy birthday!" exclaimed Helena's father, who for all his air of innocence knew how to cash in on a good mood.

Helena had found the casket key on a skein of wool. Even the key was a delight, a tiny three-pronged fancy set into a finger ring. "There's a note inside for you, Marcus." She tossed across a scrap of recycled scroll. I did not wish to communicate with Pa; I pretended to glance at it, then I burned it on a handy lamp.

Helena delved inside the box, deep in its handsome interior. I was in two minds to glide off somewhere, pretending to look for the latrine. Manners won; I bit a pastry instead. Honey oozed down my chin.

I saw Helena's face change. There must be more; the amazing box had contents. My heart started bumping angrily. She began lifting something out, and immediately I realized what it was. Unexpected gold scintillations flickered on the casket's lid. Light fluttered like butterflies over her skin. Helena exclaimed in astonishment, "Oh!" Then she lifted an object of breathtaking beauty.

Around the table silence fell.

Slowly, as if terrified she would damage something, Helena placed her gift on the table. Light still glittered from a hundred minutely teased pieces of gold. Helena turned to me. Everyone else was looking at her present. I didn't need to. My concern was watching her.

It was a crown. It was very old. It was Greek. It had once been a prize at some classical games, in the era when athletes were perfect in both body and mind. It was composed of exquisitely suspended leaves and acorns, held on gold wires so delicate they trembled merely in the air. Among the glittering twigs that formed it crouched perfectly shaped insects, and a small golden bee perched over the clasp.

Helena's mother tried to pull herself together. "Oh, Helena Justina, I am not sure you should accept this. . . ." Her voice faltered. "Marcus, you have an extremely generous father."

There was no doubting the reproof: It was too much. The common Didii had behaved crassly. From a mere relative of a purely unofficial son-in-law, such a gift was gross.

I smiled at Helena gently. Her soft dark eyes were full of tears. She knew. She was touching her little finger to one iridescent cicada as it hid beneath an oak leaf, caressing it as gently as if it were a newborn baby's cheek. "Pa has his moments," I told her quietly. "He has style, and taste, and, as your mother mentions, he can be extremely generous. Thoughtful too. He's obviously gone to a lot of trouble to find exactly the right box."

"The crown is wonderful," she said.

"You're a wonderful girl."

"She cannot possibly accept it," insisted her mother, more firmly.

I raised an eyebrow. "Well, can you, fruit?"

Helena Justina smiled at me. She paid no attention at all to her family, but suddenly they understood.

The moment, which had become precious and tender, disintegrated with a lurch. Quintus had roused himself, his face lightly dusted with honey and cinnamon. "Marcus, a message. Your father says sorry he made you sweat. He had to get the crown back from the man he had sold it to." What an unspeakable degenerate. Justinus burbled on as I ground my teeth. "There won't be any comeback—Geminus told the silly bastard he was retrieving it because he'd just seen on a vigiles' listing that it's stolen property. . . ."

Well thank you, Pa!

Helena giggled. Some members of her family may have found that unexpected. She said to me gravely, "I wonder, purely from commercial interest, whether your father screwed as much out of the silly bastard as some other seller had already squeezed from you?"

"Probably not. The disreputable Damascan whose retirement in comfort I've asssured could see I was buying out of love."

I stood and raised my winecup formally, calling upon everyone to join in my toast. "According to the Damascan, this crown was once a prize in the Nemean Games. A prize worthy only of the finest, my darling."

Her noble family had the grace to murmur agreement, pretty well spontaneously. We drank to Helena Justina in the robustly acceptable Guaranum that her father had saved to celebrate her special day. "Helena Justina, daughter of Camillus Verus and heart's joy of Didius Falco, greetings on your anniversary!"

"Happy birthday, Helena," cried Julia Justa. After which, since she could not reach her daughter, whose dining couch was too far from her, the noble matron shed a seemly tear, then turned on her scented elbow and kissed me.

XLV

It was a night to remember, but once we returned to our own apartment I had to drag myself back to the real and sordid world.

The two watches of the Fourth Cohort must have spent those hours of darkness prowling the violent Aventine Hill, expecting to meet horror again. I knew Petronius would be out with them at least part of the time. Martinus, his deputy, would bestir himself to cover another section of the night watch. Fusculus would be there as well. One or other of them might take Porcius, the recruit. Sergius, their man with the whip who enjoyed his job, would be along somewhere looking for careless householders to thrash—and hoping to try his talents on a killer. I had a good idea that if they ever found out who had murdered the brother of Scythax, someone would simply disappear off the streets. The Fourth were in a mood for rough justice. Maybe that was why, when I found I could not sleep, instead of walking out to join them in their grim patrol I stayed at home in bed.

Eventually, my restlessness disturbed Helena.

"Hush, you'll wake the baby."

"Not this one, love."

"Then you'll wake the dog."

The dog, who was squashing my feet again, shuffled to reinforce the point. "Watch yourself, furry! One false move, and I'll turn you into bootliners."

Winding herself into my arms more closely, Helena lay silent. I knew her well enough to hear her thoughts working, well enough to know what thoughts they were. "Your mother's right. When we have time to give to the babe, we'll find him a home."

Unconvinced, Helena went on quietly worrying.

I tried again. "Don't fret. The baby's safe here. Let's worry about Tertulla. Tell me how you got on today with Gaius Baebius. How many parents did you manage to talk to? Any success?"

"Not much." In a low voice, Helena recounted her adventures. "There are five families on the list which Petronius gave me. I managed to speak to someone at four of the houses. Only one refused me entry altogether; they are extremely superior."

"Why do they live on the Aventine then?"

"They must have lived here since they looked down their noses at Romulus."

"Well if anyone can tweak noses, it's you! What about the rest?"

"I saw one mother personally. She met me in a room on her own, as if she did not want anyone to know. But even then she just hissed angrily that it was all sorted out now. She was sorry for our troubles, but could not involve herself."

"Was she frightened?"

"Very, I should say."

"It fits. Kidnappers tend to say don't go to the law or we'll be back. Did she let you see the child?"

"Oh absolutely not! At two other houses I ran into a reception committee of slaves—polite but distant, and no help. At the fourth house the mother refused to see me, but I happened to meet a nursemaid. As I was being seen out by a steward, she was taking the child for a walk."

"What age was the child?"

"A three-year-old boy. I followed his nurse from the

house, and inveigled her into conversation as we went down the street. She was horrified to hear of another case, and let me engage her sympathy. She admitted the boy had been taken away—on a similar walk, so she was escorted everywhere now by slaves. That meant they were breathing down our necks, and I only had a short opportunity to talk to her. Her story was quite helpful, and it confirms Petro's theory as far as it goes. The child was snatched when her back was turned, as she bought something at a garment shop. She turned around seconds later, and little Tiberius had vanished. There was complete panic in the household overnight; the vigiles were informed, as we know; the father also had all his slaves out combing the streets. Then next day everything abruptly cooled down. The nurse was never told why. The child's parents became withdrawn and secretive. There was a great deal of tension in the household, but the street searches were ended. She thinks the family banker visited."

"That's significant." Lucky too; the father could as easily have arranged a ransom with the banker in the Forum, and we would have missed this. "It's a useful detail. How was little Tiberius returned?"

"The father went out with the banker, and came home carrying the child. The household were informed that someone had found him by accident. Afterwards they were discouraged from gossiping. That was all I could learn."

"It's enough. Was the child old enough to talk about what happened?"

"He looked a dim little overfed soul. I suppose he can talk, but we'd never be allowed to get at him, especially now. There's a close guard kept, and the escort soon became twitchy about me conversing with the nurse. I was lucky to find out what I did—and lucky Gaius Baebius had the sense to keep out of the way."

"The great pudding."

"He means well, Marcus. He's terribly concerned about Tertulla, and very angry that her own father has never put in an appearance to look for her."

"This must be the first time one of my brothers-in-law despises another even more than I do! All right, so Gaius Baebius can't choose a wife or a watchdog, but he has a heart of gold. Anyone who'll bat his head against a wall trying to complain about Lollius deserves a laurel wreath. Is he coming to help you tomorrow? Are you intending to tackle the fifth house again?"

"Gaius is scheduled for shift work at Ostia. Yes, I'll try the last family a second time."

"Not on your own."

"I wasn't intending that. These are the snooty ones. This time I'm taking Mother's litter and a train of Father's slaves. I'll experiment with announcing myself more formally as a woman of respectable background."

Helena had spoken seriously, intent on her task. Trusting her good sense and flair, I could afford to be frivolous. "Try wearing your Greek crown!"

She chortled. Then Helena Justina set about thanking me for her antique treasure from Damascus in a way that cleared my mind of most of its troubles, and eventually let me find peace and sleep.

If we needed confirmation that a kidnap gang was active, it came first thing next day. We were still at breakfast. Light footsteps scuffed the stairs outside, then, while I was wondering whether to grab a bread-roll knife in case the Miller and Little Icarus had returned, young Justinus bowled in.

We relaxed.

"Quintus! Greetings, you bibulous rascal!"

"Falco, there's been a terrible mistake!"

"Drinking with my father always is. Cool off. Your purse is deep enough; you'll get over it."

He looked sheepish. "I think I've endured enough reproaches."

"I bet."

"There's been a misunderstanding, one that concerns you."

"What's new?"

"No, listen," he burst out excitedly. "We owe you an apology."

"I'm all ears, Quintus."

Then he told us that while we had been dining at the Camillus house last night, a strange messenger had called.

He brought a note, which the Senator's secretary took in and read. Since there was a family party in progress, the secretary dealt with it himself. The note asked for money for the return of the child; the child's name was unfamiliar to the scribe. He angrily sent the messenger away, and only when the strange story was mentioned this morning had Camillus Verus realized the truth. Luckily we had been talking about Tertulla during our visit.

"Jupiter! At least we can tell Galla she's probably alive. But what a cheek! Helena Justina, someone has been trying to put pressure on your father to ransom my niece!" As if our relationship did not entail enough embarrassments.

Needless to say, no clues had been retained. The ransom note had been thrust back at the seedy messenger; there was no useful description of the man; and nobody had watched to see which way he went after he was turned out of the house. Maybe the kidnappers would try again. Maybe they would have the sense to approach Helena Justina or me. Maybe they would lose patience, and just hand Tertulla back.

Maybe.

XLVI

At the Thirteenth-sector patrol house moods were as dour as mine. It had been a quiet night on the Aventine. A normal one, anyway. Apart from eighteen house fires, arson in a grain warehouse, a rash of burglaries, several street fights related to the festival of the Armilustrium, three suicides dragged from the Tiber, and two more angry women whose nicely airing counterpanes had been stolen from balcony parapets, nothing had disturbed the peace.

I told Petro what we had discovered about the kidnaps, and he told me what I could do with my news.

"Don't fob me off. Tertulla is an official case, Petro. Galla demands an inquiry."

"She's on our daily list."

"Damn the list. This needs a vigorous follow-up."

"Give me a name or a suspect house, and I'll send in men."

"It's someone with good information. It's someone who knows enough to connect my ghastly sister's snotty truant with the fact that my girlfriend comes from a family with status." Not enough information, however, to realize that the illustrious Camilli had no spare cash.

"They could have heard it at any barber's or bread shop."

"Are you sure? Someone out on the streets knows more than Helena's father's secretary does. He sent the runner away!"

"I presume you've made sure next time he'll put a leg ring on the messenger and pass him to us."

"She's a seven-year-old girl. She ought to be a priority."

"My priority is set by Rubella. My priority is eliminating the gangs."

His scowl told me different. Petro had fathered girls himself. He knew all the doubts and dreads when a female child went missing. He quieted down, told me Helena had done splendidly over questioning the other families, and remarked that I didn't deserve her. With her help, and now the attempt to involve her father, at least we knew what was going on.

"That's no consolation to my sister, and you know it!"

Petro promised that as soon as he had time he would look into it. As things were, he would never have time. We both knew that.

There had been no more raids and no more murders. That was a relief—yet it meant we had no more to go on. Petronius and the squad were back with the dire, depressing task of flogging once more through old evidence. Worrying at empty details. Trying to tease an extra ounce of significance from useless facts.

"Where's the black boy?" Petro demanded suddenly. "The Nonnius slave?"

"With Porcius."

"Then where's Porcius?"

Porcius was summoned from fending off counterpane victims. He came into the interrogation room nervously. He must have known Petro was the calmest man on the Aventine, but he could sense short temper tingling in the air like the night before a blinding storm.

"I thought I told you to make friends with the squealer's attendant?"

"Yes, Chief. I'm doing it."

"Well?"

"He's very timid, Chief."

"I don't care if he wets himself every half-hour. Mop him dry and keep up the pressure. I want to know what he saw."

"He talks a lot of gibberish, Chief."

"We can find a translator if he lacks Latin—"

"It's not his Latin—"

"Don't nitpick. Porcius, this is Rome. We can find a trustworthy translator for any language in the world."

"Chief, he's just terrified." Like himself, Porcius could have said.

"So he's no use? I don't accept it. Surely if he was hiding right under the couch where we found him he could have glimpsed a few feet. Did he hear anything said? Can he not suggest how many abductors came to the house? Were *they* talking any foreign languages?"

Porcius blinked a bit, but pulled himself together. He must have acquired some feeling of responsibility for the tiny slave who had been placed in his care. Now he tried standing up to Petro—not a good idea. "Chief, I'm working on him. I've got a plan to lure him into talking usefully. He was brave enough the night it happened, actually; he must have gone into shock afterwards. He loved his master. He was loyal. So far I've found out that when Nonnius was taken, the boy ran after the group who grabbed him—"

Listening from the sidelines, I felt myself wince. Petronius Longus leaped to his feet. Already under stress, he picked up the last sentence and broke into a froth. "What's this? I don't believe I heard you!"

Porcius realized his error and stopped.

Petronius had needed an outlet for his frustration. The well-meaning recruit made an easy target. Petro was beside himself. "How long have you been holding this information, Porcius? Are you looking for early retirement? We have dead men and stripped buildings all over Rome, and you're prancing about like a circus horse 'working on' the only witness! Get this straight: If you serve in this cohort's investigation unit, you're in a team, a team headed by me. You don't bury yourself in private schemes; you report every detail—relevant or irrelevant—to your colleagues and to me!"

"You'll burst something," I muttered.

"Stuff you, Falco!" The interruption had calmed him

slightly. Even so, he slammed his hand against the wall. It must have hurt. "Porcius, don't stand there buckling like a bale of felt. I want to hear exactly what the slave has told you—every detail—and you'd better be fast. After that I'm going to hang you from the Probus Bridge by your boot thongs just low enough to drown you slowly when the tide comes in!"

He was still so angry he had to do something more vigorous. It was either hit Porcius or break the furniture. He seized a stool and flung it splintering against the door.

There was a long silence. The entire station house grew still. The normal ranting of victims pleading for urgent inquiries and the racket from last night's prisoners abruptly stopped. The prisoners thought some suspect was being hurled around a cell. They thought they might be next.

Porcius had his eyes closed. He knew if anyone got pounded it was going to be him.

Fusculus and Martinus, who were tough nuts, appeared in the doorway looking openly curious. I commented gently, "What with the seating that's broken by flying boulders thrown in by your neighbors and the bum props you destroy yourselves, the Fourth's office equipment bill must be rocketing these days." Petronius, red in the face and ashamed of the lapse, fought to calm down.

Porcius, to his credit, did not waver. He was white as ash. I could see his knuckles shining as he gripped his fists beside his tunic seams. He had just been bawled at and attacked by a man who was famous for never losing his temper. He knew Fusculus and Martinus were playing about behind him, pretending to give his achievements admiring looks.

He took a deep breath. "The slave boy saw Nonnius being dragged into a house."

I watched my old friend forcibly restrain himself. "Tell me about it," said Petronius, ominously quiet.

"He doesn't know whose dwelling it was. He was a house slave. Normally he hardly ever went out."

"But we found him the next day in his master's place. If

he had followed the abductors, how had he got home again?"

"He says he wandered about for hours, then found his way back by accident. When we arrived to investigate he had only just reached home. The front door had been smashed to pieces, so he crept inside without anybody seeing him."

"Right. So go back to the moment it first happened. He witnessed the abduction. What exactly did he see?"

"He was sleeping in a side room and ran out when he heard the noise. He then saw Nonnius dragged from his bedroom by several men. At that point Nonnius was gagged with something like a scarf. He was rushed out of the house, and marched through the streets. He was taken into this other house. The lad hid outside for a long time, then saw a body dragged out backwards by the feet. That was when he panicked. He guessed it must be his master. He was so afraid that he ran away."

"He didn't see the body dumped in the Forum Boarium?"

"He says not," declared Porcius.

"Believe him?"

"Yes. My guess is that if he had known where the body ended up, we'd have found him crying beside it instead of back at home."

Petronius Longus folded his arms. He threw back his head, staring at the stained daub of the patrol house roof. Porcius managed to remain silent while his chief pondered. Martinus, Fusculus, and I exchanged looks.

Petronius lowered his gaze and applied it to the stricken recruit.

"So you discovered all this in the course of your independent plan to 'lure' the witness into telling more. Now we're all going to help you resolve things, Porcius. So tell us—what exactly was your plan?"

"I thought"—Porcius gulped miserably—"I could attempt to get the slave boy to identify the house where Nonnius was killed. I thought, so as not to confuse him by going through a lot of streets, I could put him in a closed carrying chair and take him to a selection of likely spots—show him the homes of specific suspects."

"I see."

As Petronius glared at their unhappy young colleague, Fusculus risked chirping, "So what's the plan now, Chief?"

"Pretty obvious," snapped Petro. "We put the black child in a carrying chair and show him suspects' homes! Our young colleague may be irresponsible, but his idea has a certain charm. Where's the boy, Porcius?"

"I'll fetch him—"

"No. Fusculus will fetch him. You'll tell Fusculus where he has to go." This distrust of Porcius seemed hard. Petronius strode from the room before anyone could attempt to arbitrate.

Porcius appealed to me for sympathy: "I thought it was a good idea!"

I clapped him on the shoulder. "Don't worry about it. But on this case, protect your back, Porcius. Don't bother having big ideas."

Fusculus started sauntering off; he turned back and beckoned slowly to Porcius, who scuttled after him. Martinus stayed, grinning at me.

"Resignation time?" I asked, nodding after the anguished figure of the recruit.

"Who knows? Nice lad," Martinus told me. "Sends all his pay home to his mother, doesn't play around with women, doesn't leer at the male scribes, doesn't have smelly feet or tell bad jokes, turns up for his shift on time. Seems absolutely nothing wrong with him."

"Oh, right!" I remarked, pretending to catch on at last. "I can see he was never going to fit in with this cohort!"

I was joking, but the angry scene had left a bad feeling. The pressure was on now. I would hate to think any part of the Fourth might be cracking up. Especially the part that Petronius Longus ran—and most of all Petronius himself.

The Nonnius slave was taken to see the houses of a couple of big gang leaders, which at least served to eliminate rivals to the Balbinus empire; he recognized none of them. He was shown Plato's Academy; still nothing. He was then asked to look at the lovely homes of Flaccida and Milvia. He saw Milvia's first, and wasn't sure. He made up his mind the minute we let him out of the chair at Flaccida's.

He was eight years old, still in shock, and incoherent with fright. There was no way we could have used his evidence in court, even if the law had allowed it. As it was, we could only quote him if we extracted his story under torture. Petro decided not to try. One glimpse of Sergius wielding the red-hot forceps, and this fragile soul was likely to drop off his twig.

There were plenty of problems with the boy's story. A barrister would tear it to shreds. Nonnius had been taken away not by Flaccida herself, but by a group of men, none of whom we could yet identify. The slave boy could give no descriptions. Petronius was in no position to make arrests. But for our own purposes, although we could not *prove* Flaccida had been involved in anything, at least we knew: Nonnius Albius had been murdered at her house. Work on the case had begun to simplify at last.

"So what are you going to do?" I asked Petro as we walked back towards the patrol house. "Interview Flaccida?"

"You said you did that, Falco."

"I wasn't able to make her sweat. It was before we had a lead on the Nonnius death. I couldn't frighten her with a witness."

"Neither can I." Petronius was a realist.

"So you leave her bust up on its pedestal?"

He stopped on a street corner, stretching his neck. He rubbed one hand all around inside the neck of his tunic, as if the hem was causing a rash. What irritated Petro was something else. He hated to see criminals getting away with a crime.

"The bust can keep its station—but I'll chuck a few stones at it. Flaccida's the one to work on, though we need something indirect. Forget Nonnius. I'll nail Flaccida for him one day. And I'll nail her for Alexander too, though as yet don't ask me how." I could see he had made up his mind. "We've made an advance on the murders. Let's go back to the Emporium and Saepta thefts, Falco. Let's see if we can trace your father's pretty Syrian glass."

I had known him long enough to recognize which approach he was planning. "You reckon our brothel prank is now safely forgotten, and you can drag me off on some new escapade."

"Exactly. Comb your hair for once, Falco. You and I are going to spend the afternoon chatting like dangerous degenerates with lovely little Milvia!"

XLVII

Milvia was at home. This confirmed my previous impression that she led a lonely life. It seemed she rarely went out. Still, staying in this afternoon had brought the lucky girl the pair of us.

"I'm getting too old for this," I joked as Petro and I waited for her to be told her good fortune. No doubt she wanted to jump into her nicest frock.

"You've forgotten how. Just follow my lead."

We sat up and tried looking like sober citizens as Milvia tripped through the door.

She seemed delighted to see us. Until she rushed in, all pleated white stoles and dainty ribbons, I had forgotten quite what a pretty girl she was. This was certainly more pleasant than exchanging barbs with that hard nut her mother. Of course we did not place too much faith in Milvia; in our time, Petronius and I had been flattered then dumped in a midden by plenty of round-eyed, honest-looking girls.

When we asked her again about the glass flagon, she told the same tale: a present from someone to Florius. Petronius demanded a sight of her household shelves. "But you have looked at them!" Milvia cried wonderingly.

"I'd like to look again." Petronius Longus could manage

to sound as stern as if he were inspecting an unauthorized standpipe on an aqueduct, yet with a subtle hint of approving comment on a woman's physique. What a dog.

Milvia was worried. This was good. Milvia would complain to her mother; Flaccida, not having been here, would find that very disconcerting. Flaccida would wonder why Milvia had been singled out for an extra visit, and what dangerous hints Milvia might have given away.

"Falco is going to take a look with me this time."

"Oh, you're the nice one!" Milvia obviously remembered me. Petronius gave me a cheesy grin, then dug me sharply in the small of the back as we marched to the kitchen.

For about an hour we gravely surveyed miles of expensive tableware on shelves, in cupboards, displayed formally on buffets, or tucked tidily into niches. Redware and lead glaze, glass and gilded metalware. It was all in sets, and the sets were meant for civic banquets of fifty people or so. It made a poor comparison with the wonky shelf of bowls Helena and I owned at Fountain Court—barely enough for a quiet one-course supper for two people, especially if they were entertaining a foundling and a hungry new dog.

There was no glass that I recognized. Since the house had already been searched by the Fourth Cohort, I expected no surprises. I gave Petro the headshake several times, but he seemed in no hurry to leave. He smiled at Milvia, who had been showing off the household goods herself. "Let's return to the salon and get some details straight. . . ."

We trooped back and sat down. It was a decorous room in whites, greens, and blues, but I hate Egyptian summerhouse furniture that looks so light the legs may snap if you wriggle. Its pert young owner was not my kind of girl either. Once I had liked the ones who smile a lot and look admiring, but I had grown up since then. I was starting to feel alone in this sophisticated attitude.

Petro had on his stubborn look. Milvia was unreliable, but just the kind of bright-eyed puppet Petro always wanted to discuss the weather with. The whole situation took me back ten years. It was like trying to drag him out of a British meadmaker's hovel once the biddy in charge had swung her golden plaits at him. As always, I was at a loss how to deal with it. When he was in this mood, tutting and mentioning other social engagements would only make him linger. I had already dragged his wife into the conversation, in some forced context to do with tureens. Any more would just make me sound like a surly prude.

I would not have minded, but as an informer I was the one who had always had to fight off a reputation for chasing women.

"Nice room!" Petronius smiled, glancing around. He was very relaxed. He spoke in a kindly, reassuring tone, and Milvia smiled back at him.

"Watch out," I muttered. "He'll try to sell you mediocre frescoes if you show an interest."

Milvia giggled at me. "You two are not like law officers at all!"

"Is that right?"

Petronius smirked at me, then set about some genuine work. "So. Let's just get this straight. The flagon you gave to Didius Falco—"

"I gave it to his charming colleague, actually. Is the glass flagon what your inquiries have all been about?"

"Charming colleague, Falco?" Petro asked.

"Helena." I owned up. Well, it wiped off his smirk.

"After all, I had been talking to her mostly," Milvia carried on.

"Had you really?"

"We all have our methods," I told Petro.

"The flagon." Petro began again with Milvia, looking dangerous.

"Was brought home by my husband."

"Was brought home by Florius. Florius had it from?"

"From somebody he knows."

"A mysterious benefactor. Have you asked him who?"

"Why should I? He seemed rather vague."

"Does Florius keep things to himself?"

"Not particularly."

"Do you and your husband discuss his daily business?"

"No, not much." Milvia glanced down at her lap, aware how her answer could be interpreted.

"That's very sad," Petronius Longus commented somberly.

"Don't be snide," I said.

"It was a straight comment."

"There's nothing wrong!" Milvia cried defensively.

"But you're not close," Petro decided, looking pleased about it.

"We are perfect friends."

"And some other friend of Florius gives him expensive gifts."

There was a small pause.

Milvia looked from Petronius to me and back again. "You *are* proper law officers."

"If you're honest that won't worry you. Was it a woman?" I inquired. There was no point now being soft on her. It was possible, if her marriage mattered to her, that we had just destroyed it in a couple of suggestive remarks. Even if Florius was as chaste as dew, we might have ruined the relationship. Suspicion is an evil ingredient in any match.

"Could your husband be taking gifts from a woman?" I pressed Milvia again.

"I didn't think so."

"But could he have been?"

"That was not the impression he gave me. Did you have any particular woman in mind?" Milvia managed to riposte proudly.

"No. But no doubt now you will ask Florius." That came from Petronius.

"I think," Milvia decided, more firmly than I would have expected, "if you want to know, you should ask Florius yourself."

Petronius smiled quietly. "I shall do that."

But Florius was not at home.

Petronius was now in a tenacious mood. Nothing would put him off until he traced the flagon right back from its arrival in this house to when I first left the glass with Pa at the Emporium. When we came out of the house he told me he intended to return there that evening to tackle Florius in person. I naturally started making arrangements to come with him, but he reckoned that unnecessary. Florius, apparently, was viewed by the watch as a soft custard; a witness would be superfluous.

"Hah! Don't come the innocent—I know what that means, you gigolo!"

Petro graciously suggested that instead of spreading slander I could devote some time to the search for my niece.

In fact I went to the Temple of Castor baths, where I gave a couple of useful hours to exercise with Glaucus. My shoulder still felt delicate, but I managed to work on the rest. I wanted to be fit. I felt we were starting to twist the tensioning cord on the whole inquiry now. I could tell Petronius shared some of this feeling, though if his idea of getting fit was a romantic interlude, he was welcome to Milvia.

We were both on the alert, with that special edge that only comes when action is just around the corner. Neither Petro nor I was the least prepared for what actually happened next.

XLVIII

When I reached the apartment, I found we had visitors who were guaranteed to undo all the benefits of my bath and training session. I had walked in before I realized, or I would have turned tail quietly and fled. Too late: I found Helena talking in subdued tones to my brother-in-law Gaius Baebius. Gaius had brought along my sister Junia. I immediately noticed they had left their dog Ajax at home. The absence of Ajax warned me of trouble. I assumed something dire had been discovered in connection with Tertulla, but there had been no further news; the trouble Gaius Baebius was bringing turned out to be worse.

Everyone had been waiting for me. It was lucky Petronius and I had not decided to bathe together and have a long session in a wine bar. (For some unusual reason Petro had not even wanted a drink.)

In the apartment the atmosphere was strained. Junia had the skip baby across her bony knees; Helena was telling her his story, as a polite way of filling in time. Gaius Baebius, sitting upright with a superior expression, was dressed in a toga. Not even this peculiarly formal character had ever been known to don traditional dress before calling at Fountain Court.

"Gaius! What are you all wrapped up like a parcel for? And why are you here, anyway? I was told you were working at Ostia."

A worrying thought struck me, that Gaius and Junia might want to foster the skip babe. It was nothing so simple, though finding out took willpower.

"I went to Ostia this morning," Gaius said. That explained nothing. Yet somehow he managed to give his routine trip to work a resonant significance.

I sighed and gave up. Persuading Gaius Baebius to tell a five-minute tale normally took about three days.

I hung my cloak on a peg, flopped on the floor (since all the seats were taken), grabbed the baby from Junia, and started playing with him and Nux.

"Marcus!" said Helena, in a light, warning voice.

"What's up?" I immediately stopped playing camels with the babe, though Nux had less sense and carried on pretending to hunt me like a wild boar. This dog would have to be put through a course on domestic etiquette. Maybe a better solution would be to get rid of the dog. (Maybe Gaius and Junia would like to foster *her*.)

"Marcus, Gaius Baebius has to visit an official. He wants to ask if you'll go with him."

"Well, I just wondered if you could tell me the name," Gaius demurred, as I was fending off the crazy dog.

"Whose name?"

"The tribune of the Fourth Cohort of the vigiles."

"Marcus Rubella. He's a misery. Don't have anything to do with him."

"I need to. The customs force have a report to make."

"In full formal dress? What's up, Gaius? Is this something sensitive?"

On reflection it had to be, if those plodders in the taxation force had sent a supervisor back to Rome before the end of his shift. Gaius Baebius was also clearly disturbed by his task.

I stood up and straightened my tunic. I gave Junia the baby to hold again. Helena quietly squashed along a bench, leaving me room to perch on the end of it close to Gaius. That big wheat pudding was sitting on a stool, so he was lower than me. It made him vulnerable to stern treatment. Gaius knew that. He was looking uncomfortable.

I tapped him on the knee and lowered my voice into friendly cajolement. "What's the game, Gaius?"

"It's a confidential matter."

"You can tell me. Maybe I already know. Is it graft?"

He looked surprised. "No, nothing like that."

"One of the inspectors made a nasty discovery," interrupted Junia.

My sister Junia was an impatient, supercilious piece. She had a thin face, a skinny frame, and a washed-out character to match. She wound her black hair into tight plaits pinned around her head, with stiff little finger-long ringlets in front of her ears and either side of her neck. This was all modeled on a statue of Cleopatra: a big joke, believe me.

Life had disappointed Junia, and she was firmly convinced that it could not possibly be her own fault. In fact, between her terrible cooking and her resentful attitude, most of what went wrong could be easily explained.

She always treated her husband—in public, anyway—as if supervising customs clerks stood on a par with the labors of Hercules, and were better paid. But his ponderous conversational style must drive her wild. Now she snorted and took charge of him: "An inspector in pursuit of unpaid harbor tax looked into a boat and found a dead man. The corpse was in a bad condition, but it carried an identification tag. Gaius Baebius has been specially selected to bring it to Rome." Junia spoke as if the trusty Gaius had flown here on winged sandals in a gilded helm.

My heart took an unpleasant lurch. "Show Marcus, Gaius," Helena urged as if she had already managed to see it.

What he unwrapped cautiously from a piece of cloth was a simple bone disc. Gaius held it out to me on the cloth, reluctant to touch it. It looked clean. I picked it up between my fingertips. A nerve in my wrist gave an involuntary twitch.

It had a round hole at the top, through which were threaded two entwined leather strings. One of them was broken. The other still held in its knot. On one side of the disc were the letters COH IV. They were very neat, centrally set, with that telling gap which showed the last two letters were the numeral four. Around the rim in smaller letters was the word ROMA followed by a spacing mark, then PREF VIG. I turned the disc over. More untidily scratched on the back was one masculine name. It was a name I knew.

My face had set. "Where's the body, Gaius?"

Gaius must have recognized the dark tone in my voice. "They're bringing it from Ostia." He cleared his throat. "We had a problem persuading a carter."

I shook my head. I could work out how many days the body might have been lying at the port. The filthy details I did not want to know.

It was clearly a matter of pride to have identified the disc and to be drawing official notice as promptly as possible. Customs like to think they are as sharp as fencing nails. Even so, my brother-in-law must have had mixed feelings even before he saw me. Officials stick together. A blow against one arm of the public service dismays them all. Always a lover of a crisis but aware of the implications, Gaius murmured, "Is this bad, Falco?"

"As bad as it could be."

"What's happened?" demanded Junia.

I ignored her. "Was the man drowned, Gaius?"

"No. Thrown into the keel of an old barge that had been stuck on the silt for months. One of our lads noticed footprints on a mudbank, and thought he might have uncovered some smuggling. He had a bad fright. There were no hidden bales, just this: a corpse hidden out on the barge. Whoever dumped him probably thought no one would ever go out there to look."

"You mean it made a safer hiding place than the ocean, which might have washed the corpse ashore?"

"Looked as if the fellow had been strangled, but it was hard to tell. Nobody wanted to touch the body. We had to, of course," Gaius added hastily. "Once discovered, it couldn't be left there." Nice to know that in the customs realm the highest standards of public hygiene ruled.

"Was the disc actually on the corpse?"

Something in Gaius' manner made me wish I had not asked. He flushed slightly. Customs have their moments.

Screwing money from reluctant importers, they have to face plenty of aggravation, but it usually stops at shouting and obscenities. Holding back a shudder, he confirmed the worst. "We spotted the thongs. I'm afraid the disc had been rammed in the poor fellow's mouth. It looked as if in the process of killing him, someone had tried to make him eat it." I swallowed air. In my mind I was seeing a boyish, cheery face with bright eyes and an enthusiastic grin. Gaius inquired, "Is anyone missing?"

"No one the cohort knew was lost."

"So was he one of theirs, then?"

"Yes." I was terse. I stood up again. "I knew him briefly. This is very important, Gaius—for the cohort and for Rome. I'll come with you to see Rubella."

I refolded the cloth gently around its significant contents. Gaius put out his hand to take it back, but I closed my fist too fast for him.

We found Marcus Rubella at the cohort headquarters. I was surprised. It was by then the hour when most people were thinking about relaxation and food. Mentally, I had had Rubella listed as the type who worked set hours—the minimum he could get away with. I had imagined he would slide out with his oil flask and strigil, bidding his clerks farewell the minute the bathhouse stokers started thrusting wood into their stoves. I thought he probably left his work behind him then, and kept a clear mind all through dinner and his recreation hours.

But he was alone in the office, a still, brooding presence, staring at documents. When we first walked in, he barely reacted. When I told him there was trouble, he opened a shutter, as if to see the problem more clearly. For a brief moment he seemed the type who faced up to things after all.

Gaius Baebius relayed his story, prompted by me when he tried to slow down. Rubella made no fuss. Nor did he decide on any action, beyond some comment that he would write in sympathy to the family. Maybe he liked to brood first—or more likely he just loved to let events roll forwards without throwing in his own spear.

"Any idea where Petronius Longus is, Falco?"

I had a good idea, and I preferred to keep it private. "He's following up an interview. I can track him down."

"Good." This was the sunflower-seed eater, neutral and standing well back. "I'll leave it to you to tell him then." Thanks, tribune!

Gaius Baebius and I left the building. With the usual difficulty, I managed to shed my brother-in-law, who always liked to cling on when he was not wanted. As the streets grew darker, I walked somberly from the Twelfth sector, where the Fourth had their headquarters, and down the hill to the Circus side of the Aventine. I could hear gulls squabbling over the Tiber wharves. They must always be there, but tonight I noticed them with resentment. Tonight was not the time to be reminded of the sea.

Everywhere seemed full of excited parties going out to dinner. Horse-faced women shrieked. Crass men chivvied their trains of slaves to trot along faster. All shopkeepers looked malevolent. All passersby had the air of would-be thieves.

A meek porter admitted me to Milvia's elegant house. I was told Florius was still out. No one seemed perturbed by it, even though respectable householders normally show up at home in the evening. If he was going out to dinner, he ought at least to change his tunic—and some wives would expect to be taken along. No one had much idea when they might expect him back, either. It seemed routine. Warily I asked whether an officer of the vigiles had visited that evening, and was told he was talking to Milvia in private.

As I feared. Another allegedly respectable husband was marauding off the leash. Petronius Longus could behave like a real boudoir bandit.

I was shown once more into the salon with the thin-legged Egyptian furniture. No one else was there. The house seemed very quiet, with not much going on. The whole time I was there, Milvia, the young lady of the house, failed to appear.

I waited. After a few minutes Petronius walked in. He was wearing a green tunic that I had last seen the night he and Silvia dined at our apartment. He had bathed and changed, but there was no special odor of unguents. I might have been wrong; this was hardly the debonair adulterer at work. He looked perfectly normal—calm, steady, utterly the man in charge. My abrupt appearance here gave him some warning. We were such close friends, he immediately knew far more than I had done when I set eyes on Gaius Baebius.

But I would still have to tell him.

"What's up, Falco?" Petro's voice was quick and light.

"You won't like this."

"Can things get worse?"

"A lot worse. Tell me, do all members of the vigiles carry identity tags?"

He stared, then took from a pouch on his belt a small bone counter, exactly like the one from Ostia. He let me examine it. On the face was the symbol COH IV, surrounded by ROMA and PREF VIG. On the reverse, being a neat, systematic character, Petro had scratched in full his three names.

"You don't wear it?"

"Some do. I don't like cords around my neck—villains can grab at them and throttle you." Well, he was right about that.

I gave him back his tag. Then I took from my tunic the other disc, handing it over in silence. By then he was expecting sorrow. His face had set into melancholy hollows. He turned the bone and read the name: LINUS.

Petronius sat on one of the delicate couches, leaning forwards, knees apart, hands clasped between them, holding the disc. I told him what had happened, as far as the customs force had worked it out. When I finished, I walked over to a folding door and stood staring out at a garden, while Petro absorbed the facts and tried to cope.

"This is my fault."

I had known he would say that. It was nobody's fault, but taking the blame was the only way Petronius could handle his grief.

"You know that's wrong."

"How can I get them, Falco?"

"I don't know. Look, we can't even start yet; there have to be formalities. Rubella is going to write a letter of sympathy to the relations, but you know what that will sound like." We had both seen how officialdom informs bereaved families of death.

"Oh dear gods! That isn't any good." Petronius roused himself. "I'll have to go. I'll have to tell his wife."

"I'll come with you," I said. I hardly knew Linus, but I had met him once, and even the brief memory affected me. I was involved.

Petro made no move yet. He was still struggling. "I'm trying not to think about what this means."

He spoke the name on the tablet he was cradling so gently. Linus. Linus, the young, keen undercover man whom Petro had placed on the ship that had supposedly taken the condemned criminal Balbinus into exile.

The death of Linus at Ostia must strongly imply that Balbinus Pius never went. In reality the ship must have dropped off passengers at the harbor mouth. Either then, or very shortly afterwards, Petro's agent was dead.

XLIX

Normally I liked widows. They are women of the world, often without guardians, and frequently adventurous. This one was different. She did not know she was a widow yet.

Her name was Rufina. She admitted us both with a hint of a simper, then offered us wine, which we refused.

"Greetings, Chief!"

Rufina looked about thirty-five, at any rate older than Linus. She dressed smartly, though her jewelry consisted merely of colored beads strung on wires. There was no spare meat on her. She was not as pretty as she tried to act. Her manner was brash and ingratiating in a way I could only just tolerate, given what I knew.

"This is about time, I must say. I hoped you would be dropping in sometime. He's famous for being conscientious." She giggled at me. I felt ill. She crossed her knees, showing ankles and toes beneath the hem of her gown. "Have you brought me news of my husband?" Things were already unbearable. She managed to make the reference to having a husband seem even more saucy than the previous comment about Petro calling on her while Linus was away.

Petronius closed his eyes briefly. "Yes."

I glanced around. Linus and Rufina lived in a third-floor back-of-building apartment that appeared to have just two rooms. They had made no attempt to redecorate what came with their lease; the usual landlord's dirty plasterwork, ornamented with halfhearted scrolls of red carried out by a painter who had two patterns and could only do one of those properly. With relief, I realized there was no evidence of children in the house.

The furniture was sparse. There was a loom in one corner. Rufina was a home-worker, though the state of the weaving—with an untidy straggle of wools in a basket on the floor and loose loom weights scattered everywhere—suggested she approached it lethargically. From a wall niche two household gods, the lares and penates, dominated the room. The dancing figures were in bronze with a very dark patina, rather heavier and more ornate than the rest of their owners' lifestyle called for.

"It's very naughty of you to take Linus from me for months, you know."

Petronius said nothing.

Doubt fluttered across Rufina's face. "What are you telling me, Chief?" She was a vigile's wife. She must have spent most of her married life half-prepared for an official visit of this kind.

When Petronius told her what had happened, she screamed so loudly we heard doors to other apartments opening in the outside corridor. At first she pretended she would not believe it, then, amid racking sobs and wild exclamations, she launched into the vilification that Petronius had dreaded.

"You should never have made him do it!"

"Linus volunteered."

Rufina howled. "He was afraid of you!"

It seemed more likely he was afraid of his own home life. I could vaguely remember Linus suggesting he wanted to leave Italy for some peace. It seemed to me things could have been worse. Still, in relationships small habits can soon multiply into monumental grievances. "He wanted the adventure," Petronius told the wife patiently. I could see he was badly shaken by the violence of

Rufina's hysteria. "He was eager to travel." Not that he managed it.

"Oh Linus, Linus! Oh my darling! Whatever am I going to do?"

"The cohort is ready to support you all it can. The tribune will be writing you a letter—"

"Will I get compensation?"

That was better. It came out smart as a crack of artillery. Petro could deal with that. "I believe there will be a modest award, enough to give you a small pension. Linus was a good officer killed in the state's service—"

"Small!"

"Of course, nothing can really replace him."

"Small, you say! He deserved better. I deserve better for acting as his only solace while he did his cruel job!"

"We all deserved better than to lose Linus."

We were achieving little, and as soon as it seemed decent we prepared to leave. Rufina then thought of more embarrassment to hurl at us: "Where is he now?"

"Not in Rome yet," Petronius rapped back swiftly. He had gone very pale. "You don't want to see him. Rufina, don't try!"

"He's my husband! I want to hold him in my arms one final time. I want to know what they did to him—"

Petronius Longus raised his voice so harshly he stopped her. "Remember Linus as he was! What they are bringing to Rome is a six-day-old corpse that has been lying in the open. It's not him, Rufina. It's not your husband; it's not the friend and comrade who served under me."

"How do I know it is really Linus, then? There might have been a mistake."

I put in weakly: "Petronius Longus will ensure there has been no mistake. Don't upset yourself on that point. He will do what is needed; you can rely on him."

That was when the widow suddenly crumpled up. With a small gurgle of pathetic grief, she fell into Petro's arms and sobbed. She was taller than the girls he liked comforting, older, and her nature was much harder. But he never flinched, and he held her firmly while she wept. I managed to find a neighbor to take over, then we slunk away.

When the carter brought the body to the Ostia Gate, Petro and I were there waiting for it. The customs people had found an undertaker to provide a lidded coffin; Linus came home sealed in state like some general who had died on an intercontinental campaign. But before we passed him on to the funeral arrangers we had brought to the gate with us, my friend Lucius Petronius wrapped a scarf around his face, then insisted that the coffin lid be raised so he could identify his man formally.

As Petronius had warned Rufina, after six days in the sun and salty air this body bore little resemblance to his bright, cheerful, fearless volunteer. The corpse was wearing the sailor's disguise we recognized. It was the right build. The features looked correct. Taken with the identification tag evidence, we accepted that this was Linus.

Balbinus had taken a stupid risk. He must have been so eager to regain land that he couldn't wait until the *Aphrodite* left the coastal shallows and found deeper waters where a corpse could be safely pushed overboard and lost. So he brought Linus back to land with him. Someone—the freedmen we had seen leave with him, perhaps—must have helped. Then Balbinus or others had killed Linus, and abandoned his body in a casual manner that was unbelievably arrogant.

I stayed alongside Petronius while he grieved; then I dealt with transferring the coffin. When the grumbling Ostian carter had removed his vehicle and the coffin had been carried away by officers of the vigiles' funeral club, we two walked back from the Ostia Gate. Once in our nostrils, the smell of putrefaction stayed cloyingly with us. In silence we found our way to the riverbank.

It was now dark. We had the complicated mass of buildings forming the granary area and the Emporium complex on our left, and the Probus Bridge along on the right, lit by dim lamps. Occasional figures crossed the bridge. We could hear the Tiber shifting, with splashes that could be fish or rats. Across the water, donkey hooves sounded sharply on a road in the Transtiberina. A breeze made us bury our chins deeply in our cloaks, though the air was humid and we were more depressed than cold.

There was no easy way to end this night. Already I felt ominous portents of how it might turn out for me.

"Do you want to go for a drink?"

Petronius did not even answer me.

I should have left him then.

We continued to stare across the river for some time. I tried again. "There's nothing you can do, and it's not your fault."

This time he roused himself a little. "I'm going to the patrol house."

"You're not ready for that yet." I knew him better than he knew himself. People never want to hear that happy news.

"I have to tell my men Linus is dead. I want them to hear it from me."

"Too late," I said. "Rumor will have rushed straight to them long ago. We've spent more hours on this than you realize. You've lost track of time. On the Aventine, this is old news. The whole cohort already know." I reckoned at least one cohort member knew about this before we did. A fact to which Lucius Petronius still seemed oblivious.

"This is nothing to do with you, Falco. This concerns me and my men."

I felt the full drag of disaster now. He wanted a quarrel. He needed a bad one. It could have been anyone who caught the eruption, but I was his best friend, so I was the rash man who had stayed at hand.

"You're not ready to see them," I told him again. "There is a situation you have to think about carefully first."

"I know what needs to be done."

"I don't believe you do."

Somewhere in the remote distance we heard the trumpet. After our years in the legions our brains took it in, though we were too absorbed to react. In the Praetorian Camp a watch had changed. I could no longer tell which stretch of the night we were in now. Normally I always knew, even if I awoke from heavy sleep. Now the darkness seemed quite different, the city's noise unlike itself. Events had been moving at an unnatural pace. Emotions had blurred everything. Dawn might be several hours or merely minutes away from us.

At my side I was aware of Petronius giving me more attention. Patiently I explained. I knew we were unlikely to stay friends.

"This job started out as unpleasant, but it's filthy now. You have to accept that fact before you make a move, or you're going to get it wrong, Petro. There are two issues—"

"What issues?" he burst out angrily.

"Linus' death throws up two stinking problems." Both seemed self-evident to me. They remained invisible to him.

"Falco, I have a heart full of grief, there are urgent things I need to do, and it's just not clever to hold me back for some piddling irrelevancy."

"Listen! First, you've got the whole black business of Balbinus Pius. You can leave that one to creep up and depress you slowly if you like, but let's not delude ourselves. Linus must have been killed to stop him reporting that Balbinus came off the *Aphrodite* pretty well while we were waving him good-bye across the harbor. There are enormous implications: The man is still here. He never left. Balbinus is in Rome. He probably fixed the raid on the Emporium, and he hit the Saepta Julia. He killed Nonnius. He killed Alexander. He killed Linus too, of course. Jove only knows what he's planning next."

Petronius would face it—and deal with it—but not now. He stirred restlessly. I put a hand on his arm. His skin was hot, as if his blood raced in turmoil. His voice was perfectly cold. "What else?"

"Balbinus knew who had to be killed. Somebody betrayed Linus."

He answered me at once. "It's not possible."

"It happened."

"Nobody knew."

"Think how he died! His identity tag was thrust between his teeth. Some swine was making a point that his true role had been exposed. Linus himself had to face up to the fact he had been spotted. He must have died knowing he had been betrayed. You can't refuse to acknowledge it, for his sake, Petro!"

Petronius rounded on me, full of hate. "Do you think I would have put him in that position? We were dealing with power and money at their most vicious. If I could have hidden him on that ship without letting him even know himself that he was there I would have done! How can you suggest I gave no thought to the risks? Do you think I would send an unprotected agent on that trip without ensuring no one in Rome was in a position to let him down?"

"Your men all knew."

"*My men?*" He was livid. "My own team, Falco! I'm not talking cohort; I don't mean the bloody foot patrols! The only ones who knew I had sent a spy with Balbinus were my own personally hand-picked investigation team."

I hated saying it, but I had to: "I'm sorry. One of your hand-picked babies has gone wrong. One of them must be on the take."

He did not explode immediately. Still, I knew he was deaf to my arguments. There was nothing for it but to carry on talking quietly, as if we were having some sort of rational conversation: "I know they're special. I see it's going to hurt. I can understand you if you say you've thought about this possibility, that you've considered it in a sensible manner and found evidence to clear them all. But a young man who didn't deserve it is dead. Somebody told Balbinus who he was. Lucius Petronius, I'm just amazed that you won't even entertain the obvious."

It was no good. Even years of friendship could not carry us through this. I heard his voice change; he demanded in a ghastly tone, "You know something. What are you telling me?"

"There's graft among the cohorts."

"Oh, nothing new!" Petro raged at me scornfully.

"All right. This is absolutely confidential: I'm on a special task."

"*Another?*"

"That's right. Investigations are being planted around

Rome like crocuses in an orchard. I'm under secret orders to find and label which of the vigiles are accepting handouts—"

Petronius was horrified. "You're spying on the Fourth."

"Oh, do me a favor! I'm spying on everything that moves. There's nothing particular about the Fourth. I had hoped to leave them out of it."

"Not according to what you've been saying to me tonight." That was when I knew I had really lost him. "I should have known; informers and law officers never mix. Your motives are far too grimy. Get out of my sight, Falco." He meant it, I knew.

"Don't talk rot."

"Don't speak to me! Take your filthy suspicions somewhere else. Balbinus is mine; he always was. I'll get him. I don't need help from you. I don't want to see you at the patrol house—I don't want to find you on my patch at all!"

There was nothing else for it. I left him and went home. The Emperor might like to think he had commissioned me for a confidential investigation, but Petronius Longus was the real force on the Aventine, and he had thrown me off the case.

There was very little time now. As soon as the body of Linus came home, we had lost our only advantage: that Balbinus had to lie low. Now he had much less to lose. Although he would have to remain in hiding, he could act much more freely. He faced the death penalty when we caught him, but he was so full of arrogance, he probably thought he could evade capture. He was planning to rule Rome from some extravagant hiding place.

One thing he would want to do would be to carry on his campaign of vengeance against those who had brought him to justice. There was no doubt about it. Extreme peril threatened Petronius Longus. Apart from hating him for the court case, Balbinus would know Petro would be looking for him. Recapturing the big rissole was now Petro's sole task. Preventing him must be his enemy's chief goal. That, more than anything, was why I felt there was so little time to act.

I had had to tell Helena that I was persona non grata with the vigiles. For one thing she would soon notice me loafing at home instead of rushing out to crises. I had to explain the reason as well.

"Oh, Marcus, this is terrible. I was so afraid it would hap-

pen. . . . Will Petronius tell his men that you have been looking for corruption?"

"He's bound to tell his own team."

"That means . . ." Helena paused. "The one who betrayed
Linus will find out what your task is."

"Don't worry."

"It looks dangerous for you as well as for Petro."

"Love, this investigation was always dangerous."

"Are you carrying on with it?"

"Yes."

"How are you going to manage if Petronius won't see
you?"

"He'll calm down."

Seeing that I did not intend to discuss the quarrel further,
she stopped talking. One thing I liked about Helena was that
she knew when not to pry. She had her own interests, which
helped. Then, if she ever did want to fight, she liked to blow
up nonsense out of nothing. Things that were really important could be handled more sensibly.

Over breakfast, she seemed rather quiet. Maybe that was
my fault. Even warm honey was failing to soothe me; I had
had hardly any sleep and felt like sludge in the Great Sewer.
I noticed Helena neither ate nor drank. That made me feel
worse. She was pregnant, and I was ignoring it. The more
bravely she endured her plight, the more guilt made me
grouse.

"Are you still being sick?" She just shrugged. I had been
decreed too busy to be kept informed. Dear gods, I wanted
this trouble to be over so I could attend to my own life. "Listen, if I want to be companionable and concerned, you might
try helping!"

"It's all right. You're a man. Just be yourself."

"That's what I was doing. But I can probably be boorish,
callous, and insensitive, if you prefer."

"I'll bear with you while you're learning to do it." She
smiled. Suddenly she was winsome again.

I refused to be charmed. "Don't worry. I learn quickly."

Helena Justina restrained herself, plainly making al-
lowances for the tetchiness that had followed my falling out
with my best friend. This only made me more angry, but she

found a new subject to talk about: "I haven't had a chance to tell you, Marcus. Yesterday when I came home another message about Tertulla was pinned in a bag on the door. And this . . ." She reached to a shelf and produced a gold object. I recognized the overflown bulla that my sister Galla had hung around her daughter's neck, the amulet which was supposed to protect Tertulla from the evil eye. Its powers had been sorely overtaxed. Now some fool had sent the useless thing to me.

"So they're telling us this is genuine. What are they asking me to cough up?" Even to my own ears I still sounded gruff.

"A thousand sesterces."

"Do you happen to know what they asked from your father?"

Helena looked apologetic. "Ten thousand."

"That's all right. When they come down to a hundred I might consider it."

"You're all heart, Marcus!"

"Don't worry. I suspect they know they grabbed the wrong child this time. There's no money, but they don't want to lose face."

"If they reduced the price once they may be weakening," Helena said. "They seem like amateurs. People who knew what they were doing would pile pressure on us, then keep asking for more and more."

"I don't belittle the situation, but we may as well not panic. Are there any instructions in the message?"

"No, just the price they want." She was so reluctant to bother me she had not even let me see the message. Luckily I could trust Helena to tell me anything relevant. It was a relief to let her handle this. Even though I was in a filthy mood, I managed to feel some gratitude.

"We'll hear from them again, I'm sure. Sweetheart, if I'm too busy, do you think you can watch for the next contact?"

"Does that mean I should stay at home?" Helena sounded doubtful.

"Why? Have you an appointment to hear an epic poem in sixteen scrolls?"

"Certainly not. I did want to try that other house where a child is supposed to have been taken."

"No luck yesterday?"

"I was told the woman was not at home."

"True, or a fable?"

"I couldn't tell. Since they were being polite, they implied I could try another time, so I shall make sure I do." She looked thoughtful. "Marcus, when the amulet was left there, I found myself thinking about the skip baby. Remember, he had a broken thread around his neck. Maybe he's a kidnap victim too. These people I haven't managed to see yet were supposed to have lost a baby. It was reported by the child's nurse. Maybe they will listen to me if I can tell them he's been found."

Suddenly I experienced a huge pang of regret that she and I were not working together. I reached for her hands. "Would it help if I came with you?"

"I should say not." Helena smiled at me. "With due respect, Marcus, at the house in question an informer would be someone to eject. I'm trying to cross the private bastions of a very important magistrate."

A thought struck me. "What's his name?"

Helena told me. My lawyers advise me not to mention it; I don't want a libel action. Besides, men like that get enough publicity.

I laughed throatily. "Well, if you can use the information, I last saw the most excellent personage in question having his fancy tickled by a high-class prostitute."

She looked worried, and then perhaps offended. One of the reasons I had always loved her so dearly was that Helena Justina was absolutely straight. The idea of blackmailing a man who was entitled to wear the purple toga to show his distinction would never cross her mind.

"Which brothel was it, Marcus?"

"I promise I've only been in one you know about— Plato's Academy."

"That's interesting," said Helena. She was trying to make it significant.

I knew that game. I had been in the inquiry business longer than she had. I let her dream.

LI

Mentioning Plato's had given me an idea.

Reluctant to work on my own if it proved unnecessary, I did take myself first to the Thirteenth-district patrol house to see if Petro would acknowledge me. Neither he nor any of his team were there. When I tried to go in, a couple of firefighters appeared. They seemed not to know about my job tracing grafters, but someone had ordered them not to admit me. I tried to look unimpressed by their surly behavior, though I confess it shook me.

I realized afterwards that Petronius and his men would be attending the funeral of Linus. The patrolmen must have thought it odd that I had not gone myself.

Had Petro and I not quarreled, I would have paid my own respects. It seemed better to avoid causing trouble, so I honored the dead man privately. He was young and had seemed straightforward. He deserved a better fate.

I walked down to the Circus, made my way to Plato's, and with more skill than I had applied at the patrol house, I talked my way inside. An expert informer is not easily thrown. I even managed to get myself taken straight to see Lalage.

*   *   *

It was still early morning, and not much seemed to be happening. The brothel was in a lethargic mood. Just a few local clients indulging on their way to their employment, and at the time I arrived, mostly leaving. The corridors were empty; it could have been a lodging house, except that at certain points stood mounds of wilting garlands or neatly stacked empty amphorae waiting to be taken out. There was some general cleaning with mops and sponges going on, but quietly. The night shift needed their sleep, presumably.

Lalage herself must have been snatching a rest between clients. Since a prostitute works on her back—well, often horizontally—Lalage's idea of a rest was not to relax on a reading couch with a Virgilian eclogue, but to climb up steps and replenish the oil in a large iron ceiling light.

"I know." I grinned. "You can't trust slaves to do anything."

"Slaves here have other duties, with my customers." She swayed slightly, nearly going off balance as she tilted her jug against the last lamp. The effect was decorously erotic, though probably unintentional. I stepped closer and prepared to place a steadying hand on her backside, though when she managed to remain upright, modesty stayed my helpful paw. "You're Falco, aren't you?"

"Fame at last."

"Notoriety," she answered. Something in her manner told me this might be the kind of notoriety I could do without.

"In the wrong quarters? I had a visit from the Miller and Little Icarus. Do you know that pair?"

"Nasty. I barred them."

"I'm not surprised. I've seen your respectable clients. . . ." She did not react. It would take a determined niggler to worry Lalage. "My two visitors came to threaten me. Obviously my name is being mentioned in rougher circles than I like." I was trying to obtain some sign that she was in contact with the Balbinus gang; her response was completely negative.

I offered a wrist to lean on as she descended from her perch, oil flask on the drip. She stepped down, brushing against me with a firm body warm through a single layer of finely woven cloth. "And what does the notorious Marcus Didius want with me?"

"Marcus? That's informal! When I called with Petronius, I don't believe we got on first-name terms. Has someone well informed been talking or might you and I be old friends?"

Lalage gave me the full benefit of those wonderful eyes. "Oh, hardly!"

"I'm crushed! By the way, you can stop flashing the peepers. They're lovely, but it's too early in the morning for me—or not early enough. I like a roll in the sheets instead of breakfast, but I like it with a woman who has been in my arms all night."

"I'll put that in our scroll of clients' preferences."

"I'm not enrolled as a client."

"Want to negotiate terms?"

"Sorry, can't afford it. I'm saving up to go to philosophy school."

"Don't bother. You ramble on enough, without paying to be taught."

She was still too close for comfort. I resisted manfully. We fought eye to eye; she must have known I was afraid she would manhandle me. The hairs on my neck were standing as stiff as a badger's bristles. It was hard to look tough when every nerve was screaming to me to protect my assets from assault—but the assault never came. For a brothel queen Lalage was surprisingly delicate.

"I want to negotiate a truce," I croaked. She received the news with a chortle, but waved me to a couch with her. Breathing more freely, I perched on the far end. She tipped her head back, surveying me. She had a long, smooth neck, today unadorned by jewelry. Her eyelashes swept down and up again with the strength and fluid grace of trireme oars.

I sighed gently. "Stop acting up like Thaïs. Your name's Rillia Gratiana. Your parents used to keep a stationer's shop on the corner of Dogfish Court."

She did not deny it. Nor did she encourage me. Appealing to old memories would be no help. "I keep this brothel, Falco. I do it well. I run the girls, I control the clients, I organize salty entertainments; I keep the ledgers and I obtain the necessary licenses; I pay the rent, and I pay the grocery bills; when I have to I even sweep the stairs and lance the doorman's boils. This is my life."

"And the past is irrelevant?"

"Not at all. My parents gave me all my local knowledge and commercial acumen."

"Do you still see them?"

"They died years ago."

"Want to know how I know all about you?"

"Don't bother. You're an informer. Even if you tell me some sob story, I won't be impressed."

"I thought a brothel was the place men told the truth about themselves?"

"Men never tell the truth, Falco."

"Ah no, we don't know what truth is. . . . So can I call on fellow feeling?"

"No," she said. That was even before she remembered how she came by her wounded ear. She was clearly not thinking about it, though seeing the scar again, I felt a warm sense of nostalgia.

We were both professionals. For different reasons we were attuned to the surges of communication—in my case talk, in hers the other thing. A cycle in this conversation had exhausted itself. By mutual agreement we gave up and relaxed.

I would have said neither of us had given any ground in the repartee stage, but then Lalage started playing with the clasp of a bracelet fretfully. Maybe she was weakening. (Maybe the arm decoration just had a tricky hook and loop.) "So what do you want?" she asked again.

"To give you a word from a friend."

"Oh?"

"You're driving me mad with that thing. Take it off, and I'll mend it." Surprised, she gave up trying to fix the bracelet and tossed it in my lap. It was a gorgeous bauble: fine gold scrollwork in sections, holding pale emeralds. Expensive, but ruined by the usual trashy clasp. "Got some tweezers?" She provided me with a handsome set, six or seven assorted toiletry tools on a ring. "Jewelers are stupid bastards." I was working on a bent piece of gold wire that needed to be reshaped. "They spend hours of labor on the fancy parts, but begrudge a decent hook. That should hold. If you like the piece, get a new fastener." I held out my hand for her arm. When I had replaced the bracelet on her scented wrist, I kept hold of her. My grip was friendly, but inescapable. She made no attempt to break away; prostitutes know when to avoid hurting themselves. I looked straight at her. "Balbinus is in Rome."

Her fine eyes narrowed. It was impossible to tell whether she was hearing this for the first time, or merely wished me to think so. Her mouth pursed. "That's bad news."

"For everyone. Have any vigiles been to see you?"

"Not since you and your long friend." I felt I could believe her when she was being factual. That could be a trick, of course.

"You can see the implications?"

"Not exactly. Balbinus is condemned. What can he do, Falco?"

"Quite a lot, it seems. The Fourth Cohort have been busting themselves trying to work out who was trying to replace him—when all the time nobody was. Everything that's happened lately could be down to him."

"Like what?"

"The Emporium raid, and the one at the Saepta. The deaths. You have presumably heard about the deaths?"

"Whose deaths are these?" she murmured, deliberately provoking me.

"Don't try it."

There was no visible hardening; she remained the polite courtesan. But she said, without any change of tone, "If you don't want to pay for mauling me, would you mind letting go of my wrist?"

I gave her a stare, then opened my hand abruptly, fingers splayed. She waited a beat, then took back her arm.

"I want to talk about Balbinus," I said.

"And I don't."

I looked at her carefully, seeing past the elegant attire, the fine paintwork on her eyelids and lashes, the allure of the gorgeous body. There were tiny lines and dark patches around those languorous, limpid brown eyes. "You're tired.

The brothel's very quiet this morning too. What's up, Lalage? Having to work overtime at nights? Why's this? Someone squeezing you? Can it be that the profit margins of the Bower of Venus are being reduced by having to pay a managing director's fee again?"

"Take a jump in the river, Falco."

"I'm surprised. I thought you enjoyed your independence, lass. I must admit, I respected you for it. I can't believe Balbinus just turned up and asked for a cut, and you gave it to him!"

"Don't even think it. I wouldn't give him half an as if he was bursting for the lavatory. Balbinus can't pressure me these days. He's condemned. If he's in Rome, he'll have to stay in hiding, or he's for it."

"Execution," I agreed. Then I challenged her: "So you're not concealing him on the premises?"

She laughed.

I decided to accept her version. I had believed her when she talked of running the brothel without a protector. "You still ought to take an interest," I warned. "Someone must be helping him, but if it's not you, you fall into the other category."

"And what's that, Falco?"

"His enemies."

There was a pause. Lalage had always been intelligent, top of the class when she went to school; I happened to know that. Finally she rasped, "You're talking about deaths again."

"Nonnius Albius," I confirmed. She must have known about his killing. "And the doctor who convinced Nonnius he was dying, the one who frightened him so much he felt prepared to turn Balbinus in. That was wrong, incidentally. The vigiles had set him up."

I was hoping to shock her into making revelations, but it was Lalage who surprised me. She laughed again, though somewhat bitterly. "Not entirely," she said. Enjoying the thrill of seeing me startled, she stretched as gracefully as a panther; the action was automatic, not meant to be enticing, but I had to control myself. She smiled wryly. "It would only have been a setup if Nonnius hadn't known about it."

"What do you mean?"

"Nonnius realized all along that the Fourth Cohort had sent that doctor to lie to him."

Luckily Petronius Longus was no longer speaking to me, so I would be spared having to tell him this depressing news.

LII

"It's old history," Lalage confessed. "What's the difference now Nonnius is dead? Who cares?"

"Balbinus cares!" I rapped back tersely. "And so should you."

"I don't see it."

"You will when a gang of killers bursts in one night, and drags you off by the hair."

"I'll wear a wig for a few days. . . ." Flippancy was not her style. She knew her limits, and it did not last. "This is a brothel. I thought you would have noticed that! We have a system to keep out hooligans."

"Jupiter, I've seen your security! Macra busy counting the money, and a half-asleep hangdog who dies if you raise your voice to him? Nonnius had an armored door. They broke in with artillery; it was a military raid."

"Well, thanks. Now I know what we have to be ready for." She was unimpressed. She stretched her leg, dangling her sandal from a lithe instep. The footgear had a light sole but a substantial upper, the kind that is completely cut out in one piece of leather, then its myriad thongs tied up on top. Not a walking shoe, but that would not have troubled her. What troubled me was that it was being dangled from a very pretty foot.

Her blasé attitude heated me more, but in a different way. "What's the matter with you, Lalage? Balbinus has perpetrated revenge killings on at least two people who brought him to trial. I was abroad at the time, but I understood Nonnius was not his only old associate to help the prosecution. You also gave evidence."

"I was pressurized."

"By Petronius Longus."

"That's the bastard's name."

"Call me simple, but it seems to me that helping to convict him puts you next on Balbinus' shopping list of corpses, Lalage.'"

"You're simple." She knew exactly what she was saying when she returned shyly, "I can think of one person who may be ahead of me." She meant Petronius. I hoped she could not see me going cold.

"He's a big lad, and avoiding villains is his job. He can take his chance. There is still a serious risk to you."

"I can deal with it."

"The oldest lie in the world, Lalage! History is littered with the corpses of fools who gurgled, 'I'm different. I can keep out of the way!' Or have you bought him off?" I was angry as the thought struck me. "One of the vigiles has been murdered too. Are you responsible for that? Did you betray Linus?"

"I've never even heard of him." She spoke calmly. I wanted to believe her.

"Have you seen Balbinus recently?"

"No."

"He must need a bolt-hole. Has he asked to hide up here?"

"That again! Don't make me laugh, Falco."

"What about his men? Little Icarus and the Miller? Do you let them come here?"

"I told you, they're barred, the lot of them."

"And none of the old gang have been in touch with you? What about Balbinus himself?"

"No." It sounded like a lie. I watched her notice me thinking that. "Balbinus is a shark." Her voice was hard. "Believe me, Falco, he knows that he's met his match in me. I'm stronger than him, and if he wants to survive in Rome, he'd better leave me alone. What—an exile who has returned in secret? He's a fool. He doesn't stand a chance." She was talking too much now. This was not like Lalage. She still had the wide-open gaze of a whore who was lying. The trouble with whores is they look like that all the time, even when spouting truths like vestal virgins.

"And what about Nonnius? How in Hades did you know he saw through Alexander's tale?"

"Alexander is the doctor?"

"Was."

"Oh, was! Failed to diagnose his own condition, didn't he? Well I know, Falco, because the whole thing was arranged by Nonnius and me. Don't worry your little head with the details, but when Petronius sent his man with the fake story, Nonnius didn't believe him. He wasn't stupid. He could tell he wasn't ill."

"So he made inquiries and found out that the doctor who was saying he was dying had a brother in the watch?"

"He was a rent collector, Falco. He could easily add up! He told me about it. He was just laughing at first because the whole idea seemed ridiculous, but I saw how we could use it. We wanted to be rid of Balbinus. I was after sole charge of the brothel, and Nonnius intended to run all the rest. We planned it together."

"Nonnius called Alexander back?"

"He had a lot of fun pretending to be terrified, and then convinced your friend the way was clear to clean up Rome."

"What about the dead Lycian?"

"He was killed here at Plato's."

"I know that." I was thinking fast. She had to be telling me that the Lycian's murder was deliberate. "It was a fix? The weasel who did the stabbing was sent in purposely?"

"No, Castus didn't need encouraging. He was a Balbinus plant. He used to hang around here and report back how things were. I didn't tell him anything; I knew how he would react if we could get a fight going. The girl was in on it, though. I didn't want her telling Castus to calm down when the row flared up."

"They still work here?"

"Only the girl."

She was horribly calm. She and Nonnius actually had the Lycian traveler killed so the watch could discover it "by accident," and so that they could provide evidence which Lalage could be "coerced" into giving in court.

I realized Lalage would never admit this formally, and hearing it today could prove fatal for me. The mood had become dangerous. I was deep within this place. No one knew I was here. If she decided to have me killed like the Lycian, I would be seriously stuck. I tried changing the subject. "Once Balbinus was supposed to have sailed away, was it Nonnius who organized the Emporium raid?"

"I've no idea. Once the court case was over, I didn't want to know anything about the street-gang side."

"Really? I wondered whether you and Nonnius had been scheming together because you were having an affair?"

Genuine amusement rocked her. "Only a man would imagine women conduct their businesses on the basis of love."

"You were no admirer of Nonnius?"

"No." She did not bother to insult him.

"You told me once you hated him—and yet now you say you conspired together over the court case."

"So? I loathed him, but I could still use him."

"You've told a lot of lies. Why suddenly start telling the truth about Nonnius?"

"Because he's dead. As soon as I heard that, I guessed Balbinus had returned. You should have known too," she taunted.

"We thought Flaccida murdered Nonnius."

"Oh, I bet she had a hand in it. The word on the streets is that it happened in her house. They say she was there gloating. They say she herself rammed that pot on his head."

"A spirited witch!" My lip curled. "Is Balbinus at the house?"

"I doubt it. He's not stupid. That's the first place the vigiles will look." She clearly meant they *were* stupid, or at least predictable.

"Well, thanks for all this. It's good of you to cooperate."

"If you hadn't realized Balbinus was here in Rome, I was going to tell you myself."

She had not done so, though.

I stood up. For a moment I half expected her to prevent me leaving. I was guarding against an attack, and this time not the erotic sort.

"You frightened of something, Falco?" She understood men. It was her trade.

"No, but you should be. Balbinus is back. You helped get him condemned. He'll be looking for you."

"Oh, I don't think I need to worry!" She definitely meant it. I was wondering why. She rose, graciously acknowledging my departure as she supplied one possible reason in a scornful tone: "Balbinus won't be in Rome for long." The smile she gave me was the sweetest available in her wide repertoire—as dangerous as a draught of aconite. "Balbinus won't even be *alive*, will he? Not now you're looking for the man!"

I told her there was no need to be sarcastic, but I saluted the lady respectfully and took my leave.

Nonnius had hoped to take over the crime empire, but Nonnius was dead. I wondered who Lalage imagined would step in once Balbinus was settled for good. I wondered who she hoped to see running things then.

She was competent and ambitious. And Lalage, as I knew from many years ago, had always been a very clever girl.

LIII

There was no chance that Petronius would welcome me with almond cakes if I came with my new information. Hearing that his ploy had been seen through by Nonnius would only make him flare up again. What was the point of harassing him? He knew Balbinus was back; he could work out for himself his own personal danger. All I had learned for certain was some unpleasant background relating to the court case. Lalage had implied she had some mysterious hold over Balbinus, but it could be bluff. If not, it was still too nebulous to be useful.

Nonetheless, I felt I had gained a better grip on the situation. The main thing now was to find Balbinus Pius. I decided to risk my neck and tackle Flaccida. Too late; when I reached her house at the other end of the Circus, the vigiles were already there. I must have spent longer in the brothel than I realized. (Not the first man to be in that predicament.) The funeral of Linus was over now. Petronius had obviously come straight from it, with barely time for the ritual purification, in order to lead a search party at the Balbinus house.

Flaccida was standing white-faced and rigid in the street, surrounded by the few slaves she had been left for personal use. No one had been arrested, but members of the foot pa-

trol were strategically placed so that interested passersby
(of whom there were many) were being held back away
from her. Despite precautions, Flaccida must have managed
to send word to her daughter, because while I was there Milvia came scuttling up, looking flustered. She was promptly
corralled with her mother. Her house would be the next target.

I also reckoned Balbinus would not be found in either
mansion. Petronius presumably knew that too, for I could
see him leaning casually in a portico with his arms folded.
When he looked over and spotted me, I made sure I was sitting against a wall chewing my thumb in a similarly relaxed
pose. I heard him give an order to have the street cleared of
gawpers, so I left of my own accord.

It would be easy to let this situation deteriorate until it became even more personal. Searching for Balbinus was already feeling like some grim competition between Petro and
me. That could be an advantage if it sharpened us up. But it
was equally likely to jeopardize our hopes of capturing the
criminal.

I went to see Marcus Rubella.

"There's been a development. Petronius has declared me
out of bounds at the patrol house, and he refuses to communicate."

"I was warned that having you two together would mean
trouble." That sounded as if it came from our old centurion,
Stollicus.

"That's rubbish!" I retorted irritably.

Rubella was watering his inkwell and scraping the in-
nards with a stick—the usual useless procedure for trying to
get a decent mix. He possessed a fancy desk set: silver
inkpot, stylus rack, sand tray, nib knife, and a sealing-wax
lamp. It looked like a gift. Maybe somebody was fond of
him. It wasn't me.

"Do you want to be taken off the inquiry, Falco?" He
knew this had thrown me. "Are you prepared to tell Titus
you're ditching it?" This was a vicious man. Sympathetic
staff management was not in his armory.

"I can't afford that. I need his goodwill. I came to see you because I hoped you might be able to mediate."

Rubella looked at me as though I were a cockroach crawling up his favorite stool. "Mediate?"

"Sorry. Did I slip into a rare Etruscan dialect? Try arbitrate."

"You're asking me to calm Petronius Longus down?"

"Subtle."

"Fly off a crag, Falco."

"No use?"

"I value life too dearly."

"You won't try."

"He's your old tentmate."

"I don't find him in a nostalgic mood, unfortunately. Well, it seems I'll be acting alone." That was what I had wanted, though not this way. I told Rubella what I had learned from Lalage; he thanked me, in his dry manner, for handing him the task of telling Petronius how Nonnius Albius had played with him. "Rubella, since Petronius won't be using my valuable talents, I'm available to take instructions directly from you."

"I like a man who cooperates. Well now, what nugget can I find for you? Petronius is in charge of finding Balbinus."

"I can help with that."

"No. I don't want your paths crossing until your feud is worked out."

"I'll keep out of his way."

"Yes." Rubella gave me his slow, untrustworthy smile. "That's best." He meant, he was making sure of it. "As I said, Petronius is looking for the escapee. What I'd like you to take on is tracing the goods stolen from the Saepta and the Emporium." Before I could protest at this menial role, he added smoothly, "Following up the raids may be another way to find a trail to Balbinus. Besides, you have connections in the fine-art world. You seem ideal for this job—much better than anyone on my own staff."

Always a sucker for personal flattery, I heard myself agree to it. "Do I get men to assist?"

Rubella flattened the stubs of his close haircut with one hand; it must have felt like abrading his palm with pumice stone. "I don't see that you'll need any initially. If you are on to something, come straight to me for backup."

I had heard that before. I knew I would be searching for the stolen goods on my own. If I found them, I would be a solitary hero timidly approaching whichever giant was hoarding them and asking if he could please hand them over and explain himself. . . . I started planning further visits for exercise at my local gymnasium.

I was ready to leave, when the tribune raised his chin more than usual. "Do I take it that you are still pursuing the request to identify corrupt officers?"

"Certainly. I'm looking all the time."

"That's interesting. You report to me on that, I think."

"What are you getting at?"

"Linus was an unfortunate loss. I've been at the funeral; I noticed you didn't go to it. . . ." I let that ride. "I've been waiting," said Rubella, with an insinuating sneer, "for you to tell me that there must be a maggot in the Fourth Cohort's inquiry team."

I managed to keep my voice quiet, though I may have flushed. "I thought you suspected a maggot all along. I thought that was why Titus brought me in!" We clashed eye to eye. Neither achieved supremacy. The sooner I stopped working with Marcus Rubella, the happier I would be. "Petronius Longus will be reporting on the traitor who betrayed Linus when we have discovered who it is."

"You told him there was a traitor?"

Not even I as Petro's close friend could pretend that Petro had been aware of it. "It seemed best for me to warn him that he needs to be careful whom he trusts, so I did discuss the subject with him last night before we parted company."

"I suppose that's why you quarreled?" The reason was between the two of us. Rubella glared. "He and I have also spoken." Relief. Petro had faced the issue. Petro had even come clean with his tribune. I wondered whether he had asked for an interview of his own accord, or whether Rubella—who was undeniably sharp in his dour way—had realized there had been an error and had insisted they discuss what had gone wrong. "No thoughts on it?" Rubella tried.

I was not inclined to share them. "I'm standing back. Petronius Longus wants to sort it out internally." I knew that without having any contact with him.

"I have agreed to his approach. He'll review events surrounding the failed attempt to send Balbinus into exile. Then he'll interview the entire team individually." For a moment I experienced the odd feeling that whatever Petro or I said to Rubella would make its way to the other. It was like conversing through an intermediary to save face. Maybe the damned tribune understood men after all. Maybe he could arbitrate.

"Keep me informed," he concluded, as if confirming it.

Then the hypocrite wished me luck (hoping I would fall flat on my face, of course) and I took myself off to apply my special gifts to the world of stolen luxuries.

Rubella had given me the lists of stolen property. I had a quick glance at the endless details of six-foot-high Etruscan terra-cotta stands and bowls, ancient Athenian red-figure, gilt and jewelry, porphyry and ivory. Then, to deal with two commissions at once, I started with the piece I knew: Papa's glass jug.

There was one character involved in this saga whom nobody else seemed to be considering. So I pulled my cloak around my shoulders and decided to meet Florius.

I had to find him first.

LIV

My brother-in-law Famia, Maia's treasure, prided himself on being a man with contacts. It was rubbish. Famia's contacts were one-legged jockeys and liniment-sellers who drank too much. He was a vet, working for the Greens. Their pathetic choice of horse doctor may account for the fact that as a chariot team they stink.

Famia was no stranger to flagons of nonvintage grape juice himself. He had a florid face with puffy eyes. Maia fed him well and tried to keep him neat, but it was hard work. He favored a long tunic of the color of estuary mud, over which went a filthy leather apron and a belt from which hung curious tools, some of which he had devised himself. I had never seen him use a single one of them on a sick animal.

I found him sitting on a barrel at the stables, talking to some visitors. A lame horse waited patiently. It appeared to know it stood no chance of attention this week if it had to depend on Famia. Hung on the wall behind it was an impressive selection of harness rings and roundels, blacksmiths' hammers and pliers, and hippo shoes.

"What ho, Falco! I hear you slipped up with your fancy piece?"

"If that's a coarse reference to my impending father-hood—"

"Don't be stupid. I presume Helena will be getting rid of it."

"That so? I like to be kept up to date, Famia. Thanks for telling me!"

"Well, that's the impression Maia gave me, anyway." Realizing he was likely to get thumped, he sniffed and backed off. Famia simply could not believe that a senator's daughter would carry an informer's child. I had long given up any attempt to hack a path through the dark undergrowth of his social prejudice. He wasn't worth trying to talk to sensibly.

The bastard had upset me. No use denying it.

It was too much to hope Famia knew Florius, but since Florius was a gambling man, Famia must know someone else who did. Prizing the information out of him gave me indigestion for the rest of the day. He enjoyed being difficult.

It took me most of the afternoon. A long stream of undesirable characters whom Famia had suggested I consult finally ended with a snooty ex-charioteer who kept a training stable near the Plain of Mars. His office was full of silver crowns he had won when he himself raced, but somehow lacked the odor of real money that I associate with retired champions, most of whom are nearly millionaires. Famia had hinted darkly there was some scandal attached to him, though needless to say he then sent me in there without saying what. Maybe the fellow tried to diddle on the slave tax when he bought his drivers, and had been found out. Many a hopeful setting up a new business assumes the fiscal rules don't apply to him. Catching them out works wonders for the Treasury's income from fines.

One reason it was so difficult to trace Florius was that it turned out he supported the Whites. "The *Whites*?" I was incredulous. No wonder he was elusive. Nobody in Rome supports the Whites. Even the Reds are less unpopular. A man who supported the Whites could well wish to remain invisible.

The ex-charioteer thought he might be seeing Florius later. Naturally he viewed me with suspicion. People never entertain the thought that an informer might be tracing folk for a good reason, such as to bring them news of an unexpected legacy. I was interpreted as trouble. It was quite likely Florius would be warned of my visit and advised to avoid me. Determined to better him, I pretended to go along with it, said I'd call back in an hour, and concealed myself in a wine bar to await developments. At least I got a drink.

The racing snob went out in his cloak almost immediately. I gulped down my tipple and followed him. He met Florius at the Pantheon, obviously a regular rendezvous. I stood back, but neither was keeping watch for trouble. Shading my eyes against the glitter of the gold tiles on the domed roof, I observed them without their even once looking in my direction. They had a short chat together, fairly unexciting and perhaps even routine business, then the charioteer strolled off again. Florius sat among the forest of columns in Agrippa's confrontational portico. He appeared to be working out figures on a note tablet. I walked across the open area in front of the temple, then slid up to talk to him.

Florius was a mess. He was a shapeless lump, too heavy for his own good and unkempt with it. His baggy tunic had spots of dried fish pickle down the front. It was untidily hooked up over his belt, from which hung a fat hide purse so old its creases were black and shiny and stiffened with use. His boots had been handsome knee-highs once, but their complex thongs were mud-splashed and needed grease. His feet were badly misshapen with corns; the thick toenails had been hacked short, apparently with a meat knife. His brown hair looked as if it had been cut in tufts by several barbers over several days. He wore his equestrian ring, plus a haematite seal and a couple of other heavy gold lumps. This was hardly for personal adornment; his fingernails were ferociously bitten, with ragged cuticles. His hands looked in need of a wash.

This neglected bundle received my greeting without alarm. He put away his notes, which looked like details of form. (I craned for a look, hoping they would be lists of stolen goods; nothing so obvious.) He was sharp enough in his obsession; as I had approached the temple I had seen him scribbling away with his stylus so rapidly that in minutes his little squiggly figures filled a whole waxed board. I determined not to ask him about racing. He was clearly one of those mad devotees who would bore you to death.

A gusty wind had driven a sharp rain shower over the Plain, so I suggested we take shelter. He clambered to his feet, and we strolled inside the temple, passing the statues of Augustus and Agrippa in the vestibule. Though I rarely entered the Pantheon, it always had a calming effect on me. The gods looked out peacefully from their niches in the lower drum, while clouds covered the open circle in the roof.

"Wonderful building," I commented. I liked to reassure my subjects with some casual chat—a few pleasantries about the beauty of concrete before suggesting that they had better talk or I'd tear their liver out. "They say it's the first piece of architecture that was designed from the inside outwards instead of the other way. Don't you think the proportions are perfect? The height of the dome is exactly the same as its diameter." Florius took no notice. That did not surprise me. The Pantheon would have needed four legs and a bad-tempered, pockmarked Cappadocian rider before Florius raised a flicker of interest. "Well! You're a hard man to catch up with, I must say!" He looked nervous. "Your friend seemed to be protecting you. Have you been bothered by any unwelcome visitors?"

Florius cleared his throat. "What do you want?" He had one of those light, overcheerful voices that always sound unreliable.

"I'm Didius Falco. A special investigator working on your father-in-law's case."

He exclaimed in considerable anguish, "Oh no!"

"Sorry, does this bother you?"

"I don't want anything to do with it."

I took a chance. "I sympathize. When you discovered what kind of family had tricked you into marriage, you must have felt really trapped." He said nothing, but made no protest. "I've come to you because I realize you're different."

"I don't know anything about what my father-in-law does."

"Have you seen him?" I asked pleasantly.

"Oh, don't get me into this!" he pleaded.

"You have? How long ago was that?"

"Five or six days ago." Interesting. It was only a week since we put the big rissole aboard the *Aphrodite* at Ostia. Florius had spoken without intending to cooperate, but now he decided to ditch Balbinus anyway. "I'm not supposed to tell anyone."

"Of course not. It's very unfair of him to put pressure on you this way."

"Oh, I wish he'd just go away."

"I hope he will do soon. We're working on it hourly."

"Oh?" Florius seemed puzzled. "I must have misunderstood. I thought you said you were a special investigator. But you're with the vigiles?"

"Can it be that you don't think the vigiles are pursuing matters energetically?"

"My father-in-law reckons they do what he likes," he answered flatly.

That was bad news for Rome. I was supposed to be looking into this. Rubella would be overjoyed. I broached the issue carefully: "Look. This is just between us." He looked grateful for the confidence. A simple soul. "The vigiles are themselves the subject of a probe at the moment. Obviously I cannot be too specific, but my role includes reviewing them. . . . Perhaps you can help."

"I doubt it!" The great booby just wanted to hide his head in a sack.

"I don't suppose Balbinus mentioned names?"

"No."

"Did he say anything about his escape from the ship?"

"The ship he was supposed to leave on? No."

"Can you tell me what he wanted with you?"

"He only wanted me to tell him how Milvia was. He's very fond of her. Actually, he wanted me to tell her he was home again, but I refused."

"If he's so close to her, why didn't he come to your house?"

"He was afraid people might be watching it."

"Does Milvia know he's here in Rome?"

"No. I don't want her to know. She's my wife, and I want to keep her out of all this. He doesn't understand."

"Oh he wouldn't, Florius. He's been a villain all his life. His wife is as bad. They wanted Milvia to have a respectable place in society, but that doesn't mean they really think there is anything wrong with their own way of life."

"Well it's made them rich enough!" snapped Florius.

"Oh, quite. Do you know where I can find Balbinus?"

"No. He just appeared one day. I used to spend time in the Portico of Octavia; he found me there. So now I come here just to get away from him."

"I'm very glad to hear your attitude." There was no harm in putting pressure of our own on him. "It's wise, Florius. I expect you realize your position could be awkward. There are people who keep saying you may work with Balbinus in some kind of partnership."

"That's nonsense!" His fists were clenched. I sympathized. Innocence can be hard to prove. "I answered all their questions before the trial happened. They assured me there would be no more trouble."

"Of course . . . Going back to Balbinus being here now, is there a system set up for you to contact him?"

"No." Florius was exasperated. "I don't want to contact him; I want to forget he exists! I told him not to bother me again."

"All right. Calm down. Let me ask you something different. Was it Balbinus who gave you the glass water jug, the one all the fuss has been about?"

"Yes."

"He approves of you, then?"

"No, he thinks I'm nothing. It was a present for Milvia."

"Did you tell her that?"

"No. I took the damned thing home, then I had to be vague about it. I don't want her to know he's here. I don't want him to give her gifts paid for from his illegal activities."

"Pardon me, but you and Milvia seem to have a strange relationship. I've been trying to meet you at your house, but you're never there. You hate your wife's family, and you seem to have little to do with her, yet you stay married. Is this for purely financial reasons? I thought you had money of your own?"

"I do."

"Are your gambling debts exorbitant?"

"Certainly not. I've been very successful." He might support the Whites, but clearly he did not bet on them—unless he bet on them losing. But no one would give him long odds. "I'm just about to buy a training stable of my own."

I whistled jealously. "So what's with Milvia?"

He shrugged. Complete disinterest. Amazing.

I gave him a stern look. "Take my advice, young man!" He was about my own age, but I was streets ahead of him in experience. "Either get a divorce, or pay some attention to your wife. Be businesslike. A racing trainer wants to impress the punters. You can't afford to have whiffs of scandal sullying your name. People you depend on will just laugh at you."

Forgetting that people would know he had a father-in-law who was a condemned extortionist and murderer, Florius fell for the domestic threat. "Milvia wouldn't—"

"She's a woman; of course she would. She's a pretty girl who's very lonely. She's just waiting for a handsome piece of trouble to walk in and smile at her."

"Who are you talking about?" It would have been tough talk, had he not been less worked up than a scallop basking open on a sandbank. Pardon me; scallops lead lives of vivacious incident compared to Florius.

"It's hypothetical." I was terse. "Let's stick with your father-in-law. It sounds to me as if you have a very strong interest in helping the officials discover him. To start with, you can assist me. I was inquiring into the glassware. It is stolen property—" Florius groaned. He was a man in a nightmare. Everything he heard about the Balbinus family—including my instructions about his wife—made him more anxious. "I don't suppose Balbinus made up a story about where he got it from?"

"He didn't have to make it up," said Florius, sounding surprised. "I was with him at the time."

"How come?"

"He kept insisting he wanted to send a present to my wife. He made me go with him to buy something."

Taking a hostile witness to a receiver's lockup sounded strangely careless for a king of crime. I was amazed. "Balbinus *bought* his gift? Where from?"

"A place in the Saepta Julia."

It was still raining, but the Saepta lies right alongside the Pantheon. I dragged Florius across the street and into the covered market. I made him show me the booth where the jug had been purchased. Almost as soon as we reached it, the eager proprietor hurried out to greet us, clearly hoping his previous customer had come back for more. When I stepped into view, the atmosphere cooled rapidly.

I told Florius to go. He already had a jaded view of life. I didn't want him more upset. And I did not want any strangers present when I spoke my mind about the glass to its slimy, seditious retailer. All our efforts to follow up the Syrian water jug had been a waste of time. It had no bearing on the Balbinus case. The "stolen" glass had never been lost. All I was pursuing here was a sleazy compensation fraud—one to which I was myself inextricably linked.

"Hello, Marcus," beamed the dealer, utterly unabashed as usual.

I answered in my blackest tone, "Hello, Pa."

"That crown of yours was a gorgeous bit of stuff. I can make you a fortune if you want to sell. I had one customer who was interested—"

"Who actually bought it, you mean?"

"I told him Alexander the Great had worn it once."

"Funnily enough, that's one of the ludicrous stories the original salesman tried out on me. You're all the same. Though not all of you steal from your own sons and go in for blatant fraud!"

"Don't be unkind."

"Don't make me livid. You bastard, you've got some explaining to do."

Frankly, now I knew the "loss" of the glass was just another example of my father on the fiddle, I did not want to hear any more. "Ah, Marcus, settle down—"

"Stop warbling. Just describe the man who came here with the limp lettuce leaf who was just with me—the man who bought the glass water jug."

"Balbinus Pius," answered Pa.

"You know that thug?"

"Everyone knows him."

"Do you know he's an exile case?"

"I heard so."

"Why didn't you report seeing him?"

"He was buying; I don't throw trade away. I knew someone would be on to him eventually. That great po-faced lump of a friend of yours, presumably . . . Come in for a drink," invited my father cheerily.

Instead I left.

LV

As I strode angrily home I felt edgy. For one thing, I had ringing in my ears various sly protestations from Pa—mighty claims that he had meant no harm (oh that old story!), and bluster that he would never have accepted compensation illegally. . . . To be descended from such a reprobate filled me with bile.

There was more to my sense of unease than that. Maybe I was growing jumpy. The knowledge that Balbinus was here and apparently flourishing, despite all the law's efforts, depressed me bitterly. What was the point in anything if criminals could do as they liked and go where they pleased, and laugh at verdicts so blatantly?

The city felt unfriendly. A cart raced around a corner, causing walkers and pigeons sipping at fountains to scatter; it must be breaking the curfew, for dusk had only just fallen, and there had hardly been time for it to have reached here legitimately from one of the city gates. People pushed and shoved with more disregard than ever for those in their path. Untethered dogs were everywhere, showing their fangs. Sinister figures slunk along in porticoes, some with sacks over their shoulders, some carrying sticks that could be either weapons or hooks for stealing from windows and balconies.

Groups of uncouth slaves stood blocking the pavement while they gossiped, oblivious to free citizens wanting to pass.

An irresponsible girl backed out of an open doorway, laughing. She banged into me, bruising my forearm and making me grab for my money in case it was a theft attempt. I roared at her. She raised a threatening fist. A man on a donkey shoved me aside, panniers of garden weeds crushing me against a pillar that was hung dangerously with terra-cotta statuettes of goggle-eyed goddesses. A beggar stopped blowing a raucous set of double pipes just long enough to cackle with mirth as a white-and-red-painted Minerva cracked me across the nose with her hard little skirt. At least being pressed so hard had saved me from the bucket of slops that a householder then chose to fling out of a window from one of the dark apartments above.

Insanity was in Rome.

When I reached Fountain Court, the familiar scents of stale flatfish, gutter water, smoke, chicken dung, and dead amphorae seemed positively civilized. At the bakery, Cassius was lighting a lamp, meticulously trimming its wick and straightening the links on its hanging chain. I exchanged greetings with him, then walked up on that side of the street to say a few words to Ennianus, the basket-weaver who lived below my new apartment. He had supervised removal of the skip. I borrowed a flat broom and swept some loose rubbish up the gulley so it was outside a house whose occupants never spoke to us.

I was still talking to Ennianus when I spotted Lenia taking tunics down from a line across the laundry's frontage. I turned my back, hoping to avoid being hailed for a boring discussion of her wedding, now only ten days away. She must have missed me; her eyes were never good. Either that or she had finally given up any hope of cajoling me into sympathy. I had no energy to spare for people who ought to know better, who dragged aggravation down on themselves. Rome was too full of trouble for me to face her tonight.

There was more trouble than I realized. When Ennianus grinned and told me it was safe to face the street again, I saw two men walking past the barber's shop. I knew I recognized them, though at first I could not remember why.

"Who are those two, Ennianus?"

"Never seen them here before."

I felt I had a grievance against them. So I broke off my chat with the basket-weaver and quietly followed them.

As they walked I applied my subtle knowledge of the world to deducing what I could about them. From behind, they were ordinary, empty-handed punters, about the same height as each other, and the same build. They wore brown sleeveless tunics, belted with old rope by the look of it, unexceptional boots, no hats or cloaks. They must be outdoor types.

They were walking with purpose, though not hurrying. These were not loafers just looking for fun in the city. They had a fixed destination, though they lost themselves on the way. They led me along on the Aventine summit towards the riverside, then discovered the crag and had to find a path down. They did not know Rome—or at least they were strangers on the Hill.

Eventually they hit the Clivus Publicus. They carried on downhill past the Temple of Ceres, then, when they reached the bottom near the Circus Maximus, they had to buy a drink at a streetside stall so they could ask directions from the proprietor. They next turned along the Circus and began walking its length; clearly they should have come down off the Hill in the other direction, towards the twin aqueducts and the Capena Gate.

We were in an area which had featured frequently in my life the past few days: that part of the Eleventh region which bordered the Circus. At one end lay the Forum Boarium, where the body of Nonnius Albius had been left on the pavement in the stink of animal blood. Along the valley of the Circus ran a narrow finger of land where stood the lavish houses inhabited by Flaccida and Milvia. Then, on the other end, was the cluster of dingy, unattractive streets which included Plato's Academy.

By the time we had gone that far, I felt unsurprised that the brothel should be where my two men were heading. I was also certain they were rogues. I could prove it: I had re-called where I first saw them, though it was not in Rome. Their names—their working names, anyway—were Gaius and Phlosis. They were the pair of fake boatmen at Ostia who had tried to relieve me of my father's glass before I brought it to Rome for that other great fraud to try stealing it from himself.

I watched them enter the brothel, greeting the girl on the door as if they knew her. They could have been clients, vis-itors to Rome who had had Plato's recommended by a friend. That was my assumption until I realized the girl had let them enter without money changing hands.

There was no doubt Lalage had customers who kept monthly accounts here. However, the kind of men who were so favored would not be lowlifes from the waterfront, but trusted people like the Very Important Patrician who came with lictors in tow. Gaius and Phlosis were here in some other, very different, context. And from the doorkeeper's at-titude, even if they had got lost on the Hill, down here at Plato's the incompetent couple were regular visitors.

I wondered whether to follow them in. I was in the wrong condition for adventures tonight. I was tired. It had been a hectic week, packed with incident, and I knew my concen-tration was slipping. Besides, Plato's was a huge warren; no-body knew I had come here tonight, and if I went inside I had no idea what I would be going into.

The situation was far too dangerous. For once, discretion won.

LVI

I needed help with this. I needed someone who would be tough if we ran into trouble, someone trained to carry out surveillance properly. If my hunch was correct, I had stumbled across something major. It would be hazardous. It needed the vigiles. The person I really should take this evidence to was Petronius Longus. Well, that was impossible.

I could ask Rubella. Pride—pride and the fact that if I was wrong I could be merely watching a couple of paltry sneak thieves enjoying themselves at a brothel—determined me to take this forwards unofficially.

There were practical problems. I did need a partner. I wanted to subject the brothel to all-day surveillance, with the possibility of tailing some of its visitors as they came and went. I wondered whether I could risk using one of my nephews. But with Tertulla still missing, I knew all the young Didii were being marched to school in convoys and supervised by anxious mothers. There was no way I could cream one off without an angry rumpus flaring up. Besides, even I could see this work was too dangerous.

Still desperate, I faced the fact that if Petronius would not help me, what I needed was one of his men. With luck, whoever I picked would not be the happy sneak who had betrayed Linus.

As chance had it, on my way back up the Aventine I ran into Fusculus. He would have been ideal. Fusculus was fascinated by the world of small-time criminals, an expert on specialist dodges. He would be full of ideas on why a set of cargo raiders from Ostia might have come to Rome. It was he himself who had inspired my belief that Gaius and Phlosis might have serious significance: I remembered that after my own close shave with the stolen boat at Portus, he had told me Balbinus Pius used to run a whole gang of craft-rig thieves along the wharves in Rome. Maybe these two were part of his old network. Maybe it was Balbinus who had brought Gaius and Phlosis here. Maybe that meant the brothel was being used to run his empire now. It looked like that good old ruse, a cover joint.

When I fell into step beside him Fusculus growled, "Get lost, Falco!"

Presumably Petronius had been unable to confide in any of his men the fact that one of them was a traitor. He needed to identify the bad apple first. So I could not call on that to justify my role in working for their tribune. "Settle down. So Petro's told you all that I'm a management nark. He says I betrayed his friendship to spy on you—and naturally you simple souls all think that's terrible."

"I don't want to know you, Falco."

"What beats me, Fusculus, is how if you're all in the clear you can take the attitude that anyone trying to oppose corruption has to be your enemy."

"You're poison."

"Wrong. What you mean is, he's your chief, so even if he wants to play silly ass you'll stick by him to protect your promotion chances. You would all do better starting a whip-round to buy Lucius Petronius a new brain."

Fusculus told me to get lost again, and this time I did.

I felt sour. Nobody likes being hated.

Luckily there was one person left whom I could safely call upon. Someone sufficiently experienced for my purposes. Someone who was hated too.

I knew where he lived: back again on the opposite side of the Hill, by the Clivus Publicus. The Fates were enjoying themselves tonight. I marched my weary feet there again, and fortunately found that he was not yet out on night patrol. It was as I thought. Petro always took the busy first shift. He left the later, quieter one to Martinus his deputy.

It was late. I came to the point. I had been hoping to avoid telling him all my suspicions, but I soon saw that the best plan was to throw the big idea at him: "How's the hunt for Balbinus going? Not well. Of course not; he's too clever. But I think I've got a lead. I'd take it to Petronius, but since he wants to play soft, I'll have to do the surveillance alone. Maybe once I can demonstrate how the Balbinus empire now operates undercover at Plato's, Petro will want to join in. Maybe I won't give him the chance. I could keep all the glory—me and whoever shares my trouble. . . ."

Martinus did not fail me. He was overjoyed at being asked to help. Well I knew why: He thought it was his great chance to do Petro down.

I told him what I had seen at Plato's, and what I reckoned we might see if we watched the place. "Does Rubella know about this, Falco?"

"I'm not at liberty—"

"Don't get pious! I know what that means."

I considered for a moment. "He doesn't know, but we shall have to tell him. You can't go missing from the official team."

"I'll see Rubella," Martinus suggested. "If he goes along with this, he can fix it. He can say he's sending me to some other cohort. The chief won't be the least surprised. It's more or less traditional that as soon as you're stretched beyond endurance on a really major case, your best man gets filched to look for brooch thieves in some disgusting bathhouse in another watch's patch."

I had no doubt that the axiomatic secondment would be easy to arrange. Whether Martinus was the Fourth Cohort's "best man" could brook more argument. That didn't matter. The pompous self-satisfied article was good enough for what I wanted. Martinus would love to spend all day just sitting in a food stall waiting for nothing much to happen. As long as I could be in a different food stall at the opposite end of the alley, I didn't care how tedious he was.

When I finally made it back there for the second time that night, Fountain Court lay in complete darkness. No one there wasted lamp oil providing light for muggers and porch-crawlers to go about their dirty work. I steeled myself and trod quietly, keeping to the center of the lane. As I walked past the bakery, I thought I heard a shutter creak above my head. I looked up, but could see nothing. The apartment above the bakery, the one with half its floor missing, could hardly have been let, and all the stories above it were supposed to be even more derelict. Once beside the laundry I looked back again to make certain, but nothing moved.

Climbing the endless steps to my apartment, I should have felt more confident. I was now on my own territory. That situation can be deadly dangerous. You relax. You assume the problems of nighttime in Rome are over. You know too much to be really observant. Your ears stop listening for unnatural sounds. You can easily be rushed by some unexpected watcher who is lurking in the pitch dark halfway up the stairs.

But nobody attacked me. If anyone lay in hiding, I never noticed. I reached my own door, opened it stealthily, and soon stood indoors.

There were no lights here either, but I could feel the familiar presence of my furniture and possessions. I could hear the breathing of Helena, of the unwanted mongrel who had adopted us, and the skip baby. Nothing else. Nothing more sinister. Everyone within these two rooms was safe. They had lived through the day even without me to guard them, and now I was home.

I said quietly, "It's me."

The dog thumped its tail, but stayed under the table. The babe said nothing, but he could not have heard. Helena half roused herself as I climbed into bed, then came into my arms, warm and drowsy. We would not talk tonight. I stroked her hair to put her back to sleep again, and within a short period I drifted into sleep myself.

Out in the streets the foot patrols would be marching, on the search for fires and loiterers. Somewhere Petronius Longus also kept watch, hearing in the sharp October air endless rustles and creaks of evil at work, but never the certain footfall of the man he sought. In the restless pulse of the city, lone thieves crept over windowsills and balconies, conspirators plotted, off-duty gangs drank and swore, lechers grabbed and fumbled, hijackers held up delivery carts, organized robbers ransacked mansions, while bleeding porters lay bound in corridors and frightened householders hid under beds.

Somewhere, in all probability, Balbinus Pius was dreaming peacefully.

LVII

One day might be enough. It could certainly be enough to make me look a fool. If we watched the brothel all day and there was no discernible criminal activity, my name would be bog weed. Whether I wanted to skulk around longer looking for a chance to apprehend Gaius and Phlosis for annoying me at Ostia would be up to me. Martinus would curse me and storm off to tell the entire cohort what incompetent, aggravating blocks of wood informers were, and how he had been taken in.

On the other hand, if there was enough to-ing and fro-ing of known members of the Balbinus gangs to suggest a link with his empire, I would be justified. Not a hero, but entitled to swank at the bathhouse. It would be a pleasant change.

Martinus and I arrived at dawn. We began by sitting in a doorway like runaway slaves. Later a sad thermopolium was opened by a creaky woman who spent ages dabbling around the floor with a flat-headed broom and a bucket of gray water. We watched her desultory efforts at wiping down counters; then she fidgeted about with her three shelves of cups and flagons, emptied some blackened pots into her counter holes, and stood a few amphorae crookedly against a wall.

We ambled up. We told her we were foxing—watching the streets for "opportunites," illegal ones being understood. She seemed neither surprised nor shocked by this notion. Martinus engaged in brief negotiations, coins chinked into her apron pocket, and we were encouraged to park ourselves indoors on tall stools. There we could look as if we were picking at olives while we watched Plato's. We bought a dish of something in cold dark gravy. I left most of mine.

Things were very quiet to begin with. Despite my good intentions I ended up staying in the same bar as my assistant (stalwartly ignoring the fact that he seemed to assume *I* was helping *him*). The only other food stall was the one where Petro and I had sat when we first eyed up the brothel before visiting Lalage, a place where we had shown ourselves to be law-and-order men. Today I wanted to pass for ordinary street grime.

I could just about trust Martinus to blend in. He must have been forty, so older than Petronius, the chief he was longing to elbow aside. As far as I knew he had remained unmarried, and though he talked about women, his relationships were quiet incidents in a fairly ordered life. He had straight brown hair, cut neatly across the forehead, heavily shaded jowls, and a dark mole on one cheek. He seemed too boring to arouse comment.

As the morning passed we started to see typical activity—locals visiting Plato's routinely. It seemed a long time since I had groaned over this with Petro, though when I bothered to work out the time scale (needing mental entertainment) I realized it was only five days ago. In those five days Rome had descended from a city where you were wise to keep your eyes open into one of complete lawlessness.

"Here we go!" Martinus had spotted suspects. From the brothel emerged three figures; a thin man in a sky-blue tunic, with an intelligent face and a scroll dangling from his waist, and two companions, one plump, one pockmarked, both inconspicuous. We had not seen them going in that morning; they must have been at Plato's overnight.

"Know them?" I asked quietly.

"The one in blue is a Cicero." I lifted an eyebrow. "A

talker, Falco. He engages the attention of men drinking in wine bars, then keeps them laughing at his stories and jokes while the other two rob them."

Martinus drew out a tablet and stylus, then began making notes in firm square Latin lettering. As the day progressed, his writing was to shrink as the tablet rapidly filled up. To make us more unobtrusive, he later produced a pocket set of draughts, glass counters in black and red that he kept in a small leather bag. We set out a board, drawn in gravy on the marble. To look authentic we had to play for real, worse luck. I hate draughts. Martinus was an intelligent player who enjoyed his game. In fact, he was so keen it would have been insulting to fake it, so I had to join in properly and attempt to match his standard.

"You should practice, Falco. This is a game of skill. It has parallels with investigation." Martinus was one of those pretentious board game philosophers. "You need mental agility, strength of will, powers of bluff, concentration—"

"And little glass balls," I remarked.

The morning continued without much incident, though we did see a limping man whom we reckoned must be on the "wounded soldier" racket and another whom Martinus had once arrested for hooking cups off drink stall shelves. He ignored the Oily Jug, our perch. At lunchtime a whole parade of men who appeared to be legitimate customers were crowding to the brothel, when my companion stayed his hand just at the moment of capturing my last viable counter. "Falco! There go a real couple of gangland educators!"

I didn't need him to point out the enforcers. Emerging from Plato's for a midday stroll were the Miller and Little Icarus. "I know them. Those are the pair who tried acting as rough masseurs to me. They must be living there."

"Seeing two from the old Balbinus setup gives us enough to mount a raid, Falco."

"You sure? We have to be certain we land the big one."

"If he's there."

"If he isn't there all the time, I reckon he comes visiting." Before we did anything rash, I wanted to watch for an evening and night at least. Martinus made no attempt to

demur. He was not stupid—far from it. The bastard was a
champion draughts player.

In the afternoon three more seedy characters caught our
attention as they emerged. We decided they were low-life.
There was a flash type in punched sandals and a niello belt,
a broken-nosed hearty who kept kicking curbstones, and a
weed who came out scratching his head as if a whole herd
of little lodgers were bothering him. I felt itchy just looking.

"Fancy stretching your legs?" I asked. Martinus swept up
his glass counters in an instant, and we set off to trail the
trio. We both had to go. One man can't follow three.

For a nicely brought-up Aventine boy it was a real eye-
opener. First two of them joined the squash in an elbow
joint, pretending to buy a stuffed-vine-leaf lunch while they
worked through the customers with a skill that left me gasp-
ing. When someone went to pay for a flagon too early,
found his purse gone, and caught on to them, out they ran
like eels. The third man was loafing on the doorstep as if
unconnected; he misdirected the robbed man, who pelted
down the wrong street while our friends met up together
and mooched off the other way. We never saw them cleaning out the purses they had lifted, but we noticed the empty
pouches flipped into a cart.

We split up to walk on either side of the street for a
while, still tailing the three. They were now heading for the
Forum. It was at its busiest, all the temple steps crowded
with moneychangers and salesmen, and the spaces around
the rostra packed. Our mark with the overactive lice paused
to kick and rob a drunk near the House of the Vestals. The
crunch of his boot going in symbolized all that was vicious
in the Balbinus gangs.

They moved on through the press of fishwives and
breadsellers, "sampling" rolls, sausages, and fruit as the
fancy took them, never paying for any of it. One was a real
reacher, adept at leaning across shop counters to grab
money or goods. In the end we could bear to watch no
longer, not without arresting them. That might alarm the
brothel; we had to hold back. They were tackling the Basilica Aemilia, the main center of commerce in Rome, which

was cluttered with itinerant sellers and tacky stalls; plenty of scope for our boys to spend a lucrative hour.

Incensed, Martinus and I walked back into the Forum. We took a breather in the shade of the Temple of the Divine Julius, reflecting on our researches so far.

"Those three were sharp little movers. What you've uncovered has Balbinus' seal stamped all over it," Martinus commented. He seemed depressed.

"What's up? Do you think we're wasting our time taking on the gangs?"

"You never wipe out thieves, Falco. If we put those three in a cell, someone else will be along, aiming to relieve diners of their purses while they're licking out their bowls."

"If you think that, why do this job at all?"

"Why indeed!" He sighed bitterly. I said nothing. I knew this mood was a hazard of life in the vigiles. I had known Petro long enough.

Sometimes the pressure and danger, and the sheer weight of despair, caused one of them to resign. The others became even more unsettled for a while. But normally they moaned a lot, got paralytic with an amphora, then carried on. Given their lousy pay and harsh conditions, plus the traditional indifference of their superiors, complaint seemed understandable.

Martinus was now watching passersby. His arms were crossed on his chest, and his fat backside was thrust out in his habitual way. His large eyes were taking in everything. I remembered that when we were waiting for Balbinus at Ostia it was Martinus who had stayed twitching at the door of the tavern, and how timely had been his warning of the escort's approach. Here in the Forum, although his thoughts seemed to be upon disheartened philosophy, he had spotted the vagrant who was drunk as a vintner's carthorse weaving a determined course towards two highly snooty types in togas outside the Julian courts. He had noted the slaves fooling about, including the one who had pinched another's inkpot and hidden it in his tunic with a genuine intent to steal. He had seen the old woman crying and the girl who did not realize she was being followed home. His gaze had finally settled on the group of young boys loitering on the steps of the Temple of Castor and Pollux, youths who were clearly looking for trouble though probably not yet committed to a life of crime.

"Of course, it's a job," he mused. "Fresh air and mental challenges. At least when you get hit on the head it's no surprise. There's a routine, if you like that, but scope to use your initiative. You have wonderful colleagues to insult you day and night. Plus the joy of knowing everyone else thinks you're just a fireman and despises you. I haven't doused a flame in fifteen years."

"You've been on inquiries most of your career?"

"Must be thought to have the knack," he replied dryly.

He had the cynical tone of a man who knew all superiors were incapable of judgment or man management. This could have made him vulnerable. But somehow I felt that Martinus was too easygoing to complicate his existence by taking bribes. He was too lazy to bother, Petro would say.

"So what do you reckon we do now?" I asked. Naturally I had my own ideas. I was convinced the brothel had been made the new center of the Balbinus organization.

"We need to know if Balbinus is inside Plato's."

I agreed so far. "Or if not, when they are expecting him."

"So we need an inside man," Martinus said.

I glanced at him uneasily. "You mean one of us?"

"Jupiter, no! Unless"—he grinned—"you fancy volunteering?"

"If that's the plan, I fancy a long vacation on a pig farm in Bruttium!"

Martinus shook his head. "We need a single-handed worker. One who looks bent enough to be accepted without comment, but who has no real allegiance to the Balbinus mob." He pointed a long finger at a pickpocket who for the past half-hour had been patiently working the crowds. "There's one I know. He'll do."

We walked across to the unobtrusive pouch-snatcher and waited until he bumped into his next victim. Martinus instantly laid a hand on his shoulder, and just as quickly the man darted off. "Drop him, Falco!"

I knocked the snatcher's legs from under him, and Martinus sat down hard on his ribs. We tossed the purse back to the victim, who blinked in surprise, then looked at us as if he feared we were setting him up for some really complicated con. Sighing, Martinus waved him away.

We stood the pickpocket upright and grinned at him.

LVIII

"Listen, Claudius—"

"Me name's Igullius!"

He was a runt. I myself would never have let him nick my purse; I would not have let this ill-favored, pathetic creature stand near enough to me to finger it. "His name's Igullius. Write it down, Martinus!" Martinus fetched out his note tablet and wrote it down. First, however, he courteously checked the spelling.

This pickpocket had a greasy face and oily hair. His breath was coming in short, frightened pants. It informed us that his breakfast had included hard-boiled eggs; his lunch was a garlic stew. The flavoring had been generous and was now pervading all the pores of his unhealthy skin.

Martinus and I stepped back. Igullius wondered if he dared make a run for it. We glared. He stayed put. Martinus explained like a kindly uncle that it was necessary for him to submit to a search.

Igullius was wearing a natural wool toga, which Martinus lifted off him, using the tips of his fingers as if he thought he might catch plague. Somewhat to our surprise we found nothing in its folds. Igullius looked self-righteous. We surveyed what was left of him: battered boots and a rather wide-necked tunic, fastened tightly round his midriff by a nipped-in belt that was nearly bisecting him.

"Take off your belt," I commanded.

"What for?"

"So I can thrash you with it, if you don't get a move on." I sounded like a watch captain. Sometimes you have to lower yourself to obtain a result.

With a filthy look, Igullius hoicked in his rib-gripper and let the clincher off its notch. Purses tumbled from beneath his tunic with a melodious clink. One bounced on his kneecap, causing his leg to kick. "Ooh look, Falco, it's snowing denarii!"

"I'll see you," the pickpocket replied defiantly, as Martinus tweaked at the tunic in case there was more.

"I don't take." The answer from Martinus came out sweetly and calmly. Igullius probably failed to realize this was the Forum Romanum district, whereas we were from the Aventine. The First Cohort ought to be in charge here, though typically none had been visible anywhere for the past hour. Martinus stooped, gathering the booty. "The game's up, Igullius. You're going to climb the tree; we'll crucify you."

"I never did nothing."

Martinus shook a couple of purses in his face. "We'll have to discuss that. Falco, let's take him to a private room somewhere."

"Oh no!" Sheer terror now gripped our captive. "I'm not going in any cell with you!" Martinus had never intended taking him to the Fourth's patrol house; apart from the fact we did not want to involve Petronius, we were too far away. But the mere hint caused an extreme reaction. Somebody somewhere in the cohorts had a formidable reputation.

In fright Igullius made a sudden break. I grabbed him and wrapped his arms around his back, holding him fast. Martinus was stuck with the flavorsome breath, but carried on bravely. "You stink and you steal. Give me one good reason to go easy on you, Igullius!"

The pickpocket had been in the streets long enough to know what was required. "Oh Jupiter! Well what have I got to do?"

"Cooperate. But you'll like it," we told him. "We're going to give you the money to go with a prostitute!" We turned the pickpocket round, took an arm each, lifted him over a screever who was begging on the pavement with a piteous message, then marched him down the Sacred Way.

As we crossed the Via Nova into the shadow of the Palatine I noticed Tibullinus, the centurion of the Sixth. We had seen him at Ostia, and he had turned up when we were looking at the corpse of Nonnius. Tibullinus was too closely involved in events to let him notice us here. I gave Martinus the nod. Alert, he took the point. But Tibullinus was patrolling the Palatine in a style that seemed to suit him—laughing and joking with fellows he recognized. He did not see us.

We took our new acquaintance back to the Oily Jug. This time we were more brisk with the woman. She had two choices—either to spend the next couple of days with a friend somewhere, or to pass them in a cell. Once again this throat worked miracles. She decided she had a sister who was longing to see her, and fled from our watching post.

Training Igullius was tiresome. We used the kind method, only thumping him when his eyes glazed. "That building over there is called the Bower of Venus—"

"That's Plato's."

"Have you been there?"

"Of course." He was possibly bluffing, but he wanted to appear a smart man about town.

"Well, Plato's may be under new management, but we're not interested in the brothel itself. There's a phoenix in Rome. A person who is supposed to be banished has come home again." Maybe Igullius knew. He was already pale. "His name is Balbinus Pius. Some of his men are hanging out in Plato's. Maybe he's there too. Maybe he's just hiring rooms for them. But if he visits his troops, we want to know. You see how it is, Igullius. You're going in, you're going to recognize a friend, or make a new one if you have to, but however you do it you're going to sit in a corner keeping quiet until you can come out and tell us a date and time when Balbinus will be available for interview."

"Oh, give me a chance, Falco! I'm dead if I try that."

"You're dead if you don't." Martinus smiled. He enjoyed playing the cruel executioner.

I took a hand again. "Now settle down, Igullius. We know you're not entirely bad, so we're giving you this fine job opportunity. You're going to be our undercover man. And to compensate your loss of earnings from your regular work, we'll find you a big ex gratia at the end of the day."

"How about paying some in advance?"

"Don't be stupid," said Martinus. "We're in the vigiles. We have to remember public accountability."

Igullius tried one last desperate wriggle. "That place is full of hard men. They'll spot a weed in the garden straightaway."

"You've been there before, according to you. You'll have to make sure you blend in," I said callously. "You're perfectly capable. Anyone who can slide up and sneak purses, even though he has breath that can be smelled at twenty paces, can merge into a nest of mostly stupid criminals."

We gave him the price of a whore to start him off convincingly, then pushed him on his way.

Success came fast, Igullius was back in a couple of hours, nipping across the street like a startled cat. Whatever he learned had left him panic-stricken. He fell into the thermopolium, then threw himself behind the counter with his head in his hands.

"Oh, you bastards! Don't make me go back again."

"That depends," sneered Martinus. "What have you got for us?"

"I've got what you asked for, and I'm not getting any more!"

I found him a drink to calm his hysteria. He gulped down the wine, which I knew was disgusting, as if he had just crawled out of a six-day sandstorm in an arid zone. "Control yourself. You're safe now. What was your girl like?"

"All right . . ." Easily sidetracked! Martinus and I leaned on the counter watching him. Crouching at our feet, he managed to slow his breath.

"I think he's there! I'm sure he is!"

"Not visible, presumably?" Martinus asked.

"I didn't see him. I mean, I didn't see anyone who looked that big a character."

"Big? Don't believe it," I snarled. "Balbinus is just a flea."

Igullius continued, talking fast as if he wanted to get this over. "The place is humming. I've never been in a barn with such a live atmosphere. I saw half a dozen faces, I mean *serious* faces. There's one big room—" He shook, unable to spit it out. That sounded like the cavernous hall Petro and I had glimpsed. It had been full of small-timers then, but when I pressed the trembling Igullius for details, he described a real thieves' kitchen, with mobsters nesting openly.

I stared at Martinus. "Something's changed. It sounds as though Balbinus has taken over and made the place his own. Igullius, was there any mention of Lalage?" He shook his head. "Well, if you've been there before, is the brothel business being run the same as usual?" This time he nodded.

While I was pondering, Martinus tried screwing more useful facts from our eavesdropper, though to little effect. I sat in silence. We certainly could not send him straight back into Plato's this afternoon, or it would arouse the suspicions of the girl on the door. Martinus decided that Igullius could be let off and dismissed.

"I want my money then."

Martinus was looking at me unhappily. I realized he lacked the authority to pay over the kind of reward we had promised, and he was even too straight to hand back the purses Igullius had stolen in the Forum (which is what I would have done, given this was a crisis). Instead, Martinus was forced to remove the back block from his note tablet and write out a chit. "Take this to the patrol house—tomorrow!" he said sternly. That would give him some grace before Petronius found out.

The pickpocket snatched the warrant, then found his feet and scurried off.

I continued thinking. It looked as if Lalage had lied to me—no surprise at all.

I did not believe she was running the crime empire from Plato's herself. Lalage was not so stupid as to do that openly.

They were still working for the old regime. After all Lalage's claims about seizing her independence, it was hard to accept that she had caved in and allowed Balbinus Pius to take over her premises. That he might even be hiding up there seemed incredible.

She would not do it. Either he had removed her—in which case I doubted that the brothel would be running as smoothly as usual—or Lalage had some ploy in hand. That boded ill for Balbinus. But it might help us.

As Martinus and I continued our vigil, we abandoned casual chat—and draughts. That suited me. It also stopped his overblown raving about men who played board games being suitable to pit their wits against major criminals. Removing Balbinus from Rome called for a sudden rush with a sharp weapon, not cerebral guile.

It already felt like a long day, and I reckoned we were heading for a big night exercise. We found some stale bread to gnaw on. We had a drink. Indigestion set in cruelly.

Towards the evening we started feeling tense. Something was going on. Men, singly or in twos or threes, walked up to the brothel. They appeared in the street as quietly as bats. Making their way inside, they might have been bound for a party with their workplace dining club. If so, they were dressed less smartly than most colleagues going out for a bash. Also, they were being asked to pay a hefty ticket price: "That's boodle, or I'm a baby!" Martinus had identified our first definite sack of swag—a bedcover knotted at the corners, from within which came the charming chink of stolen silverware.

We both knew what we were watching. I had discussed this when I first tried to involve the deputy, and now as the early dusk fell I was being proved right. The starlings were roosting. All the day shifts were closing, and their operators were reporting in with their take, cashing up, making their way here with their takings from all the corners of the Aventine, the waterfront, and the Forum. The snatchers and grabbers, the confidence tricksters and bluffers, the strangling muggers, the dirty alley girls with thugs for minders, the robbers of drunks and schoolchildren, the mobs who held up ladies' litters, the thieves who beat up slaves. It was mainly money that was pouring in. Salable goods would be passed to receiving shops or metal furnaces. I had to slip out to a stationer's to buy more wax tablets, as Martinus had run out of space to note down all the criminals he knew. There were many more we could not identify—or not yet. Most of them left again shortly after arrival, clearly lighter of baggage.

We had to decide what to do. "Balbinus could have an accountant working at Plato's. A sidekick who just keeps the ledgers and pays off the workmen."

"What would you do, Martinus, if your most trusted collector had been Nonnius Albius, and he put you away?"

"I'd do the reckoning myself after that."

"I bet he agrees! If so, then he's in there."

"He's in there, Falco. Now he is. But if I was him, I'd move about."

"So you're saying let's nab him before he hops?"

"Don't you agree?"

Of course I agreed—but I wanted to go in there in strength. In particular I wanted Petronius among us. It was partly old loyalty. But more than that, if I was going into Plato's knowing it was full of evil men and hoping to find the worst of all calmly sitting there with a glass in his hand and an abacus, then I wanted someone at my back I could trust.

"So is it a jump?" Martinus demanded impatiently. From his tone it was clear that if I declined tonight, he would not continue to work with me. I could live without his draughts game, but not with whatever chaos he might wreak if he started working on his own.

"It's a jump if Rubella will give us some backup."

Even Martinus, with his high opinion of his own quality, could not consider a raid at Plato's with just the two of us. He went off to consult his tribune. I had to stay on watch. Things were so lively we no longer dared to leave together, in case we missed something.

I sat there for some time. I had taken one of the spare noteblocks, and was drawing a map of the brothel based on what I remembered from my two visits. One thing I knew

was that the place was very large. It occupied at least three
stories, each with numerous corridors. It had probably
grown from a single house, taking in those on either side as
success enabled expansion. Although there was one main
door, we had noticed that some of the gangsters knocked and
were admitted to a more innocent-looking hole in the wall;
they had a family entrance for criminals. In the other direction was a similar house door, much less used. Women occasionally slipped in and out. Once one emerged with two
small children; it must be the prostitutes' private exit. Not
many had freedom to come and go. I wondered where that
would place them in a fracas with the law.

Sometimes the prostitutes received their own visitors. All
were women. I made up some pretty reasons for these intriguing social calls. Some involved special entertainers
who lived elsewhere but were hired in. Some involved the
sort of tales adolescents tell each other about high-class
ladies working in brothels for high-spending favored clients.
Some of my theories were purely daft. Then two women
called whose behavior convinced me I knew what sometimes happened behind that private door.

They had come in a litter. It waited for them at the corner.
They climbed out slowly, looking up and down the narrow
street. Their skirts were long and full, their heads muffled in
quite heavy cloaks. After a brief hesitation they straightened
up and marched arm in arm to the mysterious door. Well-
heeled sandals clipped the pavement. One of them rapped,
so loudly I could hear it. Soon there was a furtive conversation with an inmate, and the two women went inside.

Of course I knew what I was witnessing. A girl with
money had got into trouble with a lover. Taking a friend for
support, she had come to the brothel in order to end her
problem with the aid of the abortionist. The Bower of Venus
was bound to possess one.

I could have lived with that. Desperate people are entitled
to risk their lives if it seems less harsh than the alternative.

What made me sick was that despite their caution I recognized those women. One was short and sturdy, with a self-
confident walk; one taller and straight-backed. The first was
my sister Maia. And the other was Helena.

LIX

They were in there for a long time. I wanted to rush in after them. Instead I remained at my post, brooding horrendously.

When they came out, it was hurriedly. The door slammed behind them. They took a few quick steps, then stood in heated discussion. I strode across to them.

"Oh gods, not still hanging around brothels!" Maia shrieked.

"Oh, you're here!" exclaimed Helena, with what sounded like relief. Her tone was urgent, tense, yet ill fitting the situation I had been conjuring up.

I was staring at Helena as she hugged her cloak around her. The girl I had loved—no; did love. With my sister, the only one I had been able to tolerate. "I'm on surveillance."

Helena compressed her mouth slightly. I realized I had hardly seen her for the past two days. This morning I had left the house before she woke. Only a dirty tunic on the back of the door would have told her I came in last night.

"Helena, I'm doing what's important. You know that."

"No, I don't know!" She actually stamped her foot. "I have not seen you to talk to since the day before yesterday. I *wanted* to talk to you—"

"I realize that." Something was wrong here. Helena knew

it too. We looked at each other in some trouble. My face seemed to have turned to wood. Anxiety and irritation jostled in hers. I croaked, "Are you all right?"

"We were very frightened, but it's better now."

"Are you hurt?"

"It wasn't like that."

It was Maia who understood first. Quick-witted and caustic, she had interpreted my clenched fists. She rammed her cloak back abruptly, so her dark curls jumped up. Her eyes were flashing.

"Juno Matrona! Helena Justina, this unforgivable bastard thinks you've just had a bodkin job!"

"Oh thanks, Maia." Everything took a very nasty lurch. "Always there with the fine and fluent phrase!"

"How could you, brother?"

I felt sick. "Something Famia said."

"I'll kill him!" Maia grated through her teeth. "Then I'll kill you for believing him!" While Helena still looked bewildered, my sister stormed off, yelling back, "I'll take Galla, I'll leave you the chair. Give my brother a good kicking, then for all our sakes, Helena, *talk to him*!"

I closed my eyes while the world rocked.

"We've commandeered a place to watch from. Will you come inside?"

"Is that an apology?" Helena was starting to appreciate that she had the right to feel insulted. I could see a faint gleam in her huge brown eyes that meant she was enjoying power. Dimly, at the corner of my vision, I was aware of Maia dragging my sister Galla from the litter and marching her away.

"What in Hades is Galla doing here with you?" I stormed. Then I warned feebly, "You gave me a bad fright. I'm in no condition to be whipped." Helena was staring at me. She looked tired and despondent. Presumably I had contributed to that. I hung my head. I was ready to try any tricks. "I love you, Helena."

"Trust me, then!" she snapped. Then she softened and offered her cheek for a formal kiss of greeting; I gave her a meek peck. As I drew back her face changed, crumpling slightly as if everything was becoming too much for her. "Oh, stop being stupid and hold me tight!" she cried.

Reprieve.

"Actually," she said, once I had hugged her fiercely and taken her indoors, "I was trying to *save* a child." I received the rebuke like a man, hiding my wince. "The people who have Tertulla sent another message yesterday—"

"Yesterday?"

"I wanted to discuss it, Marcus; you gave me no chance!" Apprehensive and annoyed with myself, I managed to signal yet another apology. Even I was growing bored with being abject. Helena growled, then herself owned up, "I decided I must do something, for the child's sake."

"Note the calm manner in which I hear this news, Helena."

"Full credit for an understanding nature." She could tell I was boiling over with anxiety.

"So instead of alerting the vigiles, you brought a couple of female bodyguards and came to ransom the child yourself?"

"What choice did we have?"

"Knowing the address they work from, Petro could have mounted a raid."

"They would have hidden the child and denied all knowledge. I'm not some frightened magistrate; I was going to report them once we had got Tertulla back."

I kept my voice level. "So you gave them the money, and of course they kept the bargain?" I had seen no sign of Tertulla.

Helena shook her head despondently. "No. I kept the money. They told me she's not there."

"They were lying. They realized you're a tough customer who will land them in court."

"I don't think so. They wanted the money. They were annoyed themselves. They say Tertulla must have run away. They can't find her anywhere. I did believe them; they even let us search—"

I was horrified. "In the brothel?"

We were both silent for a while. Bravery had always been

Helena's strongest quality, but I knew what she must have undergone. Since she had escaped unscathed, there was no point screaming over it. "The Fates only know where Tertulla has got to. Are you angry, Marcus?"

"No, but dear gods, it's my turn now to be held tight!"

Time was passing. In the city streets a new, more bustling mood took over as the evening activity began. Men had bathed. The sleek and the sleazy were leaving their homes and their places of business. This lane was growing darker; not many lamps ever burned around here.

I would have to send Helena home soon. Now we had settled down, I was enjoying our short time together. I needed her. Being alone with Helena refreshed me. Even in a tense situation I could open up, be frank, put aside the caution that must always be present with anyone else. While I was on duty with Martinus, I had to disguise my own intentions and to stalk his ambition. With Helena I soon felt clear-headed again.

"I suppose," I ventured thoughtfully, "you didn't see a man with a balding pate and self-deluding eyes, who looks as if he sells embroidery that will fall apart?"

"I tried to avoid the men." I bet plenty of men stared at her.

"Oh good! A girl who ignores brothel etiquette."

"Do you want me to go back and try to spot this man?" she asked. Always keen for adventure. The thought made me sweat with anxiety.

Luckily my stomach gave an enormously loud rumble. I confessed how little I had eaten that day. Helena Justina decided that although looking in the brothel for Balbinus would be a boon to the state, it had been superseded by her domestic responsibilities. She marched off to buy me some food.

As I ate, Helena was adding details to the map I had drawn. Martinus came back while I was still working through her lavish supplies, but I continued to munch without a conscience. Martinus had been missing so long, I had a good idea the deputy had shamelessly found himself a full dinner before he visited Rubella. "So what's the tribune going to do for us?"

"Bad news, Falco. Rubella's sole interest is the fact that this street lies in the Sixth Cohort's empire."

"He wants to bring them in? That's ridiculous. I don't trust the Sixth."

"Well, Rubella intends to discuss things with the Prefect before he'll authorize a raid—"

"Rubella's a fool."

"His plan is to go in tomorrow."

"That's a plan I'd like—if it was tonight."

Helena was still sitting quietly at my side. "What about Petronius?" she asked.

"Oh, hadn't you heard?" Martinus looked quite cheerful, so I knew it would be bad news. "He's off watch. There was an attack on the patrol house yesterday night. The fire-watchers were all out on a false alarm, but the chief was in there working. Someone rammed the joint with the old "run-away cart" trick—a cart full of rocks and rubble. Brought down half the doorway, but the back part of the building stood up to it, and Petronius escaped injury. Rubella reckons it was a direct attempt to get the chief. He thinks Balbinus was behind it, so he's declared Petro sick and sent him to the country."

"He won't take kindly to that."

"He handed in his resignation."

"Oh Jupiter!" For a calm man, my friend could do some pig-headed things.

Martinus grinned. "Rubella broke the tablet in half and handed it straight back." The tribune had some sense, then. But it meant tackling Plato's without our best man. "While I was on the Aventine I did speak to a few of the lads," hinted the deputy.

"What does that mean?"

"Sergius and four or five others may be along later."

"*Four or five?* Out of the question," I replied at once. "We can't go into Plato's without saturation coverage. Tell them not to bother."

"Tell them yourself!" retorted Martinus. He sounded petulant. Then someone tapped discreetly on the counter, and I found myself looking into the ridiculously handsome face of the whip man, Sergius. He had a long head, with a strong nose and chin, and flashing, even teeth. He was staring at Helena; she fixed her attention on counting the olive stones I had left after my repast.

Events were moving faster than I liked. They were out of control. With a thug like Balbinus, that could have fatal results.

Behind Sergius were several other men from the Fourth. At least now I knew that Petro had been sent on a goat-grazing holiday I could forget that they might have sneaked here in some mood of disloyalty to him. They were defying Rubella; I could allow that.

What I would not accept was any kind of crackbrained exercise against orders, without planning or backup, and really without full reconnaissance. I was determined to resist Martinus on this. Not that my common sense came to anything. The lads, as he called them (though they were large, fit, and ugly apart from Sergius), had piled into the Oily Jug like schoolboys invading a pastry shop. I was groaning and trying to say good-bye to Helena, so it was Sergius who spotted the development. He hissed, and quickly snuffed our lamp.

I heard the noise he had noticed. Two pairs of feet walking briskly in concert, accompanied by the disturbing chinks of heavy chains. They came from the direction of the Circus. The feet stamped with a cheerful energy in thick-soled, businesslike boots.

The men those feet carried so purposefully were known to most of us. They were Tibullinus and Arica, the centurion and his sidekick from the Sixth—two upstanding officers whom we all believed were taking bribes. They were marching into Plato's like conquering hunters, carrying on their shoulders a long pole of spoils. Suspended from the pole in chains was a male figure I recognized.

"Oh gods!" murmured Martinus. "I forgot to tell him we're the Fourth. He's gone and taken his damned chitty to the Sixth."

The trussed man was Igullius. He looked alive—but only just.

"Scatter!"

I heard my voice without expecting it. Somehow I made them all jump from the Oily Jug before the two men from the Sixth came out again to look for us. We managed to whip out of sight around the corner just in time, and heard a commotion as a group from the brothel turned over the dump we had left. Helena had had the sense to bring the still-warm bowl from which I had eaten my food. Tibullinus must have thought Martinus and I had gone home much earlier. They gave up after a short time, and retreated back to Plato's.

We were still there, however. And naturally there was just one thought on the rash deputy's mind: "They've got Igullius. If they don't know our plans already, he'll soon squeal to them. We have no time. Balbinus will be leaving any minute."

"Helena—"

Helena turned and banged the map we had drawn against my chest. Her voice was taut. "Don't apologize again. I don't want the last thing I remember to be you saying you were sorry. Oh, don't explain, I know!" she raged. "You've lost your surprise; you have no support; no one knows if the man you want is even in the brothel—but *you're going in*!"

LX

I took charge.

I passed the map around quickly and told them to get in without fuss, then disperse through the building fast. Forget thieves. Forget hard men. Forget even Tibullinus and Arica. Say nothing and hit no one, unless there was no choice. Save Igullius if it were possible, but keep filtering through towards the top and the back and the farthermost rooms of the brothel until we found Balbinus Pius.

"What then?"

"Yell your head off for the rest of us."

I like to keep plans simple. At least when this went wrong there would be only a minor body count. Only seven of us were going in.

We slipped inside in ones and twos. Paid the tally and winked at the doorkeeper.

"I'm Itia, and I'm here to see you enjoy yourselves."

"Thanks, Itia."

"Are you being joined by friends tonight?"

"Just a few."

"Maybe we'll give you a discount, then."

I was right. The brothel side of the business was reserving its position. But I did not imagine our discount would take the form of help.

I had gone in first. I walked quickly but with a casual manner. I went straight past the ground-floor rooms, the cloak pegs, and the washing facilities. There was a louder hum of masculinity than on previous times I had visited. From the big room where conspirators gathered came a full-throated wave of men drinking and talking. I did not look in. He would not be there, among the throng.

The place was already warm and hazy with lamp oil and taper smoke. Farther on it seemed quiet. Once, something attracted attention. I stepped into a room and found normal commerce in action. The girl was in the saddle. I quipped, "Glad to see you're on top of things!" and whipped the door shut on them.

Reaching stairs, I started climbing. At the landing I paused to listen. Behind me all sounded normal. No shouts of alarm. Martinus and the others must so far be undiscovered. It would not last.

Still no sign of Tibullinus and Arica. I opened more doors, more gently this time. I found either empty rooms or flesh trade of one kind or another. More kinds than I had ever heard of, in fact, though I had no time to make detailed notes.

The brothel seemed busy, but not in flourishing party mode. No one stopped me. No one even challenged my presence. Balbinus would have guards, the Miller, for instance. I would have to get past them; I had not even seen them yet.

The longer I was in there, the more urgent became my feeling that I needed to escape. I had come so far that if anything went wrong, fighting my way out would be impossible. I had been a spy scouting in hostile citadels many times before, but then I had stood some chance of disguising my identity. I was too well known here. Helena had been right. We were probably walking into a trap. My skin crawled as I began to feel the certainty that someone was fully expecting me.

There was a faint odor of incense in the air. I thought I recognized my location. I hit a wider corridor, where I remembered that the rooms were grander, though I felt no need to investigate now. I could hear music. I discerned light, and laughing voices. My stride increased. At the last moment, memory failed me, and without warning I crashed into the large room with the sunken entertainment area where Petro and I had reckoned orgies might be staged. I pulled up short, facing the certainty that something grossly pornographic had either been enacted in the recent past or was about to take place. As the braziers wreathed, burning an exotic fuel, the atmosphere hit me in the gullet; the inescapable message was that nobody who entered here would want to plead he was too honest to participate.

Candelabra stood all around the upper seating bank. Garlands of roses and other musky flowers coiled and writhed from every surface. There was a small band of musicians idly tuning up: a hand drum, panpipes, tambourines, and a curled flute. The musicians wore pleasingly friendly expressions and diagonal wisps of see-through drape. A smiling man in satyr's costume approached—the full gear of hairy trousers, goat hooves, highly visible naked working parts. His face, with its paint and fragile smile, was a disturbing contrast to the prominent masculine attribute. He gestured a welcome to me with a dreamy air. In the center of the floor four exquisite young girls, none of them older than fifteen, were performing warm-up stretches with a languid grace that spoke all too strongly of the nature of their act. They wore no clothes, even before their tableau commenced.

On the outer rim, men waited. Some tasted wine; others prodded at the serving staff or picked their teeth.

Opposite me stood the doorway that led to Lalage's rooms. There was another door. Either side of it were two long torches thrust into waist-high urns, blazing with a sweet odor of something akin to applewood. Before it lay an irregular, striped mat, the skin of some dead carnivore. To one side an extremely muscular man was chatting up a stripling who was holding a bronze ewer.

The music started. The audience stirred with a low ripple of lecherous anticipation. My eyes went automatically to the floor area. It was time to leave or be seduced. I had made my choice.

I walked around the edge of the room, I was keeping my eyes fixed on the slow and intricate patterns being wrought by the gleaming bodies of the quartet of girls. All around me were the heated faces of men looking shy while they fervently hoped we would soon reach that moment when a member of the acrobatic display would call for a volunteer from the audience.

It was certainly better than watching a grizzled Egyptian in a long nightgown performing "Where's my snake?"

I stared with the same eagerness as the rest of them, despite myself hoping to be shocked by the writhing hot properties. I was still staring as I leaned on the bronze ram's-head door handle and backed quickly through the door.

I closed it as I turned. It was solid and ornate, muffling the music instantly. Whatever I had entered was pitch black. A short distance away I could hear a shuffling noise, joined at one point by a metallic clink. Could this be Igullius?

I slipped the door ajar again and reached out for one of the Dioscuri torches. The brief inflow of light from the entertainment room gave me a second's warning. I sensed movement. Spinning back, I flung the torch to the right. Then from the left came a noisy snake of heavy chain, thrown by an expert who lassoed me and then dragged it tight. My torch had crashed onto a mosaic floor. By its quaking light Tibullinus the centurion flung another chain across the room so Arica could help hold me.

I had one chance. My arms were pinioned with bruising force. I threw myself backwards, jerking the second chain so that Arica fell off balance as he was catching it. Pain seared my arms, and my spine jarred badly. Arica dropped towards me. I had both feet up ready, and kicked into him with all my might.

Not hard enough. He yelled, but staggered upright. The bastard must have ribs like iron. As for me, I was on my back now, trapped in a mesh of links that Tibullinus was threshing tauntingly. Arica relieved his hurt feelings by stamping on my face. I managed to roll aside, but his great boot creamed down my scalp alongside one ear, tearing off skin and hair. They pulled me around the floor, knocking into the torch, though it failed to ignite me. There were enough restraints on me to subdue a maddened elephant. As I fought to resist, I roared out a name or two when I could, hoping help would come. I should have known better. My own name is Didius Falco, and help for me is the last gift the Olympian gods toss down.

In the end my dead weight must have tired them. I lost track of the kicks I had received. They lashed me up and attached part of the cold knotwork to a pillar. Tibullinus produced his centurion's vinewood stick, and amused himself by describing in picturesque terms what he would do with it. I pretended to be a pervert and slavered eagerly. If he came near enough at least I could spit on him.

Again, no such luck. They knew there were others with me. They promised a feast of torture later, then left with an appearance of urgency. Not long afterwards the fallen torch spluttered and went out.

I was in despair, but worse followed. How long I lay in the dark with my arms going numb I cannot say. It must have been an hour or so. There had to be time for Helena Justina to rush to the Aventine and take action she thought appropriate. The person she sent here had to start searching for *me*, and Tibullinus had to find and overpower *him*. By the time the door opened, I had heard the musicians in the room outside drive themselves into a frenzy—matched no doubt by the girls and their customers. I had also wasted considerable effort calling out to the exhausted company after the noise died down. Whatever their perverted tastes, they had no interest in a shackled man.

Then the door cracked open. Tibullinus did not bother bringing light into the room. He flung his captive headlong, gave him a good kicking, chained him up, spoke his usual attractive oration, and marched out again.

"Brisk," I said into the familiar darkness. "Though comforting in its warm predictability."

My new companion groaned. Maybe he was suffering from being kicked. Maybe he was just happy to be sharing his captivity with me.

After a few moments he recovered himself sufficiently to

break out into banter. "This is the last time." His voice was hoarse. He forced himself to have a rest. "This is the last time, Falco." I laid my head against the pillar behind me and sighed reflectively. "Next time you're in deadly danger, I'll stay at home and stroke the cat."

"Thank you," I said, inserting a quiet note of humility which I knew would drive him wild. "I'm touched at you coming to assist me—though it's not much use if you get yourself trussed up as well. But thank you, Lucius Petronius, my loyal friend."

LXI

Time passed.

Something dangerous was happening to my arms. I mentioned it to Petro. He was not so tightly shackled as me, probably because he had been chained up only after being knocked downstairs, hammered, and hit into the middle of next week with a large vase. He had not had my opportunities for increasing the torque by wild acrobatics. He expressed kind concern for my predicament, followed by the logical question of what did I expect him to do about it?

More time passed.

"Petro, where are your men?"

"What men? When Helena Justina had finished berating me, I ran straight here."

"Wonderful."

"Anyway, how could I call for reinforcements? I'm not here. I've been sent to the country."

"You didn't go."

"You bet I didn't. Not once I heard you'd cajoled that fool Martinus into some disastrous scheme."

"Well, I'm glad you're here," I told him warmly.

"Go to Hades," he instructed, though in the tone of a friend.

After a while I said, "I heard about the attempt to get you."

"Stupidity."

"Balbinus is not stupid. He knows you're the one he should worry about."

"You're right. I should have expected trouble." Petronius agreed to discuss it. His personal danger had been preying on his mind, and there was no one else with whom he could share his thoughts. His wife Silvia would have run amok in distress, and presumably Rubella thought imposing temporary exile showed sufficient sympathy. "The false fire alarm was a setup, of course. Someone knew I was working late that night."

"Any ideas?" I inquired, with caution.

"Someone in the team. Whoever set up Linus, presumably." The merest change in his voice acknowledged at last that I had been right about the cohort containing a traitor.

"Know who it was?"

"I've had suspicions for some time. I haven't tackled the issue yet."

There was a silence. He did not tell me the name of his suspect. Well, that was fine. Nor did I tell him mine.

"So," I exclaimed brightly. "Why were you working late? Reports?"

"No. While you and Martinus were playing hide-and-seek in a chop shop, some of us had work to do. Well, Rubella's idea of it. I've been caged up with the Temple of Saturn auditor—you know, the one who was working on the confiscation of the Balbinus estate."

"Anything useful emerge?"

"Not unless you want to split your sides at the news that Plato's Academy is a lease Balbinus had laundered. This henhouse had been given away as part of his daughter's dowry. So its landlord is wimpy Florius." We laughed.

Probably Florius had never realized. He would not be the first clean-living, self-righteous equestrian whose portfolio, unbeknown to him, was bursting with legendary brothels and cover joints.

I shifted. It was agonizing. I was yearning to escape. "When you got here, did you see Martinus, Sergius, and the rest?"

"Martinus was hustling out some half-dead pickpocket—an informant, I presume."

"Igullius?"

"If you say so. I didn't see the others." Petro's voice was clipped. "And if they had any sense they'd make damn sure they weren't near me to be seen."

Tibullinus must have left the door on the catch. A draft had blown it ajar slightly. All noises had ceased in the entertainment room now, as though the night must be well over. The audience and performers had gone home. Well, they had slunk off somewhere more private, anyway.

Nobody else had been brought to join us. Maybe that meant the others from the troop had found nothing of interest; maybe they had abandoned us. Typical of Martinus, Petro commented. I said nothing. In view of my presuming on his deputy's disloyalty, I was treading with care.

Tread was the wrong word. I could hardly move. Any attempt was torture. My flesh had swollen, and my arms felt as though they would never work again. I tried various ways of manipulating my body, but there was only one that permitted any kind of relief. So, if only to help my bruised feelings, I let out a mighty belch.

Then a small female voice outside the door whimpered, "Uncle Marcus, is that you?"

I heard a sharp intake of breath from Petro. Keeping down hysteria as much as possible, I managed to sound like an uncle who had a pocket full of honeyed dates. "Tertulla! Goodness, you'll be my favorite niece for this. Tertulla, pick up one of those big torches. Make sure you don't touch the flaming part, then bring it in to us . . ."

"I don't want to play this game."

"But come in and say hello to us," Petro said. "Anyway, we haven't told you yet what the game is."

There was a pause that made me ache with irritation, then a squeak, then the door widened, and in came a frightened little figure. She wore a dress that even her mother would disapprove of. She was dirty and exhausted, but she had the mournful air that told us she was terrified of being in trouble yet now wanted to go home. If we promised her a big enough bribe—for instance, protection against her distraught mother—Tertulla might be on our side.

LXII

Petronius Longus had always possessed a special smile, which he kept for certain situations when whatever he was planning did not require my presence. Now I learned that with this smile, subtly applied while talking quietly in that slow and friendly manner, Petronius could make a woman forget entirely that she did not want to cooperate. It was probably practice. He was, after all, the father of three little girls.

Somehow Petronius engaged Tertulla in the game of unwinding the chains that trussed him, then he and she together worked for a much longer time on the vicious cat's cradle that had been pinioning me.

He jerked my arms up and down. "Does this hurt?"

"Ow! Yes."

"That's good," he said. "You've still got some nerves left."

The entertainment room was deserted. Its floral decor had suffered a pounding. Behind the large obscene statue of the peculiar group intertwining, we spotted a window. It led onto a roof, which gave onto the street. I had to admit that my arms were unlikely to take weight yet; the pain was ex-

cruciating as the blood came back. So it was Petro who carefully lowered himself outside, who prayed that the tiles
would hold him, and then dropped to the ground. Tertulla
needed no encouragement to trust herself to the open if this
wonderful man would catch her. Now his fervent devotee,
she was soon out of there and jumping into his arms. I had
had to grab her dress to hold her back until Petronius was
standing in place.

We had agreed it was time to be sensible. I waited until I
saw Petronius hoist my niece in his arms and lope away. He
would carry the child to safety, then come back with reinforcements—this time convincing the sober Rubella that the
Sixth Cohort had no sensibilities we needed to respect. Left
alone, I too would be sensible. I would just wait quietly out
of sight.

As soon as he had gone I tossed that thought aside, and
crossed to the doorway which would take me to Lalage's
room.

It was all very quiet. I knocked gently, in case she was engaged in work of a sensitive nature, then I ventured in.

She was standing opposite, against a curtain. She appeared to be alone. Though she had not replied to my knocking, I was welcomed in with a deliciously courteous wave of
one arm. The room was deeply scented with its usual perfumes. Lalage was wearing the bracelet I had mended. Her
gown was of glowing golden silk, so fine it both covered
and expressly described the magnificent womanhood beneath. Straight-backed and bejeweled, this fabulous creature
had come a long way from the girl I had once known. I was
angry and battered, but I warmed to her dangerous magic.

"Marcus Didius! Why do I feel that I should have expected you? Welcome to my bower."

I paused, staring around. There could be no one behind
the curtain. It was attached to a rod that would allow it to be
drawn modestly to hide a bed in an alcove I had never seen
before. Maybe it was her own bed. Even prostitutes have to
sleep. Maybe once she lay flat just to dream, a prostitute of
her caliber earned the luxury of privacy.

The curtain was now gathered up in a tasseled cord

against the wall. Nobody was concealed there, as I said. It was not clear why Lalage continued standing up. But she did, erect as a javelin, with one slim hand catching onto the embroidered folds. Her fingers were buried so deeply in the material I could not see whether she was wearing rings.

I folded my arms. The air in this place was alive with danger of all kinds tonight. My eyes wandered to all the furniture, continuing until I was satisfied. I could see floor space beneath the bed in the niche, and also under the couch where she normally sat. Tables, stools, display shelves, all looked innocent. No windows. The ceiling was solid plaster, no rafters to crouch in. I searched the walls for doors; none visible. The frilled rose-colored fittings were too flimsy to hide a fugitive.

Lalage smiled. "Done like a professional."

"We all have skills. I know how to use mine."

"Are you working tonight, Falco?"

"Afraid so." I knew that tonight we were on equal terms. I permitted myself a rueful grin, which she took up with a quiet incline of her head. "Where is he?" I asked in a low voice.

"Not here. He fled."

"Are you prepared to explain?"

"Do I need to?" Her voice was arch. "The big villain was so powerful he conquered and swept me aside. Balbinus took over the establishment, while I languished helplessly."

I had to laugh. "I don't believe that!"

"Thank you." Her eyes were bright, though her sigh seemed weary. "You have good manners, Falco. In addition to a desirable body, attractive intelligence, and gorgeous eyes."

"You're playing with me."

"Oh we all have skills!"

"Where is he?" I asked again stubbornly.

"Gone to a place where he holes up. He's probably in disguise. His hideaway is on the Aventine. I don't know where. I was trying to find out for you."

"Not for me."

"For myself then. The plan—oh yes, there was a plan, Falco—was that I pretended to be terrified of what he would do to me for speaking against him in court. I let him use the brothel, so that I knew where he was."

"If you're claiming to be helping, why did you not call in the vigiles as soon as he arrived?"

"Here? The contemptible Sixth?"

"You could have contacted Petronius. He's straight. He told you he would buy the information if required."

"It was not for sale." I believed that. If Lalage chose to betray anyone, it would be for her own reasons. Reasons she felt were strong enough to put the whole contract outside mere commerce. Selling was what she did with herself. She would do something else with her enemies.

"So what has gone wrong, Lalage?"

"You, mostly." She said it with diffidence, as if sorry to be involving me. "Tibullinus told him tonight that you were outside watching Plato's. Balbinus blamed me."

"It was nothing to do with you!"

"Does it matter?" She closed her eyes briefly. It was a shadow of her alluring glance, but almost too slight to count. I glimpsed a woman for some reason pushed beyond her normal strengths. She almost looked ill. "Anyway, Balbinus left at once. I ordered Tibullinus and Arica to get out as well—so that's us finished here."

"Don't worry about them. Tibullinus and Arica—and the entire Sixth Cohort if needs be—will be under judicial review for corruption in the near future."

"I'll believe it when I see it, Falco. Better hop off quick. They're still in service, and I reckon they will be coming back with their whole cohort."

"What about you?"

"Don't worry about me."

I was worrying about something else. The curtain hanging above her began to pull away from its fixings. A small shower of plaster dust scattered on her hair. Instead of letting go of the material, she held on more tightly.

"Oh Jupiter, girl—"

I leaped forward with my arms open and caught Lalage against my heart.

The curtain rod collapsed. She had dragged it from the wall with her weight as she tried to support herself. I managed to buff aside the pole with my shoulder. The cloth engulfed us for a moment, then fell to the floor.

Lalage crashed forwards onto me. My knees bent as I braced myself. She suppressed a cry, then I stood there aghast, clutching her under the armpits and trying not to yell. Deep in her back was a knife blade. Once I looked over her shoulder I was seeing blood everywhere—soaking her gown, pooling the floor, staining the curtain now draped around her feet.

She was still alive. The gods know how, "Ah, Falco . . . Sorry about this. Balbinus, of course—in case you're too shy to ask. How will you put me down?"

"Well, not on your back, for certain. You're the expert in fancy positions. What do you suggest?"

"Have to be on top . . ."

"You're enjoying the situation."

"Always a game girl . . ."

"Well, I realize some of your finer clients would pay a lot for this." I had sunk on one knee. Bringing her with me, I managed to lower her carefully. Then there was only one thing for it. I had to stretch out on the floor myself, balancing on one elbow and holding Lalage above me in my arms. That way, I could keep her weight off the knife. She laid her head against my collarbone with the small contented smile of a sleepy child. "Oh, this is nice."

"I'll get help."

"No, stay with me, Falco."

"I'm doing you no good. It's ridiculous."

"Just be patient. It'll be over soon. How like a man!"

"I must be tired today. Not at my best . . ."

She was smiling. For some hideous reason I was smiling myself. "Ask me questions, Falco. Take the chance." She was right. I ought to be demanding last-minute information. Not indulging in crass witticisms while she lay dying in my arms.

"It doesn't matter anymore."

"Why should I die for nothing? I told you about Balbinus. Listen, who was that young officer you asked me about?"

"Linus," I forced out obediently.

"Linus. I can tell you how Balbinus found out about him being on the ship—Tibullinus and Arica."

"They're damned for it, then. Did he tell you who told them?"

"Someone in another cohort. A youngster they got friendly with . . ." She was fading. People always say the eyes glaze over, but Lalage's were so bright it broke my heart. "I wanted to ask you—"

She began but never finished. I thought I knew what she might have been wondering. When I pulled out the knife and turned her over gently, I touched the scar that still strikingly marred her ear. I straightened her limbs and her clothing, then partly covered her in the rich material of the curtain. Although she lay upon the floor, she looked as stately and comely as any queen in a mausoleum.

Stumbling to my feet, I crossed to her couch and sat. For a moment I stayed there remembering. Rillia Gratiana: the astonishingly pretty daughter of the snooty stationer, whose first day at school had been on the Ides of October, twenty-five years ago. A day that had been turned into a local scandal when a small boy who was frightened she was going to steal his school fees had reacted just a little too quickly and found his snarling teeth had met female flesh long before he was ready to cope with girls. I wanted to tell her. I had been wanting to tell her ever since that day when we were seven: Biting her ear had been an accident.

Well, it was too late now.

LXIII

The commotion burst out as I made my way downstairs. Things had been quiet, so much so that I even entertained the wild hope that Balbinus might still be in the brothel, convinced that by murdering Lalage he had secured his hiding place.

It had been *too* quiet. At some point during my long captivity with Petro, all the lads who had come in with me had been rounded up and locked away. No one could believe so few of us had invaded the place, so a protracted search must have ensued. Goodness knows how many outraged males had their evening of delights interrupted by Tibullinus, Arica, or the bunch of thugs who had been secretly living there. The annoyance of these mere customers was ignored—a highly misplaced piece of arrogance.

Enraged at losing money, Plato's customers became a defiant lot. Lalage would never have denied their push-and-shove in this outrageous way. Promising them refunds only produced a sullen crowd at the door, half of them still in their undertunics as they went on hoping for entertainment. After an hour of haggling with Macra, the inevitable happened: By some process of natural democracy, a leader emerged. He roused the rest, then led them back into the brothel for a tiff.

Their first action was to find Sergius and the lads, and set them free. Sergius explained the position, and naturally made it plain (with a wink) that his duty to the public compelled him to advise the disappointed customers to run for home. As I may have remarked, Sergius was a big, handsome fellow whose main talent was thrashing folk. He only had to be thinking about this to give others the idea. A wink from Sergius was enough to turn Plato's normally furtive customers into marauding Gauls.

When I came down, a fierce battle had broken out spontaneously all over two floors of the brothel. If I wanted to get through to the outer door, there was nothing for it but to join in.

I wound my belt around one hand with the buckle end free, and grabbed a torch in the other fist. Flailing viciously, I drove a path down the remaining stairs through people grappling untidily. It was unclear who was what. I ran the gauntlet of a corridor full of half-clothed screaming women, then met a faceful of what I hoped was washing water from a crazy man who was giggling repeatedly in a high-pitched monotone.

The main action surged within the large, refectory-like room. It was a sea of madly working limbs and tousled heads. One fellow singled me out. He had a tapered waist and shoulders so wide he looked as if he had been hung up like a tunic with a pole through its sleeves: a gymnasium freak. It did him no good. Without waiting for his carefully rehearsed approach, I kicked him below the belt, banged the stub of my torch down hard on his neck as he doubled up, and flung him back into the scrum. Across the room, Sergius grinned. I had no time to grin back, for someone else ran at me with a stool, legs first. I snatched one of the legs and yanked it aside, going in with my elbow and knee.

The girls who worked here were clustering together, some hanging in the doorways of the refectory. A small group rushed in with bigger ideas, spitting, chucking trays and cups about, pinching, scratching, and pulling hair. I could not tell which side they supported—perhaps any that enabled them to get even with men for once. One mighty dark-skinned amazon chose to come at me, huge breasts thudding as she ran. The charge petered out, to my relief, and she sank her teeth into my hand. I grabbed her nose and twisted it hard until she let go.

Two of the lads were working well together, knocking criminals out in a well-coordinated routine. But elsewhere others were suffering. We were greatly outnumbered. We soon ran out of both energy and flair. There was a thunder along the main corridor. Prostitutes raced past, screeching. Martinus came into the room backwards, using crossed broom handles to fend off three or four attacking heavies. Behind him, laughing as they chose victims to slaughter, were the Miller and Little Icarus.

The small snarling form of Icarus hurtled straight at me. I grabbed an unconscious street villain by the shoulders of his tunic and used his body to block the impetus. Icarus had a knife. Well, it might be illegal, but I'm the kind of law-abiding citizen who fully expects to meet the other sort, so I had one as well. Sparks flew as we clashed hasp to hasp. I gripped his spare wrist with my free hand and banged against his knife arm to break the deadlock of our weapons. Then Martinus sent one of his own attackers flailing into Icarus. I disarmed him and knocked him over. He was still kicking, but after living in a Smaractus tenancy, I knew how to stamp on beetles.

As soon as Icarus gave up and just prayed that he could die now, I tried to help my comrades. The Miller was mashing bodies left and right; Sergius had been crowded into a corner by some street slime, but was keeping the honors even. Martinus was down; he was covered in blood, though still jabbing with his brooms. Identifiable customers were thin on the ground. Our chance had gone. We were facing a massacre. At that moment I saw in the doorway the bemused-looking figure of the Very Important Patrician who had been Lalage's best customer, hot for an evening of exotic massage with the sinuous proprietress.

No one could have told him Lalage was dead; only I knew. The magistrate (to allude to him with courteous vagueness) was finding it hard to comprehend that his gilded boots had stepped into the dark outer suburbs of Hades. As usual, he was followed by his lictors. They were shrewd men, trained to spot trouble two streets away. They grasped what was happening at once.

Martinus muttered, "Oh gods. Do us all a favor, Falco—march the marble-prancer out of here before he knows what's happening!"

I had no need to bother. Macra, bright girl, was already wheeling him off somewhere. The lictors, having gaped at the blithe anarchy before them, rushed up the corridor after him, already forming into a protective phalanx. Well, all except one rushed off. *He* had spied the Miller, who at that moment was raising a table above his head with the aim of squashing Sergius like a rabbit beneath a wine-cart wheel. With a roar of delight, the lictor unfastened the gold ribbon on his bundle of rods. Then he hooked out an axe.

To those of you who may have wondered, I can now reveal that the axe in a lictor's ceremonial bundle is a real one—and sharp. The honed edge glittered briefly. The lictor had only had time to grip his weapon by the far end of its handle, but he knew what to do. He swung low. He swung his axe in a wide, beautiful half-circle like a scythe. He swung to cut the Miller off at the ankles . . . I looked away.

I never saw what happened to the lictor. I reckon he escaped. I doubt if he wanted any credit; there was a man who had truly enjoyed himself.

The omens suddenly grew more bleak for us. Tibullinus and Arica had returned with a century of men. They were fresh, and they were mean. They burst in ready to kill us all. For a few hairy moments Tibullinus and his patrolmen squared up to clear the party. I managed to scramble across the wet, bloody floor toward Sergius, who was smashing down shutters at a window. The other lads forced their way through to us, dragging Martinus. Opposite, the two narrow doorways both filled with ugly vigiles. Any criminals who could move were dragging themselves aside to leave room for these heroes from the Sixth to charge. We lined up to do our best. The shutters would serve us as weapons. Maybe one or two of us could climb out to the street. There were more troops in the street, however—we could hear that.

Someone said something to Arica. He passed it on to Tibullinus. Next minute the two doorways were empty, and so was the outer corridor. Girls rushed past again, this time in the other direction, jostling to reach the street door. We stood feeling abandoned; then we tore outside after them.

We fell out into a streetfight. It looked like some crazy public service exercise. There were vigiles everywhere. They were fighting each other. Suddenly I realized that in their midst were Petronius, Fusculus, and Porcius. These were not the Sixth Cohort attacking themselves, but the Sixth being set upon by the Fourth. Nothing like it had happened since the civil wars.

A man adept in violence crashed across the street towards me. He was locked in a hold with Tibullinus, a hold of painful illegality. As I winced, stepping back to give him space, he broke a bone somewhere in the centurion with a horrendous crack, then put in a punch like a pile hammer. Tibullinus lay still. His assailant stood up. He jerked his chin up derisively, as if despising the weak opposition.

Across the road, Petronius clung in the doorway of the Oily Jug, catching his breath. He grinned at me wryly. The vanquisher of Tibullinus looked at both of us.

"Nice work," I said. I meant it too.

Whatever we thought of him, Marcus Rubella had come good.

The turmoil continued. It was a head-to-head conflict of the foot patrols now; I stood back, near the tribune, and watched. Then I glimpsed through the fighting that Petro had someone with him. He was talking to Porcius.

The lad looked confused. He was shaking his head vigorously. Even though not a word was audible I knew what I was witnessing: My old friend had chosen this moment of grief and commotion to put his raw recruit through a disciplinary interview.

I knew why. Petronius had remembered the time when Balbinus Pius, awaiting sentence and his legal right to exile, was under house surveillance by the Sixth Cohort. He had been guarded by Tibullinus and Arica, whom we now knew were in his pocket. An officer of the Fourth had been assigned to them as an observer. That man was among the party, led by Tibullinus and Arica, that had brought Balbinus to Ostia. Presumably that officer had known Linus would be on watch once Balbinus joined his ship. The observer had been Porcius.

Petronius must have been suspicious for some time. This explained why he had been so hard on the recruit; why, too, when he needed the little black slave Porcius had been looking after, Petro had been so insistent it was Fusculus who fetched the child, protecting the witness against "accidents." It explained why Petronius had lost his temper so badly with Porcius.

He was angry again now.

I saw Martinus and Fusculus conferring as they kept Petronius under scrutiny. They too had worked out what was going on. Marcus Rubella, completely expressionless, stood at my side with his arms folded, watching them all. Ex-centurions are the hardest men you can meet. When Martinus and Fusculus began walking grimly towards Porcius and their chief, Rubella and I both turned and left the scene.

LXIV

For days Rome reveled in the stories: how down in the Eleventh region fighting had broken out among the vigiles, leaving several dead and many sorely hurt. It had been necessary for a Very Important Patrician, horrified by the breakdown of order, to send one of his own personal lictors to the Praetorian Camp to call out the Urban Cohorts, who, with the advantage of being armed to the teeth, speedily put down the riot. The Very Important Patrician was reputed to have composed a scroll for the Emperor denouncing the lax discipline of the foot patrols, the astonishing complacency of their officers, and the possibility that the whole event had been orchestrated by undesirable republican elements in the vigiles in order to distract attention from some sinister web of public service fraud. . . .

My contacts said that the Emperor was delighted to be supplied with the great man's views, though Vespasian was already taking action on the basis of another report that had been slapped in fast by Marcus Rubella and the official anticorruption team.

Crushed by this rebuff, the Very Important Patrician had adopted a new interest. He was now devoting himself to opposing obscenity and reforming prostitutes. Obviously, this meant he would have to force himself to survey brothels personally. Some of us thought that this had its hilarious side.

The Sixth Cohort were to be broken up and re-formed under new officers. Their tribune and several centurions had resigned. Petronius Longus was delighted by this, because Martinus was now devoting all his efforts to trying to get promoted into one of the vacant postings in the Sixth. Martinus was of the opinion that his talents for relaxed inquiry and demonic draughts would fit in well in the prestigious Palatine and Circus Maximus regions. Like a decent superior, Petronius was strongly supporting his bid to have these talents recognized.

The Fourth Cohort had been formally reprimanded by Rubella for running wild. They had been confined to their patrol houses overnight to calm them down. This had the useful side benefit of allowing Rubella to visit each station and ensure that the official story of their incursion into another cohort's district was understood by all. Luckily, most civilians were unable to distinguish between one cohort and another anyway.

Among the dead, the Fourth had lost one of their youngest officers, Porcius. The burial club was to provide him with a basic funeral, though his tribune had to tell the family that regretfully his short time in service, and other factors, meant that no claim for compensation could be allowed.

Official annoyance about the disturbance had been mitigated by the night's other results. Arrested at the brothel called the Bower of Venus were an astonishing number of criminals. It was estimated that tracing and returning stolen property recovered would take the vigiles three months. So many runaway slaves had been rounded up that the Prefect of the Vigiles held a special all-day session for owners wanting to reclaim them (those owners, that is, who were prepared to give house room to a sullen slave who had been exposed to bad company at Plato's). The power of a notorious organized gang had been broken. Among the street operators rounded up were every kind of hustler, cat burglar, and cudgel boy, and in addition there was evidence of a kidnap racket operated by some of the prostitutes.

The main evidence of this pin money racket had been provided by Helena Justina. There was one intriguing aspect that we did not make public: Helena had obtained a confession that the baby I found in the rubbish skip had been stolen by the girls. One of the hags at Plato's had realized he was deaf. When his family refused to ransom him, he was taken up on the Aventine and dumped there by a one-time doorman at the brothel. Macra told us this was the man who did all their snatching—Castus, who had also stabbed the Lycian when Lalage and Nonnius were setting out to betray Balbinus Pius. Castus no longer worked at the brothel; he had been a Balbinus stooge, and Lalage had sent him packing after the trial. He had been apprehended and was awaiting his turn for detailed questioning.

Helena Justina knew who the stolen baby's family were. The last people on the list had finally spoken to her: they denied that they had ever had a baby, let alone that the child was missing, even though a frightened nurse had originally reported it. And who were these forgetful parents? None other than a certain Very Important Patrician and his well-connected, extremely wealthy wife. According to gossip, the woman was now pregnant again. Helena and I had decided not to insist on restoring their son to them. We did not even tell them he had been identified.

The famous brothelkeeper at the Bower of Venus had been discovered dead. As a result, the authorities believed that one of Rome's most sordid bordellos might now lapse into decline. (Not everyone shared this fond hope.) Its landlord had promised to take action, anyway.

I had met Florius standing outside Plato's Academy with a long scroll in his hand. He had been informed by the Prefect of the Vigiles that this was one of his properties. Horrified, he told me that he had called for a full list of the sites he had acquired with Milvia's dowry. Obviously, as a decent equestrian he would now inspect the estate, and do everything possible to clean it up.

There was only one failure among all this fervent reform. We had scoured the brothel, and other places named to us by arrested criminals. Nowhere had we found any trace of Balbinus Pius.

Petronius and the Fourth Cohort spent all their time searching Rome for him. Balbinus had lost his empire. His wife and daughter were under surveillance. He had no regular income, though we knew all too well he would never lack funds. Petro looked hard at any property where he was known to have had connections, but if he had any sense he would take out a lease anonymously somewhere else. He could be anywhere. He could even by now have left Rome altogether. All the ports and all the provincial governors had been notified, but he could have slipped away to anywhere in the known world. Lalage had warned me he would have adopted a disguise.

For days the search continued. I helped, whenever I was free from the eternal writing of reports. I also spent a great deal of time at the gymnasium, trying to get in shape. For one thing, it was my belief that the big rissole would never leave Rome, which was his natural territory. If we cornered him, it would be highly dangerous. In addition, I needed all my strength for a domestic event; on the day before the Kalends of November, Helena and I, Petro, his wife and children, his inquiry team, my family, and many of my relatives were going to a wedding.

It had been planned for the Kalends, but at the last minute my mother took charge of the chaotic arrangements. Her first action was to change the date. She pointed out to Lenia that it is regarded as unlucky to marry on the first day of a month. Lenia burst into tears, them plumped for the last day of October instead.

Some of us thought that for marrying Smaractus the unlucky day would have been far more appropriate.

LXV

Two days before the Kalends, I was going crazy trying to obtain a cheap white sheep. All it had to do was behave nicely while I cut its throat and skinned it—a task which as a town boy I viewed with distaste, though for Lenia's sake I would grimly go through with it. She wanted all the trimmings. Auguries, and the bit where the bride and groom sit together on the sheepskin—the sheepskin that I had to provide. Yes, I had to skin it neatly because everybody would be watching, and I also had to keep the blood off so none marred the bride's highly expensive wedding gear.

Those with an aptitude for logistics will have worked out that to avoid disaster it was necessary to choose and purchase an animal the day before it was needed. I could not risk ending up as the wedding priest who had nothing to sacrifice. Having bought it, I then had to find somewhere to keep the thing.

Maia made Famia agree it could go to the Greens' stable. The laundry yard would have been a more sensible overnight billet, but by then Lenia had become hysterical at the thought of any action that might bring bad luck. I could have stowed the woolly one with a neighbor, but I was afraid

I would wake to the tantalizing scent of roast mutton with garlic and rosemary.

I had to take the sheep to the stables myself. And on the morning of the wedding, I had to cross the city to fetch her back. I made a nice little lead for her. I felt like a clown. From the Plain of Mars to the top of the Aventine is a damned long way.

On the way home I decided to stop at the Temple of Castor baths, so I would be sweet-smelling and ready to put on my clean outfit. As a gesture to Lenia, I took the sheep through with me and washed her as well. For some reason Glaucus was horrified. Don't ask me why. There was nobody important there in the morning, and I had paid her entrance fee.

Returning home I ran into turmoil, as young women rushed around trying to deck the laundry with garlands while old crones sat sipping strong drinks and discussing other people's bowel problems. The facade on Fountain Court had been hung with elaborately painted sheets. The doorway was almost impenetrably blocked with a prickly fringe of branches and flowers. Unlit torches lining the street outside were crying out to be sabotaged by passing youths.

The whole neighborhood had been disrupted by this ridiculous fling. Lenia and Smaractus had taken to heart the dictum that a good wedding should advertise itself. The backyard of the laundry was being used for huge bonfires, already slowly roasting various whole beasts. Fountain Court was full of delivery men and curious onlookers. As a temporary measure the unhappy couple were even using the empty apartment above the bakery, the one I had rejected summarily. There they had stored the amazing number of presents given to them, together with little parcels of sweets that would be bestowed on guests (in return for their ordeal, no doubt) and the nuts which Smaractus would fling to any onlookers watching the torchlight procession (as a symbol of fertility: dreadful thought). Smaractus was coming to live at the laundry after the marriage, so for one night they were even using the place opposite as a token "bridegroom's house." Workmen had mended the floor and installed a bed.

Since the bride had no relations to support her, she had borrowed most of mine. I met my mother and Maia staggering in with the bloodless offering (a dry piece of ritual bakery) and the wedding cake. This gross item, oozing fried almonds and warmly redolent of wine, had been baked by Ma, apparently using a fish kettle the size of a small shark.

"Get your fingers out of there!" As Ma whacked me for picking off crumbs to taste, I dived indoors with the useless hope that I might find a quiet corner to tie up the sheep. "That's right. Stop sneaking around looking for trouble to cause. Pay your respects to the bride."

I found a woman I didn't recognize. Lenia, who normally looked like a sack of turnips, was neatly dressed in the traditional rough-woven gown and orange slippers, with a big fat Hercules knot on her girdle prominent under her bust. Her raging hennaed hair had been tamed by determined female friends, divided with partings into seven clumps, braided tightly over wooden fillets, crowned with a garland of glossy leaves and flower petals, and topped with the traditional flame-colored veil. The veil was turned back so that her friend Secunda, frowning with concentration, could complete the task of outlining her eyes with a sooty cosmetic. To go with the dramatic elegance she was adopting an expression which mingled a simper with haughtiness. I guessed that wouldn't last.

"Oh rats, here's a bad omen on legs!" roared the immaculate vision.

"Got your distaff ready?"

"Give over, Falco. Maia's gone to find me one."

"What, a bride who doesn't own her own? Does Smaractus realize he's getting an incompetent housewife?"

"He knows he's got a brilliant businesswoman."

"I'm not sure about that!" I grinned at her. "Rumor has it you're spending the wedding night in that run-down wreck of an apartment above Cassius. Can this be wise? What couple wants to be holding back in case the floor gives way beneath the nuptial bed?"

"He's shored it up."

"What are we talking about?"

"Oh, go and jump in a cesspit, Falco!"

"Now, that's enough insults. This is the moment when you have to lay aside childish things."

"Oh, good. It can be the last I see of you, then. . . ."

I showed her the sheep, gave her a congratulatory kiss that had her reaching for a napkin to wipe her face, then bounded cheerily upstairs.

There were a few hours to go yet. In the peace of my own apartment I lay on my bed, pretending to lull myself into a contemplative mood for the augury. Helena appeared and stretched alongside for a rest. "Hmm, this is nice." I put one arm around her. "Maybe I'll get pregnant myself. I'd like lying around all day."

"We could compare notes of our symptoms. You wouldn't like being sick, though."

A silence fell. After a moment Helena rolled over so she could look at me. She held my face between her hands, inspecting the half-healed physical scars from my recent ordeal at the brothel. Though she said nothing, her expression was concerned. She understood that beneath the facade of merriment my real mood was dark. Always the first to sense depression in me, she also knew what was wrong: We had cleansed Rome of plenty of dross, but the task remained unfinished. We had swept up shoals of criminal life, and purged corruption in at least one cohort of the vigiles; I myself had even received a hefty fee for doing it. I ought to have been feeling pleased with myself.

How could I, though? Balbinus had escaped. He was dangerous. He was still out there plotting. Given time, he would revive his empire. He would go for Petronius, and maybe for me. Nothing would have changed.

The death of Lalage had had a disturbing effect on me too.

When Helena had read my thoughts to her own satisfaction, she kissed me gently, then settled down again. We lay close, both awake. The familiar sound of her quiet breathing calmed me. Her contentment became infectious. Her steady enjoyment of my presence worked its magic, filling me with amazement that she had chosen to be mine.

"I'm sorry, my love. I have not been with you enough lately."

"You're here now."

"Tomorrow I'm going to start painting the new apartment."

"We need to clean it first."

"Trust me. It's to be done tonight. I've struck a bargain with some of the vigiles."

"But it's the wedding! Had you forgotten?"

"Sole reason for choosing today! I can see two advantages, Helena my darling. If I hate the wedding," which seemed highly likely, "I can run off to assist the floor-washers. Or if the wedding seems too good to miss, I can stay with the celebrations and avoid getting my feet wet."

"You're incorrigible," said Helena, with a warm mixture of admiration and mockery.

We lay still again. Up here near the sky I could feel quite cut off from the noise and press in the streets. I would miss that.

"Are we giving Lenia a wedding present?"

"A nice set of snail picks," said Helena. For some reason I found that hilarious.

"I hope you didn't buy them from Pa?"

"No, from that second-hand gift shop down the street. It's got a lot of well-made horrors in terrible taste—just right to embarrass a bride."

I refrained from mentioning that I had nearly bought her own birthday present there.

A few minutes later our soothing interlude was disturbed by visitors. I went out from the bedroom first, Helena following more slowly. Junia and Gaius Baebius glared at us as if they assumed we had been indulging in dalliance. There was no point protesting that we had merely been talking. "What do you two want?" I saw no reason to pretend to be delighted that my sister had deigned to climb the stairs.

"Gaius has brought you his priestly veil."

"Oh yes, thanks, Gaius."

Without being invited, Junia and Gaius plonked themselves on the best seats. Helena and I found space on a bench, deliberately snuggling up like lovers to embarrass them.

"I hear you're pregnant!" Junia announced with her customary verve.

"That is correct."

"Was it an accident?"

"A happy one," Helena said stiffly.

I glanced at her. She refused to meet my eye. Helena Justina had accepted the situation but was not allowing anyone to gloat. I turned back to my sister with a shameless grin.

"What about the other little one?" asked Junia. She colored slightly. "You can't be wanting him as well?"

I felt Helena's hand grip mine abruptly. Gaius Baebius rose and walked to the basket where the skip baby lay dribbling. He lifted out the child. I noticed that Gaius held the baby with the care of a man who was unused to children, yet his grip was firm and although he was a stranger the babe accepted him. He walked back to Junia, who was not quite ready to approach us with whatever she had come to say.

"You two ought to be getting married now," she instructed us instead.

"What for?" I asked. My intention to marry Helena had immediately sprouted rose-pink wings and flown off the balcony.

"Oh, it's a decent institution," Helena protested teasingly. "A husband must maintain his wife."

I handed her an apple from the fruit bowl. "A husband is permitted to chastise his wife if she shows him too little reverence."

Helena biffed me on the chin. "Each party has the right to the society of the other." She chortled. "I haven't seen much of that lately!"

Junia's face was set. Her voice was tense. "Gaius and I have been talking about this baby, Marcus." She had a knack of sounding as if she was informing me she knew I had been pinching pastries behind our mother's back. Gaius continued to stare at the deaf babe (who dribbled back at him thoughtfully). Becoming more confident, Gaius wiped dry the dribble. My sister carried on talking: "He needs a home.

In view of his difficulty, he needs a rather special one. Obviously he cannot remain with you and Helena. Of course you are kind-hearted, but your home life is chaotic, and when your own child is born there will be too much competition for your love. He needs people who can look after him more devotedly."

She was monstrous. She was arrogant and rude—but she was right.

"Gaius and I are prepared to adopt him."

This time Helena and I could not look at each other. We had had him for two weeks now. We did not want to let him go.

"What about Ajax?" I quavered weakly.

"Oh don't be ridiculous, brother! Ajax is just a dog." Poor old Ajax. Yesterday, this would have been blasphemy. "Besides, Ajax loves children."

"For lunch," I muttered, while Helena pretended not to hear.

Junia and Gaius were assuming that once their sensible suggestion had been voiced we must have gratefully agreed to it. Of course we had. The child would be given every possible advantage. Apart from the comfortable home that my brother-in-law's customs salary ensured, whatever I thought of my sister I knew that she and Gaius would dote on the babe. Both would make every effort to help him communicate.

"Is his parentage known?" Gaius found his voice now.

I opened my mouth to supply the glorious details. "No," said Helena at once. "We tried, but it has been impossible to find out." I took her hand. She was right. She and I could always break the news if necessary. Otherwise, better for him and everyone if there was no chance of recrimination, no danger of false hope.

"I expect you've grown very fond of him," said Junia in a kindly tone. This strange softening upset me more than anything. "You'll be very welcome to see him again, anytime you like."

Helena managed to disguise the hysterical giggle in her voice. "Thank you very much. Have you decided on a name for him?"

"Oh yes." For some reason Junia had gone red again. "It seems only right in view of who found him—we're going to call him Marcus."

"Marcus Baebius Junillus," confirmed my brother-in-law, gazing proudly at his new son.

LXVI

LXVI

In case the sight of me veiled as a priest failed to cause a sufficient sensation, I had decided to attend Lenia's wedding in my Palmyrene suit. Frankly, there were not many other occasions in Rome where a decent man could appear in purple-and-gold silk trousers, a tunic embroidered all over with ribbons and florets, cloth slippers appliquéd with tulips, and a flat-topped braided hat. To complete the picture, Helena had even found me a filigree scabbard containing a ceremonial sword, a curiosity we had bought from a traveling caravan in Arabia.

"I wanted an auspex," complained Lenia. "Not King Vologaeses of the bloody Parthians."

"In Palmyra this is modest streetwear, Lenia."

"Well in Rome it stinks!"

The ceremony began a little late. When the bridegroom's friends delivered him, they were staggering and yodeling; unnerved by his coming ordeal, he was so drunk we could not stand him up. As the ritual demands, a short verbal exchange took place between the bride and groom.

"You bastard! I'll never forgive you for this—"

"What's the matter with the woman?"

"You've ruined my day!"

Lenia retired to sob in a back room, while the guests helped themselves to amphorae (of which there were many racks). While Smaractus was sobered up by his mother and mine, we all started gaily catching up. Members of the public had learned that there was a free-for-all, and found excuses to call at the laundry. Members of the wedding party, who were not paying the bill for refreshments, greeted them with loud cries of friendship and invited them in.

When Petronius arrived things were humming along warmly. It was late afternoon, and there were hours to go yet. After he and his family had finished laughing at my dramatic attire, Helena suggested we all go out for a meal in a decent chophouse to give us strength for the long night ahead. Nobody missed us. On our return, there was still nothing much happening, so Petronius jumped up on a table and called for quiet.

"Friends—Romans—" This address failed to please him for some reason, but he was in a merry mood. As well as the wine we had drunk with our dinner, he had brought a special alabastron of his own. He and I had already sampled it. "The bride is present—"

Lenia had been elsewhere in fact, still weeping, but she heard the commotion and rushed straight out, suspicious that her wedding was being sabotaged.

"The groom," proclaimed Petro, "is practicing for his nuptials and having a short lie-down!" Everyone roared with delight, knowing that Smaractus was now unconscious in a laundry basket; he must have found himself more wine and was completely out of it. Petro adopted an oratorical stance. "I have consulted among those with legal knowledge—my friend Marcus Didius, who has frequently appeared in court, my colleague Tiberius Fusculus, who once trod on a judicial praetor's toe—"

There were impatient cries. "Get on with it!"

"We are agreed that for a marriage to be legal the bridegroom need not be present in person. He may signify consent through a letter or a messenger. Let's see if we can find someone who can tell us Smaractus consents!"

It was his mother who betrayed him. Annoyed by his continuing indisposition, she jumped up and shouted, "I'll an-

swer! He consents!" She was a fierce little body about as
high as my elbow, as round as a tub of oysters, with a face
like a squashed sponge and flashing black eyes.

"What about you?" Petronius asked Lenia.

Fired by her previous success, my landlord's mother
screamed out hilariously, "I'll answer for her too. She consents as well!"

So much for the exchange of vows. Petro swayed and fell
off the table, to be caught safely by merrymaking strangers.
A hubbub arose again, and it was clear we were in for much
longer delays before I could impose enough order to begin
the sacrifice and augury. Being in no hurry, I went out and
across the street to inspect what was happening in my new
rooms.

A group of patrolmen were sitting in the apartment discussing whether rats were more dangerous than women. I
concealed my irritation, added a few philosophical comments, then offered to show them where the nearest fountain
was. They picked up their buckets fairly agreeably (the fee
they had negotiated with me was, to put it mildly, adequate)
and followed me down to the street. I told them the way, but
I stayed in Fountain Court. I had seen someone I knew.

He was standing down by the barber's, an unmistakable,
untidy lump. He had a bundle of scrolls, and was writing
notes against one of them. When I came up, I could see the
same intense concentration on his face and the same little
squiggly lettering that I had seen once when I interrupted
him outside the Pantheon making detailed comments on
racehorses. It was Florius. Across the street, detailed to tail
him everywhere in case he was contacted by his father-in-
law, stood Martinus; he had stationed himself by the baker's,
pretending he could not decide which loaf to choose. He
looked an idiot.

"The barber's is closed, Florius. We have a wedding lo-
cally. He wore himself out this morning snipping the
guests."

"Hello, Falco!"

"You remember me."

"You gave me advice."

"Did you follow it?"

He blushed. "Yes. I'm being friendly to my wife." I tried not to speculate what form his friendliness might take. Poor little Milvia.

"I'm sure your attentions will be happily received. Let me tell you something else: Whatever trouble it causes, don't let your mother-in-law come to stay in your house."

He opened his mouth, then said nothing. He understood exactly what I meant about Flaccida.

I was curious. At the same time, I was beginning to feel I knew what he would answer when I asked, "So what brings you here to Fountain Court?"

He gestured to the scrolls he was holding under his elbow. "The same as when I saw you at the brothel the other day. I have decided I ought to go around and take a look at all the properties which Milvia and I were given as her dowry."

I folded my arms. Together we stared at the place he had been inspecting. "You own the whole block up to the roof?"

"Yes. Most of the rest of this street belongs to another man." Smaractus. "There are domestic tenants on the upper floors. This small shop was leased out recently, but it's not open and I cannot make anyone reply."

He was talking about the cave of delights that offered second-hand "Gifts of Charm." The place where I had declined to buy Helena a birthday present, though where she had found a refined set of eating tools to give Lenia as her wedding gift. I had seen the snail picks now; they were bronze, big heavy spoons with pointed ends, probably from the fine workshops of central Italy. I had a similar set myself, though of more refined design. Lenia's looked like consular heirlooms, but were sold to us extremely cheaply. I knew what that could mean.

"Don't knock anymore." Florius looked surprised by my sharp tone. "Wait here. I'll fetch someone."

Back at the wedding, Maia had arrived. Her sons Marius and Ancus and Galla's son Gaius sat lined up on a bench, ready to act as the three escorts when the bride went in procession to her new husband's house. Marius was looking cross; he probably knew the torchlight procession would be an occasion of rude songs and obscene jokes: not his style.

Gaius was pretty sullen too, but that was just because Maia had insisted the young scruff should be clean. Ancus, who was only five, just sat there with his ears sticking out and wished he could go home.

I waved to them, then found Petro. "Sober up!"

Without a word, and without revealing that he was sloping off, he slid out with me. We walked back down the street to the jumble shop. My heart was knocking. I began to wish I had drunk less. When we reached Florius, he straightened up slightly at the sight of Petro; Petro gave him a polite official nod.

I explained to Petro what the problem was. He listened like a man whose concentration needed help. I recounted my visit to the shop when it was open, describing the kinds of items I had seen. His initial disinterest gradually faded. "Are you suggesting what I'm thinking, Falco?"

"Well, booths of old clutter are everywhere, and some of them probably contain the odd thing that was bought in a legitimate sale, but they are ideal cover for receiving. One reason I'm suspicious is that I saw Gaius and Phlosis, those two boat thieves, in our street not long ago. I now think they may have been up here to hand in swag they'd pinched. And there's something else, Petro: The man who ran this joint was called Castus."

Petronius made the link far quicker than I had done: "Same as the weasel who stabbed the Lycian at Plato's." He was no longer as drunk as he seemed.

"Exactly. That Castus was a Balbinus man. He had been booted out by Lalage but he was still helping the girls who ran the kidnap scheme. My niece Tertulla was snatched very near here. And I found the baby in my skip just along the street."

"Castus was one of the men we arrested at the brothel," said Petro. "In view of his past history, the Prefect has kept him in close custody. Which explains why there is no one here." He screwed up his mouth. "Of course," he went on reflectively, "I'm spending my time checking over all the places we know that had links to Balbinus. I haven't finished the dowry properties. I'm kicking myself."

I said quietly, "I told you what Lalage reckoned: Balbinus was living 'somewhere on the Aventine.' "

Petronius took a deep breath, flexing his wide shoulders. Then he shook his head like an athlete trying to concentrate before a big race. "Jupiter, I should have been sober for this!" He signaled to Martinus and ordered him to fetch Fusculus from the wedding. At that moment my helpers came back from the fountain, so they were summoned too. They set down their buckets carefully and began to size up the shop. Florius asked us what was happening. Petro looked grave. "Let's say that as a concerned landlord whose tenant may have done a bunk, I assume you would like us to break in?"

"Try not to do any damage," protested Florius at once. As a landlord he was learning fast. Then he paled. "What are you expecting to discover?"

"Loot," I said. "Stolen goods. Everything from luxuries robbed at the Saepta Julia and flagons pinched from food shops right down to all the bedcovers old ladies have been losing from their balconies recently. And if I'm right about how the premises have been used, I think we'll find a foundry at the back where precious metal has been melted down."

"And your father's glass?" inquired Petro dryly.

"Oh Lucius Petronius, I have to tell you honestly—I fear not!"

"Do I need to be here?" Florius was feeling nervous.

"Better slide off home." Petronius gave him a kindly pat on the shoulder. "I don't like to see trouble in a family; you'd best not be involved. One of the items I'm now hoping to recover is your missing father-in-law."

Florius looked more interested. "Can I help?" Clearly the worm had turned. From being a passive victim of Milvia's parents, he was now eager to see Balbinus recaptured. In view of the situation, with Balbinus under a death sentence if he was found on Roman soil, that meant mild-mannered Florius was longing for rather more than a mere arrest. The keen glint in his eye said he knew very well what recapture meant.

We broke in at a rush. The vigiles are trained to smash their way into buildings during fires. Even without their heavy equipment, they can go through a door without raising a sweat. Making Florius wait outside, Petronius, Martinus, Fusculus, and I followed the patrol straight in. We marched through the premises without stopping to investigate. It was evident, once you viewed the place as a possible receiving shop, that it was packed with items of interest—and I don't just mean potential Saturnalia gifts. As I had suspected, beyond the curtain at the back lay a cold furnace and plenty of encrusted crucibles.

"A melting pot—and they've been painting the Emperor's picture for him too!" Fusculus held up a mold for counterfeit coins.

We searched the shop, and the attached living quarters. Then we left a guard and searched every apartment upstairs, breaking into any where nobody replied when we knocked.

We disturbed a lot of people doing things they would have preferred to keep private, but we did not discover any trace of Balbinus Pius.

"Ah well. Just have to keep looking." Petronius managed to sound neutral. But I knew his true feelings. Hope had been raised for a moment. The disappointment that followed was twice as acute as our gloom before. "I'll get him," said Petro quietly.

"Oh yes." I thumped him on the shoulder. "You'd better. Old friend, there's still a nasty chance that he's hoping to get you!"

We walked down to the street. We gave Florius the news that his wife's father was still at large, told him to report anything suspicious, and watched him leave. Martinus sauntered after him, still pretending to be unobtrusive.

I had a dark sensation as Florius loped off with his scrolls and stylus. The thought of him so carefully researching his father-in-law's property made me wonder if one day he might want to research other aspects of the Balbinus empire too. Clearly he meant to expand his business interests. He had told me he wanted to start a racing stable, and I already knew from Famia that the partner Florius had chosen had an off-color reputation. Why stop there? His wife came from a notorious criminal family. Florius had never seen any need to abandon her once he realized this. Maybe I had just wit-

nessed the beginning of another depressing cycle in the endless rise and fall of villains in the underworld.

Well, it should take him a few years yet to establish himself.

LXVII

LXVII

I was in disgrace. Back at the wedding, Lenia had called for her augury to be taken. This was the ceremony I had promised to supervise. Nobody could find me. Nobody knew where I was. It was, of course, considered untenable to proceed without the inspection of the sheep's liver. Respectable people would be shocked. Luckily, the imperturbable Gaius Baebius had seized upon my absence and stepped into the breach.

"Oh I'm sure you did it better than I would have done, Gaius!"

And at least the head veil fitted him.

"He gave me some very nice promises," said Lenia sniffily.

"I had never realized that Gaius Baebius was such a liar!" Helena whispered. Gaius explained to me very soberly that as part of his preparations for trying to join the priestly college of the Augustales, he had been taking lessons on sheepskinning.

The bride was by now ensconced on her neatly hacked-off sheepskin, side by side with the slumped form of her husband, newly removed from the laundry basket. She was gripping his hand, not so much to symbolize union as to stop him falling onto the floor. A friend of Smaractus' was going around trying to get up ten witnesses for the contractual tablets, but most of the guests tried to wriggle out of this duty and privilege with weak excuses such as they had inadvertently left their seals at home. Nobody wanted to be blamed if the marriage failed, or be called upon to help sort out the dowry afterwards.

We all decided we had suffered enough and wanted our presents. This meant sending the bridegroom over the road to get them. It was obvious we would only get him over there once, so we combined this trip with sending him to sing the Fescennine verses (a raucous litany that nobody sober could remember, let alone your average bridegroom). Soon he was lighting the torches along the route for the bride's procession. Somebody supplied him with his fire and water for welcoming Lenia to his home. Smaractus revived enough to cry loudly that she could go to Hades for all he cared. Lenia had in fact gone to the lavatory, or the divorce could have been ratified that very day.

We kept the bride's procession short. This seemed wise, because by then the bride herself was drunk as well as tearful. With no mother of her own from whose arms she could be dragged protesting, Lenia, overcome by a last-minute realization of her stupidity, decided to cling to Ma instead. Ma told her to stop messing everyone about. Heartlessly jovial, we hauled Lenia away and set her up in proper fashion, with Marius and little Ancus taking her hands while Gaius gingerly carried the whitethorn torch ahead of them. Her veil had slipped and she was limping, as in her left shoe was one of the traditional coins she must take to her husband. "As if I hadn't given him enough already!"

It had grown dark enough to lend some mystery. A hired flutist came to lead the happy throng. Throwing nuts and yelling, we all jogged up one side of Fountain Court, then danced inelegantly back again, tripping on the nuts. Children woke up and became really excited. People hung out of upstairs windows, watching and cheering. The night was still and the torchlight flickered handsomely. The air, on the last day of October, was chill enough to sober us slightly.

We reached the bakery. Jostling up the narrow outer

stairs, I joined the group of delirious attendants who pulled
the bride up the last few steps to the nuptial rooms. Smaractus appeared in the doorway, with one of his friends loyally
propping him up from behind. He managed to cling onto his
ritual torch-and-water vessel while Lenia spilled oil down
her dress as she made an attempt to anoint the doorframe in
the time-honored way. Petronius and I braced ourselves,
then linked hands under her backside and heaved her indoors.

Smaractus rallied abruptly. He saw Lenia, leered horribly,
and made a sudden grab. Lenia proved a match for him. She
let out a shriek of salacious delight and lunged for him.

Appalled, Petronius and I made a break for the outside
and left hurriedly. Most of the other attendants followed us.
Any tradition of witnessing what happened in that nuptial
bed was too ghastly to contemplate. Besides, the remaining
wine was in the laundry across the road.

The street was packed with singing revelers. It took sin-
gle-minded desperation (and thirst) to force a passage
through. We made it as far as the laundry's garlanded doorway. We found Arria Silvia shrieking to Petro over the noise
that she was taking their young daughters home to bed. She
asked if he was going with them, and of course he said yes
but not yet. Helena, looking wan, told me she was going up
to our apartment. I too promised to follow my dear one
"very soon"—as the old lie has it.

Something made us look back across the road. Lenia had
run out onto the first-floor landing, waving her arms about.
Her veil flapped wildly, and her gown was half off. A raucous cheer rose from the crowd. Lenia shouted something
and raced back in.

It was dark. There was plenty of smoke from the torches.
Almost immediately the distraught bride reappeared in the
doorway of the nuptial home. People had quietened down,
most of them looking for something to drink. Lenia spotted
Petronius and me. In a voice like a grindstone she shrieked
to us: "Help, help, you bastards! Fetch the vigiles! The bed's
collapsed, and the apartment is on fire!"

LXVIII

Guests who had been prepared to fill the street when there was hope of free food and liquor found a sudden urge to go home quietly once they realized they might be asked to form a bucket chain. Others made sure they didn't help us, though they still hung around in doorways having a good gape.

The smell of real smoke had become apparent. Lenia had vanished again back into the first-floor apartment with a wild cry of "My wedding presents! My husband! Help me get them out!" It was clear that the presents were to be given priority.

There was one saving feature: As soon as someone cried "Fire!" out from my own new apartment came a group of vigiles. My Fourth Cohort helpers were soon spotted by the excellent Petronius and chivvied into action. They smartened up immediately. Someone went running to the patrol house for equipment; the rest were ordered straight into the laundry, where there was a well and plenty of water carriers too. Petro and I then raced across to see what we could do for the disrupted bridal group.

Lenia was scuttling about the outer room, uselessly gathering armfuls of gifts. We shoved her outside, fairly roughly, for fire has to be taken seriously; things could end up worse

than she realized. In the second room we were met by a pitiful sight: the nuptial bed, complete with exotic purple coverlet, had crashed partway through the floor. My landlord,
even more disheveled than usual, was clinging onto one corner in terror. He was afraid to move a muscle in case the bed
slipped completely and fell into the bakery store below. That
was where the fire was, started when in the midst of his uncontrollable passion for Lenia, Smaractus had pounded his
bride so heavily that the props beneath the floor had given
way. A bridal torch had then rolled across the collapsing
floor and fallen through the jagged hole onto the baker's
well-dried logs.

"Dear gods, Smaractus, we never knew you were such a
hot lover!"

"Shut up and get me out of here!"

Below us we could already hear battering as the vigiles
tried to break into the bakery. Petro and I began to cross towards Smaractus, but the boards lurched beneath us too dangerously. We had to stay where we were, trying to calm the
stricken bridegroom while we waited for helpers with
proper equipment. At first the smoke seemed slight enough,
and we were not too worried. A pillow slid slowly across the
tilting bed, then tumbled down into the fire, showing what
could happen to Smaractus. He squealed. He was looking
dangerously warm. Petronius started bellowing for help.

A setback occurred. Instead of dousing the fire immediately, the vigiles allowed themselves to be lured from their
duty by the tragic spectacle of a heartbroken bride: I won't
say Lenia offered bribes to them, but overcome by good nature (or something), they came galloping upstairs to save her
precious wedding gifts. By the time more help arrived and
operatives started flinging water and mats over the logs in
Cassius' store, lively flames were at work. Upstairs with us,
Smaractus was now screaming as the mattress he was
clutching caught light from the flames beneath. That was
when Petro and I really started worrying.

Luckily a centurion with sense turned up, bringing more
men with grappling hooks, axes, and mattocks. A party
below us were clearing space in the log store, although one
side of it was now raging with fire. Before they were forced

back, the landlord's prop was replaced beneath the bed, along with poles they had brought themselves, to give him more security until someone could rescue him. Ordered to this task, vigiles pressed past Petronius and me, at last working with speed and efficiency. They flung a huge esparto-grass mat across the room and commanded Smaractus to throw himself onto it. Just in time, he obeyed. They hauled. We helped. We dragged him clear at the very moment the flames shot up through the floor and devoured the bed. We all leaped back into the outer room, and heard the floor fall in, accompanied by a huge roar of fire and sparks.

The blaze went racing up the walls. Smaractus had collapsed. He was picked up as if he were light as a leaf, and rushed outside. A terrific gust of heat and smoke rushed through the building. Petro and I found ourselves coughing. The foul-tasting smoke was so thick it was difficult to find the door. As we fell outside, covering our mouths and retching, a member of the vigiles ran up the stairs, axe in hand, gesturing upwards.

"Who lives in the other apartment?"

"No one. They're even more derelict than this one."

"Quick then. Get out of here!"

We all staggered down to street level, relieved to be out of it.

A siphon party came running up, towing their pumping engine. They forced a passage into the laundry, and soon there were more buckets being passed out at a fast pace. More foot patrols arrived. When Petronius found his breath, he began organizing these into crowd control, gradually moving the sightseers back. A recruit with a bucket went up the street, dousing the wedding torches. We had enough light now without them. A ballista was dragged to the corner, though it got stuck trying to turn into the narrow lane. Smaractus saw it, panicked, and began wandering about drunkenly, threatening to sue if anyone made a firebreak by knocking down any other buildings owned by him. He was so much of a nuisance, the vigiles arrested him for failing to keep fire buckets, interfering with their duties, and (just to make certain) arson with his bridal torch.

The fire was now being contained, but with difficulty. One problem was the outer stairs. They had been rickety to start with, and the weight of heavy patrolmen thundering up in gangs with their buckets proved too much. The broken stonework gave way, luckily without too much damage to the firefighters. Petronius rushed forward to help them, and was knocked flat by a blazing shutter as it fell from above. I raced to pull him clear. At least he was conscious. Two patrolmen took charge of him, flapping cloths to give him air and checking him for broken bones. They knew their stuff.

I saw Cassius, standing with his arms folded, glumly watching the loss of his premises. Leaving Petro for a moment, I went over to commiserate.

"Could have been worse. You could have been in there asleep."

"Not with Lenia and Smaractus pounding all Hades out of the ceiling! But thanks, Falco." I had turned away. "By the way," asked the baker, "has anyone checked the upper floors?"

"Nobody lives there, do they?"

"I've seen an old woman going up a few times. Could be a new tenant—Smaractus will lease anything. Or a vagrant."

"Dear gods. Any idea whereabouts she snuggles down?"

"Who knows?" Cassius shrugged, too absorbed in his own problems.

I stepped across to the centurion to warn him there might be a person trapped. At the same moment he noticed for himself: Two floors up a shutter opened, and through the smoke we glimpsed a frightened face.

The vigiles had brought up ladders after the stairs collapsed. Without a word the centurion and I ran for a spare one, praying it would be long enough. We dragged it forwards and raised it below the right window. It barely reached the ledge. Whatever was in there had disappeared. We yelled, but there was no response.

The centurion swore. "We'll make a bridge from across the street." I had seen them do that, raising and lowering ladders on ropes to form a dangerous crossing point. Sooner them than me.

But it would take time to organize. There was nothing for

it. The centurion had turned away to give orders. While his back was turned I sprang onto the lower rungs of our own ladder and started up.

I was wearing the wrong clothes for this. The thin material of my Palmyrene suit shriveled into little burned holes every time sparks hit me. I kept on the hat, in the vague hope that it would protect my hair from being set alight. Below me I heard gasps as people realized what was happening.

I arrived below the windows and shouted, but nobody appeared. Carefully I climbed higher. I reached up and managed to get one arm over the sill. Then it was necessary to climb with mere tocholds, knowing I had little chance of making my way back again. I pulled myself up, got halfway through the window, and felt the ladder move away from the wall. I let it fall back.

Now I was stuck clinging to the window. No choice but to go in. With a supreme effort I scrambled inside, falling headlong. I stood up, testing the floor beneath me nervously. "Is anyone there?"

The room was full of smoke. It had seeped up from the two blazing stories beneath, finding its way thickly through cracks and crannies in the ill-maintained building fabric. The air felt hot. The floor beneath my Syrian slippers burned the soles of my feet as if its underside must be smoldering like red-hot cinders. At any moment everything around me could explode into an inferno.

In the back of this apartment fire broke through. The noise was appalling. Walls and floors cracked open. Flames roared up as they gave way. Light flickered wildly through an open door.

Now I saw a human figure. Someone crouched in a far corner. Shorter than me, of course. Flowing female drapes. The head tightly wrapped against the smoke.

To calm any feminine fears I tried jovial reassurance: "Madam, you need to get out of here!" I strode across. I was all set to do a shoulder hoist, though I was not sure where to turn with the burden afterwards.

Then I saw the glint of a knife. It was no time for being soft on frightened virginity. With a hard blow of my wrist I knocked the blade to the floor. A foot kicked out frantically.

Alert for the knee-in-the-groin defense, I glanced down-
wards ready to protect myself. Beneath the flounced hem of
a matronly skirt lashed a dark gray leather traveling boot—
on a foot as big as mine. It was a boot I had seen before
somewhere—the quay at Ostia. This was Balbinus Pius.

I wrenched aside the stole. A hand was grabbing for my
throat. I banged that upwards with my forearm. He ought to
have used my surprise, but he was still fumbling at his disguise. He underestimated the threat. If Petronius had stumbled in here, Balbinus would really have gone for him; Petro
would be dead. I was safer. Balbinus had not bothered to remember me.

But I knew him. I drew my Arabian blade. The scabbard
was pure decoration; the weapon was vicious. I set the point
straight against his ribs and rammed home the sword.

I heard my voice grating, "Time to depart, Balbinus!" But
he was already dead.

LXIX

Something crashed against the window. From far away across the street I could hear shouts. Wiping and sheathing my sword, I staggered to the sill. On the opposite side of the lane, which was fortunately narrow, the vigiles had somehow raised a ladder, balancing it precariously on a balcony parapet on their side and lowering one end to where I was. If I could find the courage, I could now crawl to safety across the full width of Fountain Court. It was no time for debate. Fire was sweeping through the apartment behind me. I took off and threw out my slippers (which had been quite expensive), then I checked that my end of the ladder was stable and set off for the other side.

I made it. Let's leave it at that. There is only one way to scramble for your life across a bowing wooden ladder two stories above the ground, and it has to be undignified. The moment when Petronius leaned out from the opposite balcony and grabbed me was one of the best of my life.

We exchanged glances. Petronius saw there was blood on my tunic, but that I had no visible wounds.

"Where's the crone you went to rescue?"

"I stuck my sword in her." He did not ask why. I think he guessed. "It was Balbinus."

"That's the last time I work with you. You've stolen my case!"

"I owe you one," I acknowledged.

"Tell me he's dead. I want to hear the words."

"He's dead," I answered, seeing it again. Then I was sick. The vigiles blamed the smoke.

With arms across each other's shoulders, Petro and I staggered down to street level. In the lane we discovered Helena, clutching my discarded slippers. She must have watched my feat with the ladder. Just as well I didn't know.

Helena was white and trembling, but she managed to sound cheerful: "Bad news, I'm afraid. In the confusion poor Lenia lost track of her wedding presents and some rotter's swiped the lot."

Well there you are. That's Rome all over. Organized crime never lies down for long.

Time for someone to compose a petition to the inquiry chief of the vigiles.

Please Turn the Page
for a Special Bonus Chapter
from the Newest
Marcus Didius Falco Mystery

A Dying Light in Corduba

Available in Hardcover
from
The Mysterious Press

ONE

Nobody was poisoned at the dinner for the Society of Olive Oil Producers of Baetica—though in retrospect, that was quite a surprise.

Had I realized Anacrites the Chief Spy would be present, I would myself have taken a small vial of toad's blood concealed in my napkin and ready for use. Of course he must have made so many enemies, he probably swallowed antidotes daily in case some poor soul he had tried to get killed found a chance to slip essence of aconite into his wine. Me first, if possible. Rome owed me that.

The wine may not have been as smoothly resonant

as Falernian, but it was the Guild of Hispania Wine Importers' finest and was too good to defile with deadly drops unless you held a *very* serious grudge indeed. Plenty of people present seethed with murderous intentions, but I was the new boy so I had yet to identify them or discover their pet gripes. Maybe I should have been suspicious, though. Half the diners worked in government and the rest were in commerce. Unpleasant odors were everywhere.

I braced myself for the evening. The first shock, an entirely welcome one, was that the greeting-slave had handed me a cup of fine Barcino red. Tonight was for Baetica: the rich hot treasurehouse of southern Spain. I find its wines oddly disappointing: white and thin. But apparently the Baeticans were decent chaps; the minute they left home they drank Tarraconensian—the famous Laeitana from northwest of Barcino, up against the Pyrenees where long summers bake the vines but the winters bring a plentiful rainfall.

I had never been to Barcino. I had no idea what Barcino was storing up for me. Nor was I trying to find out. Who needs fortunetellers' warnings? Life held enough worries.

I supped the mellow wine gratefully. I was here as the guest of a ministerial bureaucrat called Claudius Laeta. I had followed him in, and was lurking politely in his train while trying to decide what I thought of him. He could be any age between forty and sixty. He

4

had all his hair (dry-looking brown stuff cut in a short, straight, unexciting style). His body was trim; his eyes were sharp; his manner was alert. He wore an ample tunic with narrow gold braid, beneath a plain white toga to meet Palace formality. On one hand he wore the wide gold ring of the middle class; it showed some emperor had thought well of him. Better than anyone yet had thought of me.

I had met him while I was involved in an official enquiry for Vespasian, our tough new Emperor. Laeta had struck me as the kind of ultra-smooth secretary who had mastered all the arts of looking good while letting handymen like me do his dirty work. Now he had taken me up—not due to any self-seeking of mine though I did see him as a possible ally against others at the Palace who opposed promoting me. I wouldn't trust him to hold my horse while I leaned down to tie my boot thong, but that went for any clerk. He wanted something; I was waiting for him to tell me what.

Laeta was top of the heap: an imperial ex-slave, born and trained in the Palace of the Caesars amongst the cultivated, educated, unscrupulous orientals who had long administered Rome's Empire. Nowadays they formed a discreet cadre, well behind the scenes, but I did not suppose their methods had changed from when they were more visible. Laeta himself must have somehow survived Nero, keeping his head down far enough to avoid being seen as Nero's man after Vespasian assumed power. Now his title was Chief Secretary, but I could tell he was planning to be more than the fellow who handed the Emperor scrolls. He was ambitious, and looking for a sphere of influence where he could really enjoy himself. Whether he took backhanders in the grand manner I had yet to find out. He seemed a man who enjoyed his post, and its possibilities, too much to bother. An organizer. A long-term planner. The Empire lay bankrupt and in tatters, but under Vespasian there was a new mood of reconstruction. Palace servants were coming into their own.

I wished I could say the same for me.

"Tonight should be really useful for you, Falco," Laeta urged me, as we entered a suite of antique rooms in the old Palace. My hosts had an odd choice of venue. Perhaps they obtained the cobwebbed imperial basement at cheap rates. The Emperor would appreciate hiring out his official quarters to make a bit on the side.

We were deep under Palatine Hill, in dusty halls with murky histories where Tiberius and Caligula once tortured men who spoke out of turn, and held legendary orgies. I found myself wondering if secretive groups still relived such events. Then I started musing about my own hosts. There were no pornographic frescos in our suite, but the faded decor and cowed, ingratiating retainers who lurked in shadowed archways belonged to an older, darker social era. Anyone who believed it an honor to dine here must have a shabby view of public life.

All I cared about was whether coming tonight with Laeta would help me. I was about to become a father for the first time, and badly needed respectability. To play the citizen in appropriate style, I also required much more cash.

As the clerk drew me in I smiled and pretended to believe his promises. Privately I thought I had only a slim hope of winning advancement through contacts made here, but I felt obliged to go through with the farce. We lived in a city of patronage. As an informer and imperial agent I was more aware of it than most. Every morning the streets were packed with pathetic hopefuls in moth-eaten togas rushing about to pay attendance on supposedly great men. And according to Laeta, dining with the Society of Baetican Olive Oil Producers would allow *me* to mingle with the powerful imperial freedmen who really ran the government (or who thought they did).

Laeta had said I was a perfect addition to his team—doing what, remained unclear. He had somehow convinced me that the mighty lions of bureaucracy would look up from their feeding bowls and immediately recognize in me a loyal state servant who deserved a push upwards. I wanted to believe it. However, ringing in my ears were some derisive words from my girlfriend; Helena Justina reckoned my trust in Laeta would come unstuck. Luckily, serious eating in Rome is men's work so Helena had been left at home tonight with a cup of well-watered wine and a cheesy bread roll. I had to spot any frauds for myself.

One thing was completely genuine at the Baetican Society: adorning their borrowed Augustan serving platters and nestling amongst sumptuous garnishes in ex-Neronian gilt comports, the food was superb. Peppery cold collations were already smiling up at us from low tables; hot meats in double sauces were being kept warm on complex charcoal heaters. It was a large gathering. Groups of dining couches stood in several rooms, arranged around the low tables where this luxurious fare was to be served.

"Rather more than a classic set of nine dinner guests!" boasted Laeta proudly. This was clearly his pet club.

"Tell me about the Society."

"Well it was founded by one of the Pompeys—" He had bagged us two places where the selection of sliced Baetican ham looked particularly tempting. He nodded to the diners whose couches we had joined: other senior clerks. (They mass together like woodlice.) Like him they were impatiently signaling to the slaves to start serving, even though people had still to find places around other tables. Laeta introduced me. "Marcus Didius Falco—an interesting young man. Falco has been to various trouble spots abroad on behalf of our friends in intelligence." I sensed an atmosphere—not hostile, but significant. Internal jealousy, without doubt. There was no love lost between the correspondence secretariat and the spies' network. I felt myself being scrutinized with interest—an uneasy sensation.

Laeta mentioned his friends' names, which I did not bother to memorize. These were just scroll-shufflers. I wanted to meet men with the kind of status owned by the great imperial ministers of olden days—Narcissus or Pallas: holding the kind of position Laeta obviously craved himself.

Small talk resumed. Thanks to my ill-placed curiosity I had to endure a rambling discussion of whether the Society had been founded by Pompey the Great (whom the Senate had honored with control of *both* Spanish provinces) or Pompey the rival of Caesar (who had made Baetica his personal base).

"So who are your members?" I murmured, trying to rush this along. "You can't be supporting the Pompeys now?" Not since the Pompeys fell from grace with a resounding thud. "I gather then that we're here to promote trade with Spain?"

"Jove forbid!" shuddered one of the high-flown

policy-formers. "We're here to enjoy ourselves amongst friends!"

"Ah!" Sorry I blundered. (Well, not *very* sorry; I enjoy prodding sore spots.)

"Disregard the name of the Society," smiled Laeta, at his most urbane. "That's a historical accident. Old contacts do enable us to draw on the best resources of the province for our menu—but the original aim was simply to provide a legitimate meeting ground in Rome for like-minded men."

I smiled too. I knew the scenario. He meant men with like-minded politics.

A *frisson* of danger attended this group. Dining in large numbers—or congregating in private for any purpose at all—was outlawed; Rome had always discouraged organized factions. Only guilds of particular merchants or craftsmen were permitted to escape their wives for regular feasting together. Even they had to make themselves sound serious by stressing that their main business was collecting contributions for their funeral club.

"So I need not really expect to meet any substantial exporters of Spanish olive oil?"

"Oh no!" Laeta pretended to look shocked. Someone muttered to him in an undertone; he winced, then said to me, "Well, sometimes a determined group of Baeticans manages to squeeze in; we do have some here tonight."

"So thoughtless!" another of the scroll-pushers sympathized dryly. "Somebody needs to explain to the social elite of Corduba and Gades that the Society of Baetican Olive Oil Producers can manage quite well without any members who actually hail from southern Spain!"

My query had been sheer wickedness. I knew that among the snobs of Rome—and freed slaves were of course the *most* snobbish people around—there was strong feeling about pushy provincials. In the Celtic faction, the Spanish had been at it far longer than the Gauls or British so they had honed their act. Since their first admission to Roman society sixty or seventy years ago, they had packed the Senate, plucked the plum salaried jobs in the equestrian ranks, conquered literary life with a galaxy of poets and rhetoricians, and now apparently their commercial tycoons were swarming everywhere too.

"Bloody Quinctius parading his retinue of clients again!" muttered one of the scribes, and lips were pursed in unison sympathetically.

I'm a polite lad. To lighten the atmosphere I commented, "Their oil does seem to be high quality." I collected a smear on one finger to lick, taking it from the watercress salad. The taste was full of warmth and sunshine.

"Liquid gold!" Laeta spoke with greater respect than I anticipated from a freedman discussing commerce. Perhaps this was a pointer to the new realism under Vespasian. (The Emperor came from a middle-class family, and he at least knew *exactly* why commodities were important to Rome.)

"Very fine—both on the food and in the lamps." Our evening was being lit with a wide variety of hanging and standard lights, all burning with steady clarity and of course, no smell. "Nice olives, too." I took one from a garnish dish, then went back for more.

"Didius Falco is famous for political analysis," commented Laeta to the others. News to me. If I was famous for anything it was cornering confidence trick-sters and kicking the feet from under criminals. That, and stealing a senator's daughter from her lovely home and her caring relatives: an act which some would say had made me a criminal myself.

Wondering if I had stumbled on something to do with Laeta's motive for inviting me, I carried on being reverent about the viscous gold: "I do know your es-timable society is not named after any old table condiment, but a staple of cultured life. Olive oil is any cook's master ingredient. It lights the best homes and public buildings. The military consume vast quantities. It's a base for perfumes and medicines. There's not a bathhouse or athletic gymnasium that could exist without oily body preparations—"

"And it makes a fail-safe contraceptive!" concluded one of the more jolly stylus-shovers.

I laughed and said I wished I had known that seven months ago.

Feeling thoughtful, I returned my attention to the food. Plainly this suited the others; they wanted outsiders to keep quiet while they showed off. The conversation became encoded with oblique references to their work.

The last speaker's remark had me grinning. I could not help thinking that if I passed on the stylus-shover's suggestion Helena would scoff that it sounded like making love to a well-marinaded radish. Still, olive oil would certainly be easier to obtain than the illegal alum ointment which we had intended to use to avoid starting a family. (Illegal because if you took a fancy to a young lady who was of the wrong status you were not supposed to speak to her, let alone bed her—while if your fancy was legal you had to marry and produce soldiers.) Olive oil was not cheap, though there was plenty available in Rome.

There was a suitably Hispanic theme throughout the meal. This made for a tasty selection, yet all with a similar presentation: cold artichokes smothered in fish-pickle sauce from the Baetican coast; hot eggs in fish-pickle sauce with capers; fowl forcemeats cooked with fish-pickle and rosemary. The endives came naked but for a chopped onion garnish—though there was a silver relish dish of you-guessed-it placed handily alongside. I made the mistake of commenting that my pregnant girlfriend had a craving for this all-pervasive *garum;* the gracious bureaucrats immediately ordered some slaves to present me with an unopened amphora. Those who keep frugal kitchens may not have noticed that fish-pickle is imported in huge pear-shaped vessels—one of which became my personal luggage for the rest of the night. Luckily my extravagant hosts lent me two slaves to carry the dead weight.

As well as the deliciously cured hams for which Baetica is famous, the main dishes tended to be seafood: few of the sardines we all joke about, but oysters and huge mussels, and all the fish harvested from the Atlantic and Mediterranean coasts—dory, mackerel, tuna, conger eel, and sturgeon. If there was room to throw a handful of prawns into the cooking pot as well, the chef did so. There was meat, which I suspected might be dashing Spanish horse, and a wide range of vegetables. I soon felt crammed and exhausted—though I had not so far advanced my career an inch.

As it was a club, people were moving from table to table informally between courses. I waited until Laeta had turned away, then I too slipped off (ordering the slaves to bring my pickle jar), as if I wanted to circulate independently. Laeta glanced over with approval; he thought I was off to infiltrate some policy-molders' network.

I was really intending to sneak for an exit and go home. Then, when I dodged through a doorway ahead of my bearers and the *garum*, I crashed into someone coming in. The new arrival was female: the only one in sight. Naturally I stopped in my tracks, told the slaves to put down my pickle jar on its elongated point, then I straightened my festive garland and smiled at her.

MEDIEVAL EVIL
FROM
ELLIS PETERS

Enter the fascinating mystery-shrouded world of the 12th century with award-winning author Ellis Peters—and her wonderful creation, medieval monk/detective Brother Cadfael.